2/13

ONE-HIT WILLIE

A Classic Rock Novel

BY

WILLIAM WESTHOVEN

Author photo: Bob Karp

For more information and updates:
visit **www.onehitwillie.com**
or the "One-Hit Willie" page on Facebook.

DEDICATION

To my wife and occasional editor, Lisa, for her endless and unconditional love, patience and support.

ACKNOWLEDGMENTS

Special thanks to my friend and longtime colleague Lorraine Ash, a truly gifted journalist, author and book editor who lent her valued expertise to this project. Also to the countless other colleagues who I have worked with in the newspaper industry for the past 23 years, whose support, encouragement, humor, dedication and inspiration over the years have helped me to earn a living doing something I truly love. They are too numerous to mention here, but allow me to honor one by name, the late Ed Carroll, who signed off on hiring a former Crazy Eddie's salesman into a profession that he had no experience in. Betting on a longshot underdog, he changed my life for the better. Indeed, he may have saved it. Thanks, Ed. And finally, thanks to the musicians who have moved my soul since I was a little child, playing air guitar in my bedroom to the hottest wax spun by Cousin Brucie on 77 WABC and spilling out of my Westinghouse clock radio.

PROLOGUE

"Did you hear the question?"

Of course he heard the question. It was still ringing in his ears like a damn church bell.

Aaron hung on as the room spun around him. *Get a grip, man, you're losing it!*

"I'm sorry, who?" he asked, stalling for precious milliseconds.

"Weekend Willie. Does that name mean anything to you?"

"Uh, no. I mean, not really. Should it?" He mustered a thin smile, trying desperately to cover his panic.

After all this time ... what, thirty years? No, it was more. *How many presidents?*

How could this be happening? How could his comeback come to this? Hadn't he suffered enough? *Come on.*

"And ... go to commercial!" he heard someone shout.

Aaron squeezed the arms of his tall chair and cautiously dropped his feet to the floor. When the room finally stopped spinning, he slowly rose and tested his legs. They seemed to work, so he aimed a shaky path towards his manager. Eli was in deep, frantic conversation with the producer, waving like he was conducting a Sousa march.

"Patty, this isn't in my notes. Who the hell is Weekend Willie, and what ... " Eli shouted, stopping midsentence when Aaron joined them. "Aaron, what the hell? Who's Weekend Willie?"

"Eli, come with me," Aaron said, leading him to an unoccupied corner of the studio. "*You* ... just give us a minute, OK?" he said, pointing at Patty Place, executive producer of "The Phoenix Café."

"Eli, they've got something on, well ... *me*. This is just ... I can't believe this is happening. Damn it! I didn't ask for any of this, you know!"

"Aaron, tell me what the hell is going on. Who is Weekend Willie?"

Aaron was a reluctant guest on "The Phoenix Café," the most popular series on the cable TV music channel YFM (Your Favorite Music). *"Y? Because you like it"* was its unoriginal, obvious and often-repeated catchphrase. "The Phoenix Café" series was a reality-based launching pad for the resurrections of has-been bands and musicians. It was partly historical documentary, with probing, in-depth interviews, and partly a showcase for a comeback tour that the show's producers would book, manage and record for CD and video release.

"The Phoenix Café" had resuscitated the careers of far more obscure musicians than Aaron Lowe, former leader of the legendary classic rock band Carnival. Some of the show's subjects earned more money in the year following their "Phoenix" episode than they ever made back in the good old days.

Aaron wasn't after a paycheck or career counseling. It had never been about the money. It was about the music. And paying a debt to some old friends. One more stroll around the block with his favorite band.

The host of the show, former network TV journalist Carrie Mann, was famous for her take-no-prisoner interviews. They produced the kind of uniquely human drama that drew huge ratings. Mann was nicknamed "The Surgeon" because she could slice through any facade and get her subjects to relive the point in their career when it started to fall apart. Her goal was confession or confrontation. Either way, it was great television.

"She could make a career Marine cry," said the agent for Bonnie Lee, the long-forgotten, big-haired country singer. The poor thing disappeared from the public eye years ago after gaining 100 pounds. When she lost the excess weight and won a Grammy for her first hit record in 12 years, she caught the attention of the "The Phoenix Café" producers. After Carrie Mann interviewed her and dwelled on the 10 years of youth, natural beauty and career momentum she had lost, Bonnie Lee gained it all back and more. You could practically see her reaching for the Häagen Daz halfway through the show.

Carrie Mann was a sexy, scrappy schoolyard bully with enough credibility to fend off the critics. She had climbed the ladder of network news the hard way. She won Emmys as a foreign correspondent and was wounded covering the war in the Gulf. She had a journalism degree from Columbia, a master's in political science from Georgetown and the legs of a runway model.

And she could dangle the lucrative "Phoenix Café" carrot in front of her targets. It was the kind of bait that pulled them in like frat boys to beers and bongs. Survive Carrie Mann and spend the next six months touring in VIP comfort, complete with a charter jet and exclusive bookings in major cities. A surge of promotion, pumped through the network of radio stations that YFM owned from coast to coast, essentially guaranteed a full house for every gig.

Carrie Mann was a broker for the great American obsession with fame. She knew the public had an insatiable hunger for fresh meat to replace the celebrities whose bones they had already picked clean. She delivered the once-famous and near-famous, the sorry lot who got more of a high from stardom than they ever could from the drugs or alcohol that so often were part of their downfall. Those who suffered the worst kind of withdrawal when their fans lost interest.

It was good business for all parties. The musicians got their second bite of the apple. YFM pocketed the profits from cheap, popular programming. The cost was typically enormous to discover, develop, polish, package and promote a new artist. "The Phoenix Café" reduced its overhead by exploiting recognizable, readily available names, pulling them out of cold storage and placing them back on the market at a relative discount. Everyone got what they wanted, and isn't that the cream filling of the American dream?

Aaron expected Carrie Mann would dredge up the awful

business in Detroit. He was ready to deal with it. After all, what happened there was not his fault, and yet he assumed more responsibility for the tragedy than any of those who should have shouldered the blame. What he did afterwards was his own business.

If Carrie Mann wanted to amputate his demons and wave them in front of the camera like severed limbs, so be it. He had survived tighter spots than this. She couldn't do anything to him that hadn't been done already.

He was different than the sad parade of weeping used-to-bes who could not bear it when they walked down the street and no one recognized them. Carrie Mann was not exploiting him. He was exploiting her. And he had other people in his corner, *important people,* who would make sure his tour was a respectable event, not some kind of nostalgia freak show.

Weekend Willie was another matter entirely. Weekend Willie had been dead and buried. A sliver of inconsequential memory. If she had somehow managed to dig up those old bones, Weekend Willie could return to haunt Aaron in ways that even Carrie Mann could not imagine.

How in the hell could this be happening?

"Back in 30 seconds. Aaron, please!" someone shouted from the set.

"Aaron, I know that name from somewhere," Eli asked again. "What's this all about?"

"You don't want to know," Aaron said as he walked back to the set.

How could this be happening? he repeated to himself as he settled back into the tall chair, holding firmly onto the arms. His only comfort was that however unreal this nightmare seemed to be, the feeling was undeniably familiar. So was the bitter, metallic taste of anxiety in his mouth.

Experience would tell him what to do. Grip the wheel and go, man. Feel the wind in your face. Watch for the signs and pay the tolls. Observe local limits. And when the world stopped, he'd find his way from there.

PART ONE

CHAPTER 1

Winnie Quinn could fill a bathing suit like treasure fills a pirate's chest, and that's only one reason why she was the crown jewel of the 1941 Miss Atlantic City Pageant.

She was a buxom strawberry blonde who tanned without freckling. She looked wholesome in the sun and sexy in the dim, smoky light drifting through the rafters of the Boardwalk Convention Center. She could sing and dance better than most. The other girls never had a chance.

With a $500 cash prize in hand, Winnie pointed her future to the West. A talent scout who flirted with her at the pageant made promises about a screen test in Los Angeles. "You're prettier than Katharine Hepburn, and that hair!" he said, giving her his card and the name of a good hotel near his office.

The pageant sponsors begged her to stay. They promised her a handsome stipend just to stick around and make a few appearances on the Boardwalk. She could have her own showcase at the Steel Pier. Winnie knew she could do better than that. She was the whole package, and she knew Hollywood would roll over for her, just like everyone did on the East Coast.

The only thing she didn't count on was a second world war and a handsome young soldier she met on the train to California.

Normally, Winnie was feisty with men who gaped and whistled at her. She loved to confront and embarrass them. It was sport to her.

"Didn't your mother tell you it's not polite to stare?" she would ask sweetly but with a firm, clear voice that everyone in the room could hear. "Well? Don't you have anything to say?"

They usually didn't. If they did manage to keep their wits and fire back, she was ready to counter. "Well, you're just as rude as everyone here thinks you are."

No, you didn't so much as stare at Winnie Quinn without paying a price. That's why she was headed to Hollywood. They paid real money out there.

But when Winnie caught a tall, handsome Marine sergeant staring at her from across the car, she found herself staring right back at him. When he stood up, ambled over and removed his hat, revealing a golden wave of blonde hair, she fought to catch her breath. He held the hat over his heart, clutching it with two hands, and slowly peeled open a gleaming white smile. She nearly fainted when he politely asked to sit down.

It was a long trip and his silly jokes broke the quickly melting ice. By the time the train reached Pittsburgh, they were holding hands. By the time it pulled into Kansas City, there was talk of love. Two hours after the train arrived in Los Angeles, they found a motel and unleashed their passion.

Two weeks later, Winnie had not yet bothered to call the talent scout. It was as if all the ambition and all the plans had been sucked out of her and her obsession with Sgt. William "Bill" Taylor had filled the vacuum.

The next few months were the happiest of her young life. Bill wasn't her first lover, but he was by far the best. Winnie rented an apartment in Oceanside, not far from the Camp Pendleton, where Bill was assigned to train Marine recruits for the war. They made friends at a local tavern, Pappy's, where Bill played an old upright piano while Winnie sang and played the ukulele. The couple harmonized beautifully on the old songs they knew from childhood and also learned some of the pops they heard on the radio. It got to the point that Pappy O'Reilly noticed his business was picking up and paid them $5 a night, plus all they could eat and drink, to entertain the local barflies and restless soldiers.

Winnie eventually got around to meeting with the talent scout, who hit on her, then threw her out of the office when she cried "boyfriend."

"I thought you were a smart girl," he said. "I thought you knew the score. There's a lot of pretty faces out here, sweetheart."

"You didn't say nothing about no boyfriend in Atlantic City," he added.

It was all true. Winnie knew the score all right, and when she got on that train, she was prepared to play ball. But she was young and the world was moving fast. After December 7, things began to change even faster, and Winnie was suddenly a responsible woman with a fiancé headed for the Pacific Theater.

Before he left, Bill got a three-day pass. They seized the fleeting moment, drove to Mexico in a borrowed truck and got married.

"I will wait for you," she promised when it was time for him to ship out. "No matter what happens, I'll be here for you." And she meant it.

Four years later, Winnie's promise was still intact, yet her marriage was ripping at the seams. The couple had a new baby boy — Bobby, named after a war buddy of Bill's who died at Peleliu. Nearly a year after his discharge, Bill had yet to pursue a steady job. Once in a while, he would get together with a few of his Marine buddies and disappear for a few days. When he came home, he always had money to catch up on the bills. Sometimes he even brought gifts, like jewelry or a fancy coat.

He always refused to tell Winnie where it all came from. "I had some business up north," he would say, or something to that effect.

This went on for better than a year, during which time Bill began to drink more and more. One night, when he came home after a two-week absence, Winnie cursed him because his pockets were empty. Her sharp tongue earned her one hard slap in the face, then another.

"When I bring it home, you get on me about how I got it. When I don't have it, you want to know where it is," he said.

Winnie told herself, "I'm still young, I'm still talented. I could look for work." But when she pulled her old dresses out of the closet, they didn't fit. She had gained a lot of weight. To make matters worse, motherhood, a bad diet and all that southern California sun had taken a toll on her complexion.

She spent the rest of the day crying into the mirror. The next morning, she woke up depressed and nauseous. She was sick again the next morning.

Bill's road trips got longer and longer as Winnie got bigger and bigger. When she went into labor on April 2, 1947, her husband had been out of town for 10 days. A month later, cradling William Taylor Jr. in her arms, she knew her husband wasn't coming back. The world was still moving fast.

CHAPTER 2

It came so very easily to Willie Taylor, Jr. Making music was as natural to him as breathing. When he was three years old, he picked up his mom's ukulele and, within a few hours, he was playing along to songs on the Philco radio in the living room.

Winnie was astonished. She pulled her husband's banjo out of the closet and gave it to Willie. He quickly mastered that instrument as well. He had never heard a banjo, but seemed to sense its unique potential. The chords were easy and he soon realized that fast-picking the strings really made people sit up and take notice.

The world kept turning and it was summer, 1954. School was out and Winnie's boys were underfoot. She was working at Pappy's, waiting tables and singing once in a while on slow nights.

During the day, before the lunch crowd began to file in, she would bring young Willie to the tavern and sit him in front of the upright piano. The old girl took him a little longer to master, but eventually he started to figure it out. Still, Winnie noticed her son seemed a little frustrated.

"Mommy, I don't know why, but it doesn't make the music I want it to," he said. "It sounds *wrong*."

Pappy had an idea about Willie's problem. "You know, it may be because the damn thing is so out of tune." Pappy was anxious to test his theory, so he paid to have the piano professionally tuned. Willie's ability on the piano progressed exponentially.

"It sounds right now," he said happily.

"Damndest thing I ever seen," Pappy said. "Winnie, the

kid's got the gift. Gift from God." Pappy was Willie's biggest fan.

While Winnie, Pappy and an increasing number of regulars fawned over his little brother, Bobby would sit at the bar, reading comics or fiddling with the radio dial. When he got bored, he would follow Pappy's black cat, Rochester, out the back door and watch him catch rats down by the pier.

Sometimes, Pappy would pay Bobby a dime to sweep up the sawdust on the floor. The sawdust reeked of stale beer, but he was eager to be noticed and earn some approval. Besides, a dime was good money for a half-hour's work.

Most days, Pappy, Winnie and the boys would lunch on whatever was left over from the night before. Pappy's cook, Lourdes, made a great pot of chili almost every day and it was always better the day after. Not a great meal for kids, but money was tight and it was a sin to waste food.

Lourdes disapproved of a young boy spending so much time in a bar, so she tried to encourage Willie to play outside with Bobby and her own two boys, who were about the same age as Winnie's. It was no use. Willie was completely lost in his music. He was starting to sing now and seemed to be blessed with perfect pitch.

"He's like an angel," Pappy told Winnie. "Sent from the heavens, he was."

Knowing her youngest son had an extraordinary gift, Winnie embarked on a campaign to develop his talent. When summer was over, she met with the Oceanside Elementary School principal, Mr. Allovus, to explain about Willie's special needs. He apologized for the school's sorry excuse for a music program, which was limited to a chorus that met once a week under the guidance of the regional music teacher, Miss Schatzschneider.

"While you are here, Mrs. Taylor, I wanted to talk to you about Bobby," Mr. Allovus said. "His new teacher says that he has trouble keeping up. We think he might need some extra help. Miss Ryan said she could tutor him after school. She already has a little group of kids that are in the same boat as Bobby. She has special training for children with reading deficiencies. We're very lucky to have her. But someone would have to pick Bobby up after the lessons."

"I appreciate your offer, Mr. Allovus, but I think Bobby can catch up on his own," Winnie said. "I don't have time to be his bus driver and I need him home to do chores. I'll try to help him along when I can."

Winnie paid lip service to Mr. Allovus while her mind was already racing ahead. What was she going to do about Willie? His gifts were going to rot without real training, the kind of training he obviously wasn't going to get in this school system.

"Tell me, is there a school around here where Willie can get more musical training?" Winnie asked.

"Well, Miss Shatzschneider can give him piano lessons. I don't know of any other music teachers in the area," the principal replied.

"I've heard her play the piano. Willie's as good as her already. I mean *serious* training."

"You know, Mrs. Taylor, Willie is very young. There's plenty of time for him to develop."

This kind of attitude drove Winnie nuts. Obviously, the principal did not understand what was at stake.

"Mr. Allovus, we all have only so much time on this earth. And those who stand still are passed by. Believe me, I know. And I don't think you realize just how special Willie is."

"All the children here are special to me," Mrs. Taylor. "Including Bobby. And with due respect, I think you should be happy that Willie is doing as well as he is and focus more on Bobby's needs."

"Bobby is fine."

"No, Mrs. Taylor, he isn't. I'm not sure how he got promoted to the third grade, but Miss Ryan tells me Bobby can barely get through the alphabet. I'm seriously considering her suggestion to put him back in first grade now before we go any further. But perhaps, with Miss Ryan's help ... "

"Mr. Allovus, you do what you think is best for Bobby. I'm going to do what's best for my Willie. He has a special gift and I will make any sacrifice I must to make sure that it doesn't go to waste. Even Bobby might have to make some sacrifices, but he understands. He loves his little brother and would do anything for him, just like me."

"Mrs. Taylor, we all want what's best for both of your children, but you're leaving me with little choice. Think of how Bobby's going to feel being put back, back into the same grade and class as his little brother. He's already a shy little boy and his social development has been slow. The older boys pick on him. This will make matters worse."

"Well, this is your school and that is your problem, Mr. Allovus. And if Bobby has any more trouble, I'm going to hold you accountable. I'm his mother. I take care of him at home. What goes on here is your responsibility."

A week later, Bobby was returned to the second grade while Winnie combed the desert to find a music teacher who could mentor her Willie. Eventually, it no longer mattered. Willie taught himself, listening to the radio and playing along on the banjo, ukulele and a guitar his mother bought him for Christmas.

One afternoon, while listening to "Cousin Clem's Country Corner" on KVLY, Willie was strumming along to Jimmie Rodgers' "T For Texas," ignoring the saucy lyrics and straining his young lungs to get the yodel right. After the song, Clem announced a talent contest to be held the next month at the San Diego County Fair. There would be a $25 grand prize for the winner of the age-12-and-under category, to be judged by a panel of the show's advertisers.

Willie made sure his mother was around the next day to hear Clem pitch the contest. When it came, they looked at each other and smiled the same smile.

"Can I mom, *please*?" Willie said, looking up and pulling down on his mother's forearm.

"Only if you promise me you'll win," Winnie answered, laughing as she hugged him off his feet and swung him around.

CHAPTER 3

Wearing an adorable embroidered cowboy outfit his mother financed from the family's meager savings, little Willie Taylor was the hit of the San Diego County Fair in August of 1955. In the weeks leading up to the fair, Winnie listened to "Cousin Clem's Country Corner" every day and monitored the other shows on KVLY as well. She was sizing up the territory, trying to get an idea what the station listeners, and advertisers, would like. She detested country music but was leaving nothing to chance.

The cowboy suit, complete with neckerchief, pointy boots and big-brimmed cowboy hat, cost almost $20, nearly as much as the first prize Willie had yet to earn. Winnie knew from her beauty pageant days that it wasn't enough to have talent. If you wanted people to notice you, if you wanted to be a star, you had to look like a star.

She turned the radio dial and noted that in addition to the country music programs, there were several evangelists preaching to the unseen flock every day and most of Sunday. Putting it all together, she chose five songs for Willie to rehearse. She allowed him to prepare "T for Texas," because he loved to yodel and Winnie felt yodeling was a good exercise to strengthen his voice. He had no idea what the somewhat risqué lyrics were about, but no matter. She would not let him perform that song in public, fearing it could offend some in the audience, especially coming from such a little boy.

Instead, she had Willie play two songs from his favorite cowboy, Gene Autry. He started off with the peppy "Mule Train" and quickly segued into "Back in the Saddle Again," adding a few yodels to its "whoopie-ki-yi-yay" refrain.

With the growing crowd clapping along, he turned to another one of his favorites, Hank Williams, singing "Jambalaya (On the Bayou)" like it was written just for him. Finally, for good measure, Winnie had him do an uptempo rendition of "Will the Circle be Unbroken?" that whipped the crowd into a religious fever. So many people joined him in singing the final chorus that nearly everyone within 100 yards of the stage had turned around to see what the fuss was all about.

Winnie beamed as Tommy O'Dowd of O'Dowd's Dairy, the leading sponsor of "Cousin Clem's Country Corner," placed a blue ribbon with a cheap, round brass medal around Willie's neck. The ribbon was cut for an adult, so the medal dangled almost to Willie's knees.

Tommy raised the microphone stand so he could formally announce the winner. He was a portly five-foot-eight, although his tall cowboy hat made him seem taller. Winnie's instincts were perfect. Willie's hat was an exact match for Tommy's.

"How 'bout that, folks!" he bellowed. "We got us a winnah right heah. Ain't this kiddie cowboy sumthin' else?"

Tommy stood behind Willie, with one hand on each of the boy's shoulders, while a photographer snapped pictures for the newspaper. After they left the stage, Tommy patted Willie on the back with one hand and handed an envelope to Winnie with the other.

"A check?" said Winnie, batting her eyelashes. "I was hoping for cash."

"Little lady, I always got deep pockets for a fine-lookin' filly like you," Tommy said. His eyes were fixed on Winnie's cleavage, which glistened with sweat from the hot sun.

Winnie smiled and said nothing for a few moments, plotting to exploit the opportunity put before her. Tommy, and his deep pockets, were ripe for picking.

"Mr. O'Dowd, didn't your mother tell you it's not polite to stare?"

The next morning, Lourdes let Bobby and Willie sleep in. Winnie was still out. It had been quite a day and a late night. When they finally woke, she fixed them scrambled eggs and tortillas for breakfast.

Lourdes was staring at her coffee when she heard a car rumbling up the driveway. She went to the window and saw a big convertible speeding towards the house, kicking up a trail of dust behind it. It was a Buick with a noisy, throaty engine that could not drown out Winnie's familiar squealing laugh.

Winnie leaned over to kiss the driver, then flipped the door open and got out. The driver turned the car around and sped away as Winnie strolled inside, smiling and humming "Will the Circle be Unbroken?" She slumped down in a kitchen chair, sighed happily and fanned herself with a program from the fair.

"You just back from church?" Lourdes asked. Winnie could not tell if she was angry or joking. Maybe both, knowing Lourdes. They did not get along very well, but Lourdes was always around and willing to baby-sit her sons. She would bring her own boys over and let them all camp out in the living room. It also gave Lourdes a chance to watch TV. Neither single mother could afford to buy a TV, but Winnie had managed to wrangle one from one of her "admirers."

"*Nooo.* Any coffee left? She asked. "I'd kill for a cup of coffee."

"It's your kitchen. Help yourself. I got to get to Pappy's and start the chili."

"It's Sunday, Lourdes. What's the rush?"

"I'm gonna start a few things then get to the noon mass at St. Peter's. It's the last mass of the day."

"Are you going to pray for me, Lourdes?"

"I going to pray for *you* and *your* boys. *Reeeal hard.*"

"Tell Jesus I said hi."

There was no question Lourdes was annoyed with her now, so Winnie changed the subject. "Where's Willie?" she asked. "Is he up?"

"Both your boys out back. Bobby wants to go fishing with Tomas and Jose."

"I need him around here today, Lourdes. We've got work to do. Tell your boys to go on without him."

Winnie shouted out the window for her boys to come in. They raced to the front door. Willie won by two strides.

"Get in here, you two. I've got some wonderful news. Willie, baby, you're going to sing on the radio!"

CHAPTER 4

Winnie had been watching her weight and Lourdes had directed her to an herbal skin remedy that cleared up her complexion nicely. She wasn't that young anymore, but she could attract the likes of Tommy O'Dowd. Even with all his money, Tommy was too fat, sweaty and clumsy to do very well with real women. He frequented the prostitutes across the border, but rarely got attention from the local ladies. Especially his wife.

Winnie could work with that. All it took was one night to wrap Tommy around her busy little finger. Not that Tommy was stupid. Winnie's kid was sensational and the perfect draw for a business pushing a product consumed largely by children. He could already picture the billboards with little Cowboy Willie lassoing a bottle of O'Dowd's Farm Fresh Milk.

He wasn't smart enough to come up with the pitch on his own, but he knew a good idea when he heard one. He would have gone along with it even if Winnie hadn't slept with him. That was just the icing on cake. A good day all around.

"You really are the round wheel," he said to Winnie the next morning when he dropped her off.

There was no problem getting KVLY to go along with the plan. O'Dowd's, the station's major sponsor, had agreed to sponsor another hour of the programming day. The station manager, Dallas Houston, had heard Willie sing at the fair. He knew the kid had talent and a lot of presence for his age. He was sure the kid could be a big hit. The only question was, for how long? *As long as the fat Duke of Dairy pays me to put the show on*, he thought to himself.

Willie was brimming with confidence after the fair and also had discovered something important about himself. It wasn't the attention he enjoyed. It was how he could make people feel things with his music. He loved to make music so much, and when he did, he could feel the people around him share that love. He didn't know what an epiphany was, but that was exactly what happened to him at the fair.

He quickly learned that playing music at KVLY wasn't nearly as much fun as playing for an audience. The studio was hot and cramped. The few people milling about had jobs to do and no time to stop and listen. Still, his mother said it was good money and good experience. And he was fascinated with all the electronic equipment.

One of the engineers, who everyone called Flash, took Willie under his wing and taught him about transmitters, amplifiers, microphones and acoustics. Certain types of voices, Flash would tell him, sound better with a little echo, and the microphones had to be set up differently for a large band as opposed to, say, an eight-year-old boy with an acoustic guitar.

One day, Flash motioned for Willie to follow him into an equipment room that many of the musicians used for rehearsal. He held up what looked like a guitar, yet it was unlike any Willie had touched in his short lifetime.

"Willie, this is a Gibson Les Paul model solid-body electric guitar," Flash said. Les Paul was Willie's favorite guitar player and he loved watching the Les Paul and Mary Ford TV program that ran on stations nationwide. He tried to squeeze the same funny sounds out of his guitar as his hero did, but never came close.

"This is Les Paul's guitar?" Willie asked.

"Well, it's not his guitar," Flash said. "He designed it. Heck, he invented the thing. This one belongs to somebody else. Wanna try it out?"

Willie nervously reached out for the beautiful, shiny instrument and pulled the strap over his shoulders, but it was too long to be useful. He needed both hands just to hold it up.

"Whoa, better play it sitting down," Flash said, laughing at Willie's ear-to-ear grin.

Willie sat down, cradled the guitar in his lap and marveled at the switches and dials he couldn't begin to understand. So he just pulled a pick from under the strings of the fretboard and strummed an open chord, then nearly fell out of the chair as he heard a thunderous blast of noise from a speaker box in the corner of the room.

"*Whoa*, what was that?"

"Easy, little cowboy. A solid-body guitar needs a separate amplifier and speaker. You don't use a microphone. See these screwy things under the strings? That's called a pickup, because it picks up the sound from the strings, kind of like a record needle. You plug it right into the amp. That's what this cord is for. And that dial is for volume. You might want to turn it down a little."

Willie tested the smooth, polished six-stringer for a few minutes, ran his fingers up and down the fretboard, then thought of a Les Paul song to play. To Flash's astonishment, Willie started plucking out a near-perfect cover of the tricky instrumental ditty "Nola."

"*Whoa*," Flash said.

"*Whoa*," Willie said.

Flash became Willie's best friend over the next three years. By 1958, though, the novelty of "California's Kiddie Cowboy" had run its natural course. Rock 'n' roll was taking over radio stations from coast to coast and O'Dowd's was redirecting its advertising dollars to television. Younger children were no longer listening to the radio after school. They were watching "Howdy Doody" and "The Mickey Mouse Club."

Willie was crushed when his show was cancelled, mainly because he could no longer see Flash three days a week. This suited Winnie just fine. She thought Flash was a bad influence, giving Willie promotional copies of Chuck Berry and Little Richard records to take home.

"Race music. Nigger music," Winnie called it. "That won't go over with proper folk."

Willie begged his mother for a Gibson Les Paul. "Les Paul doesn't play rock and roll," he argued.

"That's a lot of money for something you don't need," said Winnie, who was already plotting an ambitious new course for her son's career.

CHAPTER 5

Tommy O'Dowd had taken Winnie on a trip to Las Vegas in the winter of 1959. She was surprised to find herself enjoying the role of trophy girlfriend. At 35, what once seemed like an insult was now a compliment. Of course, Winnie had an ulterior motive for taking the trip. She had been reading a great deal about the booming desert town and the opportunities it presented for entertainers looking for lucrative and steady work.

Evenings, Winnie accompanied Tommy to the craps tables at the Riviera Hotel, then slipped out on her own during the day when Tommy played golf or disappeared to a private suite for high-stakes poker. She suspected there were prostitutes up there as well, but she didn't really care. Tommy would be that much more preoccupied, leaving her free to roam on her own for hours.

She studied the layout of the Riviera lounge, which hosted some of the world's most famous entertainers on the weekends, then settled for mostly local talent during the week. She hopped cabs and made her way around the city, visiting more than a dozen casinos downtown, in and around Fremont Street and on the rapidly developing Las Vegas Boulevard, better known as "The Strip."

Some of the bigger, newer resorts had two or three performance spaces, including showrooms reserved for resident revues that played year-round. The smaller rooms were busy day and night with every kind of entertainment imaginable. There were small combos and big bands for dancing. There were comedians of every shape and size; washed up Borscht Belt comics and energetic young bucks who seemed to favor impersonations. There was a magician whose Hungarian accent was so thick you couldn't understand a word he said, but his tricks were terrific.

There were a few rock 'n' roll combos that didn't seem to draw much of a crowd. *Not what I call music,* Winnie thought to herself.

One evening, Tommy took Winnie to the Tropicana for the Folies Bergère, a spectacular, colorful song-and-dance revue that featured topless showgirls. Tommy, drunk as usual, whistled and hooted his way through the whole show, as did many of the other cigar-chomping men. Winnie admired the production, thinking to herself how smart the show's producers were. This kind of thing was no big deal in Europe, but in Eisenhower's button-down America, topless dancers were relegated to seedy bars in the worst part of town.

Playing in the plush, brass-railed showroom of a big resort, it could be passed off as an international cultural event. Men, even with their wives in tow, could ogle the breasts and fannies of beautiful women without an ounce of guilt.

That alone was worth driving hours through the desert. And when the show was over, they could indulge in another taboo vice — gambling — without fear of the law.

This is the future, Winnie thought to herself. Why knock yourself out traveling around the country, sleeping in cars and rickety motor inns, when you could play Las Vegas, where the crowd came to you?

June came and Willie and Bobby had just finished sixth grade. They were growing out of their clothes at an alarming rate. Willie was a lean five-foot six, with thick, wavy blonde hair and a toothy smile that reminded Winnie of his father.

Bobby was five-foot-eight and chubby from his toes to his red cheeks. His hair was strawberry blonde, just like his mother, and rarely combed. He would wear the same clothes over and over unless Winnie told him otherwise, although sometimes she didn't bother.

"I gave birth to a rainbow and a mudslide," Bobby once overheard her say to Lourdes.

He favored a white T-shirt with horizontal red stripes. When his tousled hair stuck up and his red cheeks glowed with sweat, he looked like a little clown. So much so that when the other kids teased him, they called him "Bozo."

That was just Bobby, Winnie thought. He was a messy, clumsy, sloppy kid. When he smiled that goofy smile of his, which wasn't very often, even she was tempted to call him Bozo.

Winnie finally started to pay attention to Bobby when he took an interest in the drums. She wasn't sure where he got that pair of drumsticks that were in his hands most of the time. He'd bang on the pots hanging in the kitchen, lampshades, the Formica kitchen counter, rocks, fence posts or anything else that he would find in front of him. At first, it drove her crazy, but soon she realized he had a natural rhythm with those sticks that he had never shown anywhere else in his life.

She bought him a small set of drums for his thirteenth birthday. "It's time you learned to do something productive with that noise of yours," she told him.

It never occurred to Bobby that he was making music, but he knew how much attention his brother got from playing music, so he threw himself into learning how to be a proper drummer. The noise was deafening at times, so Winnie bought him a pair of brush sticks.

With Bobby's volume turned down, Winnie could finally think again. The idea came to her quickly. With some more practice, she could pair the boys up as an act. A very pragmatic idea. This would solve the problem of what to do with Bobby while she was managing Willie's career. Besides, he was getting to be a big, strong boy and could help with the suitcases and the equipment should they go on the road.

Sure enough, the Taylor family unit was evolving. The only question was, where to go?

Nowhere for the time-being. Winnie had met a promoter who booked big shows at ballrooms in southern California and needed local acts to warm up the crowds. He wasn't keen on a "kiddie act," as he referred to the Taylor Brothers, but Winnie made them available on short notice, so he used them a half-dozen times that summer. Willie enjoyed playing with Bobby and was glad to see his big brother look so happy. Bobby wasn't exactly Gene Krupa, and he wasn't all that comfortable in front of a crowd, but he got the job done. He laid down a simple beat with his brushes and Willie did the rest.

In July, Winnie lied about their amateur status, and their address, and entered the boys in the nearby Orange County Fair talent show. The boys won the competition, then were promptly disqualified when someone said to the judges, "Don't you know the singer is the Kiddie Cowboy from the radio?"

The judges, one of whom actually was a circuit court justice, were quite angry. He threatened Winnie with prosecution for fraud. Winnie just returned the medals, and the money, and told them what they could do with their contest.

"And don't bother running me out of town, because we're leaving anyway," she snapped.

On the ride home from the fair, Winnie announced calmly, "Tomorrow, you boys start packing your things. The people around here think small, and we are not small people. We're moving on to bigger and better things."

"Where we goin' Ma?" Bobby asked.

"We're going to Las Vegas. There's plenty of room for us there."

CHAPTER 6

Winnie handled all the money Willie made on the radio and had saved most of it for just this kind of opportunity. There was still nearly $2,000 left after she had purchased a slightly used 1958 Rambler American station wagon, which was large enough to hold most of their belongings.

She packed some of their extra stuff into boxes and left them with Pappy to send when she had an address to forward them to. She gave away many of their possessions, turning over the plush winter coats her husband had given her to Lourdes. "I don't think I wore any of them more than once," Winnie said.

"That's because they're too warm to wear around here even in February," Lourdes sniffed silently, wondering what the hell Winnie expected her to do with them. Winnie had also given her some much-needed furniture, including beds for her boys, so she bit her lip and forced a smile as she waved good-bye. Maybe she could sell the coats.

Pappy was much sadder at the prospect of his "family" leaving town. "What am I going to do without my Big Bobby and my Little Cowboy," he said. "And who's going to make sure your mother behaves herself?"

Once the Rambler was packed, they all shared a final chili lunch at the tavern before the Taylors headed up the coast to Los Angeles, and then northeast on Route 15. They got a late start out of town, so Winnie drove all night with the boys asleep in the back seat. The sun was rising over the flat desert horizon as she crossed the California border into Nevada.

"Wake up, you two," Winnie said, repeating herself twice before the boys began to stir.

"Are we there yet?" Willie asked, rubbing his eyes and looking in every direction for a sign of civilization.

"Just about. You boys ready to be stars?"

"*Maaa*," Willie said. "I just hope they like us."

"Are we gonna stop for breakfast?" Bobby said.

"Just be patient. We'll be there soon. Then we'll find something to eat."

"I gotta go," Bobby whined.

"Bobby, just … be patient,"

Willie hated when Winnie blew off Bobby so easily. He was almost a teenager now and keenly aware that he enjoyed preferential treatment from his mother. Willie loved his brother dearly and felt guilty when his mother brushed Bobby off. He felt sorry for Bobby in general and always tried to help him out any way he could.

"Ma, I gotta go, too. Can't we stop somewhere?" Willie lied for Bobby, then realized with a smile that he actually did have to go.

"All right, all right." She stopped the car and the boys ran about 20 yards into the desert. Willie squinted into the sun as he peed on a scrubby little bush. As his sleepy eyes began to focus, he thought he saw a big sign in the distance near the road.

When they got back on the road, the sign came up quickly, standing tall in the middle of the highway.

"Welcome to Fabulous Las Vegas, Nevada," the sign said.

Winnie didn't really have much of a plan from this point, and what little she did was miscalculated.

In dusty San Diego County, a safe distance from Los Angeles, Willie's talent was more than enough to stand out against the meager competition. In Las Vegas, there were hundreds of hopeful stars with the same idea as Winnie. It didn't take her long to realize that the booking agents in Vegas weren't going to line up and beg to sign her kids. Talent was more plentiful than water in the Nevada desert.

In late August, she finally enrolled the boys in school. It hadn't occurred to her they would have the time, but the only public appearance the Taylor Brothers had managed was at the Clark County Fair, a small, dreary affair except for the talent contest, which overflowed with unemployed musicians. The boys did manage to finish third. First place went to a family that wore matching costumes and sang "Mr. Sandman" in five-part harmony.

Winnie was beyond thinking this would be easy. Quickly running out of money, and with no Tommy O'Dowds to help support her family, she was forced to take a job as a cocktail waitress at the Full House, a large casino hotel on the south end of the strip. The money was decent, but there were a lot of rules for cocktail waitresses. Winnie had never been very good at following rules. She wasn't getting any younger, either. Even worse, without Lourdes' magic potions, the hot desert sun was wreaking havoc on her ever-fragile complexion. For the first time in her life, Winnie had wrinkles.

She also landed on the bad side of Mr. Lumpkin, the food and beverage manager. Benny Lumpkin like to grab ass and Winnie knew the girls who got the better shifts let him grab even more. To add insult to injury, Benny hadn't even tried to offer her a "promotion." She still had a fine, full figure, but her weathered face gave away her age. Benny favored the young ones and treated Winnie like she was in the way.

Winnie fended him off by ingratiating herself with some of the regulars, teasing them with flirtatious patter and occasionally shocking them with bawdy comebacks. Some of these men had connections that Benny wouldn't mess with. Benny was from Chicago, knew the rules and understood his place in the Las Vegas pecking order. He had a wife, three daughters and a nice house in North Las Vegas. He had his pick of the waitresses. He ate lunch and dinner for free.

So he wasn't going to mess with those goombas' favorite cocktail waitress, no matter how much he disliked her.

"Bitch thinks she runs the place," he would mutter to

himself, but no one else.

He had no idea how right he was. Winnie's situation had not tempered her ambition. She still had a way with men, and there were plenty of those in Las Vegas. And she was still holding Willie as her trump card. When the time was right, she would put his talents on the table.

He's just a little young for this town, she thought. *He just needs to grow up a little and polish his act. Then we'll grab this town by the balls until it screams for mercy.*

CHAPTER 7

Willie took to Las Vegas like a brand-new guitar. The next two years breezed by like a vacation. His mother had backed off a little. For the first time in his life, he was allowed to just be a kid.

Franklin D. Roosevelt Middle School had a great music department. There were two classrooms big enough for a small orchestra and instruments lying around everywhere. The school didn't have a football team, but it did have a marching band. The band didn't need a guitar player, so Willie learned to pay the saxophone and trumpet. Bobby was a natural to carry the big bass drum with "F.D.R.M.S." written in bold red letters stenciled on each side.

The best part of his two years in middle school was meeting Mr. Rush, the music teacher and band director. Andy Rush was cool. A beatnik disguised in a short-sleeved white shirt and black tie. He was rapidly balding at age 25, but he was handsome, lean and well-groomed. The boys in his class, who were just beginning to notice girls, noticed that the female teachers really seemed to like Mr. Rush.

Like Willie, Mr. Rush played all kinds of instruments, including a Wurlitzer 112 model electric piano that he owned and kept at the school. Willie had never seen one before and loved its tone. He would sit for hours after school, playing the Wurlitzer until Mr. Rush said it was time to lock up.

Mr. Rush also turned Willie on to blues and modern jazz. He knew he had a prodigy in Willie, and was amazed how many of the complex Les Paul instrumentals he knew by heart on the guitar.

"Les Paul can really play, but he's all gimmick," Mr. Rush

argued. "Listen to Wes Montgomery or Tal Farlow. Johnny Smith. Earl Hooker. Those guys are where it's at now. Muddy Waters and B.B. King. B.B.'s a bluesman, but he's got a big jazzy band, with horns and everything. And I have some old Charlie Christian records that would blow your mind."

Willie sopped it all up. He practiced jazz to please Mr. Rush, although he really preferred the blues. Some of it sounded kind of country and had the danceable rhythms that Willie always preferred.

"You could hurt yourself dancing to jazz," Willie often said. He and Bobby would try to dance to a Miles Davis record, get all twisted and then fall on top of each other, laughing like hyenas.

Winnie was relieved that Mr. Rush didn't like rock 'n' roll. He said rock 'n' roll was bourgeois and only played by musicians who couldn't play anything that required real talent or discipline. Willie kind of liked it, and Bobby loved the beat, but something about rock music really rubbed Winnie the wrong way, so he mostly stuck to what pleased her and his favorite teacher.

Mr. Rush, who also taught at the high school, had a lot of talented students. Some were even working in town. Still, he knew Willie would someday play rings around them all. All he needed was some direction.

"You know, Willie, this isn't a great town for serious musicians," he told him one day after school. "Music is work here, not art. It's product. Musicians turn music out like factory workers build cars. Follow the blueprint, put it together just like it says on the instructions. No surprises. Make it sound like it's supposed to sound. Over and over. Night after night.

"You keep telling me your mom is going to get you and your brother a job. And that's great. But you have something special. You could be a real musician. A real artist. But you have to dedicate yourself to training and practice. Develop your own style. Learn to be a leader, so you're the one who shapes the sound. You have to remember that, even if you get a job here. A musician has to follow his muse."

"Muse? You mean like music?" Willie asked.

"No, your *muse*. Your inspiration. What inspires you to make music?"

"Well, my mother says ... "

"No, Willie, your mother can't be your muse," Mr. Rush said, chuckling. "Especially *your* mother. No, what makes you *want* to play music?"

"People like it when I play," said Willie, trying to understand. "And that makes me feel good. I feel like I'm sharing."

"That's fine. Now, what makes you *have* to play?"

Willie looked up at his teacher. He wanted to say something, but his mouth was empty.

"John Lee Hooker. There's another happening guitar player. Bluesman. Got his own style of playing boogie-woogie. Totally gone. He put it this way: "The music is in him, *and it got to come out.*"

Willie began to understand. "I feel like playing right now. Is that what you mean?"

"Kinda," said Mr. Rush, smiling. It wasn't the revelation he was hoping for, but he was starting to get through. "Yeah, let's play. I have a surprise for you."

Willie got behind the Wurlitzer and noodled a bit while Mr. Rush left the room and headed for the parking lot. He returned with a long, flat instrument case and laid it down on the floor. "Open it," he said.

Willie got up and came around the piano, dropping to his knees in front of the case. He flipped the latches and opened the case to reveal a shiny, gold electric guitar.

"A Les Paul! A Gibson Les Paul!" Willie hollered. "Can I try it? *Pleeease?*"

"I don't see why not. It's yours." Mr. Rush stared at the young boy, really a young man now, making sure he did not miss the reaction. Willie's eyes nearly popped out of his head.

Then his jaw dropped open. Mr. Rush thought for a minute that Willie might start drooling, or stop breathing altogether.

Once again, Willie tried to say something, but his mouth was empty. He couldn't even feel his tongue.

A few syllables finally made their way through. "You mean it? For real, for keeps?"

"You bet your b-flat, my little Mozart. Just one promise."

"Yeah, yeah, *what*?"

"None of that rock and roll shit, OK?"

Willie's mouth still wasn't in full function. He nodded his head up and down about five times, smiling from ear to ear.

Mr. Rush later told him he won it in a poker game from a musician in Chubby Checker's band. "I made it my mission to rescue this beautiful axe from that amateur." Word was out that Chubby fired the guitarist when he showed up for a gig at the Dunes without his instrument.

They didn't call it Lost Wages for nothing.

CHAPTER 8

That was it for Willie. The music was in his blood. In his breath. In his soul.

It was in him, and it had to come out.

It all stayed with him. More and more, he practiced jazz and other more sophisticated instrumental arrangements. His old influences, though, stayed with him. Les Paul, Hank Williams, Gene Autry. None of it was pushed aside. Willie was a sponge and once he soaked it up, it was with him forever.

Mr. Rush just sat back and marveled. From a technical perspective, Willie, now all of 14, could play as well as anyone he knew. And he was already developing a unique sound of his own. There were elements of Chicago blues, country and jazz. He sounded a lot like B.B. King, but his smooth, rhythmic phrasing was more of the western swing variety. Sometimes, it would morph into rockabilly, at which point he could feel Willie pull back as though he'd crossed some sort of unholy line. Then he would pull out a banjo and just let loose, playing chords so fast his hand would blur to the naked eye.

Willie wasn't quite as advanced on the keyboard, but Mr. Rush thought he was good enough to make a living playing a piano. He also was the best saxophonist and trumpet player in the band, and could even write horn charts.

He was a much better drummer than his brother, although that wasn't saying much and he would never say so to Bobby's face. Drumming was the only thing Bobby was good at, good being a relative term in this instance.

Willie's voice still hadn't fully matured, so he could still sing high notes with crystal clarity. His ever-expanding musical experience, however, allowed him to warble like a world-weary crooner. *Soul and control,* Mr. Rush called it. A scary combination. Sometimes, he sounded like Peggy Lee. Other times, he sounded like Sam Cooke.

"Sometimes, you just sound like Willie Taylor," Mr. Rush would say with a wink. It was the best compliment the boy had ever received.

Willie was, indeed, the real deal. He could be one of the leaders of a new generation of music.

The future, though, would have to wait. Winnie's dreams always trumped any hand, even in Las Vegas. Especially in Vegas. She had been patient for two years, waiting for the right time and place to grab the brass ring.

Mary Murray had been the featured attraction in the Regal Lounge, the largest of the two lounges at the Full House. It wasn't as big as the Royal, the feature showroom where big stars would play to more than 1,000 high rollers at a time. The Regal could fit maybe three hundred people, nearly three times the capacity of the Rascal Lounge, which the waitresses called the Rathole because the tips and the floor show were usually lousy. Benny Lumpkin loved to send Winnie to work back in the Rathole whenever her fans from Chicago weren't asking for her at the Regal.

Mary had the looks of a debutante. She favored blue taffeta dresses and a beehive for her honey blonde hair. Her voice was thin yet pure, and she had a following among the regulars, especially the oil-rich Texans who would fly in and take over the strip on a Saturday night. The *goombahs* liked her, too, and could always be relied on to fill a few seats.

Winnie noticed that Mary had been missing a few gigs of late and looked like she was gaining some weight. Winnie put two and two together, but said nothing to management. Instead, she took Willie and Bobby shopping for clothes. White shirts, white sports coats, white dress shoes. Tan trousers and bright blue knit ties.

Then she told the boys to start putting a show together. She wanted them to write it all down. Three 45-minute sets. Songs, arrangements, a few jokes she stole from comics who had left town.

At work, she sucked up to Benny and managed to wrangle a few extra shifts out of him at the Regal. She kept her eyes and ears open, making sure to knock on the office door to see if anyone needed anything. This gave her a chance to eavesdrop.

About three weeks later, on a steaming-hot Tuesday in July, Winnie was standing outside the office door and overheard Tony Seville, aka Tony Sevilia, shouting into the phone. Tony was the assistant general manager of the Full House, second in charge overall, and booked all the talent.

"God damnit, I didn't knock her up! ... Look, I really don't give a shit, just get me another singer. By tonight!"

Winnie waited until later, about four in the afternoon, the time when Mary Murray would stroll in for her 6 o'clock show.

"Where's the band, Tony?" Winnie asked. "They going to need dinner back there?"

"No dinner, sweetheart. No Mary, no band. Gonna be dark and quiet here tonight, I'm figgerin.' You want off tonight? Tips are gonna be slow."

"Tony, I have an idea," Winnie said. "You want a band in here tonight? I can have you a band onstage in two hours."

"Honey, just stick to pushin' the booze, OK? I ain't in the mood."

"C'mon Tony, what do you have to lose? I swear, they're really good."

"What? Ya gotta boyfriend who plays in a band? All you dames go ga-ga over musicians. Like to shoot the whole fuckin' lot of 'em."

"Well, yeah, sorta. My two boys. My sons. They've won talent contests and everything."

"Kids? I don't need the Everly Brothers in my room.

People here hate that rock and roll shit."

"No rock and roll. Absolutely not." Winnie sensed exhaustion and weakness. If she pushed him too far, he might lose that famous temper of his. But she already had him on the ropes. She wasn't going to back down now.

"Tony, they play country and the pops. My youngest plays the guitar and banjo and sings like Caruso. Tony, they got matching costumes and everything."

"They did fill-ins last month at the Hacienda," she lied for good measure.

Tony picked up the phone and made another call. "Nothing? No one?" he said to someone. "Jesus Christ."

He hung up the phone and sighed.

"Alright, Winnie, you win. Bring 'em in. You swear to me they know what they're doin'? Cause if they don't, I'm holding you responsible."

"Tony, you won't regret this."

"Two hours, Winnie. Tell Benny to get another waitress up here."

Oh, she would love that. *Gotta go, Benny. I'm bringing in a band for Tony.*

CHAPTER 9

Willie didn't expect to see his mother motoring up the driveway at four-thirty in the afternoon.

"Put your suits on, boys, it's time to play!" Winnie said, bouncing through the living room like a pinball.

"What's going on?" Bobby asked.

"Come here and pay attention to what I say," his mother said, still pacing back and forth. "I've got you a job. You're going to play the Regal tonight. It won't be that crowded on a weeknight, but it's a job. And we have an hour and a half to get you on that stage. Bobby, pack your drums and put them in the Rambler. Then, clean yourself up and comb your hair."

Willie was prepared for this.

"Willie, what do you need?"

"My Les Paul, the Sears and the banjo. And my amp."

"They have amplifiers at the lounge. Forget the amplifier."

"I'm used to my amplifier. I can't do the Les Paul stuff unless I have the right settings."

"Fine, pack your amplifier. And don't get those clothes dirty. Please make sure your brother is clean, too."

"Maybe the uke, too. I could do the Hawaiian thing. And my binder! I need all the music and notes."

Willie was so excited, and so eager to please his mother, that he forgot about Mr. Rush and his muse. It was a paying job. His mother taught him to respect that, and he knew this wasn't the kind of audience that wanted Wes Montgomery and B.B. King.

He packed the car, leaving his muse in the closet, and practiced knotting his bright blue tie on the drive over.

Winnie pulled the car around to the back entrance and banged on the large metal door. One of the bouncers opened the door and helped the boys unload. Mario, the stage technician, was helping the boys set up when Tony rushed in and pulled Winnie aside by the forearm.

"Winnie, these kids are … *kids!*" He said. "What have you got me into here?"

"Tony, please, trust me," Winnie said. "I swear you won't regret this."

"You just remember what I said. Jesus, what a day!"

There never was anything to worry about. Bobby was petrified, but Willie was in complete control. He patiently bobbed his head up and down until Bobby picked up the beat of the first song, "Twelfth Street Rag," a peppy Les Paul instrumental with a simple rhythm.

The rest of the night was easy. The crowd was bigger than expected. About half-full, then a little more by the third set after word had spread around the hotel.

Willie even surprised himself. The audience reaction was so positive that he couldn't help enjoying the adulation. Drunk with confidence, he jumped off the stage, grabbed a tall hat from one of the Texans and started doing some Gene Autry songs that he and his brother hadn't even rehearsed. Somehow, Bobby was able to follow along.

The end was a thing of beauty. They had rehearsed it for days — "Jambalaya," first played slow and sweet, then a full-tilt rave. Everyone was clapping along and the Texans up front were stomping their feet as well. One of them grabbed a waitress and danced with her right in front of the stage. More couples followed until you could hardly see the boys on the small platform stage, which wasn't more than eight inches off the floor.

Winnie leaned against the back wall and started to cry. Tony walked over to her, arms spread wide apart. He gave her a bear hug, wiped a tear from her cheek and smiled.

"Go tell Benny you're fired," he said. "Then come back

here tomorrow. Not too early, maybe around noon. Bring those boys of yours. We'll all have lunch. Tell them to bring their suits. They can have a swim in the pool while we talk."

"*Talk?*" Winnie was at a rare loss for words.

"Contract talk. I'm gonna need them for at least two months. After that, we'll see. OK?"

They turned their glances to the stage as the song ended and the crowd roared. Winnie could barely see them, but knew her boys were standing together, taking a deep bow that also was thoroughly rehearsed.

Tony pulled a wad of cash from his pocket and gave her five hundred-dollar bills.

"In the meantime, you keep an eye on those boys. And make sure they get a good night's sleep. They're gonna be up late tomorrow."

The crowd was slow to file out of the lounge and the boys had to fight their way through to reach their mother. Some of the Texans stuffed five-dollar bills in their hands as they passed by.

When they got to the back of the room, Winnie hugged Willie until he couldn't breathe. Still holding onto Willie, she smiled at Bobby and mussed his sweaty hair.

I'm so, so proud of you boys," she cried, looking Willie square in the eye. "You're going to be bigger than Elvis."

CHAPTER 10

Willie and Bobby rarely got the chance to be regular kids. The Taylor family business always came before play. So even after last night, when they stood tall as Texans on the Regal stage, an invitation to swim in the huge Full House Hotel pool brought the little boys out of these young men.

Thoughts of Marco Polo and cannonball dives quickly vanished as a pretty young towel girl escorted them to the pool. "Betty, show these boys where they can cool off," were Tony's instructions. "And be careful with them. They're famous."

Willie thought he recognized Betty from the school bus. She was already in the high school but had stopped taking the bus in the spring. *Probably got a boyfriend with a car*, Willie thought. Anyway, she sure was pretty, with her platinum-blonde hair bobbed and pinned behind her ears with pink plastic ribbon clips. She was wearing a white T-shirt and shorts that revealed the outline of a two-piece swimming suit. Her round, pink cheeks glowed when she smiled. Even squinting into the sun, Willie couldn't miss her bright blue eyes.

She smiled at Bobby, then smiled a little longer at Willie. Her pink lips curled like Cupid's bow. "C'mon," she said, turning down a steamy hallway with signs that said "Spa," "Locker Rooms" and "Pool." "You guys from around here?" she asked.

"Um, yeah. Well, actually, we're playing at the Regal. We're a band," said Willie, trying to hide his nerves.

"You're in the band?" she said.

"Well, we, *are* the band, actually," he stammered.

"We're the Taylor Brothers!" Bobby blurted out rather boldly. His voice cracked as he said it, and he turned red with embarrassment.

"Well, I'm just sure you are," Betty replied in a kind voice that reassured Bobby and impressed Willie. Her sweet southern drawl had both boys fighting off daydreams.

Betty was just the tip of the iceberg. When they got to the pool, an Olympic-length quarter acre of blue ripples, their teenage fantasies suddenly seemed insignificant. There were dozens of white folding lounges, and at least every fourth one held a beautiful girl baking in the sun. *Women*, actually, as Willie observed. *More than girls*, he chuckled. *Much more.*

Betty lowered her eyebrows and smirked. She had seen men react like this here many times before. She tossed a few towels over their shoulders and went back to work. Willie turned around and said, "Uh, thanks. Where do we, uh … "

"Anywhere you want, sugar," Betty said. "Just pick a chair and take a load off."

Willie smiled and thanked her again. He lingered as he watched her walk away, her blonde hair glowing in the sun. On second thought, she was much prettier than a lot of these *women*, at least by his measure. Funny, he had started to notice girls in the last year or so, but hadn't considered favoring a *type*. This girl was his type, he decided then and there.

She noticed him staring and turned back around.

"Was there something else you needed?" she said, enjoying the attention.

"Uh, no, I guess. This is great."

"What's your name, Taylor Brother?"

"Willie. Willie Taylor. I think I know you, sorta. I go to Valley Memorial. I mean, I'm going to go there. I've seen you on the school bus."

"Oh, that smelly thing. I've got my own car now. I'll be a junior this year."

Great. She was probably two years older than he was. His fantasies began to cool. The day was getting warmer. He started to think about the pool.

"You and your brother really play at the Regal?"

Interest! Could this be possible? Was she teasing him?

Maybe she didn't have a boyfriend. She said she had her own car.

"Well, we did last night, and my mom, I mean, my mother, is talking to Tony right now. All I know for sure is that we're playing again tonight."

Betty looked him over, slowly. "My name is Betty, by the way, thanks for asking. Elizabeth Anne Tilden."

"My name is Willie."

"Yes, I know. Willie Taylor. You play at the Regal. You're one of the Taylor Brothers."

Now she was teasing. Or was that flirting? He really didn't know much about this sort of thing.

"Yeah," he said. She was still smiling. Willie had to laugh at himself. At the same time, he noticed he was at least four inches taller than her. That gave him some confidence.

Still, he had no idea what to do. Would she go out with him? Willie wasn't ready to find out. He wasn't sure he was ready to date a real girl. Surely his mother would have an opinion.

That was a sobering thought. His confidence waned.

"I guess I should let you work," he said.

"Should you?" she said.

An older woman called for Betty. Her boss, maybe. "I'll see you around, Taylor Brother," she said, smiling as she skipped off.

Good God! Willie was sweating, but at least he could breathe again. He turned to look for Bobby, who had been watching the exchange from the edge of the pool. "Who is that?" said Bobby, who was breathing a little heavy himself. "She looked familiar."

"Betty, from the bus," said Willie, staring in the direction that Betty had disappeared.

"I didn't know you knew her. Is she nice?"

"Nice. Yeah."

Time for a cold swim. Snapping out of his fog, Willie pushed Bobby in the pool, then dove in himself. They spent the next hour in and out of the pool. Betty never came back.

Tired from the night before, both boys eventually chose a lounger and napped into a deep sleep. Willie woke to the sound of his mother's voice calling his name.

"Oh, for God sakes, look at you two!"

What? *Ouch!* Oh. Willie and Bobby were beefsteak red with sunburn.

"Well, come on," Winnie said. "We'll pick up some Noxema on the way home. Bobby, how could you let this happen? Don't you boys have any sense?"

"We were asleep," said Bobby, trying not to wince. "It's OK."

"Well, you'll just have to grin and bear it," Winnie said.

The Taylors piled into the Rambler and headed for home. On the way, Winnie told the boys about their new contract to play the Regal. Tuesday through Friday, four shows a night, seven at night to one in the morning. One hour on, 20 minutes off. If no headliner was booked for the weekend, they would play from six until two on Saturday night, and the usual hours on Sunday.

Winnie negotiated a salary of three hundred dollars for the week, double when they played the weekend. Winnie wanted more, but Tony said they were just kids and should be thanking him for the chance of a lifetime. Winnie grudgingly agreed, with a few riders: full dinner every night for all three of them, a private table for Winnie in the back and their name on the neon roadside marquee out on the Strip. All of that cost Tony very little, so it was a good deal for everyone.

The contract locked them in until Labor Day. Mary Murray was only about six months along and couldn't stand more than half an hour without her ankles swelling up like tree trunks. She wasn't going to be of any use to Tony for a long time.

The Taylor Brothers were a smash hit upon their return to the Regal that evening. As stipulated by their new contract, they had to play an hour longer than their tryout gig. Midway through the last set, they ran out of rehearsed songs, so Willie was forced to wing it. He slipped in covers of two songs that were popular in that summer of 1961: Ricky Nelson's "Travelin' Man" and Elvis Presley's "Are You Lonesome Tonight?" Willie could hear his mother's voice in his head, commanding him not to play rock 'n' roll. But it was either those or country gospel tunes, which Winnie had told him weren't really big with the casino lounge lizards.

Although Ricky Nelson and Elvis were rock 'n' roll stars, those popular hits had enough melody to fit in nicely with the other songs they played. Maybe Winnie wouldn't even notice, Willie hoped. For the first time in his life, he smiled at the thought of fooling his mother and taking some control over his career. After all, he was a professional now, making ... *how much were they making, anyway?* Winnie hadn't said anything about the money.

The crowd loved hearing the Taylor Brothers put their take on the top 40. Willie hadn't rehearsed either number, but had memorized the words and melodies after hearing them played over and over on the radio. All Bobby had to do was follow along, quietly swishing the brushes over the snare drum without causing too much of a commotion. Willie had gotten used to Bobby's rather predictable style. He'd learned to play with the beat when Bobby was on and over it when Bobby was lost.

Willie thought for a moment about doing "Hound Dog" then saw that their time was almost filled. They saved "Jambalaya" for the closer, got everyone on their feet and finished once again to a healthy ovation.

As people filed out, the boys made their way to the back of the room, where Winnie was sipping a glass of wine at her table. Just like the night before, a few of the patrons slipped them tips along the way. One woman, wearing a tight gold party dress and too much makeup, slipped Willie a five-dollar bill and a cocktail napkin with a phone number on it. She appeared to be alone and looked older than Winnie. *Egad,* Willie thought to himself.

The boys sat down, exhausted. Bobby grabbed a large burgundy napkin and wiped the sweat from his face. Winnie snatched it out of his hand. "Bobby, that's disgusting," she said, then she turned to Willie and beamed.

"That was great, great," she said. "You boys were just wonderful. Maria, can we get some Cokes over here for my boys? They're dying of thirst."

"Mom, how much are we getting for this?" Willie asked.

Winnie's smile disappeared and her lips drew tight. That's the way she looks when she's about to yell, Willie thought.

Winnie, though, bit her lip, then looked down at the table. "I don't want you to worry about that," she said calmly. "You boys need to focus on your music and your show. My job is to take care of the bills. The family. I'll tell you this. The money is enough to put food on the table. We might even be able to buy a nicer house. And you'll both get an allowance."

"Really? How much?" said Bobby.

"Why don't we talk about it tomorrow?" Winnie said. "We're all tired. Let's just go home. And both of you will take a shower before you go to bed. Those suits are smelly, and you both reek of Noxema."

"Maybe you should wash them before we play tomorrow," Willie said.

"Maybe we need to go to the men's store and splurge," Winnie said, perking up a bit. "I want my boys to look and smell nice."

CHAPTER 11

Labor Day came and went and, with school back in session, Winnie and Tony had to negotiate a new agreement. Keeping the boys onstage past midnight, every night, was not going to fly with the administrators at Valley Memorial High School, where both were enrolled as freshmen.

Tony was in a bind. If this were any other band, dictating terms that messed up his entire schedule, he would have tossed them out on their ass. But in just two months, the Taylor Brothers had become such a draw for the hotel that people were being turned away at the Regal. Sometimes, the overflow "settled" for the headliners in the Royal. Sometimes they just headed for the casino. But Tony knew it was Winnie's kids who brought them through the front door.

Tony was able to take credit with top management for the boost in business. Credit was important to him. As rough as he was around the edges, Tony had brains and ambition. He wanted to run the Full House someday. The Taylor Brothers were a feather in his cap. He needed to lock them up before some other hotel stole them away.

Still, schoolboys could not do six hours a night. This meant he couldn't even offer them steady work, which put Winnie on his back. "You need to work something out, Tony," she nagged him. "They're too good to be filling in a few weekends a month. They've got a following. If you can't use them, there are plenty of other hotels on the Strip."

So much for loyalty and appreciation, he thought. He thought briefly about getting her out of the way, then quickly thought again. She was a woman, for Christ sakes. Hell, she was their *mother*.

Even worse, she was right. Tony was screwed. And he didn't need another headache right now. Danny Benvenuto, general manager of the Full House, had all his underlings sprucing up the operation top to bottom. They were all about to get an inspection from Patsy Bucco.

"Maybe you could talk to Patsy about your scheduling problem," Danny said to Tony. "I'm sure he'd love to sit down and help you work it all out."

Tony didn't appreciate Danny's mocking tone. He was well aware that Patsy Bucco didn't have time to talk about the floor show in his lounge. The Full House was a fairly small duchy in the Bucco family kingdom, which stretched from Chicago to Mexico to the Atlantic Coast.

Tony would figure it out by himself.

He arrived at a pragmatic solution. They didn't need out-of-town weekend headliners at the Regal. The Taylor Brothers could fill the Regal any night of the week, including weekends, for a fraction of what it cost to hire and fly in a "name" act for the bigger weekend crowds.

Cutting back on pricey weekend headliners would free up his budget to hire a few mid-level names to come in during the week, when the Taylor Brothers had to go to school. Over-the-hill crooners who still had a loyal following. Faded vaudeville stars who could make more out here than in the Catskills. He'd still have enough money to hire a public-relations assistant to dust these dinosaurs off and sell them to the middle-class weekday tourists.

A new advertising campaign was initiated to support his strategy. The hotel leased a billboard on Highway 15 leading into town. "Come see why the House is full every night. Your favorite entertainers, all week long, only at the Full House!"

That's what everybody called the Full House. The *House*. It was all about family, after all.

On the top right corner of the billboard, the sign would be updated to list the headliners and the dates of their appearance. Just below were the words, "Every Fri.-Sat.-Sun.:

The fabulous Taylor Brothers."

Winnie drove the boys out of town just to stare at the billboard. They stopped the car about fifty yards from the sign and admired it while the setting sun behind them turned it a bright orange.

"I'm so proud of you boys," she said, not even trying to hold back the tears. "This means so much to me. You know, I thought my name might be up there like that some day. But you never know what fate has in store for you."

She looked up again at the sign, dwelling on the name "Taylor." For the first time in years, she thought of her husband. Her tears dried quickly in the warm desert wind. She could feel the wrinkles on her face tighten up.

"Fate was not kind to me," she said, her mood quickly festered to anger. "But I've made sure that fate is something you won't have to worry about."

The new contract called for eight hours Friday and Saturday night, five hours on Sunday. Six hundred dollars a week. An extra thousand to play straight through the Christmas and Easter week vacations.

Willie settled nicely into the routine. Nothing made him happier than to play music and make people happy. Sometimes, though, all the attention was too much, especially coming from a bunch of noisy, drunken adults. And there were more older women and more napkins with phone numbers. *Egad*, he would think as he tried to avoid inhaling their toxic perfumes.

At school, things were a little more normal. Their new status wasn't that big a deal, especially since their classmates were too young to get into the Regal. It wasn't as if the Taylor Brothers were on Ed Sullivan. All they knew was what they heard from grown-ups.

Besides, Willie and Bobby weren't the only working professional entertainers in the school. Valley Memorial was filled with the children of musicians, actors, magicians, animal trainers, comics, even showgirls. A lot of these kids had show business in their veins. They had connections staring at them from across the dinner table. Willie knew of one girl who played violin in Liberace's orchestra. Two boys were in a family of acrobats that had worked in several big shows. There were rumors that several of the senior girls were kicking their heels in chorus lines. Another was said to be dancing topless in the Folies.

Mr. Rush, who also ran the music department at the high school, was disappointed when Willie didn't go out for the varsity marching band. Bobby still had the time to bang his bass drum up and down the field. Willie had to spend weeknights working on the act, choosing new songs and charting arrangements. Sometimes, Mr. Rush came over to help him out and the jam sessions would go on until they frayed Winnie's nerves. Winnie hid her mistrust of Mr. Rush, a rival for her favored child's affection, because she believed Willie still needed a musical mentor.

When his mother wasn't around, Willie turned on the rock radio stations coming out of California and played along. The energy and the beat of rock music was hard to resist. He was a big fan of Roy Orbison, who sang in his key. He also liked Chuck Berry, the Everly Brothers, Marty Robbins and Jerry Lee Lewis.

Orbison's "Running Scared" had already made its way into the Taylor Brothers' playlist. They were learning his latest hit, "Dream Baby (How Long Must I Dream)." Willie had to be very careful about sneaking rock numbers into the set, although Winnie actually liked "Love Me Tender." She also allowed them to play "Itsy Bitsy Teenie Weenie Yellow Polka Dot Bikini" because it made people laugh.

Winnie realized Willie was taking more and more charge of the show. She not only accepted this, she encouraged it. He finally seemed to accept that, at the Regal, there were songs you could do, and songs you couldn't. On the increasingly rare occasions when he pushed a song she didn't like, she knew she still had the final word. And he was developing a knack for identifying newer songs that might rock a bit, but would still be appreciated by the older crowd that he played to.

Willie was more frustrated about the good songs they could not do because it was just the two of them. No backup singers, no harmonies, no piano. No horns. Willie was itching to expand some arrangements, but without a larger band, there was no point.

He wished he could convince Winnie to hire a few pieces for the band. He knew it would be a waste of time. Truth was, if it were feasible, Winnie would have Willie on that stage all by himself.

At school, Willie caught up with Betty, who he had not seen the rest of the summer. She worked early at the pool and he worked late, so their paths had not crossed. He found out she was a junior. More significantly, she had a boyfriend, Steve, a straight-laced senior who wore neatly pressed khaki slacks and starched shirts. She always greeted Willie with a smile when they passed in the hall and there was occasional small talk about work and such. Willie was still too scared to pursue her. He knew he had no chance.

Spring came early that year. One morning, as Willie and Bobby were waiting for the bus, an old red Plymouth convertible came speeding up to the corner. Willie was thrilled to see Betty behind the wheel. She was wearing dark black sunglasses and a white scarf on her head.

"Hey there, Mr. Taylor Brother. Want a lift?" she said.

The other boys, including Bobby, were speechless. Willie smiled and got in. As they drove off, Willie realized they were not heading towards the school.

"What's going on?" Willie asked. Real smooth, he thought.

"I like to get out of town sometimes, where I can drive fast," she said. "Clear my mind so I can bear seven dreary hours cooped up in classrooms."

"Where's your boyfriend?" Willie asked, regretting the

question immediately.

"We broke up," she said. "Such a tragedy. Steve is a nice boy, and he's going to make some girl a nice husband someday. His family is loaded. His father runs the Stagecoach downtown. But he was *soo* boring."

Willie was mute as he tried to figure out what was going on. Betty broke the silence as she turned the car around, using a well-worn curved path off the shoulder that she clearly was familiar with, and sped back to town, leaving a cloud of dust in her wake.

"Actually, if you want to know the truth, he broke up with me," she said. "I don't think his parents approved."

"I find that hard to believe," Willie said. She smiled. He smiled back, having finally scored a point with her.

"Why Mr. Taylor, I do believe that's the nicest thing you've ever said to me," she said, her Georgia drawl making music out of every syllable.

"Steve is going to Stanford in the fall," she said. "I'm afraid I may be stuck here forever. So I decided I'd better find some new friends who might stick around with me. What do you think?"

"What do I think?" For a young man with such a command of melody and rhythm, Willie still hadn't learned how to make time with a girl.

"Do you want to be my friend?" Betty asked. "Goodness, Willie, relax. I'm not going to bite you."

"That would be nice. To be friends," Willie said as they pulled into the school parking lot, just as the homeroom bell was ringing.

Betty parked the car, took off her sunglasses and stuck her hand out.

"Then it's settled. We're friends," she said.

Willie shook her hand, savoring the feel of her slim, manicured fingers. Her hand was cool. He was feeling flush. "Friends."

"You know, I'm not supposed to, but I snuck in to see

your show a couple of times when I got stuck with a double-shift," she said. "You are really, really good."

"You did?" said Willie, starting to feel a bit woozy. "You really think so?"

Betty hesitated, then gave him a soft, swift kiss on the lips.

"You are *soo* adorable," she said.

CHAPTER 12

Winnie was predictable as always. "How old is this girlfriend of yours?" she asked.

"She's not my girlfriend. She's my friend. A friend," Willie said. He wasn't really sure what Betty was.

"How old is she?"

"Sixteen, I think. She's a junior."

"Sixteen! Young man, we need to have a talk," Winnie said.

Betty's car horn signaled Willie's reprieve. "That's her. We'll be late for school. Gotta go, bye." Willie kissed his mother, grabbed his books and dashed out the kitchen door of their new home, a small, comfortable bungalow in one of the older neighborhoods on the north end of town.

"Take your brother with you," said Winnie. She looked at Bobby, who was still eating breakfast. "Go!" she said. Bobby wiped his mouth, grabbed his books and ran after his little brother.

Girlfriend or not, Betty was a good friend. That alone was a new experience for Willie. As long as he could remember, his only real friends were his family and the adults he had worked with.

Flash had been a good friend. Mr. Rush was a good friend. Betty was different. When she talked about her feelings, her dreams, her problems at home, Willie could relate, which made him comfortable enough to talk with her about his own feelings. His mother. The nagging belief that he was missing out on a normal life.

Willie also learned that Betty would not turn seventeen until November, so she was only about a year and a half older than him. She also didn't have her driver's license yet, but her mother let her drive because she had a job.

Betty, like Willie, had her own unique set of problems. She was being raised by her mother, Amanda, one of the first female blackjack dealers in Las Vegas. Her mother and her father, Ed, who was twelve years older than Amanda, had moved from Atlanta to Reno during the war. Ed knew someone there who promised him all the construction contract work he could handle. But in late 1943, he developed a serious heart condition and could no longer work. A heart attack killed him a few years later, leaving Amanda alone with a young daughter and another, Betty, on the way.

Circumstances during the war years favored independent women willing to risk their femininity and standing in the community. Displaced from her southern roots, and faced with the burdens of being a single mother, Amanda had no trouble swallowing her pride. The shortage of men had created all sorts of opportunities around town, including Harold's Club, which had put out the word they were willing to hire women dealers in the casino.

Amanda sent for her own mother, a widow herself, to join in her in Reno. Nana could watch the kids while she worked double shifts at Harold's. Once the gamblers got used to a woman dealing their cards, the stigma wore off and Amanda was in demand to deal at the private, high-stakes tables where the hours were crazy but the tips were fat. When she took time off because Nana broke her ankle, one of the regulars even offered to hire a visiting nurse so she could get back to the table.

Betty's sister, who was five years older, ran off with her boyfriend in 1960. Nana had died the same year, leaving Amanda in a deep depression. Betty was old enough to take care of herself by then, and home had become a dreary prison. She found jobs to keep her busy and boyfriends to give her the attention she craved.

The boyfriends never stuck around very long, especially

when Betty laid down the law. She was a lovely, funny, vivacious young woman, smart and open-minded. She also was a virgin and determined to stay that way until marriage. That was a promise she made to her beloved Nana.

"Save yourself for that special man, and you will always be special to him," said Nana, an old Southern belle who passed blonde hair, a Georgia peach accent and impeccable manners on to her youngest granddaughter.

In some ways, though, Betty was like most girls her age. The idea of dating a musician — a local celebrity at that—was exciting. At the same time, she was tired of fending off the raging hormones and clumsy gropes of the older boys she was always able to attract.

Willie was an artist, a prodigy who was too modest to appreciate or exploit his incredible talent. He also was an innocent, a quality she spotted quickly upon their first meeting. She could also tell he was lonely.

Sure, some of her girlfriends snickered at the thought of her dating a younger boy. He was tall, nearly five-foot eleven now, although his high-pitched voice and the peach fuzz on his cheeks gave his age away.

His youth and innocence made him easy to control, which was part of her plan from the beginning. She enjoyed teasing him, flirting with him, watching him squirm when she "dripped some honey," as Nana used to say.

She hadn't counted on falling for him, but he was so sweet, and so willing to listen. They would drive out into the desert and talk for hours. It didn't take long before they became inseparable, which drove Winnie up the wall.

It took a little longer for their friendship to evolve into a genuine romance. At first, Willie was too shy to put the moves on her. He didn't even *have* any moves. And Betty was in no hurry, either. Steve had dumped Betty after one particularly eventful evening when, in a drunken haze, he tried to force himself on her. She defended herself by grabbing his crotch and giving it a hard-fist squeeze.

Nana had taught her that one, too. "You're so lovely, you're going to have to beat the boys off with a stick," Nana had said. "But there's never a stick around when you need one."

Spring gave way to summer, and school was out again. The Taylor Brothers took over the Regal six nights a week. They were now making a thousand bucks a week, although Winnie was the only one in the family who knew that.

One Saturday night, Willie was about to sing Bobby Vinton's "Roses are Red (My Love)," the biggest hit of the summer and Betty's favorite song. He hesitated when he spotted her peeking through the standing-room-only group along the back wall. She didn't realize he had seen her.

Willie had practiced the song by playing it to her in the desert, adding his own dreamy guitar arrangement. Now, he had a chance to sing it to her in public.

"Ladies and gentlemen, this next song is for a very special someone. She knows who she is." Willie had a flair for introducing songs and this personal note delighted the older women in the crowd, who fanaticized about making a man out of this sweet-singing teen.

He stared straight at Betty as he made the dedication. He was pleased to have caught her off-guard. Across the room, he saw her blush for the first time.

He sang the song, slow and sincere, improvising a beautiful guitar solo in the bridge that threw Bobby off for a minute since they had not rehearsed it that way. Willie closed his eyes and swayed as he played. The crowd hushed and swayed along with him as it felt the softness of the sweet notes floating out of his guitar.

The audience roared as he finished, and Willie took a deep bow. Betty dabbed her eyes. *Was she crying?* It sure looked that way to him.

With the crowd in his hands and the last set nearly complete, Willie was feeling the moment. He strapped on his Les Paul, turned up a few knobs and whispered to Bobby,

"Runaround Sue." Bobby protested for a few seconds, then obeyed as he always did.

Willie fought to control his voice, which was finally starting to mature but had a habit of breaking when he sang too loud. The coarse growling that the song demanded help him keep control. Besides, he was feeling it tonight. He was fearless. On this rare occasion, he couldn't care less about his mother's attitude toward rock 'n' roll. Mothers matter less and less when a young man is in love.

It was the night he found his muse. And Betty was standing in the back, clapping and dancing with abandon along with the rest of the standing-room-onlys. The couples at the tables soon jumped up and joined the *"hey, hey"* chorus.

"Yeah! Those are the backup singers I've been waiting for!" Willie shouted.

Even Bobby was getting excited, banging hard to make sure his beat wasn't lost in the ruckus.

Willie wrapped up the song with a loud *"whooo!"* and took his bows. As was their habit, the Taylor Brothers made their way through the middle of the room to Winnie's table in the back corner, shaking hands and pocketing tips as they pushed through the crowd.

Winnie started right in on "Runaround Sue" until Tony, who was standing nearby, came over and put an arm around both boys. "Winnie, take it easy. Lighten up on these boys. Look at this place. They know what they're doing."

Willie scanned the room and saw Betty at the main door. She pointed down the hallway, as though he should follow. Then she melted into the swirling crowd.

"Uh, Mom, I'm going to stick around for a while," he said. "I need to check some wires and stuff. I think I heard something buzzing, like something isn't grounded."

"We can wait," Winnie said. "Bobby, go help your brother."

"No!" Willie said. "I mean, no, it might take a while."

"How will you get home?" his mother asked.

"I'll make sure he gets a ride," said Tony, who saw the exchange between Willie and Betty. "Let the boy take care of his business." Tony winked at Willie, who wasn't sure what Tony was talking about, but was grateful for the cover.

Willie went back to the stage for a few minutes and pretended to fiddle with the microphone wires. When he saw Winnie turn her back, he ducked out the door behind the stage.

Tony watched the performance with amusement.

"Bobby, you look bushed. Why don't you take your mother home?" he said.

Willie headed for the equipment room, which the boys also used as a dressing room. He hung up his jacket, took off his tie and went out the other door, which opened to a hallway leading to the pool.

Normally, the pool door was locked at this late hour, but not tonight. The full moon provided enough light for Willie to spot a woman's figure treading water in the pool.

"Betty?" he asked in a low voice.

"No, it's your aunt Tillie," she replied. "Come on in, the water is *wonderful*."

"I don't have a suit," Willie said.

"So what?"

"I see you have a suit."

"I work here. I have suits in my locker. Come on."

Willie laughed nervously, pulling off his shoes and socks. He rolled up the legs of his pants, and stepped out on the low diving board. Carefully, he sat down and dangled his feet in the warm, quiet water.

"Is that all you want?" said Betty, dripping sweet honey into the water, which smelled faintly of chlorine. "The water is just so perfect right now. And it's so romantic."

Romantic! Up until now, Willie and Betty had done little more than cuddle and kiss. They had yet to explore their deeper desires. "Just hold me for a while. Please, I need to be held," Betty would often say when she felt her resolve was about to melt.

Both of them had carefully avoided words like *boyfriend, girlfriend, date* and, especially, *love*. Each needed a friend more than a lover and were scared to jeopardize the friendship with romantic complication.

Tonight was different. The moon was full and the water was perfect. Willie had sung a special song for her in front of hundreds of people. Funny how he could function so well in front of an audience, take command of a room full of adult strangers, and still find it so hard to form a complete sentence just a few minutes later in the presence of his girl.

Betty floated on her back, her arms spread wide for support. She slowly drifted toward him and let her toes touch his. Willie watched the ripples in the water that danced away from her body. He had never seen her in just a bathing suit. Her smooth, wet skin glistened in the moonlight.

"C'mon. Come swim with me," she said. "You're all hot and sweaty. It'll cool you off."

Willie's desire made short work of his modesty. He stripped off his shirt and trousers and dove in. Betty swam to the other side of the pool and lounged on the low, wide stairs leading out of the shallow end. Willie followed until they were side by side, half in, half out of the water.

"You were wonderful tonight," she said. "How could any girl resist you?"

She kissed him, long and full. "Was I that special someone you told everyone about?" she asked. She was breathing heavy and looking him straight in the eye.

He moved closer to her, their bodies touching from shoulder to toe.

"You're my muse," he said, kissing her neck and stroking her bare arms. Willie's wet boxer shorts were matted to his skin and failed to hide his excitement. Betty giggled and brushed her hand lightly across his hips. "C'mon. I know where we can go," she said, jumping up. "*Hurry.*"

She led Willie by the hand to the towel room. They

emptied a bin of freshly laundered towels in a corner and bundled themselves a soft nest, where they both made love for the first time.

"Don't you give up on me, Mr. Willie Taylor," Betty said afterwards. Willie wondered what she meant by that as she fell asleep in his arms. She was a morning person, and it was so late. He was used to working nights and stayed wide awake, reliving the last hour over and over in his mind.

Soon enough, he saw the orange glow of sunrise peeking through a small window. He woke his muse gently. She smiled, her eyes only half-open. They dressed quickly, gathered the towels and ran to Betty's car, looking around to make sure no one had seen them.

Heading up the empty Strip, Betty started to laugh. "I have to be back here in about an hour."

Willie was silent, wondering what he would tell his mother when he got home.

CHAPTER 13

Stephen "Sonny" Simpson had seen it all, from the El Rancho to Bugsy Siegel and his Hollywood mob fraternity, to the bulging resorts that put the Strip into play in the late 1950s.

You could read all about it in his column in the Las Vegas Telegraph. If you wanted to know who was hot, and who was not, it was all in "The Sonny Side of the Strip."

Sonny dished gossip gathered like crumbs from gaming tables, dressing rooms and board rooms. He interviewed the over-the-hill and rising young stars, and rubbed shoulders with the builders, bankers and bankrollers who had turned this dreary desert town into the fastest-growing leisure destination in the world.

Building and expansion had slowed a bit in the early 1960s, so of late, Sonny focused his quill on the entertainment beat. He was also nearing retirement and gradually cashing in on his reputation. The word was out. Sonny could be bought. Even a small mention in his column about a new singer or a revue could double business overnight. Managers, agents and even the artists themselves were often willing to pay his price. Sonny's "gratuity" was peanuts compared to the bill for a billboard.

For the last two years, Sonny had resisted writing about the Taylor Brothers. He was waiting for someone to place an "order." Winnie nagged Tony about Sonny. He was just one of the things Winnie nagged Tony about. Tony didn't see the point. The Taylor Brothers didn't need any press. If they needed anything, it was a bigger room.

Eventually, Sonny could no longer sit on the fence.

Everyone in town except him was talking about the Taylor Brothers. The Telegraph had already printed a letter from a reader accusing Sonny of being out of touch with the "new" Las Vegas since he presumably had not discovered what was going on at the Regal.

Sonny picked a slow week and finally trekked down to the Full House to see for himself. He wore a short-sleeve white shirt, a black tie and the same weathered hound's tooth fedora he wore in the picture that ran with his column. The fedora covered his shiny bald head. Large, black-rimmed glasses completed the cliché image of a weary, ink-stained wretch.

Once proud of his thin, wiry frame, Sonny now had a small potbelly and the posture of a question mark. He sat at a table in the back, all by himself. Now that he was "collecting" for retirement, he no longer enjoyed the thrill of public recognition. He knew he was a fraud and when people stared at him now, Sonny couldn't help but wonder how much they knew.

Sonny was impressed with the preshow buzz about the room. He amused himself watching well-dressed men with glamorous dates argue in vain with the door manager, who kept pointing to a full reservation list. He recognized a speckling of local luminaries, including a councilman and a table full of executives from the Sands. *Looking to raid the House*? Sonny wondered, and scribbled a few lines in his thin spiral reporter's notebook.

Still busy with his visual reconnaissance of the room, Sonny didn't really pay much attention to the start of the show. When he did, his first reaction was, "Big deal, they're just a couple of local yokels playing popular tunes of the day. Dime a dozen, 10 cents a dance."

By the end of the first set, he had happily joined the converted. Willie Taylor was the goods. Sure, the Taylor Brothers played other people's songs. So did Caruso. The young one sang like an angel. He could play anything with strings like he had four hands. And the boy enjoyed the music so much, anyone watching him had no choice but to do the same.

Willie reminded him a bit of Howdy Doody, with his long, gangly limbs and schoolboy face. It was a charming disguise for a sophisticated musician who seemingly could take any song and make it sound like his own. He did the same with the audience. His bright smile, "aw-shucks" demeanor and relentless enthusiasm really did a number on the women in the audience. They didn't know whether to mother him or seduce him. Maybe both.

Sonny spoke to a few of the ladies who had been coming to the show for two years. "I feel like I've watched him grow up," said a woman with too much mascara who wouldn't give her age. "He's in the same class at school as my daughter. I can't wait until he gets a little older."

"You want to fix him up with your daughter?" Sonny asked.

"No," she said, licking her lips. "I want him for myself."

Sonny gulped, excused himself and scribbled down a few more notes.

The next day, he called the high school. The principal, Mr. Finley, told Sonny that Willie was an above-average student who never let fame go to his head.

"He's just like every other student in this school, no better, no worse," Mr. Finley said.

"How does he get his schoolwork done working all those late hours?" Sonny asked.

"Well, he doesn't work during the week when school is in session," Mr. Finley replied. "He only works weekends. Willie's a real weekend warrior. Monday morning to Friday afternoon, he's just another kid."

It all went into Sonny's Sunday column, including how Willie hadn't forsaken his education and the Full House was not exploiting child labor. He was a weekend *warrior*, a weekend *warbler*. Sonny, who wrote for Variety before settling in Vegas, loved alliteration.

"That's why some of the people around the Full House call him Weekend Willie." Sonny made it up. That was how he wrote.

That night, Willie learned he had a new nickname.

"Hey, Weekend Willie!" the valet hollered across the lobby. And the bellhop. And the concierge. And the bouncer.

And Bobby. Bobby's tone of voice, though, had a different ring to it. He was angry. Bobby's name was mentioned exactly once in the column.

Sonny Simpson had successfully coined a nickname for the hottest act on the Strip. He still had a long reach. Whether he had done a favor for the Taylor Brothers was another matter.

CHAPTER 14

Over the next year, Willie and Betty continued to discover each other.

Bobby discovered beer. And trouble.

Sophomore year at Valley Memorial had been tolerable enough, but now he was a junior and Betty had graduated. At least his brother wasn't lonely at school. Bobby had made some new friends of his own. He bought an old pickup truck with the tips he'd been stashing away and still had enough coin left over to keep his buds in suds.

Willie, who was rapidly maturing both mentally and physically, worried about the rowdy, raunchy crowd Bobby was hanging with. But not that much. He'd spent a good part of his life sticking up for big brother. It wasn't his fault that Bobby was slow. Willie had done his share to help him. Bobby was still one of the locally famous Taylor Brothers, even if most people now referred to their act as "The Weekend Willie Show."

Bobby had an easy life because Willie and Winnie worked their tails off. Sure, Winnie could be hard on Bobby. He was old enough to stick up for himself for a change.

Betty needed Willie a lot more than Bobby did. Bobby still had his gig. Betty's mother had been fired, most likely for being drunk on the job. Once Betty graduated, Amanda lost what little motivation she had to carry on. She had lost her husband and her mother. Her oldest daughter was God knows where.

Now, her baby girl had a high school degree and a steady boyfriend with prospects. Amanda didn't have anyone left to be strong for. It was time to rest.

There was a suicide attempt that no one knew about except Betty and Willie. They found her in the garage, in the car, with the top down and the engine on. A broken window and a crooked door jamb let enough air into the garage to keep Amanda from doing any permanent damage. Still, the incident scared the life out of Betty.

"I don't know what I'm going to do," Betty said. "I can't watch her every minute. I have to work."

Betty had been promoted to assistant pool manager at the House a few weeks after graduation. The money wasn't great, but she could pay the rent and put food on the table. Willie helped out when he could, but Winnie was still minding the checkbook. He still hadn't summoned the nerve to ask her how much the Taylor Brothers were being paid.

Faced with two more years at Valley Memorial without Betty, Willie threw himself into his studies with the intention of graduating after three years. His guidance counselors argued against the plan. Willie held his ground. He was making money and had no interest in college.

He was allowed to take a few extra courses. Mr. Rush took care of the rest. Willie signed up for summer school music credits before and after his junior year. Mr. Rush rubber-stamped his passing grades. He knew Willie could have taught the classes that he didn't always have time to attend. Those final credits allowed him to collect his diploma in August of 1964.

Bobby stayed on for the start of his senior year, majoring in truancy. By early November, he was suspended. He never bothered to go back.

Winnie tried her best to manage both her boys while she bore a few crosses of her own. She had battled skin problems her entire adult life and they were beginning to catch up with her. She finally had a diagnosis: chronic psoriasis. The pain and embarrassment about her appearance kept her home more days than not. Just after Valentine's Day, she went to a spa in Florida for a few months of treatment, leaving the boys on their own for the first time in their lives.

Bobby took advantage of his mother's absence and hosted a series of noisy parties at the Taylor home. Willie couldn't work with all the traffic and horseplay, so he spent most of the time living at the Tilden residence.

Winnie had arranged for Tony to hold their paychecks until she returned. But Tony never told his secretary. One day, the secretary found three envelopes made out to "W. Taylor" and handed them over to Willie.

By then, the Taylor Brothers' post-graduate rate had risen to fifteen hundred dollars a week. When Willie saw the numbers, he was furious. Furious at Winnie for holding back. Furious at himself for letting her get away with it. Furious that Winnie wasn't around to experience his blinding rage.

He cursed and yelled so loud and long that Tony ran out of his office to see who was making such a scene. Then Willie cursed at Tony, who was shocked at the boy's unprecedented disrespect and firmly ordered him to take it outside or he would knock some sense into that foul mouth.

The next day, Willie rifled through Winnie's "bill box." He found a statement for a savings account with nearly eighteen thousand dollars and a pile of stock certificates he couldn't put a price on. *Well, at least, she hasn't spent it all*, Willie thought, wondering how much his mother was spending in Florida.

Willie thought about all the work he had put in on the act. All the sacrifices. He thought about Betty and her mother, living in a run-down stucco shack with no air conditioning, tattered screens and peeling paint.

He was embarrassed for himself, realizing what a child he still was. He had a high school diploma and a high-profile job. He didn't cause or get into trouble. He was respected by his peers and a city full of adults. Yet he still lived with his mother. She paid him an allowance from the money that *he* earned. She controlled what he did, what he wore and where he worked. He was arguably the best musician in town and his mother still dictated what songs he could and couldn't play.

He didn't even have a car. Once in a while, Winnie let him borrow the Rambler. Most of the time, she drove him where he needed to go or he took the bus.

He thought of a phrase that Moe, the desk manager at the House, liked to use after certain people checked in.

"What a schnook."

It was time to change all that.

That afternoon, he went down to Franklin National Bank and requested a withdrawal of $5,000. He waited about five minutes before he saw a familiar figure, Mr. Rollins, come up to greet him. Mr. Rollins was an officer at the bank and a Regal regular. He knew Winnie quite well and even sat at her table on a few occasions when his wife wasn't with him.

"Well, if it isn't our Weekend Willie," Mr. Rollins said cheerfully. "What can we do for you? What's this about a big withdrawal?"

"I'm taking care of some business for my mother," Willie replied. "She hasn't been feeling very well, you know."

"I know, I know, the poor thing." Mr. Rollins shook his head. "You know, Willie, that's a lot of money."

"She's going to buy a new car," Willie said.

"We can make all the arrangements for that, no problem. Just have her tell us the exact amount and we'll issue a cashier's check."

"Well, Mr. Rollins, she's not buying the car from a dealer. And the guys she's buying it from, I don't think they take checks. If you know what I mean." Willie tried to smile like a lawyer. The banker smiled back.

"Sure, sure, I get it. But you're not authorized to accept a withdrawal. Perhaps we could call your mother and … "

"That would be difficult. She's in Florida right now. But she'll be home by the weekend. And to tell you the truth, Mr. Rollins, I need some of that money right now. We also need some new amplifiers, and the new drums that Bobby ordered have come in. The shop needs payment in full before we can take them. I'm just trying to take care of some of this stuff before she comes home. So she doesn't have to worry. Gotta make sure the Taylor Brothers are in top form. All that money they pay us. They expect the best."

Mr. Rollins didn't want it getting back to Tony that Franklin National was not cooperating with his meal ticket. Willie knew all this. He had it all organized in his head like the second set on a Saturday night. He had Mr. Rollins eating out of his hand, just like the napkin ladies.

"Sure, sure, kid. I'll take care of everything. You just wait right here."

Mr. Rollins hurried off. He stopped short when Willie called after him.

"Mr. Rollins, better make that six thousand."

Willie didn't need the bus to get home. He drove there in a brand-new Ford Mustang convertible. He had drooled over the Mustang prototype when he attended the 1963 automobile show at the Convention Center. Willie thought it was the coolest car he'd ever seen.

In the spring of 1965, there was still a waiting list for the Mustang at Clark County Ford and a longer wait for the convertible. A bright red demo model parked on the edge of the road at Clark County Ford turned Willie's head every time they drove by. It wasn't nearly as exotic as the bullet-shaped prototype, but Willie dreamed about being behind the wheel of one just the same.

Fortunately, the dealer's sales manager was a fan of the Taylor Brothers and a friend of Tony's. When Willie entered his showroom and said he wanted a Mustang, the sales manager immediately called his salesman son-in-law away from a customer. "Gimmie the keys to the Pony. I just sold it," the manager said.

"You said I could drive the demo. You said it would be good for people to see it around town!"

"You're arguing with me? *You're arguing with me?* Gimmie

the goddamn keys before I bust you to the car wash."

Weekend Willie was starting to enjoy this little shopping spree.

Next stop: the florist. He went to the one that supplied the House and collected another hefty discount. Four dozen roses nearly filled the Mustang's sorry excuse for a back seat. Then it was off to the jewelry store. Everybody knew Myra, the ubiquitous owner of Hillman's, the biggest jewelry store in town. And she knew everybody.

Myra was another fan. Myra was a *napkin lady*.

"You want to buy a necklace?" she said, feigning disappointment. Young man, if this isn't for your mother, I am going to be crushed."

Willie picked out a beautiful, diamond-crusted gold heart on a delicate gold chain. Even with the discount, it cost him almost five hundred dollars.

That was enough for now, he thought. He throttled up the Mustang and drove over to Betty's house to give her the roses and the necklace.

"Tomorrow, we can go out and pick up a few things for the house," Willie told her. "A few things for your mother."

He looked at Betty. She was glowing. "Anything else you need?" he added.

"Just hold me for a while. That's all I need."

And so he did, feeling like a grownup for the first time in his life.

"You are my knight in shining armor, Mr. Taylor Brother. I'm the luckiest girl in Las Vegas."

Lavishing gifts on Betty and tooling around town in his new Ponycar made Willie feel like a king. *Enjoy yourself while you can*, he told himself. *The queen would be coming home soon.*

CHAPTER 15

Pasquale "Patsy" Bucco had no regrets. He made no apologies. It was a different world. A different time. Men with power made their own laws. They took what others could not protect. If you got in their way, you had better be prepared to play rough.

Things were different now. More people. More government. More laws. More lawmen. More lawyers.

Fewer places to hide.

These days, muscle only got you so far. Money, not fear, was what made a man powerful.

Patsy was built like a coal furnace. Five-foot-seven, nearly as wide, with a cast-iron stomach inside and out. Shoulders wider than the alley that cut from Division to Elm in his native Chicago. Round biceps the size of coconuts. Knuckles hard as lug nuts.

He had a face that only a blind mother could love. Rough and red, with jowls like a bulldog. Even his eyebrows had muscles, which left him with a perpetual squint. He grew old-man moles on his cheeks and temples before he was 30.

As a young *cugine*, eager to earn his stripes on the streets of Chicago, Patsy was a fearless and uninhibited soldier. He would do anything they asked of him. Murder, robbery, bootlegging, hijacking trucks, he did it all. No discussion, no complaints.

He accomplished his missions with a ruthless efficiency, thanks in large part to an even temperament that was quite unusual to his profession. Even while beating up gamblers who couldn't pay their tab, Patsy never lost control. It was business. It was his job. He never committed violence in anger or for revenge. Unless it was revenge that his bosses ordered him to collect. Only on rare occasions did he need resort to violence in self-defense. Everyone knew you didn't mess with Patsy Bucco.

Behind this Spartan, Neanderthal facade was a keen mind that always kept him one step ahead of everyone, even the old men in charge. He kept his mouth shut and his eyes and ears open. He remembered everything. And nobody had a clue.

This came in handy when the lieutenants in the Bianco crime family would get drunk and start flapping their gums about this and that. About how much they had pocketed on the side from the last bank job. That what Aldo Bianco didn't know wouldn't hurt him.

What he learned from these men, and what he understood better than most, was that most criminals lacked character and honor. *Big surprise.* They were not to be trusted, so Patsy trusted no one. And when the time was right, he didn't have any trouble blackmailing these men of low character, then murdering them after they paid his price.

Patsy was under no illusions. He was no better than they were. He was only smarter than they were. Smart enough to get them before they got him. Family loyalty was a myth. It was every man for himself. Family and loyalty was the dope they pumped into the veins of the uneducated, simpleton foot soldiers to keep them in line. Ironically, those who exploited that loyalty often rose to positions of higher authority.

As Patsy climbed the family ladder, he patiently played the role of a trustworthy underling with just enough intelligence to follow orders without screwing up. In 1941, he earned a coveted spot in Aldo Bianco's private posse. From this vantage point, he was able to slowly build his own network of loyalists.

His big break came during the war. The end of prohibition had cut into business, so there wasn't as much to fight over. Americans were more interested in fighting the Axis. A lot of mobsters, including his bosses, let their guard down.

No one was all that surprised when Aldo Bianco and his four closest capos were indicted for the murder of a federal judge. No one, not even the FBI, suspected it was Patsy who anonymously supplied them with the incriminating evidence that hung the Bianco inner circle out to dry.

It was a brilliant plan. With the head of the organization chopped clean off, a large faction of the gang nominated Patsy to seize control. Begged him, really. He was the only family member who had the trust of the soldiers and the respect of the old guard, who weren't up for a fight. A few renegades attempted to stage coups of their own, but the majority had spoken. At the age of 31, Patsy Bucco was running the entire operation.

His first order of business was to find new streams of revenue to replace the losses from bootleg liquor sales. Patsy already had his eye on Las Vegas. He was in love with the idea of people coming to him to give up their money. He was more than happy to show them a good time in return.

It took nearly a quarter of the family holdings to build the Full House. When they ran over budget, Patsy sold pieces of the hotel directly to the old guard. They were taken by his persuasive argument. Patsy had learned a lot in a short period of time, they thought.

Patsy wasn't through teaching them. The agreements were sealed with handshakes and kisses on the cheek. One by one, the old men died and Patsy folded their shares back into his. Surviving relatives didn't dare to challenge him for reneging on deals they had no record of.

Mob wars and bathtub gin were the past. The future was in gambling, which was legal in Las Vegas, or drugs, which were dirty business in any neighborhood. He wasn't the first criminal to realize this. But he was the smartest, and made the smart choice.

Patsy's only regret was that he never found the right girl. Women, at least the kind of women who might interest Patsy, were usually frightened of him. He longed for someone he could share his secrets with. He dreamed of finding an intelligent, trustworthy soul mate who might be able to understand, perhaps even appreciate, his complex and enigmatic mind. A few ambitious floozies tried to dig their nails into his wallet. He typically brushed them off.

He found a small measure of comfort on the Jersey Shore. Patsy spent as many summers as possible in Atlantic City. He loved to stroll the Boardwalk and wander through the attractions on the Steel Pier. He spent long days on fishing charters that went for bluefish in the summer and tuna in the fall. Ten miles off the coast, he could relax and enjoy the great outdoors without fear of assassination or arrest.

Patsy and a few close friends would pack one ice chest with beer and another with food. At dawn, they would drink steaming coffee from a thermos as they began a long day of smelly bait, cigars and pickled eggs. When the fish were hitting, there was plenty of action. When they weren't, he would nap to the sound of the waves lapping gently against the hull. When the day was over, he took to the bow to let the sea spray cool his leathery, sunburned face on the long ride in, and watched the seagulls that followed the boat, snapping up the pieces of bait tossed into the wind by the boat mates.

Every once in a while, they would spot a few dolphins following the boat. Once, Patsy was startled to see a small whale swimming off in the distance. Small for a whale, anyway. From dorsal fin to tail, it was almost as large as the Staten Island Ferry. No doubt big enough to sink his forty-foot charter boat if it chose.

Patsy didn't know what kind of whale it was, and didn't give a shit. "Badass nature," he called it. Magnificent creatures. They had power, purpose and a peaceful life. Nobody messed with them, at least around here. *Nice work if you can get it*, Patsy would always think. God, did he envy them.

Nighttime was spent patrolling the Boardwalk, walking off rich lobster dinners at the Hob Nob. Then, he and his cronies would retire to the Ambassador Hotel. They kept a suite there just for him. Some of the men would start a poker game in the parlor. Others headed for the poolroom or the bar. Patsy preferred the lobby, where a pretty girl would play soft music on the biggest grand piano he'd ever seen. Soothed by the melody, he would read a magazine or simply watch people come and go.

Unlike Chicago, there were a few women for Patsy in Atlantic City.

Patsy had needs like anybody else. There was nobody special, just the occasional Uptown party girl who was classy enough not to get on his nerves. He preferred to keep up a Spartan image in Chicago. He didn't trust anybody there. Too many enemies. Too many Delilahs.

The women in Atlantic City knew he was a rich and powerful man. They weren't stupid, and Patsy knew his status was the only reason they gave him the time of day. Still, in this tarnished jewel by the sea, the women were more honest than most about their motives. All they wanted was to be shown a good time and treated like ladies. They weren't fixing to become the queen of North Chicago.

Atlantic City girls were much prettier than Chicago girls, too. Strolling the Boardwalk in shorts and sundresses that billowed in the ocean breeze. Lounging on the beach in next to nothing. Maybe there was something in the air, a tonic that let Patsy forget his enormous responsibilities.

Summers in Atlantic City were always too short and Patsy's usually ended early. Sometimes, he was so depressed on the train back to Chicago that he would cry like a baby, alone in the darkness of his sleeper cabin. To pass the time on the long ride home, Patsy would remember his first trip to Atlantic City. It was the summer of 1941, just before the war. He was riding shotgun for Aldo Bianco, who was attending a summit of bosses from everywhere east of the Mississippi. He remembered strolling down the Boardwalk for the very first time. The smell of the steaming clams, roasted peanuts, taffy and salt air was intoxicating.

One night, the entire Chicago delegation was given VIP seats for the Miss Atlantic City Pageant. Patsy was bored until a leggy strawberry blonde took her turn on the stage. She was the most exquisite example of femininity Patsy had ever seen.

Patsy wasn't a ladies man, but he had a good eye. She won the race by 10 lengths. Her image, and her name, were burned in his brain for life.

"Now there's a dame that could really get me in trouble," he said to no one.

CHAPTER 16

Florida had done miracles for Winnie. Her complexion had cleared up completely. Her hair was a bright new shade of red. She had lost at least 20 pounds and was dressed to make sure everybody knew it. The canary yellow rims on her butterfly sunglasses matched her new dress. A straw hat with a wide, floppy brim, high heels and a patent leather purse, all white, completed her tropically themed ensemble.

Willie decided the best way to handle Winnie was to be casual. He picked her up at the airport and didn't say much of anything until they got to the Mustang.

"Where did this come from?" Winnie asked in a demanding tone.

"I make a lot of money, mother," Willie calmly replied. "I'm a celebrity. People expect me to look like a celebrity. I look good in it."

Winnie paused for a moment. She tried in vain to read her son's face. She couldn't read his voice, either, except he had never called her "mother" before.

Winnie decided to lie in the weeds until she figured out what was going on. *Something* was going on.

"Well, anyone would look like a celebrity in this car," she declared.

That was the beginning of a cool but civil standoff between Willie and Winnie. She took a few days to get settled and do some business in town, some of which involved the bank. She never mentioned the withdrawal, even though Willie was sure she had received a full report from Mr. Rollins.

The following Monday, with Bobby out of the house, she

sat Willie down for a private chat in the kitchen.

"I did a lot of thinking while I was in Florida," she began. "You've both grown so much, and it's due time you took on some more responsibility. From now on, I'd like you to take care of the finances. The money. *Your* money. Here's the deal. I'll arrange for Tony to pay you from now on, including the back pay from the last few months. You give me half the income, and you can keep the rest. Do with it what you will, although I suggest you open a savings account. The Taylor Brothers make fifteen hundred dollars a week. Half of that is still a lot of money."

Willie listened quietly, waiting for the rest. It didn't come.

"And you get half?" Willie asked after a long pause, emphasizing the "you."

"I'm going to take half of what you give me and manage it for Bobby," Winnie said. "I'll pay him a salary out of that, probably two hundred or so a week, and put some more in a savings account. For him. For his future. He's never going to make the same kind of money as you, Willie."

"And the rest?" Willie asked.

"You wouldn't begrudge your mother a salary, would you? After all I've done, all *we've* done together?" Winnie spoke sweetly, with a hint of hurt in her voice. "You boys are men now, and you're going to do what you're going to do. A lot of that won't involve your mother. That's fine. That's the way things should be. But I have to live."

"Mother, what about the rest of the money, the money we've already made?"

"Oh, I've been saving. For all of us. There's enough to buy a much nicer house. I've already talked to a Realtor. It's time to get out of this dusty old rat trap."

She could read her son's face now. Her explanation was falling short of satisfactory.

"There will still be some money left over. We could take a trip. I don't know. Do you need some money? I could write you a check."

Willie was tempted to laugh in her face. Instead, he chose to let sleeping dogs lie. He'd have more than seven hundred bucks a week coming in, plus tips. He could live large, still help Betty and avoid an escalating confrontation that he might not have the stomach for.

He accepted her terms with a single exception.

"No mother, I don't need any money right now," he said. "Just one thing. Go ahead and buy your new house. Bobby and I will stay here."

"Now Willie, that gets complicated. There's still a mortgage, papers, utilities."

"You can sign it over to me. I'll pay the mortgage."

Winnie had planned to sell the house and use the equity for a down payment on the new one. It really wasn't enough money to argue about. Not enough to spark a confrontation that could cost her even more.

It was an acceptable compromise and completed a successful negotiation.

"OK, Willie, if that's what you want," Winnie said, reaching her arm across the kitchen table to touch his hand.

It wasn't what he wanted. He had no intention of opening a frat house with Bobby. *Tappa Kegga Bru? No thank-you.* Willie just knew it was time that both of them made a break from the smothering influence of their mother. He could stay mostly with the Tildens and pretend to be Bobby's housemate. This way, Willie would always have an excuse to come around the house and keep Bobby from going too far over the edge. Bobby still needed someone to look after him. Willie couldn't trust Winnie to do the job. She had never shown any interest in it before.

"One more thing, Willie."

Here it comes, Willie thought. The other shoe. This ought to be good.

"I don't want Bobby to know about any of this," Winnie said with a stern voice. "He doesn't have to know. He'll have more than enough money to live on and I'll make sure he has savings to fall back on. If he thinks you're getting something he isn't, this will never work.

"You boys will have your house, I'll have mine, and you'll both have a salary, a nice salary. As far as he is concerned, all the money is going through me, just like it always did."

Willie could feel the tension exit his body in one clean wave. *Had she noticed*? The other shoe had turned out to be a warm, fuzzy slipper. He and his mother were of one mind as far as Bobby was concerned.

"If that's the way you want it, mother. We'll do it your way." He wouldn't give her the satisfaction of being right. Still, the eight-hundred-pound gorilla in the room had hopped off his back and was heading for a new jungle.

If only the United Nations could settle arguments this easily. Willie laughed at the thought of Khrushchev banging a slipper on his desk in front of the U.N. General Assembly.

CHAPTER 17

Bobby was thrilled, Betty was thrilled. Both mothers were thrilled.

Willie was held hostage by his own second thoughts.

Everything had happened so quickly. Only a few weeks ago, he was content with the status quo. His mother's heavy hand smothered him on occasion, but they had a system that worked. She handled the business and he handled the music, at least to a degree. Bobby had a mother and a brother looking out for him.

Things were different now. Willie had so many more responsibilities. Bills. A new family to take care of. He'd assumed sole responsibility for Bobby's welfare. Oh, and he had a high-profile nightclub act to perform and manage.

Willie thought several times about asking Betty to marry him. Then that nagging feeling he'd missed out on his childhood would come rushing back. He had enough responsibilities without being a husband. He needed a safety valve to let a little pressure escape. So he held on to his bachelor status. Betty sensed his tension and didn't even bring the subject up.

Winnie still held court at her table at the Regal and delivered her unabashed critique after every performance. Willie still caved in on some of her demands, mostly those involving the songs they played. He was writing songs now and felt the urge to test them out onstage. Winnie seemed to enjoy reminding him that people preferred popular, recognizable melodies, which would by definition eliminate his own compositions.

Rock 'n' roll, of course, was still taboo, although even

Winnie had to agree that some of those Beatle tunes went over quite well. Ed Sullivan had inspired her latest idea. She had seen Ed wear a Beatle-esque mop wig during one of the Fab Four's appearances on his show, and showed up the next night at the Regal with similar wigs for her boys to wear.

"They'll love it," Winnie said. "It'll be cute."

Willie just rolled his eyes. Bobby agreed with Winnie.

"Fine, you wear one, then," Willie said to his brother. Bobby, who had developed a taste for bugging Willie, went ahead one night and put the wig on during a Beatles medley in the second set.

Willie cut the medley short and went back to Roy Orbison. Joking around was one thing. Being the joke was another.

Playing the Regal was becoming a joke in general. Winnie was right. Nobody wanted to hear his new songs. Since he left school, he hadn't had that much contact with Mr. Rush, whose lessons kept playing through his mind. Mr. Rush had warned him that to grow as a musician, sooner or later he would have to risk rejection.

"If it's in you, it's got to come out, even if nobody else wants to listen," he said more than once.

Willie used to listen with rapt attention as Mr. Rush told him stories about the great bluesmen, some of whom lived in poverty their entire lives. Some of whom spent much of their careers playing on street corners for spare change. The many who suffered the humiliation of prejudice, or felt the wrath of prison guards at infamous Parchman Farm prison.

Willie thought about his own childhood. It wasn't easy growing up without a father, and with a mother who orchestrated his every move. Still, here he was, not yet old enough to vote, and he was driving a Mustang convertible. Somehow, it didn't seem to measure up. Maybe he did need to suffer a little before he could write songs that people would be interested in hearing.

Playing the same songs six nights a week was becoming a bore. Now that he actually needed a job, being the star of the

Regal Lounge was a grind.

"Not exactly the kind of suffering that Blind Willie Johnson was singing about," Willie said to Mr. Rush as they strummed through Johnson's version of "Lord, I Just Can't Keep From Crying." Johnson was blinded at age seven when his stepmother threw lye in his face. That was about the same age when the Kiddie Cowboy started his career.

If Willie felt guilty about his lack of character-building life experience, he didn't need to for much longer. The blues were coming to Las Vegas, and they had big plans for him.

CHAPTER 18

Major expansion and renovations began at the Full House in the late spring of 1965. Business was picking up and competition was booming. Big new casino hotels were opening up and down the Strip and many of the established properties were expanding.

The Full House was adding a 15-floor tower with 300 new rooms and 20 luxury suites. There would also be a new wing with a big restaurant and conference rooms for the convention trade. When they finished the casino expansion, it would be the largest in Las Vegas, at least for a while.

The Royal and the Regal both were getting top-to-bottom makeovers. The rooms were a mess during the day, with contractors coming and going and the sound of power tools grinding away.

At one point in early June, the Regal became unusable and was to be closed for at least two weeks. Willie took the news rather well when he realized it meant his first real vacation in nearly four years.

He and Betty took the opportunity to get away. They hopped in the Mustang and headed for California. First, they spent a day in Oceanside, where the only familiar person Willie could track down was Tommy O'Dowd. He didn't bother to call on his old sponsor. He found out that Pappy's had closed and later burned to the ground. Pappy, Lourdes and her boys were long gone. KVLY was now a rock 'n' roll station staffed by strangers. One person there told him that Flash had gone east.

He told the manager at KVLY that he used to be the Kiddie Cowboy. "Kiddie what?" the manager asked. There were no archives, no photos, no recordings or any record of the station's old shows.

"It's like I never existed," Willie sighed as they hit the highway and headed north to San Francisco.

Willie and Betty quickly fell in love with the City by the Bay. They took picnic lunches into Golden Gate Park and checked out a few clubs in the evening. Willie brought his guitar along and became acquainted with some of the friendly, long-haired folkies who were plugging their instruments in and experimenting with wild new sounds. They were also experimenting with drugs and a free love, both of which Willie and Betty politely declined.

They did accept an invitation to stay with one young couple, Astrid and Val, who lived in a houseboat in nearby Sausalito, just across the bay and the Golden Gate Bridge. Willie and Betty slept on the floor with a few other couples that Astrid and Val had taken in. Musicians jammed, girls walked around naked and everybody shared whatever food or drink they could get their hands on.

As crowded as it was, Willie treasured those few days on the houseboat. It was a much-need change of pace, a chance to bond with fellow musicians, people who didn't want anything from him except kinship.

Betty got into the spirit of things and even learned to be comfortable walking around in the nude. She also enjoyed telling everyone what a big star Willie was in Vegas. Eventually, she tried some marijuana, liked it and talked Willie into taking a few tokes. All it did was make him cough.

One night, the entire group went into the city and caught a set by a guitar player named Frank Zappa and his band, the Mothers. It was an amazing show. The band played wild, complex compositions that mixed rock, jazz, classical and the avant garde exploration that Mr. Rush liked. Betty found the music grating and the band's humor a little vulgar. Willie's finely tuned ears found the purpose in the chaos, all orchestrated by the keenly focused Zappa.

Now, here's a musician who doesn't care if people are listening, Willie thought. *He's playing what's in his head. He's got a vision and he's directing the band towards that vision.*

Willie also noticed that Zappa didn't look like he was suffering. He was having a ball. So was the crowd, which was no surprise considering the cloud of pot smoke that filled the club like an ocean fog.

The week went by like a daydream and it was time to go. Betty gave their phone number out along with invitations for their new friends to visit Vegas.

"My mother would love to have you over," Willie joked, earning a punch in the shoulder from Betty.

On the way back home, they drove through the desert at night, leaving the top down so they could enjoy a clear sky full of brilliant stars. Willie wondered how such a beautiful drive could end in a place as ugly as Las Vegas seemed to him now.

"The ocean, the bay, the waves. That's for me," he told Betty, who was sleeping peacefully with her head on his shoulder.

The Regal was still a royal mess when they got back to town. Tony wasn't sure when the Taylor Brothers would get their stage back. The pool was open, though, so Betty had to get right back to work, leaving Willie at least several more days with nothing to do.

A few days hanging out with Bobby and his friends drove Willie out of the house back and to the Regal to see what they were doing to his stage. When he arrived, he saw an unfamiliar face who seemed to be in charge of something. He was a tall, dark-haired young man wearing an expensive suit, shiny shoes and a sharp scowl. He carried a large binder and moved from one end of the room to the other, stopping every few steps to yell at someone.

"Tony, who's that guy, and when did he buy the joint?" Willie asked.

Tony frowned and held a finger to his lips.

"Keep your mouth shut around here," Tony said. "That's Carlo Bucco. Patsy's nephew. He's in charge of the renovations."

"Of the Regal?"

"Of the whole fuckin' hotel. He's supposed to be some muckety muck with the unions, the contractors. *You know.* He's driving me crazy, and everybody else. But whattaya gonna do? He's Patsy's guy."

"Hey Tony! What the fuck?" Carlo hollered over.

"Now what?" Tony muttered. "Do yourself a favor, kid, find another place to do nothing."

Willie didn't need to be told twice. He would hang out at the pool with Betty.

CHAPTER 19

Willie found more trouble at the pool. Her name was Tina.

Betty had already tangled with Tina Bucco. Tina wanted bigger towels. All of the towels were the same size. The water was either too hot or too cold. The sun was in her eyes. And all those kids in the pool making such a racket! All of this was Betty's fault and Tina let her know all about it.

Tina had arrived with her brother, Carlo, to spend the summer at the Full House. She hated it here. Las Vegas was dusty enough on a good day, more so when you lived on a construction site. She was a night person and complained that she could not sleep at the pool during the day with all the hammers banging and cranes clanging steel beams together. Also Betty's fault.

Tina also was bored, so she passed the time by harassing the prissy little blonde pool manager. She had asked around and learned that Betty's boyfriend was the big star attraction at the Regal.

Willie and Betty didn't act like boyfriend and girlfriend when they were at the House, but Tina could feel the electricity when she saw them together for the first time. She jumped right up and sauntered over to the couple, smiling behind a dark pair of sunglasses.

Willie could feel Betty's mood darken as the glamorous, raven-haired beauty approached them.

"Oh God, what does she want now?" Betty whispered.

"Why Betty, darling, when were you going to introduce me to this handsome young man?" Tina said sweetly. She sounded sincere enough, at least to Willie.

"Tina, this is my boyfriend, Willie Taylor," Betty said, cool as a Popsicle. "Willie, this is Tina Bucco. Her uncle is Patsy Bucco. She's come to stay with us for the summer."

"You mean this is the famous Weekend Willie?" Tina said, stroking Willie's arm as she sized him up. "I'm very honored. I can't wait to see your show. Everybody says it's the biggest thing on the Strip. Uncle Patsy says you make a lot of money for us."

"Us?" Willie thought. Who exactly did he work for? He knew about Patsy and the family, but never thought much about them. They used to keep a low profile at the House. He had never even met Patsy, who came out about once a year for a quick inspection. Now, Carlo was busting balls inside and his sexy little sister was making waves outside at the pool.

"Nobody told me how handsome you were," Tina cooed. "Betty, when I heard you were dating one of the Taylor Brothers, I just assumed it was the chubby one."

Betty blushed easily and turned the same shade of red as Willie's Mustang.

"Oh, that was a terrible thing to say," Tina said, brushing beads of water off her chest, which was barely contained by a black bikini top. "Willie, you must think I'm awful for saying such mean things about your brother. Let me make it up to you. I'll order lunch for all three of us. Betty, can you call room service for me?"

"Room service doesn't cover the pool," Betty said.

"Then get me *whatever*, Betty," Tina snapped. "Let's have some champagne!"

Willie just smiled and kept his mouth shut. He knew enough about women to know that anything he said right now would piss off at least one of them.

CHAPTER 20

With the exception of the new tower, all the renovations at the Full House were completed just after Fourth of July weekend. The grand reopening of the Regal was scheduled for Friday, July 16.

The renovations helped Willie to convince Winnie that the Taylor Brothers had to spruce up their act and their extended vacation was the perfect time to take action. Willie started by adding two members to the band and quickly arranged dozens of songs for the new quartet. Sammy Llanes played both upright and electric bass and had a deep voice perfect for harmonizing with Willie. Winnie argued against hiring a Mexican, but Sammy was light enough to pass for white. Turns out he was really from Columbia and his father was Spanish.

Completing the new quartet was a slight, bespectacled young man named Joshua Rosenberg, who went by the stage name Jimmy Rose. Jimmy's main job was to play a small electric piano. He could play saxophone and trumpet as well. Willie also was hoping that he could convince Mr. Rush to sit in with the band every once in a while on guitar, violin or trombone.

Reopening night was a blast. Willie's mixed feelings about going back to work dissolved once his loyal audience welcomed him back to the stage. He enjoyed playing the new, fuller arrangements and the many new songs he had been able to add to the set. He appreciated the enthusiastic applause that greeted the new band members and took it as a sign of approval. Step by step, his musical world was expanding and he was learning how to be a leader, just as Mr. Rush predicted he would someday do.

Carlo, Tina and another woman, presumably Carlo's date, sat front and center for the show. Tina and the other woman had a great time. Carlo looked like he wanted to be somewhere else.

Near the end of the final set, they were joined by a short, muscular middle-aged man. He wore a shiny, tailored pinstripe suit. He kissed Tina on the cheek and whispered a few words in Carlo's ear before he sat down.

Was this Patsy? Willie hadn't heard about him coming into town. His face looked like it had stopped a truck. Still, Willie sensed the man was not nearly as threatening as Carlo. Or Tina, come to think of it.

Willie wrapped up the night with "Everybody Loves Somebody," a popular Dean Martin hit from the year before, and a peppy cover of Roy Orbison's "Oh, Pretty Woman," which got everybody up on their feet for the big finish.

Tony always loved how Willie did that.

"They used to hang around after the show just to look at Mary Murray," Tony laughed. "I had to throw her ass out the back door just so I could empty the room. You Taylor boys get them to conga their coolies out the door and right into the casino. That's the way it's supposed to work."

Tony followed the boys back to their mother's table. When they got there, Willie realized they were being followed. He turned and saw the group from the front table. The middle-aged man smiled and stuck out a thick, meaty paw.

"Tony, how are ya? So, this is the famous Weekend Willie I've been hearing so much about. Good to meet ya, kid. I'm Patsy."

Willie smiled without opening his mouth. He wasn't sure if he was allowed to speak.

Tony broke the silence and attempted to break the ice.

"What did I tell ya, Patsy? Ain't they somethin'? This kid really helps keep us in beans. Been doin' it for nearly four years."

"What, did you have him out there in diapers, Tony? He's just a *bambini*, eh?" Patsy laughed, patted Willie on the cheek and mussed his hair. "Relax kid, you're among friends. I hear you've already met my niece, Tina."

"Um, yes, yes, sir, we met, out at the pool. Hi," Willie stammered.

"Take it easy, kid. I don't bite. Not like *she does*," Patsy said. He gave Tina a stern, paternal look, then turned to Carlo.

"And Carlo. Have you met my nephew yet?" Patsy asked.

"Yeah, how ya doin'," Carlo said, looking the other way as he offered his hand.

"Nice to meet you," Willie said, nervously accepting Carlo's firm, cold grip.

"Willie, where are your manners?" The voice came from behind him. It was Winnie, still sitting on her throne.

"Oh, sorry. Mr. Bucco, this is my mother," Willie said

"Mr. Bucco, I'm so pleased to finally meet you," Winnie said. I've heard so much about you."

"Nothing bad, I hope, Mrs. Taylor."

"Nothing I can't handle, Mr. Bucco. And please call me Winnie."

"Well, I do love that name. Tell me, Winnie, do you like champagne? Tony, can we get some champagne over here?"

"Only if you'll join me, Mr. Bucco."

Willie wondered what Tina was smiling about. She wasn't looking at him. She was looking at her uncle. Her uncle was looking at Winnie. There was an unfamiliar grin pasted on his face. Winnie smiled right back and let Patsy light her cigarette.

Willie looked at Tina again, then looked at his mother. *Uh-oh*. This was not a good idea.

Patsy sat down next to Winnie, who quickly preened her hair and outfit. She had spent the day in the new spa and beauty parlor at the Full House. She was wearing a blinding red dress and perfume you could smell all the way to the casino. She looked as good as she had in years, Willie thought. And her timing was typically perfect.

"The first thing you'll have to tell me is how such a young woman could have two grown sons." Patsy's smooth talk was a little rough, yet sincere.

"Why Mr. Bucco, are you flirting with me? "

"I guess I'm just feeling the occasion. Everybody seems so happy out here. Where I come from, people ain't always so happy."

"And where is that, Mr. Bucco?"

"All over, really. I have business all over the country. Too much travel, I suppose. Mostly I'm from Chicago, although I spend a lot of time in Atlantic City."

"Well, then we do have something in common. I've spent some time in Atlantic City myself. It's been quite a while since I've been back."

Willie watched closely as Patsy's eyes suddenly bulged and his jaw dropped. He stared at Winnie, then smiled so broadly that his eyes nearly disappeared. "No, it couldn't be!"

"Couldn't be what, Mr. Bucco? Is there something wrong?"

"Not at all, not at all" Patsy said slowly. "It's just ... tell me, Winnie, tell me about Atlantic City."

"Well, Mr. Bucco, I don't like to toot my own horn, but in my younger days, I was something of a beauty queen. I was Miss Atlantic City in nineteen ... well, some years ago."

"Winnie Quinn!"

"Why, I haven't been called that in ... yes, how did you know my name was Winnie Quinn, Mr. Bucco?"

Patsy's grin was so wide that even Tina was confused.

"I've always known," Patsy replied. "You have no idea."

Willie was smiling now. His mother had always had a talent for wrapping men around her little finger, and she was obviously going to work on Patsy. Somehow, Patsy had turned the tables. Willie rarely got a chance to see Winnie tilt back on her heels. *What could this mobster from Chicago possibly know about her?*

"Mr. Bucco, you are an interesting and mysterious man."

Winnie had enough experience to hang on to her composure and stay in character.

"Call me Patsy," said the principal owner of the Full House, pouring champagne for his new lady friend.

Chapter 21

Betty continued to live life on the bad side of Tina Bucco. Willie was sympathetic. He was on the wrong side of her brother.

Carlo didn't seem to like anyone, even his girlfriend. Still, he clearly had a serious problem with Willie.

It probably started during the grand reopening. He didn't like how everyone, especially the women, fussed over Willie. Now, Patsy was chasing after Willie's mother and his sister was chasing after this skinny kid musician.

Problems at the construction site hadn't improved his mood. Patsy had steered Carlo away from the rougher side of the business. He knew his nephew was as tough as they come and fearless in a fight. That was what worried Patsy. Carlo enjoyed the violence like a hobby. He could be a sadist at times. He had a temper, too, and too many enemies for such a young man. Patsy didn't want Carlo to suffer the same fate as his father, Nicky, whose temper got him killed. He wanted to see Carlo grow old, have some kids and keep the family name alive.

So Patsy got Carlo involved in the "executive" level of the construction industry. When he protested, Patsy told him he needed to learn this side of the business if he ever wanted to lead the family. Since Patsy had no heirs of his own, the job was his to lose. The way to keep it, Patsy counseled, was to be smarter than the enemies who would inevitably surface to challenge you.

Even in a tailored Italian suit, Carlo managed to keep collecting enemies, so much so that Patsy decided to get him out of Chicago. The expansion of the Full House was a perfect place to hide him out, cool him off and gain him some practical experience. If all went well, Carlo would be put in charge of acquiring and developing additional Las Vegas properties in the future.

Patsy sent Tina to Vegas along with Carlo, ostensibly to keep an eye on her brother. In reality, Patsy knew Tina had fallen in with a bad crowd and appeared to lack any sense of self-control. He knew she had been taking drugs and was hanging around with some dangerous characters. After two of his better soldiers got into a bloody fight, leaving one dead and the other in prison, word got out that Tina had been dating both of them. She might have even planned the whole mess on purpose.

Not even 21, Tina was on the fast track to a bad end. Patsy made the tough choice to break his sister-in-law's heart and send both her children out of town. He begged her to go with them. Dahlia was a neighborhood girl, though, and could not bear to leave.

Still, there was no choice. If Patsy didn't do something soon, Dahlia was going to go from widow to widow with two dead children. *Maybe she'll change her mind*, Patsy thought. *Maybe we'll all end up out there.*

Tina eventually took to Las Vegas. Once she got to know her way around, she had to laugh at the irony. "Uncle Patsy sent me to Las Vegas to curb my wild ways," she giggled. "I'm not sure he really thought that one all the way through."

Carlo saw a different side of the city. Heat. Dust. Lazy contractors who didn't speak English. He knew Chicago like the back of his hand. In Las Vegas, there wasn't much beyond the Strip and downtown, and he still got lost all the time. Pockets full of cash couldn't buy him a decent Italian meal.

In Las Vegas, he wasn't much more important than the next suit. The only reason he was feared was because of his uncle. He was under orders not to indulge in the kind of behavior that made him a target in Chicago. And he resented every minute of it.

Worst of all, this Weekend Willie kid and his family were infesting the Bucco family like fleas. The kid and his redneck oaf of a brother ruled like kings in the Regal. And Winnie was walking around the joint like she was Carlo's godmother-in-law.

Patsy extended his stay in Las Vegas to spend more time with Winnie. It galled Carlo to see his ferocious, focused uncle behaving like a teenager in heat, lounging by the pool with Winnie, laughing and snuggling with her at the Regal. He bought her expensive gifts, including a new Chrysler Imperial LeBaron, designer dresses and a necklace with a diamond large enough to find work as a paperweight. Winnie loved to show them off and rewarded Patsy with public displays of affection that left no doubt of her upward status.

Before he finally left, Patsy made it clear to everyone that Winnie was to be treated like family.

Willie was the featured attraction around here, so Carlo tried to leave him be. Bobby was an easier and more enjoyable target for his anger. Carlo would torment and insult Bobby every chance he got. When Bobby would unwind at the lobby bar after the show, Carlo would yell to the bartender, "Hey Sam, make sure the fat boy pays his tab."

Inevitably, there was an incident with some of Bobby's friends. They had been drinking pretty heavy at the lobby bar one night when Carlo came by and said to Bobby, "Fat boy, you and your little faggot friends are blocking the bar. Why don't you scram and let the paying customers get by."

One of Bobby's well-lubricated buddies said, "Who the fuck is this?" Bobby grabbed his friend and tried to hold him back, but it was too late.

"*Who am I?*" Carlo said. "I'm your worst fucking nightmare, you scumbag redneck *gavonne*. Now you and your faggot friends can get the fuck out of here before I cut off your dicks and serve them in the buffet."

Bobby's friends started to close ranks and move towards Carlo until they saw a larger huddle of men moving quickly to

Carlo's side.

Bobby tried his best to become a peacemaker.

"Let's get out of here, guys," he said. "Carlo, I'm sorry, they don't know who you are. This is my fault. We'll just get out of your way."

Too late. Carlo and his posse followed Bobby's group outside. With a simple nod, his boys started in on Bobby's friends, punching, kicking, stomping until they all lay on the ground, bleeding, crying and curled into fetal positions.

Carlo pulled Bobby aside and pulled out a switchblade. He pushed Bobby against a wall and slipped the tip of the blade inside Bobby's quivering nostril. Carlo could feel an adrenaline rush as a small stream of blood flowed from Bobby's nose.

"Now listen here, you fat fuck," Carlo said, the spittle from his mouth spraying Bobby in the face. "I'm getting sick of you and your whole fucking family. From now on, you come here, you do your little kiddie show and you get the fuck out. *Capish*?"

Maybe it was the liquor. Somehow, Bobby chose this time and place to stand up for himself. His timing was as bad as Winnie's was good.

"Hey, I got friends around here too, you know." Bobby started his defense with a whimper and gradually built up some resolve. "If you hurt me, your uncle's gonna be real pissed. My mother sees everything that goes on around here. You just leave me alone, or I'll make trouble for you."

Carlo smiled, let go of Bobby and took a step back. He mockingly straightened out Bobby's jacket collar and brushed the dust off his shoulders.

"Well, well, maybe I underestimated you," Carlo said, still smiling. "Come on, boys, we've been threatened. We better get out of here before these cowboys come back with a bunch of Indians. We could all lose our scalps."

He closed the switchblade and tossed it to Bobby as he walked away. "Here, you might need this. You never know when someone might want to hurt you."

The next day, Willie got a call from Bobby, who said he was sick and couldn't play that night. No matter how irresponsible he was in general, it wasn't like Bobby to skip a gig. Willie quickly lined up Mr. Rush to play drums.

Bobby's absence continued through the weekend. In the meantime, Willie heard about the fight in the parking lot. He asked Tony for advice.

"I already talked to Carlo about it," Tony said. "Told him beating on Bobby was bad for business. He understands and he's sorry for what he did. I wouldn't worry about it, Willie."

"Should I talk to Carlo, Tony?" Willie asked. "Try to apologize, smooth things over?"

"I wouldn't do that if I were you," Tony said. "Let Carlo cool off for a while. Let me take care of it. I know how to handle this sort of thing."

Willie nodded his thanks and started to leave. Tony stopped him.

"One other thing, Willie," Tony said. "While you're at it, you may want to steer clear of Tina. Just until things cool off."

Willie had no problem with that advice. Avoiding Tina had become a part-time job for him since their first meeting at the pool. She just had a talent for showing up wherever he did. It had become impossible for Willie to visit Betty at the pool without Tina interrupting. The poolside was now her office. She had a whole corner of the patio area reserved just for herself, with a phone and an assistant who hurried in and out, running various errands.

"What does she need an assistant for?" Betty grumbled. "What is it she does that requires assistance?"

That was something Willie was sure he didn't want to find out.

Tina also showed up every night at the Regal, claiming the same front-row table she had shared with her uncle. During breaks, she would follow the band out back and hang on Willie until the others were too uncomfortable to stick around.

Bobby had finally returned and was especially uneasy around Carlo's little sister.

One night, about two weeks after the fight, Tina came out and bummed a cigarette from Bobby. Bobby gave her the whole pack and quickly went back inside. Sammy and Jimmy finished their smokes and joined Bobby inside, leaving Willie and Tina alone in a corner of the new wing that was hidden from prying eyes.

"You know, Willie, I think I make Bobby nervous," she said. She moved closer to Willie and put her arms around his neck. "Do I make you nervous?"

"Tina, I like you just fine, it's just … "

"I didn't ask if you liked me, Willie. I asked if I make you nervous."

"No, you don't make me nervous."

"Since you brought it up, do you really like me?"

"Yes, I said I did. You're very, uh, you're a very nice girl."

"What exactly is it that you like about me, Willie? I mean, I am terribly spoiled, and I'm such a bitch. Just ask your girlfriend."

Tina let her hands drop down to Willie's chest. She played with the top button on his shirt. "So what is it exactly that you like about me? Is it my body? Do you want to touch it?"

"Tina, you are a very attractive woman," Willie said, trying to find the right words.

"Do you want to touch me, Willie? You can if you want to," she said, rubbing against Willie with greater force. "I can tell you want to."

She reached down below his belt to gauge his response. Then she stretched up on her tiptoes and stuck her tongue in his ear. Willie grabbed her by the shoulders, but did not push her away. He just stood there, passively, wondering what this raven-haired vixen would do next.

Just then, Sammy opened the back door. "Willie! Back on!"

Tina kissed him on the cheek, let him go and slipped past

Sammy back inside. Willie took a deep breath and headed for the door as well.

"Willie?" Sammy said as Willie walked past.

"What?"

Sammy wiggled a finger at the side of his face. "Lipstick."

CHAPTER 22

The long, hot summer dragged on almost to Christmas. At last, Tina and Carlo went home to spend the holidays with their mother in Chicago. The collective exhale at the House was enough to kick up a sandstorm in the nearby desert.

Willie, Betty and Bobby spent Christmas Eve at Winnie's luxurious new home. Willie and Betty then spent Christmas Day with Amanda. Amanda was feeling better these days. The Tilden home had been fixed up quite nicely. Willie supplied the finances and Amanda threw herself into supervising the repairs and decorating a new kitchen loaded with modern appliances. All three of them had a lovely time stringing colored lights on the porch and trimming the artificial tree in the living room. Natural Christmas trees were hard to come by in the desert.

Willie and Betty helped out by taking care of the landscaping, pulling rocks and weeds and planting new grass and flowers. Willie found lawn work to be very therapeutic. He habitually watered every morning with a hose and a simple, handheld twist sprayer. Betty kept asking why he didn't buy a sprinkler. He said he enjoyed the simple process of drenching his hungry half acre and watching the blades turn a rich shade of green. The grass still grew slowly in the desert, so he always looked forward to the days it was high enough to mow. He bought a power mower from Sears and dutifully manicured the lawn from corner to corner. When he was done, he raked up the clumps of grass and swept the new sidewalk until the entire property was spotless.

Betty had to forbid Willie from mowing on Christmas day. "Nobody wants to hear that noisy motor today," she said, amused at Willie's one domestic obsession.

Willie hadn't felt this comfortable since their vacation trip to California. The break helped him to clear his head and make a few decisions. One decision in particular.

Amanda had been up since dawn cooking the Christmas feast and went to bed right after dinner. It was sweater-cool outside. Willie and Betty took an open bottle of wine from the dinner table and went outside to find the North Star.

They spent a few quiet moments holding each other and laughed about the Beatle's "A Hard Day's Night" board game that Winnie bought Willie for Christmas.

"Speaking of presents, I have one more," Willie said, leading Betty to the bench on the porch.

"What are you up to now, Mr. Willie Taylor?" Betty asked.

Willie pulled a small box out of his sweater pocket and handed it to her. Inside was a large diamond ring. Not as large as some Betty had seen at the Full House, but big enough that she could not miss its meaning.

"Oh, *Willie*. Oh, no," she said, looking at the ring, then looking away.

Her reaction was curious and unexpected. Willie had already braced himself for one of her patented bear hugs. Instead, she went still. She looked down at the ring, up at Willie and down at the ring again.

"Betty, I think we should get married. I think it's time. Will you marry me?" Not terribly eloquent, Willie thought. He still had trouble finding the right words when he wasn't onstage.

"Oh, Willie," Betty said again. "I don't know about this."

"You don't know?" Willie was shocked. Something was wrong and he had no idea what. "What don't you know? Don't you want to get married?"

"*Yes*, I *do* want to get married," she said. That sounded better until he saw the tears. "I want to marry you. I want to spend my life with you. I want to have your children. But ..."

But?

"Willie, I don't think you're ready to do this," she said, looking away from him. "I think you still miss not having a childhood. That you didn't get to do all that stuff other boys do."

"I'm not a child anymore," Willie said. "I don't want to play catch and race cars."

"I know you don't," Betty said. "But I know you resent how you've never been able to do what you want. First your mother, then your brother, then us. Sometimes I feel like I'm just another chain around your neck, and if you can't at least feel like you can get away from all this, you'll end up resenting us. *Me.*

"Oh, I can't believe this is happening. Please, please try to understand. I want us to stay together. I couldn't bear it if I lost you. I just wasn't expecting this. I wasn't ready for this."

"I want us to stay together, too. I don't understand what the problem is," Willie said, his voice giving away hurt and confusion.

Betty blew her nose and tried to find some composure. She took a deep breath and reached out to hold Willie's hands.

"Willie, I love you very much. And I think you love me. And I think we could have a good life together."

"So what's the problem?"

"Willie, we've been together for four years. We've been mostly living together for almost a year. *And you've never said it.*"

"Said what?"

"You've never said that you love me."

"Of course I love you. You know I love you."

"Then tell me why, Willie. If you really love me, how is it possible that you never told me so?"

He wasn't even sure she was right. Maybe she was. How very strange.

Of course she was right. At first, they both avoided the word. After a while, she didn't. He remembered that moment.

He knew he was afraid to say it then. He didn't realize that he was still on the fence.

Betty was good about that sort of thing. She didn't push him. When he didn't know what to say, she let him stay quiet.

So he did.

"Betty, I'm sorry. I don't always express myself very well."

"Willie, you're a musician. A true artist. You have no trouble expressing yourself onstage. You're so sure of yourself up there. Do you know why? It's because you know in your heart that you belong there. You can be confident, knowing that you want to be on that stage. You want to be playing music. Everybody can see it. That's why they come. That's why they love you so much.

"I don't think you are really sure about anything else. If you were as sure about us, I don't think you would have so much trouble expressing your feelings."

She was beginning to make sense and Willie didn't like it. There were so many things he was unsure of.

Betty moved closer to him and put her head on his shoulder. They sat there for a long time, savoring the rare quiet of a Christmas evening in suburban Las Vegas.

Willie broke the silence. "I don't know what to do."

"Willie, I'm so sorry. Please try to understand. I'm not saying *no*. I'm saying *not yet*."

"So what am I supposed to do now?"

"Just try and understand. And please, please, don't give up on me. Don't give up on us."

Betty looked at Willie. He looked so lost, so alone, and she didn't know what she could say to make it better.

"Why don't we try and get some sleep," she said.

They went back inside, turned off the Christmas lights and went to bed. Neither one of them could sleep. They both stayed still, trying not to disturb the other.

So much for Christmas, Willie thought. *Ho, ho ho.*

CHAPTER 23

Musicians draw inspiration from their muse. Songwriters write about their muse. So Willie tried to write some songs about Betty.

He spent a long time thinking about what Betty had said. Ever since he was a child, Willie had trouble speaking his mind. Somehow, it was different onstage.

English was his second language. Almost since birth, music had been his first.

He could sing about love. He just couldn't talk about it. Maybe if he started writing about Betty, the perfect words would come to him, just as he could always pluck the perfect musical notes out of the air. No one else could see them. He could see them floating by like balloons. All he had to do was reach out and grab them with almost any musical instrument that might be handy. That was the essence of his talent.

Willie sought counsel from Mr. Rush. They would drink a few beers and talk about women and music. Mr. Rush didn't have a lot of advice about women, but he knew all about the blues. And he knew about the healing power of music.

Mr. Rush tried to help Willie understand the connection between words and music. "They are both ways to communicate," he explained. "You have to understand that is what you are doing every time you speak or sing. You're also communicating when you play your guitar. There is a big difference, though. Music is far more abstract than language. Sure, language is often abstract. But music *always* is. And that makes it a safer way to communicate. At least for the lucky geniuses like us who can play musical instruments.

"In other words, my little Mozart, you're a fraud. You and

me both. We dazzle people with our talent and artistic expression, and leave our adoring audience to fill in the blanks. There's no effort on our part to plainly state what we mean and no obligation to stand by it.

"They listen to us play and get to think what they want. Their thoughts turn to fantasy, and the guy on the stage gets the starring role. Anyone who can play such beautiful music must have the soul of a poet, right? Bullshit.

"What we do takes talent. Telling someone what's really in your heart takes guts. Very few of us have both. You have very few weaknesses as a musician. So you know what you have to work on, don't you?"

Mr. Rush finished his beer and opened another. He sounded like he had left a few things unsaid.

"You know what? There is something I've been wanting to tell you," he said to Willie, looking him straight in the eye.

"Yes?" Willie asked.

"I'd really like it if you stopped calling me Mr. Rush."

Andy agreed that writing more songs would be a good outlet for Willie. He reminded his student that to validate his songs, a real songwriter must perform them, preferably outside his living room. That presented a problem for Willie, who had a stage of his own to play other people's songs, but no showcase for the bleeding-heart laments of a love-struck teenage boy.

Patsy Bucco, of all people, solved Willie's dilemma.

Winnie had convinced Patsy to take an extended vacation in Las Vegas. "Really breaks up your winter," she told him, promising to keep him warm if it fell below sixty degrees.

By February, 1966, the new hotel tower was ready to open. Patsy had Winnie design the interior of the top-floor suite he had reserved for his own use. Tina moved into another suite at the opposite end of the hall. Carlo took the one in the middle.

Patsy made a sincere effort to befriend Winnie's boys. Willie began to like and even admire Patsy. He certainly appreciated how he distracted Winnie from meddling in his increasingly complicated life. And how Patsy was nice to Bobby without patronizing him like so many others did.

He tried not to think about what Patsy did for a living.

Bobby was still keeping a low profile around the House. He would show up a few minutes before the gig and leave right after.

Most people could not tell that Willie and Betty were having problems. They still lived and slept together. Willie still watered the lawn every morning, sometimes standing out there for more than an hour. He still visited Betty at the pool every afternoon on his way into the Regal.

Willie worked on a few songs about his girlfriend, but he never played them for anyone else, not even Betty. The sad fact was that he was communicating with her less than ever. Ironically, now that he was no longer sure if they were in love, he used those words every day. And every time he came close to opening up about the hurt he felt when she turned down his proposal, he pulled back.

They were still so very young and could only hope that time would help them find a common ground to build a foundation for the future.

Willie fell into a routine of stopping by the pool in the afternoon, then joining Winnie and Patsy at the hotel's fancy new restaurant. Trattoria Dahlia, named after Patsy's sister-in-law, finally introduced authentic Chicago-Italian cuisine to the Strip. Patsy had brought in a famous chef from Chicagoland and spared no expense in supplying him with the best meat, fish, cheese and produce available west of the Mississippi. When Patsy was in town, he personally approved all of the specials.

One night, Willie was nibbling on the veal special while Winnie munched a salad and sipped some expensive red wine. Patsy was working on a thick T-bone and asking Willie a lot of questions about the music business.

"You know, there's a lot of money in making records

these days," he said. "I've been looking into that. There's a small record label in New Jersey, Harrison, I think it's called. You ever hear of it? I know the guy that owns it. He's thinking about selling it. He's got some debts to settle."

"That'd be great, Patsy," Willie said, wondering how much trouble the owner of Harrison Records had got himself into.

"They got some rock and roll hits, and they've had some luck with the race music, you know, that rhythm and blues stuff. Like that Ray Charles guy, you ever hear of him?"

"Sure Patsy, Ray Charles. He's a big star, although he's doing country music these days."

"No kidding? A *moolenan* singing Country and Western? Winnie, did you ever hear of such a thing?"

"Well country and easy listening," Willie said. "Anyway, he doesn't sing a lot of R&B these days."

"So how come you don't make records, Willie? You sing better than a lot of the shit I hear on the radio."

Winnie stopped eating her salad.

"I don't know, Patsy," Willie said. "No one's asked me to, I guess. I'm so busy, anyway. And I don't know of a single record company working out of Vegas."

"So what about it?"

"What about what?"

"Why don't you make a record?"

Willie stopped eating and looked at his mother. She was way ahead of him.

"Patsy, you're a genius!" Winnie exclaimed. "You could make a fortune. We could make a fortune. This record company. Do you really think you want to buy it?"

"Well, *buy* ain't quite the right word," Patsy said.

The next day, Patsy made a few phone calls and, just like that, he was in the record business.

CHAPTER 24

Harrison Records took its name from the tiny, crowded industrial New Jersey town in which it was located. Just north of Newark and a short ride from the river crossings, Harrison offered accessibility to New York and cheap rent for business owners.

Second-generation Russian immigrants Viktor Chernev and his brother, Mikhail, whose friends called him Mickey, had some success running jazz nightclubs in Newark and took advantage of their contacts by starting a record label. To avoid the increasingly troublesome ties to their family's homeland, they also changed their last name to Harrison, which helped to reinforce the commitment to their new home town.

Viktor handled the care and feeding of the musicians. Mickey had the head for business and had scouted out the perfect spot for their new venture. In 1955, he bought a bankrupt funeral home and mortuary at auction for pennies on the dollar. The building, located on Main Street in downtown Harrison, was two blocks from the rail station. Built around the turn of the century, it was as sturdy as a bomb shelter, with thick walls and a maze of rooms. The huge basement was sectioned off by cinder block walls into five large spaces, which Mickey knew he could easily convert into recording studios. There was more than enough room upstairs for offices and storage. He could even provide bedrooms on the second and third floors where the musicians could crash while they were in town.

Viktor brought in a lot of talent, but few of the jazz recordings on the new Harrison label made much of an impression on the charts. Mickey decided to gamble on rock 'n' roll. By 1961, a string of modest hits by the Arthur Kills, named after the narrow waterway running between the Garden State and Staten Island, had put Harrison Records in the black for the first time.

Mickey's gamble had paid off. Too bad Viktor's gambling habit did not. Viktor liked the ponies and had built up a large debt betting on losers at Monmouth Park and Yonkers.

The debt found its way to the desk of Patsy Bucco, who had taken interest in the music business. He came up with a win-win solution for everyone who mattered. Patsy would assume ownership, leaving Mickey in place to run the business as a salaried employee. Viktor would get lost, debts forgiven and with the promise that next time, Patsy wouldn't let him off so easy.

Mickey feared the worst when just a few weeks into the new arrangement, Patsy was flying in a new musician he had signed to the label. All Mickey knew was that the kid's name was Weekend Willie and he was some sort of hot-shit lounge act in Las Vegas. None of it sounded very promising.

Patsy overruled Winnie regarding Bobby's participation in the sessions. He had spoken to Mickey, who explained how these things generally worked. The company had writers and producers who supplied the songs, arrangements and studio musicians. Most of the new rock bands only had one or two members with any real talent. The rest of them got in the way. Weed out the amateurs and the whole process went a lot faster, which meant cheaper. It also meant the label could hold onto publishing rights and charge the artists for production costs, keeping most of the proceeds in-house and piling up the tax deductions.

That's how Patsy saw the Taylor Brothers and Band. A bunch of amateurs trying to keep up with the genius. If Patsy was going to do this, he was going to do it the right way. Bobby was out. So was the hired help. Willie had the name, the looks and the talent. Patsy trusted Mickey to supply the rest.

Willie felt guilty leaving his brother behind. They had been a team for so long. Yet Bobby had never shared his brother's dedication to their craft. He could keep a beat. That was about it. Willie remembered something that Mr. Rush had said. "A great musician must find other great musicians to challenge him. Otherwise, he will never reach the next level."

It was time that Willie tested himself and see if he could play with the big boys, the kind of pros who cut the hits he was covering in Las Vegas. He could spend a few days out east, gain some valuable experience and be back in time for the weekend action at the Regal.

He just wished that his troubled mind would allow him to enjoy the adventure a little more. Most musicians would consider this akin to winning the lottery. Bobby, Sammy and Jimmy were seething with jealousy and equally confused about how Willie spoke of the trip as an accountant would discuss an audit.

Willie quietly packed his Les Paul, a notebook full of songs and a few days' worth of clothes. Winnie also was surprised that her son was not more excited about this once-in-a-lifetime opportunity.

"I can hardly sleep," she told him at the airport as they waited for his Eastern Airlines flight number to be called.

"Records are a shot in the dark," Willie told her. "Some of my favorite records are collector's items now because nobody else bought them. Besides, chances are I won't even get to do any of my own songs. I haven't even heard the songs I'm going to be doing.

"The Regal is a sure thing. I'm not going to mess it up. Too many people depend on me. I'll be back in a few days and that will be that."

Willie was depressed to hear himself speak in such practical terms. *Mr. Rush would shoot himself if he heard me now,* Willie thought. *I must be getting old.*

Things went better in Harrison than Willie could have

hoped for. Mickey was pleasantly surprised to learn that Willie was a world-class talent. He introduced Harrison's new star to his top songwriting team, Jerry Miller and Angie Metz. Miller and Metz had written nine Top Forty hits, including all of songs charted by the Arthur Kills. They spent the first night and day jamming with Willie and trying to get a sense of his style. The next day, they brought in a pile of songs they thought might suit his talent. Willie chose four of them and a group of musicians was brought in for the session. Twelve hours later, six sides had been recorded, including two of Willie's compositions.

One of them was called "So Far Away From You," which was the first song Willie wrote after his falling out with Betty. It was a bittersweet ballad, with lyrics that spoke the feelings he could never express.

> *I'm so far away from you*
> *And I don't know what to do*
> *It's not easy when the one you love*
> *Has turned and walked away*
>
> *I could follow but I'm afraid*
> *Of losing all the love we made*
> *If I don't let you find a way*
> *To decide for yourself that you want to stay*
>
> *I'm so far away from you*
> *And my life has turned a shade of blue*
> *Bluer than the morning sky*
> *I wonder if you're coming by*
>
> *I could try to find the words to say*
> *I love you in that special way*
> *But the words can't help me anyway*
> *Cause I'm so far away from you.*

"Sweet and sad, the girls will love it," said Angie Metz, who told Willie she was a lesbian. "You must really have the girls falling at your feet out in Los Angeles."

"Las Vegas."

"Sure, honey, wherever."

The other Weekend Willie original was a peppy little rockabilly number, "Betty Are You Ready?"

Betty, are you ready to go?
Betty, are you ready to go?
You're the only girl that
Makes me oh-oh-oh
Betty are you ready to go?

Betty, at the down town station
Waiting for the train full of anticipation
Leaving all her dolls and toys behind
Betty, she going off to college
Ivy League sweaters and higher knowledge
Wondering when she gets there what she'll find

Betty, she don't want to go away
Betty has a fella and he begged her to stay
But daddy he don't care how much she cry
Begged and pleaded with her mean old dad
He's the best boyfriend that I ever had
And if you make me go I just might die

Betty, are you ready to go?
Betty, are you ready to go?
You're the only girl that
Makes me oh-oh-oh
Betty are you ready to go?

Betty, sees her train a-comin'
Then around the corner sees her fella runnin'
Betty stops to hear her fella say
Betty, please don't say good-bye
Swear that if you give your fella one more try
You'll be happy every single day

Betty, traded in her ticket
For a little gold ring with her initials in it
Betty said college would have to wait
Betty and her fella were bound by fate

Betty, are you ready to go?
Betty, are you ready to go?
You're the only girl that
Makes me oh-oh-oh
Betty are you ready to go?

The songs weren't quite up to the standard of Miller and Metz. Willie's originals were recorded only to be used as B-sides. Mickey said it was too expensive to burn professionally written songs for the B-sides, at least until Willie had sold some records and built up a following.

Regardless of their intended use, Willie was thrilled to hear his own songs brought to life in the studio. Up until now, he had only strummed them to himself on a guitar. Betty didn't know they existed.

He decided to keep the songs a secret until the records came out. Maybe he had found a way to tell Betty how he really felt about her. Maybe hearing Willie sing her name on the radio would help to bring her around.

The trip to New Jersey also gave Willie some time to think on his own. Sitting alone in his room at night, he was able to explore his feelings without any distractions. He tried to objectively examine both sides of their relationship. Despite their problems, Willie felt incomplete without Betty at his side. She was still his best friend. She understood him better than anyone. She was beautiful and kind and, in a town full of phonies, she was completely lacking in pretense.

Willie loved everything about her. Maybe the problem was that he didn't feel worthy of her love.

He also worried that it might be too late for them. That she wasn't going to wait around forever for him to change.

Then again, maybe it was time he gave himself some credit. Here he was, a budding star getting the VIP treatment from some serious players in the music business. Even though Patsy had set the whole thing up, Willie knew that he had earned the respect of his new friends at Harrison Records. They spoke about doing another session in a few months. He was sure Patsy had nothing to do with that.

The final sessions wrapped up the day before his flight back to Vegas was scheduled to leave from LaGuardia. Willie hoped to jam with the group one last time, but they had a gig lined up in the city that evening.

He was about to ask if he could tag along when someone called downstairs and said he had a visitor at the front door.

"Says her name is Tina," the woman said.

CHAPTER 25

"I was shopping in the city and Uncle Patsy asked me to check up on you. Make sure you weren't getting into any trouble out here. So here I am!" Tina was a lousy liar because she really didn't try.

"I wasn't in trouble until now." *Did he say that out loud?*

"Now Willie, I come all this way to see you and this is the thanks I get? How rude of you!"

"Seriously, Tina, what's going on?" Willie was being rude. He had so enjoyed his trip up to now that he was thinking of excuses to stay longer. Of the many things he dreaded returning to, Tina was near the top of the list. Now she was *here.*

"Seriously, Willie, I was shopping for spring styles on Fifth Avenue, just like I always do this time of year. When I heard you were going to be so close I just thought to myself, 'how perfectly fabulous!' Maybe I could show him around New York, we could have a nice time and maybe he would realize I'm not such a terrible person. I'm sorry if you think that, Willie. I know I can be a real bitch sometimes. But is it so terrible that I like you and want to be your friend?"

She almost sounded sincere. *Almost.*

"Of course not, Tina. And I guess it was nice of you to come all the way here to say so. But as it turns out, I'm leaving in the morning, so there's not that much time to be a tourist."

"Well, then, I guess we better not waste any more time," she said, grabbing his hand and leading him to a black Cadillac Fleetwood limousine parked out front. A uniformed chauffeur stood motionless next to an open door to the back seat.

"Tina, I can't," he protested. "I've got to pack. I was going to go to this gig and ... "

"Nobody invited you to the gig, Willie." Willie turned around. It was Miller and Metz, grinning like Cheshire cats. "I think you better take this beautiful young woman up on her proposition," Jerry Miller said.

Tina smiled at her new friends, thankful for their support.

Willie gave them a dirty look and let out a heavy sigh.

"Let me get my coat."

Willie had to admit he was having a good time. Tina knew Manhattan and was a determined tour guide. She walked him through Greenwich Village and Chinatown, where they gorged on a lunch of dim sum, green tea and some other Chinese delicacies that Willie had never heard of. Tina then ordered the driver uptown, past Lincoln Center, Radio City Music Hall, Carnegie Hall and Columbus Circle, all the way into Central Park.

They left the limo and strolled through the south end of the park. Wollman Rink was still open for skating, so they rented skates and hit the ice. Neither one had ever skated before, so they spent the next hour slipping, sliding and falling on top of each other. Their pitiful efforts to stay upright gave way to a fit of unrestrained laughter. Finally, holding each other tight for support, they managed to reach the middle of the rink. Willie steadied himself against Tina as he turned in every direction, taking in the spectacular view of skyscrapers rising above the tree-lined landscape.

"See that one right there? Tina said, pointing high into the urban horizon. Willie wasn't sure which building she meant. The towers were quickly turning to dark silhouettes against a bright-orange setting sky. "That's where I'm staying. The St. Moritz. It's *very* elegant."

Willie looked at Tina. Her cheeks were red from the cold and her long, shiny dark hair was dusted with snow flurries. As she tried to keep a grip on Willie with her puffy knitted mittens, her legs wobbling with uncharacteristic uncertainty, she almost seemed vulnerable. And very desirable. Out in Vegas, her reputation preceded her. Despite her beauty, nearly everyone looked for a place to hide when she entered the room.

Wandering anonymously around sophisticated Manhattan, Tina stopped traffic as men strained their necks for a better look. Here at the rink, men were bumping into each other and falling to the ice as they skated by. All these strangers knew for sure was that this tall, blonde young man was a lucky guy.

"This really isn't so bad, is it?" Tina seemed to know what he was thinking.

"No, this is great. I've never done anything like this before," Willie said, smiling back at her. "I've never even see real snow before."

"I'm really glad you're enjoying yourself, Willie. I really wanted you to be happy. You seem so unhappy most of the time."

"I'm not unhappy. I'm just, well, preoccupied a lot of the time," he said.

"Especially when I'm around. The evil she-devil, out to steal your soul."

"I don't think of you like that, Tina."

"Well, you're nice to say so. Maybe we can be friends after all."

"Yeah, maybe, if you continue to behave yourself." He was comfortable enough to tease her. He really was having the time of his life.

They were in another world and Tina was an entirely different person. Maybe Willie was, too. He certainly felt different out here on his own in the big city, with a beautiful, glamorous woman hanging onto him for dear life. Other men were looking at him with envy. They certainly weren't looking at him like some kid who didn't know what he was doing, which is how he often felt at home when he wasn't onstage.

It was getting dark and the flurries had turned to a steady snow. Thick clouds consumed the daylight before sundown could arrive.

"You know, I think we're in for a storm," Tina said. "Why don't we go to my suite, warm up and order some dinner?"

"Are you serious? I'm still full from lunch," Willie laughed.

"Maybe we'll find a way for you to work up an appetite," Tina said, turning away and skating off before Willie could ask her what she meant. Willie noticed that all of a sudden, she was quite steady on those skates. He followed slowly, falling twice before he reached the wall.

There were plenty of luxury hotels in Las Vegas, but none could match the opulence of the St. Moritz. Tina's suite offered a breathtaking view of Manhattan, Central Park and the ice they had just tried to skate on. There was Italian marble everywhere, from the floor to the columns in the dining room to the spacious bathroom, complete with a bathtub large enough for two.

Willie took off his coat and fell into a plush easy chair. Tina knelt down next to him, pulled a lever and laughed as the recliner unfolded under him.

He laughed, then winced in pain.

"God, I think I must be one bruise from head to toe. We must have fallen a hundred times."

"You poor thing! You know what you need? A nice hot bath."

Tina got up and pulled a long piece of cloth hanging like a ribbon near the front door.

"Watch this," Tina said. A few seconds later, he heard a knock on the door. Tina opened the door and a pretty maid came in, smiling politely. "Yes, ma'am?"

"Can you run a hot bath for my gentleman friend, please?"

"Very good, ma'am, right away." The maid hurried off to

the bathroom. Willie could hear the water running.

"I just *love* this place!" Tina said.

After the maid left, Willie explored the cavernous bathroom, which had a separate shower, two sinks and a makeup station. There were bottles of mouthwash, cologne, creams, oils and bubble bath in every corner. The bathroom window of their corner suite offered yet another postcard view of Manhattan.

Willie found two thick, white robes hanging near the shower. His and hers, or so they appeared. He took off his clothes and tried the large one on for size. It was warm, plush and roomy.

"I'm just going to soak for a while. Is that OK?" he called outside.

"That's what it's there for, sweetie," Tina called back. "Indulge yourself. I'm certainly going to."

Willie sat in the tub for nearly half an hour, soaking his aching muscles and quieting his bruises. He scooped the frothy bubbles and leaned back until the water touched his chin. *I just might sleep in here*, he thought, closing his eyes.

He started to drift off, then opened his eyes when he heard the bathroom door open. It was Tina. She was wearing a silk, pearl-white robe and held a bottle of champagne in one hand, two glasses in the other. At least he thought it was a robe. It barely covered her waist, and Willie could clearly see the outline of her breasts through the smooth, sheer fabric.

Willie gulped. He was tired and sore, yet too comfortable to tense up the way he thought he should. He shifted higher in the tub, happy for the camouflage of the bubbles. He hoped he didn't look too silly.

"Relax, Willie. I'm not going to bite you. I was just lonely. You've been in here forever."

She put the glasses down by the sink, poured the champagne and handed one glass to Willie. He sipped, enjoying the cool liquid massaging his throat. The rest of his body, inside and out, was warm and steamy.

Tina refilled her glass, placed it on the edge of the tub and slipped out of her robe. She smiled and stared straight at Willie as she stepped into the far end of the tub. She sat back on the opposite end, and let her feet slither their way up Willie's legs.

"Isn't this just the living end?" she asked.

Willie's mouth went dry. He drank some more champagne.

Tina gathered some bubbles and slowly rubbed them on her shoulders and breasts. Willie remained still, watching her every move. He watched her empty her glass. Then she pulled her legs in, spun around and slid back into Willie's lap.

"I could really use a massage. Will you rub my shoulders?" she asked sweetly.

Willie obeyed without saying a word. His hands slid easily around her shoulders and neck. Her skin was slippery and smooth. She leaned back and let her hands dance up and down his legs.

"I could get used to this," she said, using the more aggressive voice that Willie was familiar with. "Why don't we just move in?"

"Tina?" Willie said, not sure of what else to say.

"Yes, lover?" Tina didn't hear a reply, so she read his mind. She reached back, took his hands and guided them to her breasts. He began to explore her soft, round curves and well-toned muscles. Say what you want about her spoiled manner; Tina had the kind of body that men fought wars over, and it was being offered to him on a soapy marble platter.

She turned again and sat on top of him, hip to hip. She leaned forward and kissed him hard, plunging her tongue deep into his mouth.

There was no turning back. After some torrid foreplay in the tub, they made their way to the bedroom. There, she did things to him that no woman had ever done before. Well, there had been only one woman who had ever done *anything* to him before. As enthusiastic and uninhibited as Betty could be, she was an inexperienced lover. Tina *knew things*. Willie didn't want to think about where she learned them. He was content to lay there and let her pass on the lesson.

CHAPTER 26

Somehow, the word got back to Las Vegas before Willie did. The day after he got home, he was drawing stares at the Regal. Some of the showgirls who hung around the pool during the day whispered and giggled when they passed him in the hall. A couple of older women who Tina liked to spend time with smiled at each other as he opened a door for them.

Tony, who always had his finger on the pulse, gave him a long look when he got to the Regal. "How'd it go in Jersey?" he asked.

"Pretty good. It was good." Willie answered, trying to read Tony's face.

"Everything OK?" Tony continued. "You feel OK? You look a little tired."

"Yeah, I guess I'm a little tired. Jet lag or something."

"Yeah, jet lag," Tony said. "How's Betty doing? She glad to have you back home?"

"Sure, I guess. She's home for a few days. Her mother is sick and she took a few days off."

"Yeah, I heard. When is she coming back?"

"I'm not sure. Maybe tomorrow."

"Tomorrow, huh?" Tony looked around, then looked back at Willie. "Come with me," he said, and led Willie to his office. Tony closed the door and sat behind his desk like he was taking a meeting.

"Kid, did you bring Tina out there with you?"

What the?

Tony didn't need an answer. He could see it in Willie's face.

"Man, you got some set of nuts on you. Fuckin' musicians. Are you crazy?"

Willie broke out in a cold sweat. How did Tony know anything about New York, and who told him?

"Hey, she just showed up. She was in New York. She said she was shopping. I didn't bring her anywhere."

"That's not what I hear."

"What did you hear? Who told you?"

"I hear you and Tina hooked up in New York and *ba-bing*. You two are some kind of item now."

"We went sightseeing! We went ice skating. We went to Chinatown!"

"Kid, you look like you been to more than Chinatown."

"Oh God! *Oh God!* Tony, where did you hear all this?"

"Hear what?"

"Tony, quit kidding around."

"I hear from Tina's friends. So did a lot of other people. It's all over the hotel. The fucking maids know about it."

"Where did they hear about it?"

"From Tina, I guess."

Tina!

"She's still in New York. At least I think she is."

"Don't really matter where she is, kid. You ever hear of a telephone?"

Willie squirmed until he could no longer sit. He jumped up and paced, best as he could, in Tony's cramped, cluttered office.

"Tony, you gotta help me. It was just … it was just … we were just sightseeing. She was trying to be nice. I didn't want to insult her. We had a good time, that's all it was. Then, well, I don't know. Betty's been mad at me, and Tina was, well, you know … she just wouldn't give up. She was all over me.

"Tony, you gotta help me. If Betty hears about this …"

"Kid, I can't help you. You are fucking *busted*. Betty's gonna hear about it. You need to figure out what you're going to tell her.

"Maybe you can lie. Deny the whole thing. That works sometimes. Never worked for me. That's why I got two ex-wives. One of them stabbed me with a fork. Which reminds me, kid. Betty ain't necessarily your biggest problem."

"What? Who?"

"Carlo."

Carlo!

"Fuckin' musicians."

Willie had been looking forward to reclaiming his stage and playing some of the new songs he recorded in Harrison. Now he was too busy to enjoy the homecoming. He was too busy keeping an eye out for Carlo as they played.

As scared as he was about running into Tina's temperamental brother, he was dreading the inevitable confrontation with Betty.

He lingered at the Regal for almost two hours after the show, then finally drove home. Betty was asleep when he got there. She did not wake when he climbed into bed beside her.

Betty had missed three days of work caring for her mother, who had a bad flu that progressed to mild pneumonia. Down the hall, Amanda slept silently. She must be getting better, Willie thought.

As he lay there in the dark, Willie reviewed the previous afternoon. Betty had picked him up at the airport, and there had been no sign of a new problem. She had been her usual self, polite and pleasant, no more or less distant than she had been since Christmas.

She had asked about the trip and if the sessions had gone well. Somehow, Willie had managed to blank the tryst with Tina from his mind, as if it had been some sort of erotic dream. He told Betty about the people he met and the songs they had given him to record. He was still keeping his own songs a secret. He still hoped they would be a pleasant surprise and would help to bridge their divide.

If she had heard anything, it hadn't showed. None of that

mattered, though. She'd hear about it soon enough. He considered telling Betty about Tina showing up and showing him the city. He couldn't be rude to Patsy's niece, right? If Betty heard anything else when she went back to work, that was just Tina being Tina.

Sounded believable enough to him.

The next morning, Willie and Betty had a long talk about his trip to New York. She said she believed him.

"I believe you have enough character not to cheat, and not to get involved with some mobster slut. I don't care what anybody else thinks."

Willie achieved new levels of guilt listening to her buy his story. Even if he got away with it, he was never going to live this down. He had broken the trust of the one person who had never doubted him. Busted or not, he was guilty as charged.

Betty went back to work that very day. Willie promised to visit her at the pool as he always did on his way in. He spent the rest of the morning helping Amanda, who was indeed feeling better. He fixed her some scrambled eggs and went to the pharmacy to refill her prescriptions.

Later that afternoon, around the usual time, he drove over to the House, parked the Mustang and headed straight for the pool. As expected, he found Betty stacking towels. Her mood was foul and her manner was cold.

"Yes, I heard plenty," Betty said matter-of-factly. Then she started to choke up a bit, folding the same towel over and over. "I know what you said, but it's just so humiliating. It's hard. The women around here are such, well, there are a lot of Tinas around here."

"What did they say?" Willie asked. "What did she tell them?"

"Why don't you ask her?"

Betty pointed to the far corner of the pool. Tina's corner. Tina was back, holding court in her usual manner.

Willie stared over at Tina. He wanted to confront her, but not here. Not in front of Betty.

Tina had no reservations about confronting them. As soon as she saw Willie, she jumped up and skipped over.

"Willie! You're back!" she exclaimed, giving him a little hug. "Betty, you must be thrilled to have him back home."

Tina smiled at Betty, smiled at Willie and took a step back.

"Oh, I must be intruding. I'll just leave you two alone." And off she went back to her corner.

For a moment, Willie thought he had dodged the bullet. Then he looked at Betty. Her face was red and her whole body was shaking.

"*You did! You two ... you did! It's all true!*" She started hitting him in the chest and arms as though she was holding a hammer.

He fended off the blows and grabbed her arms. Then she went limp in his grip and started to cry. He tried desperately to hold her up.

"Betty, I told you we *didn't*."

"You *did!*" she cried. "All I needed was to see you two together and I *knew*. Don't tell me you didn't because I know you did! How could you? How could you sleep with her? And then lie to me about it?"

"Betty, let's go inside and talk about this." Willie had lost complete control of the situation, which wasn't surprising. He never had control in the first place.

"Why? Why? What are you going to tell me in there? More lies? *Oh, Willie!*"

"Betty, let's not do this here."

"Yes, let's not do this here. The famous Weekend Willie might be embarrassed in front of his precious fans. What about *me*? What about me, Willie? Do you have any idea how humiliating this is?

"Oh God, oh God! What am I going to do? I loved you Willie. I trusted you. You asked me to trust you and I did. Don't I mean anything to you?"

"Betty, I ... I'm sorry." He couldn't pretend any more. Maybe he could explain ... no. He couldn't.

"I'm sorry!"

"Is that all you have to say? *You're sorry?* Oh God, this can't be happening."

"Betty, I made a mistake. A bad mistake. She just showed up. I swear I didn't know she was there, she just showed up and, well, it didn't mean anything. I didn't even want to go. I was stupid and I made a mistake."

Betty just stood there and stared at him. Slowly, she gathered herself.

"I can't do this. I can't do this, Willie," she said softly. "I can't compete with all these ... people. If it were just one girl, even *her*, I might be able to understand. But I'll never matter as much to you as all these people, these women, all these people who come to see you. They love you and you love them. There's no room for me."

"Betty, that's not true," Willie protested. "I love you. I don't love her, or anybody else."

"Maybe you don't love Tina, but you'll obviously do anything she says, just like you'd do anything for that roomful of people who come to kiss your feet every night. Don't you see? That's the problem. They can always count on you. I can't. Not anymore."

"Betty, you can. I swear it will never happen again. *Please.*"

"No. I can't do this anymore. I can't ..." Betty started to sob again and ran inside. Willie stood motionless, looking at his feet. When he looked up, there were at least 20 people staring at him like he was naked.

Must have been quite a show, he thought. He wanted to scream those words at the gaping mob. Then he decided that his dignity had been battered enough for one day.

He looked over at Tina, who had gathered her belongings and was walking by on her way inside. She stopped, smiled at Willie and shrugged her shoulders.

"*Whoops!*" she said, then she disappeared through the same doors that Betty used for her dramatic exit.

CHAPTER 27

After a quick round of negotiations with management, Willie had a new address — Full House Casino Hotel, Grand Tower Suite 12-E, 1110 Las Vegas Boulevard, Las Vegas, Nevada.

It had been almost six weeks since he removed his belongings from the Tilden residence and moved into the hotel. It certainly was convenient, and it didn't cost him a dime.

Tony and Danny Benvenuto both took pity on the poor boy. They had four ex-wives between them. They knew how it was, and they wanted to make sure their top attraction knew they were behind him.

"It'll be easier the next time," Tony told Willie.

Willie didn't appreciate the humor. He was angry, embarrassed and heartbroken. Angry with Tina for seducing and betraying him for her own amusement. Embarrassed for being so easily duped. Heartbroken that Betty wouldn't have anything to do with him. She tore up the checks he sent her to help care for Amanda and the house.

He didn't dare visit her at the pool. Even if she agreed to listen, Tina would probably show up to throw gasoline on the fire.

Tina did offer an apology of sorts. She assured Willie that her feelings for him were genuine, and she only told a couple of girlfriends about their tryst because she was so happy.

Willie didn't buy a word of it. Tina continued to offer herself to him, saying he might as well make the best of a bad situation. She obviously didn't understand, or care, how much trouble she had caused. She just wanted what she wanted.

She cornered him one night after the show as they took the elevator to the tower suites. "She doesn't want you, Willie, and I can't imagine why you want her," she said. "She's got you all messed up. I can set you right again."

"That's not what I need right now," said Willie, trying to remain diplomatic until she lost interest.

"I know what you need," she said, backing him into the corner of the elevator. "I know how to make you feel better."

Willie's disapproving scowl and rigid body language told her she was fighting a losing battle.

"Well, maybe it's for the best," she said. "My brother already wants to kill both of us."

"Gee, thanks for trying to cheer me up," said Willie as the elevator doors opened. "This is my floor. I'll see you around."

"Count on it," Tina said, smiling as they separated to neutral corners.

Willie somehow managed to push Tina's brother out of his thoughts. Carlo had returned to Chicago before Willie came back from his trip. No one seemed to know if and when he was coming back. The tower was finished, so there wasn't much left for him to do in Las Vegas.

Tina's warning was the first he had heard about Carlo knowing anything, and at this point, he really didn't care. If Carlo showed up to beat the crap out of him, he probably wouldn't even fight back.

All he could hope was that Betty would one day forgive him and take him back. He knew he didn't have the words to bring her around, so he put faith in the quality of time to heal all wounds. In the meantime, he asked Andy Rush to keep an eye on Betty and make sure she had someone to talk to. She trusted Andy. He was the unofficial pastor of young local musicians, having taught so many of them since middle school.

The only thing that made Willie feel any better was to play his music. Betty knew him so well it was scary. Nothing mattered more to him than leading his band and mesmerizing his loyal fans like some sort of desert Pied Piper. The connection between musician and audience was sacred to him and, no matter what was going on in his personal life, he would never betray that trust. Especially now.

A few more weeks passed and Willie slowly adjusted to the new routine. Living in the hotel meant no commute, no home chores, not much of anything at all to do during the day. Most of the time, he slept late and took meals in the kitchen at Trattoria Dahlia. He was friendly with the staff and they enjoyed cooking for him.

Once in a while, he would meet Winnie in the dining room for lunch. His mother tried to discount the breakup. "Plenty of fish in the sea," she said. "You're a handsome, successful young man. Any girl would be crazy not to want you."

Mostly, Winnie talked about Patsy and where he was, what he was doing and when he was coming back.

"He's supposed to be here by the end of the week," she told him while slurping down a shrimp cocktail. "You know, this might be the time. I think he's going to propose."

Willie still liked Patsy and was dreading that confrontation as well. Did Patsy know about him and his niece? And what would *he* do about it?

Patsy arrived, on schedule, that very Friday in early May. He commented that it was still winter in Chicago while it felt like mid-summer in Vegas. The three of them grabbed an early dinner that night before Willie had to go to work.

Willie chewed silently on his steak while Patsy and Winnie caught up. When Winnie got up to powder her nose, Willie figured he would excuse himself and escape to the Regal. Patsy asked him to stay.

"Willie, I hear you got some woman trouble," he said. "And I hear some of it has to do with Tina."

Willie swallowed some air and winced from the pain in his chest. Patsy chuckled and gently put his hand on Willie's arm.

"Relax, Willie. Whaddaya think, I'm going to whack you?" He laughed out loud. "I know you hear things about me and my business. Believe it or not, I don't go around *whacking* people. I don't know how these rumors get started."

Patsy stopped laughing and took on a paternal posture.

"Willie, I'm gonna let you in on a few things. The first thing is that I am in love with your mother, and tonight I'm gonna ask her to marry me. That would make me your stepfather, and nothing would please me more. I think you're a fine, hard-working young man. So talented. So polite. So sensitive. You have the soul of an artist. You may not believe it, but I respect those qualities in a person. And I respect you.

"I'll let you in on something else. As much as I love my niece, I know better than anybody else what she can be like. And I blame myself. When her father was killed, I spoiled her out of sorrow and guilt. I did the same with Carlo.

"And now, both of them, when they don't get their way, *whoo boy*, you better watch out. What really breaks my heart is that both of them have a mean streak a mile wide. That I do not accept the blame for. But I am somewhat lacking in character myself, and I can only do so much. That's all any godfather can do. Sooner or later, we all have to find that character in ourselves, and be true to it.

"*You* have character, Willie. And, God bless her, I don't think it came from your mother. Or your father, from what I hear. It's all yours. And, as I see it, your character shows through in almost everything you do.

"One bit of advice. Keep away from Tina. For your own good. Until she grows up, she's really no good to anybody. Take it from me. I can't tell you how many times I've had to clean up the messes she makes."

Willie was so touched by Patsy's kindness and wisdom that he forgot to be relieved.

"I appreciate everything you've said, Patsy," he said. "But I think you're giving me too much credit. I've really made a mess of things all by myself."

"Don't be so hard on yourself, kid," Patsy said. "I'm sure you never meant to hurt anyone. Am I right?"

"Well, sure. But I knew better. I knew it was wrong, and I did it anyway. I didn't mean to hurt Betty, but that's exactly what I did."

"Well, you're learning. Life experience, son," he said. "There's no substitute for life experience. Too bad it's so damn expensive. We all pay the price.

"Look at it this way. The next time, you'll know better."

Willie managed a smile. "Somebody else gave me the same advice. It sounds a lot better coming from you."

"Tell me, how's the girl? How's Betty?"

"It's been nearly two months and she still won't talk to me. I don't think she'll ever forgive me."

"Well, I'm sorry this has been so hard on both of you," Patsy sighed. "So much unhappiness. You can tell Tina's been through this way."

Just then, Winnie returned. "Well, what have you men been talking about? Women, I'll bet. My ears are absolutely burning."

For the first time in weeks, Willie was having a good night. The House was packed, the Regal was breaking occupancy codes and his stepfather-to-be was a well-armed guardian angel.

Winnie was so wrapped up with Patsy that she rarely bothered him about the show any more. That gave Willie the freedom to expand the set list, explore his own maturing musical repertoire and play more rock 'n' roll, which interested him more every day.

He still couldn't shake the feeling that trouble was following him like a loyal dog. His intuition was still barking the next morning when the phone woke him up. It was Andy Rush. He was so excited that Willie couldn't make out what he was saying.

Oh God, he thought. *Betty! What had happened?*

"Slow down! What's wrong?" Willie shouted into the phone.

"Nothing's wrong, man! I just talked to a friend of mine in Philadelphia. Weekend Willie is breaking in the Northeast!"

"What are you talking about?"

"Your record, man! It's all over the radio! It's a hit!"

CHAPTER 28

"Time for a Change" would have been a great song for the Arthur Kills. Too bad they had already broken up by the time Miller and Metz wrote it. The band's lead singer, Arthur Van Houten, decided to quit music and go back to college. His parents had raised him to be a doctor. They were never comfortable with his "hobby."

The Van Houtens held their breath when the Arthur Kills went from playing proms to packing the Palladium after their unlikely run of hit records. The Beatles came to their rescue. The British Invasion buried the Arthur Kills and their folky pop sound. Just like that, they were yesterday's news.

When the Harrison label dropped the Arthur Kills in 1965, Arthur's parents issued the ultimatum. If he quit now, they would still pay for medical school. If not, he could try paying the rent playing the lounge at Holiday Inn.

Off he went, killing off the Arthur Kills and leaving Miller and Metz without a voice for their songs. Harrison Records hooked them up with a few "girl groups" and they charted a few more songs, but Harrison could not compete with Phil Spector and his big-budget "Wall of Sound" empire. The old stone walls in the basement studios at Harrison Studios were covered on the cheap with slabs of plasterboard that ate the high end and made drums sound like metal garbage cans rolling down the driveway. Miller and Metz, perpetually frustrated by the sonic quality of the recordings, often grumbled about Mickey Harrison and his "Drywall of Sound."

"Time for a Change" had been sitting around for a year when Weekend Willie showed up at Harrison Records.

Everyone there loved the song and had been anxiously awaiting a singer who could do it justice. At first it seemed like a bad fit for Willie, but the Harrison gang was so impressed with Willie's talent that they thought he could make it work.

Although it was a pleasant song with a toe-tapping rhythm, it would not accept an arrangement that translated Willie's energy and enthusiasm on record. No one was satisfied with the final results, but given the tight production schedule, they all said "good enough" and pressed it onto a 45 with "Betty Are You Ready?" on the B-side.

Harrison pushed the record best it could and even paid a few radio stations in the Northeast to put it into rotation. Sales, however, remained slow and the reaction from listeners was tepid at best. A few stations quickly dropped the song from their playlists. WAX-AM in Philadelphia was about to do the same when one DJ, Ricky "The Waxman" Reynolds, played the B-side by mistake.

"Betty Are You Ready?" had an infectious chorus and a bouncing rhythm that was easy to dance to. It sounded great on a car radio and was fun to sing along with. With the warm weather approaching, listeners on the East Coast were waiting for a new "summer song" they could sing while speeding down the highway to the seashore. "Betty" was ready to fill the order.

Listeners began to flood WAX with requests for "Betty" and ran to the record stores looking for the song. Before long, Mickey Harrison had to subcontract a few record-pressing plants to keep up with the demand. By Decoration Day, 1966, "Betty" was the top seller on the east coast and had cracked the Top Forty on the Billboard charts. By late June, it was the Number Two record in the nation, second only to "Monday, Monday" by the Mamas and the Papas. A month later, it finally hit Number One, where it remained for four weeks before being replaced by Donovan's "Sunshine Superman."

By Labor Day, "Betty" was a certified million-seller. The

title of the song had become a popular catchphrase. Johnny Carson even used it one night during his monologue.

And the youth of America were asking, "When do we get to see Weekend Willie?"

It was going to be a long wait. All Willie could think about during his climb to the top of the charts was the irony. The song that he hoped would melt Betty's heart was falling on deaf ears, at least where it mattered. He waited and waited for Betty to call. She never did.

Willie was also fuming about the songwriting credits for the song, which went to Miller and Metz. When he called to complain, Mickey told him "That's how the business works when you are a rookie. You got your name on the record. I was the producer. Miller and Metz were responsible for the arrangements and the band, and having their names on your record helped to sell it. They were as much a part of the record as anyone, so I gave them songwriting credit. How else are they going to get paid? Would you deny them that?"

Willie also groused that he had never been told of the record's release. "These things happen fast, kid," Mickey said. "I paid people to press and push the thing and the rest of us went to work on the next record. I didn't even know it was out myself until I heard it on the radio."

None of this remotely sounded like the truth. Andy Rush had warned Willie that a lot of new artists get ripped off early in their careers until they have a big enough name to make demands. Truth was, Willie didn't really care. Mickey pleaded with him to come east to play some dates. He would fix him up with a professional band and get him top billing on a concert tour. He might even get to play "American Bandstand."

Already holding the short end of the stick, Willie wasn't about to give up his lucrative job at the Regal to work for nothing more than a handshake.

"If people want to see me, they can come here," said Willie, years before Elvis perfected the strategy in Vegas.

Those who did make a pilgrimage to the desert went home wanting. "Betty Are You Ready?" haunted Willie and he flatly refused to play it, even when the crowd would chant "Betty! Betty! Betty!"

Willie changed the station every time heard the song on the radio. He could not bear to hear his voice pledging love and devotion to the girl he lost. He could only imagine how Betty felt when she heard it.

Willie had never been comfortable being a celebrity, at least when he wasn't onstage and caught up in the moment. Now, a hit record had expanded his audience and taken the fun out of playing at the Regal. It wasn't so bad during the week, when the crowd was comprised mostly of familiar faces. Then, the weekend crowd would come in, including an armada of "Betty" fans who wouldn't take no for an answer.

For the first time in his life, Willie was hearing boos.

"This jerk has one hit song and he won't play it? What is he, some kind of *moron*?" That was the typical reaction. More than a few fans demanded their money back. Tony begged Willie to reconsider.

"I know how you feel, kid, but this is bad for business," Tony told him.

Word of the uneasy situation got back to Chicago. Unhappy fish leaving the Regal were skipping the casino and swimming straight for the parking lot. As "Betty" kept moving up the charts, the bottom line at the House was dropping like a Whitey Ford spitball.

That was all Carlo needed to hear. At Patsy's request, he had spent the last several months in Chicago, gaining experience in the construction business. The plan was for him to go back to Vegas the next year to oversee two new casino hotels that the family was planning to build there.

Carlo had heard all about Willie and Tina. He was aching to teach Willie a lesson once and for all about messing with the family jewels. That was only one of the reasons Patsy was keeping him collared up in Chicagotown. He didn't want

Carlo damaging his fiancé's son and a good earner for the family.

But Carlo believed Willie was adding insult to injury and was screwing up a good thing at the Regal. Something had to be done before this punk kid, this fag musician, fucked up the entire operation.

Carlo was the last person Willie expected to see when he opened the door to his suite one morning in early September. It was just after Labor Day. "Betty" was finally sliding down the back end of the hit parade.

"Uh, hey, Carlo. I didn't know you were back." He wasn't sure what Carlo was doing there, but he was sure it couldn't be good.

"Hey, big shot. How ya doin'?" Carlo smiled and walked past Willie into the suite. He surveyed the messy room, cluttered with clothes, musical instruments and notebooks. Then he cleared a pile of laundry from an easy chair and sat down.

"So, you're a big rock and roll star now. You got any chicks in here?"

Willie remained mute and sat on the bed.

"I'm just trying to stay out of trouble, Carlo."

"Well, you ain't doin' a very good job of it. In fact, you're causin' trouble for a lot of people. You're causin' trouble for me."

"I don't understand."

"That stupid 'Betty' song. You're pissin' people off. A big draw like that and you don't play it? What the fuck is your problem?"

For once, Willie was finding it hard to be scared of Carlo. He was actually getting annoyed with this slick-haired goon. He was sure Patsy wouldn't approve of Carlo being here to give him the third degree.

"Carlo, no matter what I play, I always pack the room, and I've been doing it for years without any help from people telling me what songs to play."

Carlo squinted, frowned and sat up in the chair. Then he smiled.

"You're a real big shot around here, aren't you? And now you got Patsy wiping your ass. But let me tell you something. I'm tired of you, your whore of a mother and that fat fuck brother of yours."

His tone helped Willie relocate his fear. Carlo stood up and paced around the room. When he came upon Willie's Martin acoustic guitar, he picked it up and started towards Willie.

"Carlo, *come on* ..."

Carlo was practically on top of Willie when he took the guitar by the neck and swung it like a baseball bat, shattering it against the bedpost. Instinctively, Willie jumped up and ran for the door. Carlo caught him from behind and pinned him hard against the door.

"You think you're hot shit? You think you can fuck with me? Do you know how many people are dead because they fucked with me? You fuck my sister and now you want to fuck me, too?"

Carlo punched Willie hard in the kidney, then again. When Willie spun around, Carlo pushed him back against the door, then punched him hard in the stomach. Willie fell to the ground at Carlo's feet, gasping for air.

"You listen to me, you little fuck. From now on, you play that song or I'll take that guitar and shove it so far up your ass you'll be able to play it with your tonsils."

Carlo kicked him hard in the side until Willie rolled away from the door. As Carlo opened the door, he offered one more morsel of advice.

"And stay away from my sister, or I'll kill you."

CHAPTER 29

Willie was too humiliated, and too terrified, to tell anyone of his meeting with Carlo. Patsy's nephew was a real pro. He had tenderized Willie like the veal special at Trattoria Dahlia without leaving a visible mark. The incident also made Willie admit something he had been trying to deny for years. He was earning a living working for violent criminals and it was only a matter of time before violence and crime touched his life directly.

Even when Carlo's boys beat up Bobby, Willie had been able to find a convenient excuse. Bobby was drunk, stupid and hanging out with people who were sure to get him in trouble.

This time, he couldn't explain his situation any other way. *Sleep with dogs, wake up with fleas.* Tony found a reason to use that saying almost every day. Of course, Tony was one of the fleas.

It was Monday, so Willie didn't have to play that night. He cleaned up his room, took a shower and tried to chew at the straps binding him to a mess the size of a landfill. He was in big trouble and he had no idea what to do. Hide behind Patsy? Carlo had already demonstrated that he wasn't worried about his uncle. Tony? Tony was a friend, but Tony had his own problems with Carlo.

Winnie?

He was really, really in trouble.

Willie was happy to follow some of Carlo's advice. He was already doing his best to avoid Tina. As for the other thing, no. He could not, *would not* play "Betty Are You Ready?"

Could he?

The next morning, Willie woke up and saw the light. He called Bobby and told him to assemble the band two hours before the show. They had a new song to rehearse.

Sammy Llanes couldn't believe his ears. Sammy was a romantic.

"Man, after all this time, I can't believe you want us to do 'Betty,' " he said. "I thought this was some big artistic taboo with you. That you were waiting for Betty to come back. That you were waiting until you actually got a royalty check."

Bobby sensed that something was wrong with his brother.

"Don't joke about it, Sammy," Bobby said. "If he wants to play it, then we play it."

"I don't know, this might be bad luck or something," Sammy said.

Everyone had heard the song at least a hundred times on the radio, so it didn't take long to hammer out a decent arrangement. All the band members quickly worked their parts. The one exception was Willie, who was just going through the motions. Sammy shrugged and went outside for a smoke with Jimmy Rose.

Bobby took advantage of their absence to interrogate his brother.

"Willie, what's up? Why are you doing this?"

"I just decided we should play it, Bobby," Willie said. "I don't know, maybe we can get it back up the charts."

"Is there something wrong? You can tell me. Did Carlo talk to you?"

Bobby's rare display of intuition startled Willie almost as much as Carlo did.

"Why would you say that?"

"I hear things," Bobby said. "I heard from one of the girls that he was pissed at you."

"Bobby, you can't say that to anybody. I am in trouble with him, and I don't want to get in any deeper."

"I knew it! Shit! That fucking greaseball!"

Willie could see Bobby was getting all riled up.

"Bobby, take it easy. What the hell did you do when Carlo was on your back?"

"What do you mean?"

"You avoided him like the plague. You took off until we dragged you back in here. I'm doing the same thing. He wants me to play the song. I'll play the song. I don't want any more trouble. I can't handle any more trouble."

Bobby saw the fear in his brother's eyes and backed off. Right now, he was the only one who could understand what Willie was going through.

"Yeah, OK, Willie," he said. "We'll do it your way. No problem."

The two brothers just sat there for a while. Bobby was the last person Willie figured he could confide in. Suddenly, he felt closer to his brother than he had since California.

"Maybe we could get mom to nag Carlo to death," Bobby said, cracking up like a little kid. Willie had to laugh as well.

"Sure is a lotta crap piling up around here, big brother," Willie sighed.

Bobby loved it when Willie called him "big brother." He didn't hear it very often. It made him *want* to be the big brother who could protect his little brother from harm. It was usually the other way around. Maybe this time would be different.

"You know, maybe we should just blow this crappy town," Bobby said. "Let's just get the hell out of here, just you and me and the boys. We can go on tour. Maybe we can still play 'Betty' on Bandstand."

Right now, that didn't sound too bad. They had enjoyed a nice run at the Full House. They had money in the bank. At least Willie did.

Winnie was set up with Patsy. She might not even notice if they skipped town. And Betty? Well, she was part of the past. She had made that clear enough. Maybe things would be different after he got settled in a new town. Maybe he could send for her and they could start a new life.

"Tell you what. I'll rent a U-Haul tomorrow and we'll pack up everything after the show," Bobby said. "We can be in L.A. by morning."

That night, Weekend Willie played his Number One hit in public for the very first time. As it was in rehearsal, the band was ahead of Willie all night. They played "Betty" near the end of the final set, with no warning or introduction. The crowd still went wild, and Willie could see Carlo pop his head out of Tony's office to see what was going on.

Willie wondered what Carlo really wanted. Did he really hope Willie would obey him, or did he hope Willie would defy him and provide the excuse to escalate his attacks? Carlo's granite face did not give away his motives.

The next day, Willie went into town and cashed out his savings account at the bank. There was almost twenty thousand dollars. More than enough to get them started.

Mr. Rollins handled the transaction personally. Willie tried to satisfy the nosy banker's curiosity with a tall tale about a real estate investment.

"Sure, sure," said Mr. Rollins, who found a small gym bag for Willie to carry his withdrawal.

Back in his suite, Willie spent the afternoon packing his life into four suitcases, two of which he bought on the way home. He filled three with clothing. The final suitcase, a hard-plastic Samsonite guaranteed not to break, held his sheet music, notebooks, harmonicas and the other music-related accessories he had accumulated over the past ten years.

Willie left out a pair of jeans and a comfortable shirt for the long ride to L.A. He planned to change right after the show, leaving his white Taylor Brothers' suit on the bed to symbolically declare his new independence.

There was no need for good-byes. He would contact everyone in due time and let them know he was OK. The plan was to lay low for a while, just in case Carlo or Patsy had any ideas about coming after them. Once everyone had a chance to cool off, Willie figured Tony would find a new act to play the

Regal and life would go on.

He removed the cash from the gym bag and repacked it in the case of his Martin acoustic. There was plenty of room in it since Carlo had smashed the prized instrument beyond repair.

Around five o'clock, Willie was ready to head down to the Regal for his final show when he heard a knock at the door. It opened before he could answer.

"*Yoo-hoo, anybody home?*" It was Tina, still in her poolside bikini and wrap.

"What's all this?" she said, spotting the suitcases on the bed and floor. "You're going on vacation and you're not taking me?"

Willie realized he would have to think fast to cover himself with Tina. Her big mouth could easily complicate the plan.

"Didn't you hear?" I bought a house. I'm tired of living in a hotel. Too many people. I'm buying a house."

"You don't say?" she said, still looking around the room. "Well, lover, I'll miss having you as a neighbor, but maybe this isn't such a bad idea. I'll be able to visit you without interruptions and prying eyes."

Tina closed the gap between them, then stopped when Willie took a step back.

"Honestly Willie, am I such a bad person for liking you as much as I do? Look, I really came here because I heard about you and Carlo. And I wanted to apologize. I'm sorry about Carlo. I'm sorry about Betty, I'm sorry about making you so uncomfortable."

Willie sat on the bed and relaxed as much as he could with Tina in the room.

"It's OK, Tina," Willie said. "You don't have to apologize."

"Well, that's nice of you to say. But I do have to apologize. I *want* to."

She started to tear up.

"I *need* to."

She came over to the bed and sat next to him. The tears, real tears, were flowing.

"I don't know why I act the way I do sometimes. I don't know. Sometimes it's just not easy, you know? What they are ... we are ... what I am ... I couldn't live a normal life if I tried. It's not easy being the crown princess of the Bucco family."

"No, I guess it wouldn't be." Willie could believe that much.

"I just want you to understand. I don't want to hurt anybody. It's just that sometimes I hurt *so much* ..." She started to sob, and Willie felt obliged to lend her a little comfort. He offered an embrace, and she wrapped her arms tightly around him.

"Oh, Willie. I just knew you would understand. You really care about people's feelings. You're the only man I've met other than Uncle Patsy who ever gave a damn about me. The only one who didn't just want my body."

"I do care about you, Tina," Willie heard himself say. She tightened her hold on him, then took her head off his shoulder to look him in the eye.

"Do you really, Willie? Do you mean it?"

"Sure I do."

She moved her face closer to his, hesitated, then kissed him softly. Willie, touched by her vulnerability, and still dazzled by her beauty, kissed her back.

Then, suddenly, both of them backed off.

"Tina, I ..."

"Willie, you don't have to say it. Just tell me we can be friends and I'll take my time." She sniffed and wiped a few tears from her cheek, then smiled shyly. "Then maybe you'll let me visit you in your new house."

"Of course you can. You can be the first one."

Tina gave him a little kiss on the cheek, then got up to leave.

"By the way, I loved hearing you sing 'Betty.' Maybe someday you'll write a song about me."

"Maybe I will," Willie said. "You coming to the show tonight?"

"I wouldn't miss it for the world."

Willie regretted the invitation and hoped Tina would find something better to do that night. She could cause problems just by showing up.

The show that evening was uneventful. Willie didn't see Tina or Carlo. Winnie's table was empty. His mother had gone to Chicago to meet Patsy's "family."

He played "Betty" anyway, just in case. After the show, the band packed everything in the U-Haul that Bobby had rented and hitched it to his pickup truck. Willie kept the Les Paul with him. He always preferred having it close by and would store it in the Mustang for the midnight escape through the desert.

He packed the guitar in its custom hard case and headed upstairs to get the rest of his luggage. When he got to his suite, he found the front door open.

He went inside and a bitter taste filled his mouth.

"Going somewhere, motherfucker?"

Carlo!

"I bought a new house, Carlo. I'm moving out of the suite," Willie said, sticking to his improvised cover story. "You guys can have it back to rent out. It's all yours."

"Is that why you took twenty large out of the bank? Must be some fuckin' house."

Shit! Mr. Rollins must have ratted him out. This was bad. *Really* bad.

It was only then that Willie saw the Martin guitar case lying open on the long windowsill. The cash was still there. Was Carlo going to rob him? Would he stop at robbery?

"Look, Carlo, I don't want any trouble. I played the song. And I thought you would appreciate it if I moved out."

"And you stayed away from my sister, just like I told you. *Right?*"

Oh, God!

"Carlo, I swear, I don't want any trouble. She came by. She was upset and I was nice to her. That's all!"

"That's *all*? She says you're her best friend. You're the only one she can talk to. She's giving me shit, saying I should be more like you!"

Carlo stood up and gave Willie a hard backward slap across the face. Willie could feel the large gold ring on Carlo's finger crack against his cheekbone. The salty taste of blood merged with the bitters as he tried to recover from the stun of the vicious blow.

"More like you! More like some little faggot musician who lies to me, lies to her and skips out on us in the middle of the night."

Whap! Willie tried to reach the front door, but Carlo caught him and slammed his head against the wall.

"You think you can just leave? Lie to my sister and leave? Skip out and fuck up my business?" *Whap!* Willie reeled across the room and tumbled over a chair.

Carlo found a piece of the broken guitar neck in the corner and held it like a hammer. He moved slowly towards Willie, who was trying to hide behind the chair. "It's time you learned a lesson. Let's see how well you play that guitar with two broken hands."

"Leave him alone, Carlo."

It was Bobby's voice. Willie's head was still buzzing, but he could clearly see his big brother's hulking form standing just inside the doorway. He was holding a small pistol. His trembling hand pointed the gun straight at Carlo.

Carlo turned away from Willie and stared down Bobby.

"I mean it Carlo. *Back off!*" Bobby said. He looked as terrified as Willie felt.

Carlo smiled. "Big man, big man. Big gun you got there. You man enough to use it?"

Carlo pulled out a bigger gun, a .45 automatic, from the small of his back.

"You want to play with guns, Hoss? Let's have a

showdown, right here."

Sweat was pouring from Bobby's brow into his eyes, making him squint. His hand kept shaking as he pointed the gun straight out.

"I'll do it! I swear! *Back off!*"

"Look at you, you fat fuck! Christ, you look like you're going to piss in your pants."

Bobby closed his eyes and pulled the trigger. Willie heard an impossibly loud *bang*. Carlo spun around and dropped his gun.

"*Fuck!*" Carlo hollered. Bobby had shot him in the side. Willie could see blood soaking Carlo's starched white dress shirt.

"I don't believe it! You fucking shot me!" Carlo dropped to one knee. Bobby dropped his pistol, stumbled back against the wall and tried to catch his breath.

"You fat fuck! I'm gonna kill you!" Carlo, still on his knees, picked up his gun and aimed it at Bobby. Willie tried to rush Carlo from behind, but he was too late. He heard another loud *bang* and saw Bobby bounce back against the wall. Carlo had shot him in the chest.

"*Willie! I'm shot! He shot me!*" Bobby screamed and sunk to his knees, then crumbled back against the wall.

Willie stumbled forward and fell on top of Carlo, who dropped his gun again. Carlo groaned and cursed softly, and offered no resistance. There was blood everywhere. After a few seconds, he was face down on the floor.

Willie got up and crawled over to Bobby, who was bleeding badly from the chest and mouth.

"I was gonna help you with your bags, and I heard Carlo," Bobby said between heavy breaths. His entire body was shaking. Willie tried in vain to stop the blood pouring from his chest.

"Am I dying? Help me Willie! *Help me!*" Bobby began to choke, then went still. His eyes remained open as his head fell to the side.

"Bobby! Come on, Bobby! Don't do this!"

Willie began to tremble uncontrollably. Was this really happening? Was Bobby really dead? Were they both dead?

All of a sudden, another loud shot rang out. He whirled around and saw Tina standing over Carlo. Bobby's gun was in her hand. Smoke was curling out of the barrel. Blood was coming from the back of her brother's head. Willie saw Carlo was kneeling. He hadn't noticed that Carlo managed to get back up with his gun in hand. Tina had come along just in time and chose Willie over her own blood.

Tina stood there in shock as Willie rose. He took the gun from her hand and laid it on the bed.

"I was just coming to tell you ..." Tina said. "I wanted to tell you ... to watch out for Carlo. We had another argument and he hit me. He's never, ever done that. He had a gun. He was going to kill you."

Tina started to cry. Willie held her for a few seconds until she pushed him away.

"Willie, you've got to get out of here, *right now*! You don't understand. *They'll kill you*! You've got to get out of here! They'll never stop looking for you!

"Tina, Carlo — he shot Bobby! I've got to do something!"

Tina gathered herself and looked right at him.

"Willie, you *have* to get out of here. Right now. I'll take care of Bobby. I'll think of something, tell them something. *Just go! Now!*"

"*I can't.*"

"*You have to.* Do you want to end up like your brother?"

Willie looked around the room. He grabbed the Les Paul and started for the door, then turned back inside. "Tina, I'm sorry. Tell Bobby I'm sorry."

Then he remembered the money. He ran over to the windowsill, closed the Martin guitar case and took one more look at Bobby. "He's dead, isn't he?"

"I think so, Willie. I think both of them are." Tina said. She had regained a lot of her cool. "You need to *go*. I'll take care of it. Please, just get out of here. Get in your car and get as far away as you can. As fast as you can."

Willie came to Tina and reached out to touch her hair. She took his hand and kissed it softly. "Go," she whispered.

"Where?" he said.

"*Anywhere*," she said. "Willie, *please*, just go."

He didn't know what else to say. He turned, stopped to look once more at Bobby, then quickly walked out the door. He never looked back.

PART
TWO

CHAPTER 30

Aaron Lowe didn't like to talk about himself all that much. He didn't really talk much at all. Mostly, he wrote. He scribbled thoughts, ideas and dreams in a spiral pocket notebook that he always kept with him. Descriptions of things he had seen, places he had been and recollections of conversations had or overheard.

He lived a behind-the-scenes existence, blending into the background. Just another face in the crowd. He took the long way around trouble. He didn't have a lot of friends. He didn't have *any* enemies.

It was easy to blend in the Haight-Ashbury district of San Francisco in 1967. It was the Summer of Love. Every man was your brother. Every woman was your sister.

Or your lover.

During the day, the bustling neighborhood swelled with colorful flower children. Speakers in the windows of homes, coffee shops and bookstores blared music for passersby. Aaron loved to wander down the middle of the road and hear a dozen different songs compete for his attention. Some of it was recorded. Sometimes, it was coming from a band playing inside.

There were musicians on every street corner. Folkies, bluesmen, bluegrass bands and jug bands. Beat poets and bongo players.

Impromptu concerts and jam sessions were a daily affair in many of the tall, narrow Victorian rowhouses that lined the neighborhood avenues like an overgrown picket fence. Their front doors were wide open. Anyone could come in and join the party. On the weekends, the entire neighborhood would migrate to nearby Golden Gate Park for joyous be-ins, love-ins and the occasional protest rally. People would share food, drugs, even their bodies, and dance to the music until the cops threw them out.

Aaron loved it here. He loved the brotherhood of this tiny hippie nation. Nobody made any demands or asked any questions. Wherever he went, they just said "welcome, come on in."

He was luckier than most. Aaron told his small circle of acquaintance that he lived off a modest trust fund set up by his parents before they died in an automobile accident a few years ago. He rented the top floor of a lovely corner house on Jefferson Street, near the Marina District. From the balcony outside his bedroom, he had a full view of the Golden Gate Bridge and San Francisco Bay.

The rent was a little steep, one of Aaron's few indulgences. He didn't fritter away money on the typical young man's vices. He lived a simple existence, exploring the Haight, the Marina and the scenic expanse of Golden Gate Park. Along the way, he filled his notebooks, jotting down anything that came to mind. One notebook was used strictly as a diary that he began the first day he arrived in town.

He furnished the curved balcony with a used set of wrought-iron patio furniture topped by waterproof vinyl cushions. He spent nearly every evening out there, sipping tea or cheap wine and playing a vintage Martin acoustic guitar he found in a pawn shop.

The balcony was big enough to seat six or seven people, depending on how well they knew each other. Most of the time, Aaron sat it out alone, strumming the blues and watching the sun set into the Pacific. He had been in town for less than a year and hadn't made any close friends. Besides, he enjoyed being alone. It gave him time to think.

He had a lot to think about. Too much to think about.

Inside the apartment, there was a small efficiency kitchen,

a living room and a large, black-and-white tiled bathroom. He loved the ancient oversize tub that sat on legs shaped like gargoyles. The best part of the apartment, though, was the circular turret bedroom, which had old, cut lead-glass French doors that opened to the balcony.

Mornings, he would grab some food at the Gold Mine Café, a small breakfast-and-lunch joint across from his corner. They fixed scrambled eggs and salsa in flour tortillas, just like the ones he enjoyed as a child growing up in coastal Southern California. Coffee bothered his stomach, so he drank tea with milk. When he finished, he would smoke a cigarette and skim the headlines in a copy of the Chronicle that was always there for regular customers.

Some days, he would spend hours walking the wharf, the marina and the park. When it rained, he would buy a cup of tea to go and head for the library.

His favorite pastime was to sample the flea market of music in the Haight. He rarely spoke at length to anyone there, yet he felt a kindred spirit to the disaffected, Bohemian sea of young Americans who had claimed the neighborhood in the name of peace and expressive freedom.

The only habits he didn't share were their love of drugs and their obsession with exploring the inner mind. Aaron didn't need drugs to find that place. He had tasted the marrow of his own soul. He'd gone farther in than anyone should go and he didn't care to go back.

Once in a while, he'd puff a joint when it was passed his way. It was the polite thing to do and he did find it relaxing in moderation. Too much and he would just want to sleep. He enjoyed the taste of wine, but it gave him a hangover, so he drank it sparingly.

In early June, the late spring sun finally cut through the mist and gifted San Francisco with a hint of summer. The string of warm, sunny days helped Aaron to emerge from his self-imposed exile. He was used to warm weather and was beginning to feel like himself again.

One day, while enjoying the full blossom of Golden Gate Park, he finally let his guard down and initiated some genuine human contact. He saw a small group of amateur musicians sitting cross-legged on a big blanket. The quartet's harmonies were light and sweet. The two guitar players were another matter. Neither could play very well, at least by his standards. One of them, a plump young woman wearing a flowing, flowered dress and beaded jewelry, could not tune her guitar.

Aaron offered his assistance and lifted the guitar to his ear. It took him all of 60 seconds to retune six strings.

"There you go. It's not easy to keep a guitar tuned in this town," he said. "Too many temperature swings. Too much humidity."

The girl offered her thanks and a broad smile. She already had a crush on this tall, shaggy-haired blonde man with a full, dark red beard and a keen ear for pitch.

"You're welcome. I'm Aaron," he said.

"Hi, I'm Andrea," she said. "And this is my girlfriend Jenny, Jenny's brother Carl and his old lady, Cassie."

Jenny was the better, and prettier, of the two guitarists. Neither of the girls could have been much more than 20 years old. Carl and Cassie looked to be about ten years older.

Jenny and Aaron made instinctive eye contact. Jenny was tall and slender, with straight, shiny blonde hair that covered too much of her pretty face and flowed to the waist of her hip-hugger jeans. She was wearing a ruffled peasant blouse and leather sandals and was playing a beautiful Rickenbacker 12-string guitar, which she offered to Aaron.

"You know, I bet you can play this much better than me," she said. "You want to join our jam?"

He accepted the invitation and they played music until the setting sun blinded their eyes. Everyone was hungry and thirsty, so they squeezed into Carl's Volkswagen Beetle and drove to Chinatown looking for dinner. Andrea was obviously enjoying the close quarters in the back seat with Aaron.

"It's easy to tell you have the soul of an artist," she said, stretching out and sliding onto Aaron's lap. "I love artists. They make love with such passion."

Aaron squirmed as much as he could without insulting the girl. Jenny sat quietly next to them, looking terribly uncomfortable.

They ate themselves silly, then said their good-byes at the restaurant door. Aaron said he would be glad to join them again soon for another jam in the park. He left feeling a little more human than the day before.

He hadn't heard from his new friends for about two weeks when the phone rang on a warm Friday morning. It was Andrea. Cassie had split town and they were sitting on an extra ticket for the big Monterey Pop Festival the next day. Aaron knew about the big three-day concert a few hours' ride down the coast. The lineup was daunting, especially on Saturday, when a bunch of the biggest bands in the San Francisco area were scheduled to perform: John Cippolina, Aaron's favorite bay area musician, and his Quicksilver Messenger Service; Steve Miller, Canned Heat and the Butterfield Blues Band; Al Kooper and the Electric Flag; Otis Redding and Jefferson Airplane; Big Brother would be playing with an amazing new singer from Texas named Janis Joplin.

Aaron was reluctant to attend such a huge event by himself. Now, he had no excuse. All he had to do was keep Andrea at arm's length.

Fortunately for Aaron, Andrea's attentions were now dripping all over Carl. Both of them had dropped acid. Aaron and Jenny declined to join them and shared a wineskin full of sangria.

While Andrea and Carl sat in their own little world, the long day gave Aaron and Jenny a chance to swap stories. Jenny's group had come down from Olympia to commune with the Haight. She was 19 and had just dropped out of college. Her brother was just back from Vietnam and out of the army. Cassie was a stripper he met at a bar and they had been together for six months until last week. When Carl ran out of money for drugs, Cassie ran out on Carl.

Jenny was just as broke as her brother and was planning to return home next week. Carl had hooked up with some old army buddies in the area who were going to help him find work. Andrea, it seemed, had hooked up with Carl right after Cassie left, leaving Jenny as the third wheel.

She confessed to Aaron, "The crazy thing about it is, when we came down here, Andrea and I were, well, *you know* ..."

Aaron tried to hide his surprise.

"Oh, I didn't realize you were ..."

"No, I'm not, really. Well, I guess I don't know. I was kind of lost back home. I was bombing out in college and Andrea was my roommate. I had never met anyone like her. She was so strong, so confident. She always seemed to know what she wanted and was never afraid to go for it. One day, she went for me, and I guess she made me feel secure.

"And besides, it's a new world, right? Why shouldn't we take pleasure anywhere we can find it?"

Jenny didn't sound all that convinced of her argument.

Aaron laughed.

"To tell you the truth, I was worried she was after me," he said. "Of course, why would she want me if she had you?"

Jenny laughed. "And why would she want me if she could have Carl?" They looked over at Andrea and Carl, who were so stoned that they were afraid to leave the blanket, as if it was suspended in mid-air.

"Well, I promise I would never dump you for your brother," said Aaron, which made both of them laugh even more.

"Seriously, though, what Andrea did wasn't very cool, and your brother doesn't seem to be looking out for you like he should," Aaron said. "If you need any help, or a place to stay, just let me know. I have plenty of room."

"That's very nice of you, Aaron," she said. "I'm not sure where else I could go."

After the festival, Andrea and Carl were happy to ditch Aaron and Jenny. Carl dropped them off at Aaron's place and sped off. Aaron and Jenny, tired from a long day in the sun, slowly climbed the long stairway to Aaron's apartment. Inside, Jenny wandered around while Aaron poured them some orange juice.

"This is a nice guitar," she said, running her hands over his Martin six-string.

"Oh, that? I bought it in a pawn shop," he said. "It's not nearly as nice as yours."

Jenny continued her survey and came upon a hard guitar case. "And what about this? She opened it and lifted up the contents. "A Les Paul. Wow! You can wake the dead with one of these!"

CHAPTER 31

Aaron and Jenny shared an obvious attraction. They spent most of the night on the balcony, talking about Jenny's sheltered childhood and her rude awakening at college.

After high school, she couldn't wait to leave home and flex her wings at college. She was a rebel who had never had a chance to rebel; a sensual woman who had yet to explore her sensual side.

Two semesters at Berkeley changed all that. She slept with the first boy she went out with. He dumped her a month later. She smoked pot and tried acid once, which was enough. She slept with one of her professors, then dropped his course when she found out he was married. Then Andrea seduced her and began to dominate her life.

Aaron knew what it felt like to be used and decided that the last thing Jenny needed was another person to treat her like an object. She would have been a willing lover and probably would have stayed with him as long as he wished.

Instead, Aaron gave Jenny his bed and slept on the couch. The next day, Jenny retrieved her belongings and brought them back to Aaron's place. Aaron spent the rest of the day giving her guitar lessons.

They retired early, woke up at dawn and went for breakfast at the Gold Mine. Then, they packed Jenny's things in Aaron's Mustang and he drove her all the way back to Olympia. They took the scenic route up the Pacific Coast Highway, stopping for the night in Coos Bay, a picturesque town on the Oregon Coast. The next morning, they took some local advice and detoured to nearby Sunset Bay to catch a glimpse of sea lions living in their natural habitat.

Jenny and Aaron parted on platonic terms. Both of them longed to be loved, yet both knew it wasn't the right time or place. Each of them had too much emotional baggage left to unpack. And unlike their brothers and sisters in the Haight, they both had learned the hard way that free love carried too high a cost.

So much for the Summer of Love.

In September, Aaron began auditing courses at San Francisco State University. He could not enroll because there was a problem producing his transcripts. No matter. Aaron wasn't after a degree, so there was no reason to wait until he could take the course for credit.

The professors at SFSU certainly didn't mind. Most of them were caught up in the spirit of the times. "The more, the merrier," said Professor Geddy Yamashta, who taught History of Music 101.

Spending three hours a week in a classroom with 20 other music lovers was the ideal therapy for Aaron. He recognized three of his classmates from a jug band he'd seen playing on a corner. He even remembered one name, Patrick Finley, a tall, thin red-headed banjo player who liked to joke around. He could really pick and watching him play reminded Aaron of how long it had been since he'd held a banjo. Before long, Aaron and Patrick became fast friends.

Hanging out with Patrick and his group, the Moonshiners, also reminded Aaron how long it had been since he had played with a real band. They knew he could play guitar, although they had no idea how well. And the Moonshiners were currently without a guitarist or a bass player, so they practically begged him just to sit in.

He still wasn't ready, so he made up some excuse about stage fright. The balcony would remain his only stage for a while longer.

The Moonshiners eventually broke up when Patrick passed a big audition for a new band that was being formed by Eric Troy, a dynamic young singer who had attracted quite a following in San Francisco after fronting several local bands. This time around, the band would be assembled around Eric, all under the watchful eye of Larry Hayes, the legendary A&R man for the National Records conglomerate.

Eric was a classically trained singer and actor who favored patterned Nehru jackets and frilly scarves on stage. Aaron had seen him at a club and found his style pretentious and overly dramatic. Still, he was tall, dark and handsome. Someone described him as "Jim Morrison without the danger." And his biggest fan was his girlfriend, Helena Guðmundsdóttir, a famous fashion model from Iceland known as the "Ice Princess."

Helena fancied herself a singer since she had dated so many of them. Now, she was with Eric, and the plan was to have them out front as lead singers backed by a band full of the Bay Area's best. The band would be called the Victorian Manner and would be the first act signed to Golden Gate Records, a subsidiary of National run by Larry Hayes himself.

Patrick Finley was signed on as the guitarist because of his versatility. He was no Hendrix, but he was formally trained and could play guitar, banjo, mandolin and fiddle. Gerald Abernathy, a conservatory-trained pianist, also passed his audition, while Garrett Townsend was hired to play the Hammond B-3 organ. A drummer was hired, then quickly replaced by Donald A. "Dewey" Davis, one of the best-known drummers in town, when his band Avocado Avenue broke up unexpectedly. At Dewey's suggestion, they also brought in Sean David from the Avocados to play bass.

Dolores Herrera, a performance artist who played soprano saxophone, oboe and a half-dozen other reed instruments, was the final piece of the puzzle. She was also a soulful singer who was hired at least in part to drown out Helena when she wandered off key, which was often.

When the Moonshiners spurned Patrick for "selling out," Aaron and he became closer friends than ever. Aaron did everything he could for his new friend, helping him learn the new material and coax the necessary sound effects out of his equipment.

Patrick and Gerald Abernathy functioned as the band's musical directors. It was a struggle for them to make sense of the patchwork arrangements Eric had attached to his strange new lyrics, which attempted to merge the musical qualities of Shakespeare's sonnets with the rhythmic rap of the beat poets.

Gerald also came to rely on Aaron's input and the two of them became close friends as well. Both were serious musicians who had been labeled early as young prodigies. Gerald was a pale wisp who had suffered badly from childhood asthma and still had trouble breathing in smoky rehearsal rooms. He was barely five foot four and no more than 110 pounds, with thinning hair and thick glasses that made him look like every high school's class nerd.

Both Aaron and Patrick towered over him, yet Gerald was the leader of this talented trio, which some referred to as "Mutt, Jeff and Mutt." When Aaron and Patrick snickered at Eric's lyrics, and swore the arrangements would never work, Gerald found the right notes and segues that made them bearable. He made chicken salad out of Eric's chickenshit genius. If the Victorian Manner ever struck the right chord, it would be because of Gerald Abernathy.

Aaron's significant consultation with Patrick and Gerald was beginning to make Eric nervous. Who was this stranger who had never been seen or heard playing music?

Patrick and Gerald argued that Aaron was just a friend who was making a valuable contribution with no expectation of being paid. At the same time, they also lobbied to make Aaron an official member of the band.

"No way," said Eric, who was uncomfortable enough with the wholesale changes being made to his songs. Lenny Hayes tried to pacify his leading man, telling him the new arrangements were necessary.

"It's still your band, big guy," Lenny told him. "You and Helena are still driving the bus. People will be coming to see you. And these are still your songs. But unless you want to give up half of your royalties to hire a full orchestra, we can't play them the way you want to."

Lenny was already worried about the Victorian Manner and its temperamental singers, so he cut a side deal with his musical directors. Aaron would be put on a small salary as an associate producer for the recording sessions. If all went well, he could join the tour as some kind of stage or equipment manager, just to have him around.

Aaron was pleased with the offer and gratefully accepted. He still wasn't ready to climb a stage and face an audience. Helping a new band shape its identity sounded like a good use for his abilities. He'd be back in the game without compromising his anonymity.

The money wouldn't hurt, either. Aaron had exhausted almost half of his "trust fund" over the past year. He could use the paycheck.

Two months after the auditions, the Victorian Manner entered the studio for the first time. The timing was bad. It was nearly Christmas. Eric and Helena were going to spend the holidays in London and then stop in Iceland on the way back to the States.

The hired hands, under the leadership of Patrick and Gerald, jelled quickly. The many influences brought in by each member were blending nicely. Gerald's classical piano gave the music a touch of elegance. Patrick contributed his knowledge of Irish and English folk music, helping the band to sound like an American version of England's Fairport Convention.

Dolores Herrera and her ethereal reeds added a hint of mystery. Dolores also was a visual point for the band's stage presence. Her dark, exotic looks and sensual choreography cast an eerie silhouette in the background when she undulated in sheer, flowing robes, backlit by smoky red light.

The rest of the band, especially Dewey, made sure that the driving rhythm of San Francisco psychedelic rock never got lost in the mix. Gerald was the brains in the band. Dewey Davis was the balls, and Sean David's bass had been trained to follow Dewey like a tethered trailer. Garrett Townsend's lush swells on the Hammond B-3 made a spicy, spacey broth for the rest of the ingredients to simmer in.

While Eric's songs made for a lousy platform, the band was coming together faster and better than anyone could have hoped for. They couldn't wait to lay down the first tracks, but just as rehearsals were completed, Eric and Helena were off to London, leaving the rest of the group to twiddle its thumbs.

CHAPTER 32

Finding themselves on vacation, Aaron and Patrick passed the time by clubbing and crashing every concert they could get to. Aaron studied Steve Miller's unique blend of psychedelic rock and authentic Chicago blues. Patrick sat through the Grateful Dead's marathon sets at the Fillmore, admiring Jerry Garcia's electrified folk guitar. Both of them went to see Jimi Hendrix. Twice. Each time they walked out shaking their heads, knowing they would have to start from scratch.

One night, the Victorian Manner entourage, sans Eric and Helena, went to the Avalon Ballroom for a special homecoming concert by the Jefferson Airplane. The Airplane had taken off during the Summer of Love to become the first San Francisco band to break both nationally and in Europe. Back in town after a long tour, the Airplane's Avalon gig had attracted most of the Bay area's musical elite.

Aaron, Patrick and Dewey were at the bar when a stunning young woman with long, wavy chestnut hair came up to them. Her name was Claire Hall and she was a journalist working for Rolling Stone, a new magazine based in the city that covered the music, lifestyle and politics of the emerging counterculture.

She recognized Dewey and was looking for a scoop on the Victorian Manner. "You guys must be so excited to be working with Eric Troy," she said. "When are we going to hear something from you guys?"

Patrick tried to impress her by introducing himself as the band's musical director. "We're working really hard, trying to make those songs represent who we are and where we are as a creative force," he said, staring into her huge brown eyes. "We know a lot of people are waiting, but good things are worth waiting for, right?"

Dewey's famous laugh rumbled from his massive belly as he witnessed Patrick's feeble come-on. Unfortunately for Patrick, Claire was already fixated on Aaron.

"And how about you? Are you with the band?" she asked him.

"No, he's just my bitch," Dewey said, trying to keep a straight face. He lost it a few seconds after everyone else did.

"I'm just helping out with a few things," said Aaron after the laughter subsided. "My name's Aaron."

Claire stuck with the group, keeping close to Aaron, while the Airplane knocked everyone out with a fierce two-hour set. After the show, the group splintered as the crowd spilled outside. Claire asked Aaron and Patrick where they were going.

"I'm beat, gonna get some sleep," Aaron said.

"I'm wide awake," Patrick said to Claire. "The night is young and so am I. Where can I take you?"

"I'm with Aaron," Claire said. "It's been a long day. By the way, can I get your numbers? In case you guys have some news I can write about? I'd really appreciate it."

Patrick was happy to oblige. He wrote his number, and Aaron's, in her notebook.

Claire wrote something down on a piece of notepaper, tore it out of the notebook, and handed it to Aaron. It was her name and number. "In case you think of something. *Anything*," she said with a smile.

Patrick sighed as she walked away. "Well, my brother, despite my valiant efforts, she made the wrong choice. Enjoy. She's a vision."

Aaron shrugged and stuffed Claire's note in Patrick's shirt pocket. "You know, she did make the wrong choice," he said. "Take it from someone who's made a few of them."

"Whoa, dude, don't tell me you didn't see what I saw,"

Patrick said. "You do like girls, right?"

"I like them just fine. I just can't afford them," Aaron said. "Hell, I can't even afford *you*."

"You got that right. I'm strictly high-ticket," Patrick said, laughing. "Too bad Brenda Starr couldn't appreciate the bargain I was offering her."

The next day, Aaron got an excited call from Patrick. "Lowe-man, pack up the Les Paul. You've gotta gig tonight," he said.

"What are you talking about? I don't even have a band," Aaron replied.

"Neither does he."

"He who?"

"Chuck Berry."

Chuck Berry rarely toured with his own band. He would book the gig with a contract stipulating that the house must provide a band capable of playing his classic songs. Many a young guitarist had started out by teaching himself the trademark Chuck Berry chords. A lucky few got the chance to back the man himself.

Berry was booked that night to play at the Matrix, a nightclub where the Airplane once served as the house band. The club's assistant manager, a classmate of Aaron and Patrick in Music 101, had called Patrick looking for a substitute band. The band he previously signed to back Berry had cancelled at the last minute.

Patrick said "leave it to me" and got on the phone. Within a half hour, he had Dewey and Gerald on board. Patrick could play bass. He wanted Aaron to join them on guitar.

"Chuck Berry, man, what are you waiting for? Jesus?" Patrick could never understand Aaron's reluctance to perform. He didn't seem the type for stage fright. "This is as close to Jesus as you'll get in your lifetime. Come on, man, time for the Lowe-man to kick out the jams!"

Aaron couldn't argue with Patrick's cockeyed Christian

logic. He agreed to pick up the sword of St. Les Paul and play backup for Jesus. Otherwise, what was the point of living?

They met to rehearse at Dewey's place, an old converted warehouse just outside the Wharf. Dewey was the biggest, baddest, blackest drummer in town and made a good living as a studio musician. He was a large man who played a large instrument, and he needed a large space to live in.

Though he could have afforded a nice house, none were big enough to his liking. This long, three-story warehouse, which filled half a city block, was the largest building he could afford, so he bought it and moved in. He had it professionally cleaned, then fashioned a small loft-like living quarter in the far corner. The rest of the wide-open floor was filled with stage risers, drums, gongs, dozens of amplifiers and towering stacks of speakers. He frequently rented the equipment to promoters putting on concerts at the colleges and in the parks. When it wasn't out for hire, Dewey loved to hook it all up and rock the neighborhood.

Chuck Berry's new backup group, which Patrick named the Imposters, spent the afternoon running through the trademark chords of "Johnny B. Goode," "Roll Over, Beethoven," "School Days" and "Promised Land." Gerald had the hardest time of it, trying to adapt his grandiose style to the simple, punchy rhythms of the great Jimmie Johnson, who played piano on most of Chuck Berry's hits. Once he got the hang of it, the band fell into a solid groove that had them bouncing with a natural high.

That night, Aaron felt like a real musician for the first time in more than a year. The Imposters got to warm up the crowd with an hour-long set of blues and rock oldies. They played John Lee Hooker songs, Willie Dixon songs and vintage rock nuggets like Van Morrison's "Gloria" and the Isley Brother's "Twist and Shout."

It took about 30 seconds for Aaron to connect with a young audience high on its toes, waiting to party with Chuck Berry. He took the lead vocals on about half the songs and thrilled his bandmates as he tossed his inhibitions to the wind.

When the set was over, the band went backstage to cool off before the big set with Chuck Berry. They were surprised to learn that, less than a half hour before the show was to begin, Berry still hadn't arrived.

Forty minutes later, the promoter exhaled as Berry pulled up in a white Cadillac Coupe De Ville. He came inside, carrying nothing more than his guitar in a case.

"You weren't worried, were you boys?" he said, flashing a broad smile as his disciples went mute. "Chuck Berry never misses a gig."

"What about the set?" Patrick asked. "We haven't rehearsed. What are we gonna play?"

Berry just laughed as he unpacked his guitar and asked which way to the stage.

"Don't need to rehearse. We're gonna play Chuck Berry songs. Come on, boys, I ain't got all night. Let's give it to 'em and get out."

The Imposters just stood there, not sure of what they had gotten themselves into. When they realized Berry was halfway to the stage, they hurried after him. By the time they caught up, he was already in the spotlights taking his bows.

He turned around and shouted to Aaron, " 'No Particular Place to Go,' in G. Just follow along and never take your eye off me. Let's rock and roll, boys!"

The next hour was possibly the most satisfying of Aaron's life. He loved the crowd, he loved the band and he loved playing behind Chuck Berry. Even on the small stage, the spry old guy did his splits, duckwalks and a few other acrobatic moves that Aaron had never seen before. There were rumors he had been going through the motions at many gigs, but tonight, he was on fire.

When it was all over, Berry went right up to the promoter and loudly demanded his fee, in cash. Aaron and Patrick were still a little intimidated in his presence, and wondered if they would be next to feel his wrath.

Dewey soothed their fears. "Hey, he loves musicians. He just hates the jiveass promoters who rip us all off. Sumbitches ripped him off for years and he just don't take it no more."

Sure enough, after Berry got his cash money, he came over to say good-bye.

"You boys OK. You can play some. You can play with Chuck Berry any time." Then, as fast as he came in, he was gone.

"What a sweet guy," Gerald said, sarcastically. "He doesn't even know who we are."

"Don't knock it, little man," Dewey said. "That was like a blessing from the Pope. You die now, your ass goes straight to heaven."

Aaron thought he was already there. His night got more interesting when he headed out to the bar and saw Claire.

"The Imposters, huh?" She smiled at Aaron. "Where did you come up with that name?"

"There's Chuck Berry, and the rest of us are imposters." Aaron smiled back at her, then frowned when she took out her notebook.

"You're not going to write about this, are you?" Aaron said.

"Of course I am. The whole world is waiting for the debut record by the Victorian Manner, and half the band is jamming in a club with Chuck Berry! That's news."

"Is it? I never thought of it that way," Aaron said. "Well, since I'm not in the Victorian Manner, you don't have to waste any ink on me."

"Good-looking, a great musician, and he's modest, too," she said. "I might as well take you home to meet my parents right now."

Aaron blushed. "I'm just, well, not all that keen on publicity."

Claire cocked her head like a confused spaniel, then smiled again.

"Say, you want to go find a cup of coffee somewhere? You

can tell me about all those secrets you're hiding." Claire could see Aaron was startled. She put the notebook back in her pocketbook. "Off the record, of course."

The last thing Aaron needed to do was open up to a journalist. But he was feeling so good, still warm from the rush of the gig, and wasn't ready for the night to end. Claire was beautiful, smart and very sure of herself. She obviously was into him and he was starting to like her, too.

None of the coffee shops were open, but they found a diner with some great pastry. Aaron ordered tea and a slice of thick apple strudel. Claire asked if she could try just one bite, then ended up eating half. They laughed and ordered another piece.

"So seriously, off the record, what's your story?" Claire asked. "I checked around town and hardly anybody knows you. Yet here you are, playing guitar for Chuck Berry and, well, I still don't know what you're doing with the Victorian Manner. What are you, some kind of coach?"

Aaron laughed, watching her nibble the crumbs on the plate. She was charming.

"Something like that," he said. "I'm a friend of Patrick's and he wanted some help. It's no big deal, really."

"A lot of musicians in town would beg to differ. How long have you known Patrick?"

"Just for a little while. I've only been in town for about a year."

"Where did you come from?"

"Las … well, I was born in Las Vegas, but I grew up south of L.A."

"Were you in any bands down there?"

"Yeah, well, not really. You know, just dances and stuff. I kind of like to do my own thing."

"I guessed that. You know, even just playing Chuck Berry songs, I can tell you're really good."

"What makes you say that?"

"I don't know, I can just tell. I can always tell. Did you see

Jimi Hendrix at Monterey?"

"No, I was there the day before. I've seen him, though."

"Well, that's the best concert I ever saw. And I knew it would be. I saw him almost two years ago in New York. He was playing in a small club in Greenwich Village. Jimmy James and the Blue Flame. I knew right there he was going to be huge.

"I just know. I can tell. It's not what they play, or how they play it. It's in their eyes. You can see they belong up there on the stage, playing whatever it is they play. I could see it in Jimi's eyes. I can see it in your eyes, too. It's just kismet, you know? It's your fate, your destiny, to give us music."

Aaron was flattered with the comparison to Hendrix. He was more impressed with how Claire could see right through him.

Aaron ordered a refill and lit a cigarette. He wanted to know more. "You see all that in me?"

"Yeah, I do. What I can't figure out is why you act like it's no big deal. Most musicians are desperate to be noticed, to be recognized as some great artist. You obviously love playing and performing. Why aren't you in a band of your own?"

"Well, sometimes it's hard. I get stage fright," he said.

"I heard that about you. I don't believe it. Not after what I saw tonight." She looked serious. "Why do you pretend like that?"

Aaron was trying to keep his cover, yet he felt the urge to open up to her.

"You don't understand. It's different playing behind a big deal like Chuck Berry. Everyone was looking at *him*. Nobody noticed *me*. Well, nobody other than you, anyway.

"It's a lot harder when you are the man in front. A lot is expected of you. It can be very lonely."

"And you know all this from playing in what, a high school dance band? What do you know about being the man in front? You are very mysterious."

She backed off when she didn't get an answer.

"I'm sorry. That's the journalist in me," she said. "But there's something you're not telling me, and it makes me wonder."

"There's really nothing to tell," Aaron said. "I've played in some bands. They never went anywhere. This is where I ended up, and now I have a pretty good situation. I'll probably put a band together eventually. Right now, I like what I'm doing."

"Well, maybe you're just modest," she said. "Maybe you're just a draft dodger making his way up the coast to Canada."

"Maybe I'm working under cover for the FBI to bust the hippie nation from the inside."

Both of them laughed. "Well, whatever," she said. "I do love a mystery."

Claire lived a few blocks away, in the heart of the Haight, so Aaron walked her home. Her house was brightly lit and full of activity at three in the morning. Aaron could smell a pungent aroma from the joint that a group of people were passing on the front stoop.

"My roommates," Claire said with a sigh. "It's hard to get any sleep around here."

She looked up at Aaron. "Would you like to come up? I've got some nice Lebanese hash I've been saving."

Aaron had enjoyed the evening. It felt good to spend time with a girl again. Still, there was only so much human contact he could handle for the time-being.

"Well, I don't really turn on that much. You'd probably waste it on me."

Someone must have bumped the stereo. Aaron could hear a song by the Doors skip to the middle of another.

"This place is crazy," Claire said. "There's noise all night long, and there's never any privacy." She took Aaron's hand and studied it, using a finger to follow the lines in his palm. "Maybe we could go to your place."

Aaron blushed and bit his lip.

"You know, it's been a long day," he said. "Maybe we should just call it a night."

Claire looked a little embarrassed.

"I'm sorry, she said. "I thought we had made a connection. I get a little pushy sometimes."

"We did, Claire," he said. "I like you a lot. I'm just a little, well, distracted."

"Is there somebody else? Do you have an old lady?" she asked.

"No. No old lady," he said. Aaron loved that phrase, "old lady." It never seemed to fit the women being described that way. At least not around here.

"Well, then, maybe we could go out again sometime for coffee and strudel."

"Sure. That would be great."

Claire hopped on her toes and gave him a quick kiss. "Groovy. How about tomorrow?"

"Groovy."

CHAPTER 33

The recording sessions for the first album by the Victorian Manner were the stuff of legend. Arguments that escalated into fistfights. Clashes of ego that threatened to compromise the San Andreas Fault. Attacks of anxiety, panic and hysteria. Walkouts and tearful reunions that ate up days of studio time.

Eric returned from Europe with a briefcase full of new songs inspired by some lengthy experimentation with LSD. It also became apparent that Helena had a heroin problem. And the happy couple wasn't very happy. Just getting the two lead singers on the same page often took half the day. They bickered constantly and were only in the studio together when absolutely necessary.

Side by side, they fought their management and the band's musical directors at every turn. Patrick and Gerald had everyone ready to lay down the first batch of songs. They begged Eric to save his new ones for the next record. Enough time had been wasted already. Eric, though, was convinced he had given birth to "a great manifesto of poetic revolution" and he needed to share it with the world.

One late-night conflict between Eric and Gerald turned ugly when Eric unleashed a string of insults, accusations and threats that drove Gerald into an asthma attack. Dewey broke it up by threatening to kick the snot out of Eric if he didn't back off.

"I don't care if your name's on the door," Dewey said with a two-hand grip on Eric's jacket. "We're a band, and nobody is that much more important than anyone else."

The sessions for the album, a two-disc opus called "The Obsessive Search for Harmony," ended just before Easter,

1968, four weeks after the record was due in the stores. The entire band splintered off into different directions for the holiday weekend. At that point, even Aaron, Patrick and Gerald had to get away from each other.

By virtue of her growing friendship with Aaron, Claire had an insider's view of the sessions, which she diplomatically wrote about in Rolling Stone.

> *"One can only hope the sweat and passion felt by members of the Victorian Manner during the sessions for 'The Obsessive Search for Harmony' will show up on what is sure to be the most anticipated record to come out of the Bay Area since the Airplane's 'Surrealistic Pillow.'"*

Lenny Hayes was so taken with Claire's writing that he hired her as the band's new publicist. Claire hoped her new job would help her get closer to Aaron. Aaron was already feeling a bit crowded by Claire and worried that this new arrangement might make matters worse.

Sure, they were by many measures a couple. After a few weeks together, their relationship finally became intimate. Aaron admired her passion for life and was a grateful partner in her energetic lovemaking. He was genuinely fond of her and they spent time together almost every day.

Still, at Aaron's insistence, they kept separate addresses. What he didn't like were the late-night phone calls and constant questions about what he was doing, where he had been and what he had planned for the rest of the day.

"I wouldn't have to ask if we lived together," she would say, then apologize once again for being pushy.

Aaron and Claire spent the extended Memorial Day holiday weekend driving down the coast through Big Sur. When they could not find an inn or a cabin to rent, they camped in the state parks. One night, they crashed a hidden ocean beach just north of Monterey. They equipped themselves with only a few essentials: sleeping bags, a jug of Gallo wine, a few snacks and a battery-operated radio. It was the perfect place to spend a quiet night, but Claire had other plans.

"I know you've never dropped acid before," she said as they watched the sun sink into the Pacific. The cool ocean breeze was a relief from the hot sun that baked them all day driving the Mustang down the coast. "I've got a surprise."

Claire produced two small scraps of paper with tiny yellow stains in the middle. "I know you aren't that much into drugs, but this is different. You *have* to try it. It opens your mind. It lets you touch those things that always seem just beyond your grasp. You know how you lose words on the tip of your tongue? When you're tripping, they all come back."

Aaron had his reservations. "Didn't seem to do that for Eric," he argued.

"Hey, if you're a jerk, it can make you a bigger jerk," Claire said. "If you're just a simple artist looking for the meaning of the universe, it might help you find it."

"Meaning of the universe? I've always wondered about that," Aaron said, giving Claire a little smile.

"Maybe it would just make you a bigger jerk, just like Eric." She was a little annoyed. "Come on, seriously, try it just this once. *With me*. It's like an adventure. And this is the perfect place to do it. The worst thing when you're tripping is to be around people who aren't. We're all by ourselves here. It's perfect."

"I saw on 'Dragnet' that heroin leads to LSD, and I haven't done heroin yet."

"Aaron, would you please be serious?"

"I'm on vacation. How serious do I have to be?"

In this idyllic setting, Aaron was unusually relaxed and up for almost anything. He swallowed the blotter acid and waited for the adventure to begin.

The first thing he noticed was that the large, round full

moon lighting up the night had taken on a crystalline aura. It looked like a street lamp with beveled glass windows. The corners acted like prisms, beaming rainbows of light in every direction.

Then, the breeze began to blow hot and cold. It felt like the current of a river. He had to force himself not to try and swim upstream. Finally, he realized he was in the same spot and laughed until he was out of breath.

Claire was laughing with him, although she didn't know why. They tried to talk, but neither could understand the other. Aaron heard himself talking. He wasn't sure if the words made any sense.

Since talking was a waste of time, they cuddled up and spent hours, or what seemed like hours, looking out to sea. They stared at the moon, rocked with the motion of the waves and wondered if there were people on the other side of the ocean staring back at them.

Aaron's mind blossomed in the dark. He wished he had remembered to bring his guitar. It would have been interesting to see if he could play in this condition. He recalled Andy Rush's lecture about communicating with music instead of words.

Mr. Rush! The image of his old friend and teacher took a front-row seat in his mind. How long had it been since he last saw him?

All of a sudden, their last meeting flashed in front of him. His hands began to sweat and shake. He felt the warm barrel of Carlo's gun in his hand. He felt Bobby's last breath on his cheek. He heard Tina begging him to leave.

The rest of that night began to replay in his mind like a bad dream. He held up the guitar cases to cover the bloodstains on his shirt as he hurried out of the Full House. He packed the cases in the trunk of his Mustang and guided it into the heavy late-night traffic on the strip. He didn't know where to go. He thought about driving straight out of town. Instead, his car brought him to Andy Rush's house.

Andy had been fast asleep when he heard the doorbell ring in the middle of the night. The cobwebs in his brain tore apart when he saw his finest student standing there, bruised and bloodied.

"Get in here," Andy said. "What happened? Are you OK?"

He sat Aaron at the kitchen table and brought him a wet towel. Aaron just sat there, shaking. Andy used the towel to clean him up.

"Willie, what happened? Are you in some kind of trouble?"

"I didn't know where else to go," Aaron said. "Can you help me?"

"Of course I'll help you, baby. Tell me what's wrong." It was Claire's voice. What was she doing here?

"Who did this to you, Willie? Who hurt you?" Andy handed him the towel.

"Who hurt you, baby?" Claire asked as she stood behind him and massaged his shoulders.

"I don't understand," Aaron said. "Bobby's dead. Carlo killed him. Carlo tried to kill me. Carlo's dead. I think I killed him. Or Tina. She was there, too. She told me to go."

"Who's Bobby? Who's Carlo?" What, was she taking notes?

"All right, Willie. Try to relax. You're safe here," Andy said. "Give me your keys. I'm going to move your car around back. If anyone is looking for you, that Mustang sticks out like a sore thumb."

"Talk to me baby. What's wrong?"

"Claire, you shouldn't be here. It's dangerous. You should go."

Andy returned and passed him the jug of Gallo. "Willie, how did all this happen?"

"Carlo went after me, in my room. He was pissed at me, pissed about me and Tina. He went after me and Bobby tried to stop him. He had a gun. They both got shot. Andy, Bobby's dead! And they'll be coming after me. The family, the cops ..."

"*Who's Tina?*" Claire was being pushy again.

"OK, Willie, we've got to get you out of here. They might come looking for you." Andy looked out the window to see if any headlights could be seen on his street.

"*Why does he call you Willie?*" Claire asked.

"Here's what we're gonna do. You can hide out at my mother's house. There's no electricity, but it's empty and there are no neighbors. You'll be safe there for a while. That'll give us a chance to figure out what to do."

Andy drove Aaron to his late mother's house, about five miles outside of the city limits. She had died almost a year earlier and Andy had not been able to sell it. The curtains were drawn and weeds had overtaken the lawn.

Unable to sleep, Aaron paced as he waited anxiously for Andy to return. Claire, who somehow managed to come along for the ride, was napping quietly on the couch when Aaron saw Andy's Plymouth kicking a trail of dust up the long driveway.

Andy brought some sandwiches, a jug of water, a six-pack of pop and two bags of ice. He wrapped some ice in a towel and placed it against Aaron's swollen cheek.

He also brought a battery-powered radio. "There was nothing in the morning papers," he said. "But there's a report on the radio about a murder in your suite. They said the police want to bring you in for questioning."

The ice felt good on Aaron's face. The pop soothed his dry mouth and throat. He was too nauseous to eat.

"Are you sure it's safe here?"

"It's safe for now," Andy said. "But we need to get you away from Vegas. You need to disappear, man."

"Maybe I should go to the cops. Maybe they can protect me."

"Willie, think about it. Think about where you live. The cops and the crooks, *same thing, man*. You're gonna need to get out of this town and even then you're gonna have to lay low. These people have a long reach.

"This is what I think you should do. I've got a friend in Los Angeles. He works with the underground. He's an expert with fake I.D.s. and has been supplying them to draft dodgers so they can get into Canada.

"I'm going to give you his name and address. I think you should go see him, get yourself a new identity and head straight to Vancouver. You should be OK there for a while. After things cool down, get in touch with me and we'll figure out what to do next."

"Andy, the reports. Did they say anything about Bobby?"

"Yeah. I'm sorry, Willie, he's dead. They said there were two bodies. They didn't say who the other one was."

Aaron thought about his brother and began to cry. Bobby, the slow, tubby albatross in the Taylor family, had come to his rescue and ended up dead.

For the first time in his life, Bobby had come up with the answers. For a few wonderful hours, Aaron and Bobby had been loving brothers, happily planning to skip out on their oppressors and search for new territories to conquer. Their dream was torn apart by a few small pieces of hot lead.

"You know, me and Bobby, we were going to leave town last night, right after the show," Aaron told Andy. "I even closed out my savings account. We were ready to go. We were *gone*, man." He opened the Martin guitar case so Andy could see the money.

Andy whistled. "Well, I guess that was a break. You're going to need that cash. But I don't know, if they investigate, it might look bad, you taking all that money. Like you planned all this."

"We didn't plan anything like this," Aaron said. "We just needed to get away from here, away from Carlo and Tina. They won't have to investigate about the money. They already know. Carlo knew all about it. The bank manager called *him*. That's what set him off. Oh, man, I can't believe this."

"Anyway, Willie, I'm really, really sorry about Bobby," Andy said. "I've got to go and see what else I can find out. I'll wait until after dark and come back with your car. In the meantime, try to relax and get some sleep."

"*Try to relax, baby,*" Claire said. "*You're having a bad trip.*"

Aaron paced for hours, stopping frequently to peer outside through the dusty curtains and dirty windows, but finally fell asleep on the couch. The glare of the sun setting through the living room window woke him. He was dying for a shower, but there was no water. Instead, he wet another towel with the melted ice and washed his face. The cool water helped him regain his focus.

After sundown, he saw two cars turn into the driveway and approach the house. Andy was driving his Plymouth. Behind him, someone else was behind the wheel of his Mustang.

It was Betty.

"*Who is that? Is that Tina?*" He felt Claire behind him, looking over his shoulder.

Andy opened the front door for Betty, who rushed to Aaron's side. "Oh, Willie. What did they do to you?"

"Betty, I never thought … Andy, you shouldn't have got her involved in all this. She shouldn't be here."

"*Betty?*" Aaron tried his best to ignore Claire. He needed Betty right now and didn't have time to explain.

"She heard the radio report and came to me, Willie," Andy said. "And I needed some help with this. Someone we could both trust."

"Willie, I want to help you," Betty said. "Please let me help you."

"Betty, I'm sorry. I'm so sorry. I've ruined everything."

Betty held him tightly and put a finger to his lips.

"Ssh. Not now. This is not your fault. Those people, those evil people, they're the ones to blame. You've done nothing to deserve this. And your brother never hurt anybody. Willie, I'm so sorry about Bobby."

"He tried to help me. He saved me."

"I know, baby. I know. Andy told me."

"Bobby's your brother? You have a brother?"
Not now, Claire!

"OK, Willie, here's the deal. Your car is all gassed up. There's a cold chest of drinks and food in the back seat. Get in the car, keep the money hidden and head west. You won't have to stop until you reach L.A."

Andy handed him a folded map. "You may need this, but if you stay on 15, you should be fine. My friend's name is Freddie Garcia. His address and number are on the map. I wrote mine down, too, in case you forget."

They all sat there for a while. Andy sat by the window, keeping an eye on the road. Aaron sat in an easy chair, slumped forward. Instinctively, Betty sat on the arm of the chair and began to rub his shoulders. Andy looked over at them and took the hint.

"You should go soon," Andy said. "I'm going to go outside for a cigarette."

Claire had disappeared, so they were alone in the musty room.

"Betty, you were right about everything," Aaron said. "I took what we had for granted. I didn't realize ... I didn't understand. I ... I played my music and they treated me like a war hero ... it was like a drug. You have to understand. To be able to do what you love best, and have so many people love you for doing it, it was like I would die without that feeling. Nothing else seemed to work for me."

Tears slid gently down Betty's cheeks. "Willie, I loved you so much. I still do."

"And I love you. I really do. But without my music, I don't know who I am."

"Willie, I never asked you to choose."

"I know, but I couldn't handle both. I was working six nights a week, taking care of my brother, you and your mother. Dealing with my mother. It was too much. I tried, but I couldn't do it ... the next thing I knew, everything got out of control."

"It's not all your fault, Willie. It was hard on me, too. I wanted to be there for you, I wanted to be happy for you, but I was so jealous."

"Betty, I know this sounds stupid, but Tina meant nothing to me. I didn't know what was happening to us at the time, but I still never meant to ..."

"I wasn't only jealous of Tina. I hated all those people who were taking advantage of you, pretending to be your friends. Tony. Tina. Your *mother* ... they were all the same, and I just couldn't compete."

Aaron buried his head in Betty's neck. "You know, I'm not even twenty years old, and I feel so ... ancient. I feel like I've never really had a chance to rest. I'm so tired ... and now look at me. I've got to drive all night alone through the desert just to stay alive."

He felt someone tugging on his arm.

"*It's time to go, baby.*" Claire was back.

"Betty, maybe after a while, we could ..."

"*She can't, baby. That's all behind you now. Just relax and listen to my voice. You're safe with me, baby.*"

Aaron heard the waves crashing on the shore. He looked up at the moon and saw it reflecting off the water. A warm breeze surrounded him like a soft blanket.

"Are you OK?" Claire said as she kneeled behind him, rubbing his shoulders. "You want a drink or something?"

"Yeah, I'm fine," Aaron said. "I just wish I had my guitar."

Chapter 34

Once the final tracks for "The Obsessive Search for Harmony" were in the can, the production and marketing departments at Golden Gate Records went into high gear. They all worked overtime mixing, editing, mastering and promoting the record. Lenny Hayes wanted this thing *out*.

Famed mod artist Adam Harlow was brought in to design the album cover and gatefold. He and Helena had run with the same crowd for a while and were rumored to have once been lovers. His work was brilliant. Bucking the trend towards wild, colorful covers, Harlow's cover was mostly white, with an abstract pen-and-ink outline of a Victorian home in the corner. The gatefold opened to a large landscape photo of an opulent Victorian drawing room, with members of the band scattered throughout. Gerald sat at an elegant grand piano. Garrett sat behind him, playing a harp. Sean David drew a bow across a cello. Patrick was strumming a lute. Dewey, dressed like a Civil War Union officer, carried a tin drum.

Eric and Helena, formally attired for the ball, waltzed in the center of the room. Dolores struck a ballerina's pose in the far corner of the dance floor.

Aaron settled for "special thanks to" credits on the record's inner sleeve. Claire got her credit for publicity.

It was a great-looking package and marketing did a terrific job building anticipation for the release. Disc jockeys, especially those on the "progressive rock" FM stations that were popping up like dandelions, were counting the days until the official drop date on the Monday before Labor Day.

Lenny rubbed his hands and dreamed about kids driving

to the shore for one last fling of summer, listening to the Victorian Manner on their radio or 8-Track.

All the pieces were in place, except for one problem.

"The Obsessive Search for Harmony" was a flat-out piece of incomprehensible crap.

Everyone agreed the band was tight. What good was tight when the songs stunk? Critics ridiculed Eric's drug-induced "visions" and snickered at Helena's off-key caterwauling. All the producers, trying to save the project in the mixing room, probably just made it worse. Too many cooks and all that.

Aaron was more grateful than ever that he hadn't been invited to join the band, which had at least six months of touring commitments lined up. The album peaked early on the charts at Number Forty, then sank quickly into oblivion. Still, the tour would go on. Guaranteed bookings had been made in writing. Tickets had been sold. Ed Sullivan was waiting to introduce them to America.

The Victorian Manner caravan, which included Aaron and Claire, jetted across the country for the East Coast leg of the tour. Their first official concert was performed in a brand-new, half-empty Madison Square Garden arena. It was worse in Boston, where the band had booked shows at three different colleges. None of them drew more than 1,500 people.

Hearing reports that promoters were losing their shirts, Ed Sullivan cancelled the Victorian Manner and hired the Doors to fill the vacancy.

Things only got worse from there. The record was barely noticed in Europe and promoters there cancelled all 12 shows in England, Ireland and France.

The only good news came from Iceland, where Helena was revered as a goddess. The record had been Number One there since it came out. Promoters begged the band to play some shows there, but it was far too expensive for the entourage to clear customs and collect peanuts in Reykjavik.

The band limped through the South and Midwest before marching home, beaten and humiliated, just before Christmas.

The cancelled European tour left them with some downtime until the scheduled West Coast concerts, where they hoped to salvage some dignity before friendly home-town audiences.

Eric and Helena split to London for the holidays as soon as they got back to San Francisco. With their king and queen out of the way, the rest of the band planned to get together at Dewey's for a big New Year's Eve party. They would also use the occasion to discuss their future.

Patrick arranged a reunion of the Imposters for an informal performance at the party. Excited by the prospect of playing with a small group of friends for a larger group of friends, Aaron was happily counting down the days to the event. He organized the rehearsals and the group prepared a loose, loud set of classic blues and hard rock. Sean David was recruited into the group, so Patrick moved over to rhythm guitar, leaving Aaron on the lead.

Claire, devastated by the terrible press the Victorian Manner had received from coast to coast, was still in a foul mood. Fortunately, most of her anger was directed at Eric and Helena. During the long nights and days on tour, she had revealed a lack of patience and nasty temper. Aaron had grown comfortable with their relationship, but learned to avoid Claire when she was in one of her moods.

Aaron sometimes wondered how much their night at Big Sur might have affected her attitude. She never said much about his "bad trip" or what he might have revealed to her about his past. All she did was ask him what *he* thought about the trip. He simply told her that he recalled a few things from his past he didn't want to remember. That was true enough.

He knew Claire wanted to know more. Thankfully, for once she didn't push. She had possession of him in the here and now. He agreed to let her move into his apartment. That seemed to satisfy her.

When they arrived at Dewey's for the party, Aaron and Claire found that the big drummer had pulled out all the stops for the occasion. He had hired a small traveling carnival that filled the block outside his warehouse. There were more midway booths inside his massive "living room." Balloons, strings of Chinese lanterns and blinking colored lights were everywhere.

A stage had been erected in one corner and was fully prepped for the set by the Imposters. A tape of the Rolling Stones blasted from the P.A. as Dewey, dressed in a tuxedo, greeted guests at the door. There were about 100 people inside, and maybe twice that outside, shooting targets with air rifles, tossing rings over bottles and taking turns on the rides.

"Step right up. Welcome to Deweyland!" Dewey gave Aaron a big hug and kissed Claire's hand. "Test your skill. Everybody's a winner."

"Dewey, this is incredible," Aaron said. "My God, you have a Tilt-a-Whirl!"

"Don't want to be on that one after everybody drinks and eats too much." Dewey's laugh rumbled louder than the Stones.

It was an unusually warm night, so Dewey had lifted the warehouse's old truck bay doors, leaving the building wide open. People were having a ball, drinking, passing joints and throwing burgers on the dozen charcoal stoves Dewey had glowing on the sidewalk.

"Dewey, you know all these people?" he asked.

"Most of 'em," he said. "Not a lot of neighbors in this part of town. Hell, if people want to crash, they can crash. Why, you think maybe I can charge admission?"

"Too late for that, brother," Aaron said. "You could have made a fortune."

"Well, brother, let me tell you," Dewey said. "It's more fun to spend a fortune than it is to make one. Know what I'm saying?" His laugh drowned out the Band's new album, "Music from Big Pink," which was now playing on the P.A. "Of course, I really don't know how much fun it is to make a fortune, since I ain't done it yet."

That was Dewey. He was large and loved to live that way.

The crowd continued to swell as Aaron began to experience a few preshow jitters.

"You know, there are more people here than there were at some of the Vic Manner gigs," he said.

"They musta heard Eric and Helena were out of town," Dewey said. "No danger of hearing " 'My Existential Existence.' "

"You were great on that song, Dewey," Claire said, straining to get in the spirit of things.

"Shit, all I got to do on that cut was bang a tambourine upside my head," Dewey said, dreading the very thought of the album's worst track. "But I'm ready to rock tonight, my brothers. We gonna wake the dead tonight, feed 'em popcorn and beer, and teach 'em how to dance."

An hour before midnight, Dewey couldn't wait any longer. He tore off the top of his tux, grabbed the Imposters and led them to the stage. People began to gather near the stage as they heard the band tuning up. The crowd was so large that it spilled out the bay doors and across the street.

Aaron took a few deep breaths and called a group huddle. For some reason, he was more nervous now than he had been playing with Chuck Berry.

"What now?" He asked.

Patrick smiled at him. "You're the man. You choose."

Now Aaron realized why he was so anxious. For the first time in more than two years, he was back out front. In the meantime, he had copped to stage fright so many times that even he was beginning to believe it.

Suddenly, the old muscles, and old attitude, kicked in.

"OK. 'No Particular Place to Go.' Worked fine the last time we played," Aaron commanded, then turned to his microphone.

"All right everybody, let's give 1968 over to history. I'm ready for a new year. How about you?"

The crowd roared. Aaron turned the Les Paul up a few notches, then counted off, "*One-two-three-four!*"

Three hours later, dripping sweat in the dead of winter, Aaron mesmerized the audience, and his bandmates, with yet another incredible guitar solo in the middle of the Beatles' "Helter Skelter." He had bought "The White Album" just two weeks earlier, on the first day of its release, and quickly put together an arrangement for the Imposters.

Aaron had already earned the respect of the band, but until tonight, they had never really heard him open up. He had a strong alto that could sing sweet soul and whiskey-soaked blues with equal aplomb. When Dewey needed a break, he played the drums for half an hour, then moved to the piano when Gerald had to get some fresh air.

However, it was his jaw-dropping guitar solos that blew everyone's mind. There wasn't a style he hadn't mastered.

He played blues, jazz, rock and even country, dazzling the crowd with an electrified cover of "Jambalaya" that had people dancing two blocks away. He pulled out his beautiful new Fender Telecaster Custom guitar, which he tuned for playing slide, and played a few Elmore James songs by himself while the rest of the band listened in awe. At midnight, he played a screaming, psychedelic version of "Auld Lang Syne" inspired by an arrangement of "The Star Spangled Banner" he had heard Jimi Hendrix improvise one night.

They wrapped the set well after two with a speedy cover of Chuck Berry's "Promised Land," during which every band member took a solo as Aaron introduced them by name. When the song ended, Dewey pulled a rope behind his drum kit and hundreds of balloons dropped from the tall ceiling.

Aaron turned to Dewey, who shrugged his shoulders. "I forgot to do it at midnight."

Everyone in the band fell down laughing as the crowd begged for an encore.

"That's all, folks," Aaron told them. "You got your money's worth."

"Man, even I got my money's worth, and I paid for this

party!" Dewey said to Aaron as the band left the stage and mingled with their audience. "Where you been hidin' that shit? And *why*?"

Even Patrick, who knew Aaron's abilities better than anyone, was speechless.

"I'm just going to give you my guitar and enter the seminary like my parents always wanted," he said. "First Clapton, then Hendrix, now you. I give up."

Aaron smiled shyly and looked for Claire. He saw her prying her way through the crowd and met her halfway. When she reached him, she grabbed him by the collar and locked him in a deep soul kiss.

"That was just … I knew you could … let's get out of here," she said, pausing to catch her breath. "I need to fuck you really bad."

Aaron quickly said his good-byes.

"Dewey, you throw one hell of a carnival," he said.

"This whole year has been a fucking carnival," Dewey agreed. "So I figured this was the only way to end it. I didn't know it would turn out to be your debutante ball."

"You two go home and get some rest, Claire," Patrick said. "We're going to put your boyfriend to work next year."

"We're going home, but he's not getting any rest," she said, flashing a wicked smile. "I just became his groupie."

The next afternoon, the group returned to Dewey's to help clean up and celebrate the New Year. There were at least a dozen people there when Aaron and Claire arrived. Some of the men were watching U.S.C. lose to Ohio State in the Rose Bowl. Dewey's older sister, Rhonda, was cooking up a big New Year's dinner. A few of the other girls were helping her, but Claire clung to Aaron's arm as the band members gathered near the stage area.

Conspicuously absent were Garrett Townsend and Dolores Herrera. Garrett had been to the party last night but declined to play with the Imposters. No one had seen or heard from Dolores since they got back in town. No one *ever* saw the reclusive "reed lady" offstage or outside the studio.

The first order of business was the upcoming final leg of the Victorian Manner's concert tour, which would wind its way up the coast from Los Angeles to the Bay for a three-night finale at the Fillmore. No one could muster much enthusiasm for going back onstage with Eric and Helena.

"I'd rather play dives with you guys than go back to that," Patrick said. "Last night was far out, man. That's where my head is at. That's the kind of music I want to play."

"Why don't we all just fucking quit?" he said.

"Look at your contract, man," Dewey said. "They got your honkey ass locked up for two years. If you quit, you won't be able to do dick. No gigs, no studio, no nuthin'."

"So, what's the big deal? I'll be back where I was a year ago," Patrick said. "I can go back to school."

"I don't know about you, but I got bills and child support to pay," said Dewey, the oldest and most experienced professional musician in the group. "I gotta work. I don't like the music, either, but I played worse. Shit, I used to drum for Neil fucking Diamond."

Once the rest of them got used to the idea of Dewey and Diamond, and stopped laughing, Gerald spoke up.

"Well, I don't know about you guys, but whatever we do, I think we should do it as a group. If we stick together, maybe we can make this work."

"I can dig that, brother," Dewey said. "You heard Chuck Berry. He said we can play some. I think we got some chemistry, you know what I'm saying? We got a connection."

Sean and Gerald nodded in agreement, then looked at Patrick.

"What about you?" Gerald asked Patrick.

"OK, my brothers, I'm in," Patrick said.

"*Right on!*" said Dewey, who quickly rediscovered his usual cheerful mood.

Patrick then turned to Aaron.

"And what about you?"

"What about me?" Aaron said.

"What do you think? What do you want to do?"

"What's the difference? I'm not in the band. I don't have a say about any of this."

Patrick jumped up, spun around and began to pace up and down the stage.

"See, that's what's so fucked up about this situation," he said. "Here's the guy we should be playing behind and he's setting up the microphones! What sense does that make?"

Gerald tried to put his new mandate to work.

"Why don't we just insist that if Aaron doesn't play, we don't play?"

Now, it was Aaron's turn to stand up. First, he had to break Claire's grip, which was holding him tightly down. She knew what he would say.

"*Whoa*, boys," he said. "I want to be in *this* band, not in *that* one. Besides, if you do this, they're gonna argue about it for weeks. It's just going to drag the whole scene out and make you more miserable than you are now.

"Let's just be patient. Be realistic. Eric is frying his brain with acid and everybody knows Helena is a junkie. How much longer before they go away all by themselves? And they hate us. When you finish the last couple of shows, they'll probably fire you or pass out. Either way, you'll all get your freedom before too long. Then we can figure out what to do next."

Patrick agreed, but continued to put Aaron on the spot.

"Well, Lowe-man, while we're talking about it, what do you think we should do then? Are you willing to join us or what? Time to get off the fence, brother."

Aaron wasn't ready to make that decision. Claire broke the silence.

"Aaron, tell them," she said.

"Tell them what?"

"You know. Your songs."

"What songs?" Gerald asked.

"He's been writing songs. And they're amazing."

Ever since he returned from the bad trip to Big Sur, Aaron had been obsessed with writing. It was like the acid lit a fuse in his head and ignited a blast of creativity. Once again haunted by memories of his past, which he had successfully repressed for almost two years, Aaron found that writing helped ease the pain.

He usually wrote in the abstract. Even Claire, who was aware that Aaron had been traumatized in some way, could not glean the details of his history from the songs. Still, they artfully documented the tortured soul of a sensitive artist who had an intimate relationship with heartbreak and tragedy.

"Claire, I told you, they're not ready," he said. Then he turned to the group. "Believe me, they're not ready."

"Then get them ready," Dewey said. "Come on, brother, what do you say? Want to run off and join the carnival?"

Aaron surveyed the anxious faces of his fellow musicians. They were offering their swords to him. They not only wanted him to join, they wanted him to lead the way. They were willing to play his songs before they even heard them.

He was humbled by their friendship. It was, he thought, his finest moment in fourteen years as a professional musician.

"OK, OK, I'm in. You guys are the best. That's what I want to be, too."

Chapter 35

Just as Aaron predicted, Eric and Helena self-destructed as the band completed its first and hopefully last tour. Eric was convinced that the hipper audiences on the West Coast would better understand what his songs were about. Just to be sure, he started to give each one a long-winded introduction. He rambled on about why he wrote it, how he wrote it, when he wrote it and where he was when he wrote it until everyone was numb.

The band went through the motions and faithfully carried out its contractual responsibilities, fully expecting to be unshackled after the Fillmore shows.

The day after the final concert, everyone involved with the Victorian Manner was asked to attend a meeting at Lenny Hayes's office.

When they arrived, Eric stood up before the assembly and apologized that things had not gone better.

"I should have listened to you more," he said to the band. "I didn't appreciate how much you guys had to contribute."

Without saying a word, Helena stood up and left the room.

"Don't worry about that. I can handle her," Eric said. "The point is, I've grown as a person in the last few months and I'm willing to let you guys have more of a say in the future. I know 'Harmony' wasn't as good as it could have been, but I really believe the next record can be a lot better."

The next record? Everyone else in the room was convinced there wasn't going to be a next record.

Aaron, sitting next to Claire in the back of the room, looked around and saw a lot of sour faces. Never had so many people been so depressed by not losing their jobs.

He looked at Claire. Her face was turning red. He would have to be careful around her when the meeting was over.

Lenny Hayes took over the rest of the meeting. He handed everyone a schedule for the next set of recording sessions. Eric handed over sheet music and lyrics for his new songs to Gerald and Patrick.

Aaron watched his friends review the material while Lenny went on about marketing and touring plans. Patrick muffled a laugh. Gerald just shook his head.

After the meeting, the Imposters faction broke away to a cafe on the corner. Sitting at an outdoor table, they could see Eric and Helena arguing in front of the Golden Gate building.

"Look at them," Claire said. "She couldn't handle him apologizing to us. Not that I believed a word of what he said."

She saw Gerald studying the songs. "Gerald, how bad are they?"

"I don't know, I'll have to see what I can do," he said, continuing to sift through the notes.

Claire needed more information, "Patrick? What about you?"

"Train wreck," he said. "The whole thing is off the rails and we're stuck on board till the last stop. What a drag."

"They've got to be kidding," Claire said. "What can they possibly hope to accomplish? They are so out of it. They don't have a clue!"

Claire's complaints weren't sitting well with Gerald.

"You know, Claire, you and Aaron aren't locked in like we are. You can just walk away."

"But what about our plans? When are we going to get to play our stuff?"

"*We* will have to wait until Eric or Lenny lets us go. Then *we* can play *your* stuff," Gerald said, clearly annoyed. I'm sorry if that gets in the way of *your* plans."

Claire glared at Gerald, then started to sob.

"I'm sorry, Gerald. I didn't mean to butt in where I don't

belong. I thought we all wanted the same thing. I know how badly Aaron wants to get involved."

Aaron put his arm around Claire and stroked her hair. He wished there were a button he could push to shut her down.

"Look, there's plenty of time," Aaron said. "Let's just do what we have to do."

"Another nine months slumming in the Vic Manner? Fuck that," Dewey said. "I think I'll go break an arm or something."

"Whose arm?" Aaron asked, trying to lighten the mood.

Claire stirred her coffee and sniffed. "Who knows, maybe Eric and Helena will O.D. and we'll all get laid off."

"That's not funny, Claire," Gerald said. "You don't joke about that sort of thing. That's not cool at all."

Claire stared Gerald down. "I wasn't joking. I wish they would just go away. And I'm tired of you hassling me."

Then she stood up and quickly walked away. Aaron looked down and played with his teabag.

"I'm sorry, Aaron, I didn't mean to upset her, but when did she take over?" Gerald said.

"Don't worry about it. She just doesn't have a lot of patience. I'm not in that much of a hurry, myself."

"Aren't you going after her?" Patrick said.

"Not this minute. I can't talk to her when she's like this. Look, don't worry about it. Remember what Gerald said? We have to stick together. Everything will work out. You guys just hang in there."

Aaron looked down the street. Claire was around the corner and out of sight.

"Maybe I better go find her," he said.

No matter how much polish Gerald applied to Eric's new songs, they were rambling, incoherent arias that could drive a dog to howl. They were train wrecks, as Patrick predicted. Everyone in the band was embarrassed to be involved.

Patrick and Gerald finally went to Lenny and begged him to face facts.

"To tell you the truth, kids, I knew a long time ago this wasn't going to work," he said. "I thought Eric had enough talent, charisma and sex appeal to lead a big-league band. My mistake. But this is still a business, and my job is to deliver another record. I would make more money if it was a hit, but I still get paid. And after 25 years of coddling prima donnas, I just don't care anymore. I'm gonna let Eric be Eric, then I'm gonna collect my money and go sailing. Catalina sounds nice. Maybe do some fishing. Read the funny papers. That Daisy Mae is some piece of ass, let me tell you.

"I'm gonna buy a new color TV and watch the Dodgers. Stay up late and watch Johnny. Watch those astronauts when they walk on the moon. Can you imagine? What a world we live in. Too bad Kennedy ain't alive to see the day.

"You boys are gonna get your money, too, so just grin and bear it. *It's a business.* Next year, you can split with my blessing and start up the biggest new band of the Seventies. I'll listen to your songs on the radio and brag to my friends in the business how I put you all together. My granddaughter will think I'm cool. Maybe you'll let me bring her backstage to meet you.

"Now, who wants lunch?"

The word was passed that Lenny wasn't going to do anything about the problem, which didn't leave many options. Aaron talked Claire out of quitting, but she remained angry and distant to everyone except him. Lenny put her to work touting the second Victorian Manner album, "Confessions of the Cosmic Candyman," which would be released in early May. A summer tour, including a huge festival being planned in upstate New York, would keep them on the road for four of the next six months.

Lenny gave in to one demand. It was Patrick's idea. Nobody would quit the Victorian Manner on one condition: the Imposters would get to open some of the shows on their own. That was reason enough for everyone to stick together.

Everyone except Claire was satisfied with the deal and

willing to endure one more go-around with Eric and Helena. The whole band spent nearly a month rehearsing the new show, then separated for two weeks to rest up before the album release and tour.

Most of the group stuck around town. There would be enough travel for everyone in the months ahead. Eric and Helena, however, planned another getaway, this time to an exclusive spa in Palm Springs.

Aaron was surprised to overhear Claire and Helena talking on the phone just before she and Eric left town. Something about supplies. Claire noticed his curiosity and explained that Lenny asked her to track down some hypoallergenic makeup that Helena would need on tour.

The next afternoon, Aaron first heard the news on KSAN radio.

> *"Unconfirmed sources are reporting that Eric Troy and Helena Guðmundsdóttir, the creative force behind the Victorian Manner, had perished in a horrific accident on the Pacific Coast Highway, about 20 miles south of Monterey near the Carmel Highlands. Sources say Troy's MGB Roadster apparently crashed into a guardrail and flipped over it, tumbling 200 feet to a rocky beach. Two bodies were found dead on the scene."*

Aaron didn't move until the ring of the phone snapped him out of shock. It was Patrick.

"Did you hear? Can you believe this?" he said.

"I just heard it. They haven't confirmed it yet," Aaron said.

"I just talked to Lenny. He confirmed it. They're dead. *Splat.*"

"Patrick, have some respect."

"Just calling it like it is, bro. The Vic Manner is history-ville. The king is dead. Long live the king."

Aaron felt bad about Eric and Helena and didn't like being tagged as the heir to a warm throne.

"Cut that shit out, Patrick," he said. "Let's keep it to ourselves for a while."

"Sure thing, bro. I'll tell you what, though. Claire sure has her mojo working. Is she out dancing in the streets?"

"She's supposed to be with Lenny. She's probably trying to call. I better hang up."

"OK. Give her my congratulations."

Aaron hung up and the phone rang right away. Claire said she was busy at the office trying to handle media inquiries about Eric and Helena.

"The police said they were drinking, smoking dope and doing God knows what else," She said. "Eric must have lost control. It's all so horrible."

Considering her mood of late, she didn't sound all that upset. Patrick was right. Claire was taking this as good news. She just couldn't help it.

That night at home, Claire and Aaron sat on the porch, watching a thick fog consume the bay. She was having trouble sleeping. Aaron tried strumming some soft chords to soothe her nerves.

"I'm sure Patrick and everyone else thinks I'm terrible, that I jinxed them and I'm glad they are dead," she said. "I won't lie. I'm glad they are gone. I'm glad they are out of the way. But I never would have wanted anything like this. I need you to believe that, Aaron."

Aaron played a few bars of somber blues and gave her a long look.

"Of course I believe you, honey," he said. "I don't think you would ever wish harm on anyone. It's just, well, that's why they say be careful what you wish for. They didn't die because of anything that anyone wished or didn't wish. They died because Eric was too wasted to drive and he drove anyway.

"But if you wish someone ill and ill becomes them, you

can't help wonder … and there's nothing you can do about it.

"It's just life, honey. Things happen. Time goes by. People die. More time goes by. All we can do is live while we can, and leave the dead behind."

"Well, it's just upsetting that some people don't think the way you do, and they would just as soon blame me," Claire said.

"Just stop blaming yourself, and don't worry about what other people think. Anyone who thinks you wished Erica and Helena over that cliff isn't worth worrying about."

"You mean like Patrick?" she asked.

Aaron laughed. "Yeah, like Patrick. No, that's just his sick sense of humor. *Splat.* That's his assessment of what happened.

"Look, Claire, you've got to stop thinking that the band hates you. Just stop trying to force them to like you. I feel guilty saying it, but things are looking up for us. Everybody's going to be excited about the new band. So just relax and go with the flow, OK?"

Claire started to cry. "OK. I'll try. It's just that I want so much for people to know how special you are. And it seems like we've been waiting so long."

"Claire, it's not me that is special. It's the band. What we do as a group can be special if we stick together and really dedicate ourselves to the music. None of us can chase individual glory. Otherwise, we'll end up like Eric, a self-centered bad joke of a musician who was finished before he hit twenty-five."

Claire held him tightly as he wiped away her tears. "I wish I could be more like you. I love you so much. I would do anything for you. *Anything.* I'll always be there for you, no matter what."

CHAPTER 36

On the fifth business day after Eric and Helena were found dead, a press conference was called at Golden Gate Records.

Nearly fifty reporters, along with camera crews and photographers, huddled in a big conference room for the Victorian Manner's funeral. The surviving members of the band, along with Aaron, Claire and Lenny Hayes, sat at a long table. A centerpiece bouquet of microphones bloomed in front of them.

Gerald spoke for the band, which wore the appropriate veil of grief. He read from a prepared statement.

"We were unanimous in our belief that the band ceased to exist when it lost its two guiding lights, and could not be the same without them. With that reality in mind, we regretfully announce the end of the Victorian Manner. I'm sure Golden Gate will still release the record, and we hope it will be a lasting tribute to our departed brother and sister. But there will be no tour. As of now, it's over."

Patrick showed up slightly drunk for the event. Aaron prayed Patrick could keep from laughing. Instead, Patrick nodded off, his head landing on Aaron's shoulder. Aaron shifted him up a bit and hoped no one would notice.

All in all, the event had gone better than expected. There was a bit of discomfort when Dolores and Garrett, who were loyal to Eric and Helena, had to unite at the table with their rebellious band mates. They knew the Imposters couldn't wait for the press conference to be over so they could explore their new lease on life.

"That was heavy, man," Dewey said as the conference

broke up. "Gerald, that was beautiful. I was balling like a baby. Inside."

"Yeah, me too," Patrick said.

"Before or after you passed out?" Aaron said, annoyed that Patrick chose to be wasted when serious business was being conducted.

"I'm grieving in my own Irish way," Patrick said. "Who wants to grieve some more with me?"

"Think I can pass for Irish?" Dewey asked.

"Davis, hmm, close enough," Patrick said.

"OK, then, I just copped some sweet Oaxacan," Dewey said. "Anybody want to join us at my place for some groovy grieving?"

"*Grievin' ... on a Sunday afternoon,*" Patrick sang to the melody of "Groovin'" by the Young Rascals.

"Maybe next time," Aaron said. "I'm glad you guys are coping."

Aaron wasn't going to waste any time grieving, either. He wanted to play some music.

"Gerald, you want to work on some songs? I could use some help," he asked.

"Hey, hey, I'll help," Patrick said.

"Patrick, you're really not in any condition to work. Why don't you just go with Dewey? Gerald and I will put some stuff together and we can all meet tomorrow at Dewey's for rehearsal. What do you say?"

"Sounds like a plan, Lowe-man," said Patrick as Dewey led him away. "Mañana, my brother."

Back at Aaron's place, Gerald experimented with some of Aaron's new material, working through the melodies on the second-hand electric piano Aaron used when he was songwriting. He tried to sing some of the lyrics, but had trouble reading Aaron's handwriting. Yet there was enough there to interest him.

Gerald still was playing the pessimist.

"You know, it would have been nice to do those opening

gigs for the Vic Manner," he said, referring to the cancelled tour. "Would have been nice to play in front of those big crowds. The others act like we're already big stars and people are going to run to see us. I don't see it that way. There's going to be a lot of dive bars and cheap motels for us between here and there. People knew Eric and Helena and the few people who come to see us because they were Vic Manner fans are going to be disappointed when we don't play their favorite songs."

"Maybe we could rearrange a few of Eric's songs and work them into the set," said Aaron, trying to suppress Gerald's bad vibes.

Gerald peered over his glasses, quietly looking for signs that Aaron was kidding. Aaron broke a smile. Gerald stuck fast to his funk.

"I'm serious," he said "We've gone back to start and we didn't get to collect $200. Lenny said we shouldn't be expecting a lot of royalties. The label spent a fortune indulging Eric and his whims. The Vic Manner went to the grave in debt."

"Well, I think we can make ends meet until people get to know us," Aaron said. "I don't mind playing clubs and bars. It's a lot more fun when there's just a few hundred people out looking for a good time. These big formal concerts are a drag. Ten thousand people sitting a mile away. How are you supposed to connect? I like the energy of a small crowd. You can feel it all around you. It gets in your face, like a good sweat. It bounces off the walls. When it's all over, you feel like you've been a part of something."

Aaron sensed that Gerald was curious about where Aaron gained all this experience and insight, so he changed the subject.

"All right. If we're going to play small, we have to plan that way. How are we going to get around? What kind of equipment are we going to need? Can we afford roadies or are we going to have to set up by ourselves? We have to have someone to work the sound and the lights. And someone's gonna have to book the shows and manage things."

"OK, who's going to do all that?" Gerald asked.

Just then, Claire walked through the door with some groceries. She planned to cook and asked Gerald to stay for dinner.

"So what are you boys talking about?" she asked.

"Well, payroll, for starters," Aaron said. "We're going to need some hired help. For one thing, we're gonna need a manager."

"No you don't," she said as she filled a large pasta pot with water. "You've already got a manager."

"Who?" Gerald said.

"*Me*," she said. "Now, come help me chop these onions."

Someone had to mind the front office. Why *not* Claire? She knew the scene, she knew the language and she had the contacts. After all the politics and business decisions that bogged down the Victorian Manner, the musicians just wanted to play music. *Their* music. Everyone, including Aaron, looked past her mood swings and agreed to hire her.

Claire would book the shows, make the travel arrangements and spread the advance word. Finding people to handle the sound and lights wouldn't be a problem. And Dewey had the equipment.

That left one thing — putting a show together.

The group already had a sound. Blues-based rock 'n' roll, with a little folk and spacey psychedelia to keep things interesting. Jams and improvisation were allowed, but the emphasis would be on ensemble play.

They would be happy to play mostly oldies and covers, but serious bands were measured on the quality of their original songs. Gerald had written several long instrumental pieces, full of intricate movements and complex changes. These songs would be great showcases for the band to show off its virtuosity. Patrick had written some fun folk tunes and rearranged some traditional Irish pub songs that would help change the pace.

The band's original work, however, would center on Aaron's new songs. He had a feel for the blues and his dark, bittersweet lyrics sounded more like the memoirs of an old sharecropper than a handsome young hippie.

One song, in particular, blew everyone's mind. "The Dead Don't Have to Worry," was a sad, slow country blues ballad. Aaron bridged the song with a searing slide guitar solo that Muddy Waters would have been proud of. But it was the lyrics that knocked everyone on the floor:

If you believe in heaven, and many people do
Death is something that the righteous can look forward to
A better world than this awaits you on the other side
The angels will descend to guide you on the magic ride

A holy man he told me, and holy men don't lie
The dead don't have to worry, the living have to worry till they die

The wicked fear the next world, the evil fear it too
If God is watching they will be the first to know the truth
Before the gate to heaven we all have to pay a toll
And money's not enough to buy salvation for the soul

The heathen hordes they understand that dogma don't apply
The dead don't have to worry, the living have to worry till they die

Virtue is its own reward my mother used to say
Heaven is for those who choose to live their life this way
How many of the mighty fail to understand that love
Lifts the weak and helpless to eternal life above

The put-upon and persecuted never need know why
The dead don't have to worry, the living have to worry till they die

"I didn't know you were so religious," Gerald said. "It's a beautiful thing, when you think about it. Even if you don't believe in God, it's nice to think the good will be rewarded, and the wicked will be punished."

Aaron had never been particularly religious. He couldn't remember ever being in a church. Music was his religion and the guitar was his cross. On those occasions when he did consider his immortal soul, he was sure it had been long lost to damnation.

To many, "The Dead Don't Have to Worry" was a song of faith and hope. Ironically, it was at best wishful thinking on the part of its author. Blues for a condemned man who longed for rewards he would never receive.

Most of Aaron's lyrics carried a similar bittersweet message. In "Shadows," he sang of a great love that had slipped through his hands. "Brother Blues" told a Cain-and-Abel story, with Cain shackled forever by the burden of shame. "Thin Ice" was a cautionary tale about a man who risks his happiness for a moment of greed. "Desert Flower" lovingly described a beautiful blossom born to wither in the hot sun. Each song celebrated the good things in life, then detailed the anguish of a man who threw it all away.

Everyone who heard them came away with a different perspective. The lyrics would never be mistaken for Shakespeare or Dylan, but they were good enough to make fans stay up late arguing about their meaning.

The mystery of Aaron's lyrics took a back seat to the music, played by a band that was shaping up as one of the best in the Bay area, if not the entire country. It could play rough and tumble, punching out catchy chords and funky rhythms. It could also produce tasteful, elegant waves of dreamy melodies. They could play fast, slow, loud or soft to equal effect. They could play serious one minute, then change the mood to light and lively with a juke-joint attitude that forced people to their feet.

By the end of spring, the band was ready to hit the road

and test its luck in front of live audiences. Rumors of their blistering-hot rehearsals, strategically spread by Claire, had generated inquiries from record companies, including Golden Gate, but the band was still smarting from the Victorian Manner fiasco and reluctant to sign away any creative control. Instead, they flaunted their independence. The band members all chipped in to fund the tour. Once they knew more about themselves as a band, they would decide what to record first, how to record it and who to record it for.

There were still a few details to be ironed out. For one thing, they had never settled on a name. "The Imposters" was rejected because they wanted to stake their claim as a new band, with no ties to anything they had done in the past. For the same reason, Patrick's suggestion, "The Ill-Mannered" was rejected as well.

Sometimes, the solution to one problem leads to another. One day, Aaron and Dewey were shopping for vehicles to transport the band and its equipment around the country. They got a great deal on a used Volkswagen Camper, which could comfortably seat six or seven and even had a bunk in the back. They also bought a delivery truck with a seven-ton capacity that would fit most of the heavy equipment.

They were searching for one more large vehicle to carry the instruments and a few more bodies when Aaron slammed on the brakes. "That's it!" he shouted to Dewey. Then he backed up the street, parked and got out. Dewey ran to catch up with him. "What? What?" Dewey asked.

"There," Aaron said, pointing to a white Wonder Bread delivery step van parked outside a small grocery market. The van was decorated with colorful balloons in every corner. In the middle, there was a painting of a packaged Wonder Bread loaf, along with the well-known slogan "Helps Build Strong Bodies 12 Ways."

A "For Sale" sign was taped in one window.

"Perfect," Aaron said.

"If you say so," Dewey replied.

They bought the van on the spot, then Aaron filled Dewey in on the details of his idea. They would need a commercial artist to finish it off.

The next day, the band gathered at Dewey's place to inspect the new fleet and discuss details of the tour, which would slowly work its way east.

"I thought you guys bought three trucks," said Gerald, pointing to the Volkswagen and the truck. "I only see two."

"Well, two trucks and a camper, to be specific," Aaron said. "Got a surprise for you."

He punched a button to lift one of the truck bay doors at the warehouse, and Dewey drove the step van outside. It still had the balloons decorating each corner, but the Wonder Bread loaves had been painted over. In their place, in ornate red and gold lettering, was the word "Carnival."

Aaron explained. "You remember Dewey talking about the carnival we were living in for the last year? Well, maybe that's who we are. Life is a carnival, man, a real circus. And we're going to be the greatest show on earth."

"*Right on!*" Dewey said, honking the van's horn for emphasis.

"Good name for a band, don't you think?" Aaron asked the group.

It was unanimous. The Carnival was in town, but not for long. It was time to conquer America.

CHAPTER 37

Carnival spent most of the summer of 1969 logging miles on America's lonely highways. The tiny but colorful convoy spent an average of 10 hours a day traveling from one gig to another.

Claire had become quite good at her new job. She sweet-talked Lenny into giving her a list of club owners and concert promoters who might have work for them. Once she booked a dozen gigs from California to Chicago to New York, she highlighted a line on a map through all the stops. As the band followed the trail, she made hundreds of phone calls on the road, trying to book more shows along the route.

Sometimes, the band would detour several hundred miles just to play one more gig. Claire kept calling and booking, calling and booking, cashing in on the new referrals and glowing reviews they earned along the way.

The first two weeks, Carnival played five shows between L.A. and Austin. The next two weeks, they played ten between Dallas and Chicago. By mid-July, closing in on the crowded Northeast, they were working almost every night.

The band grumbled when Claire booked two shows in one day. If Carnival was scheduled to play a weekend club date, she would look for a nearby festival or fair that could give them a daytime gig. If the crowd were large enough, Claire would even agree to play for free. Carnival needed to be seen and heard.

Claire assured them the hard work would pay off. Carnival was drawing positive publicity and encores in nearly every town they played. Word of mouth was traveling faster than they were.

They were even starting to make some money, clearing six thousand dollars or more on a good week. They weren't living like headliners but Dewey was making his child support payments.

Aaron had rekindled his love for the stage and the band was really stretching out. Carnival would rev up with a Chuck Berry or Willie Dixon tune, then settle into a long, intense jam. Then they'd do one of Aaron's songs, which were coming to life on the road. He couldn't wait to record them.

Still, after two exhausting months, the tour had become a grind. Onstage, everyone got along. Offstage, they were preying on each other's nerves. Even the usually unflappable Aaron was longing to return home for a little break after Labor Day.

One weekend in mid-August, the band was booked for two nights at the Joint in the Woods, a large club in northern New Jersey, about thirty miles out of Manhattan.

They arrived early in the busy suburban town, so there was plenty of time to kill before the gig. Everyone slept late, then the band members gathered in Aaron and Claire's room for beer and pizza.

They were watching the local news on television when reports started to air about the Woodstock Music and Arts Festival in Bethel, New York. They knew about the festival because the Victorian Manner had been one of the first bands signed to appear there.

No one had imagined the scope of the event until they saw the reports. There were hundreds of thousands of people already there for the first night of the three-day festival, and God knows how many more on their way.

The New York Thruway was shut down and thousands of young people were abandoning their vehicles to hike the rest of the way. Aaron and the rest of the group howled as reporters interviewed local farmers and townsfolk who feared for their lives with the hairy hippies invading their quiet, rural kingdom. Some of them wanted to string up their neighbor,

Max Yasgur, who agreed to let the promoters use his farm for the event.

"So close, and yet so far," Dewey sighed. "What a scene, man. What a scene. And to think we were supposed to be there."

"And where are we?" Patrick said. "Seriously, where are we?"

"Parsippany," Claire said, nibbling on a slice. "New Jersey."

Patrick pointed a finger at the TV. "And how far away is that from here?"

"I don't know," Claire said. "Couple hundred miles, maybe."

"Shit, let's just hop in the VW and go, man," Patrick said, cracking open another beer. "That's where we should be, jamming with Jimi."

"Patrick, even if we didn't have to work here, the roads are closed," Aaron said.

"Claire, get 'em on the phone," Patrick said. He was slurring his words. Aaron realized Patrick must have had a few before the beer and pizza. "Tell 'em who we are. Maybe they can send a helicopter or something."

Claire ignored Patrick, so he started to yell, "I want to jam with Jimi! I want to jam with Jimi!"

The men continued to ignore him. Claire yelled back.

"Who are the 'them' you want me to call, Patrick? And who do you think you are that they should give a damn? You are not the Victorian Manner. They don't want you. They don't even know who you are."

"Shit, Aaron, your old lady is a real bummer," Patrick said.

"Don't bring me into this," Aaron said. "Why don't you just go lay down for a while? We've got to play in a couple of hours."

"What, you don't think I can play?" Patrick said. "Pull out your axe, man, I can outplay you right now!"

"Why don't you just cool it, man," Dewey said. He had that stern tone that meant you better be listening. "Look, it just ain't the right time or place for us. We payin' our dues, just like everybody does. Vic Manner never had to pay no dues, and where are they now? Don't that tell you something?

"Brothers, you all listen to me. Our time will come. This ain't it, but our time will come if we don't screw it up. So Claire, keep your mouth shut. And Patrick, do like Aaron say and go take a nap. Then take a shower. We got our own gig to worry about."

Patrick put down his beer, shrugged his shoulders and left. The whole scene worried Aaron, who had noticed Patrick was drinking a lot lately. He knew the road had been particularly hard on him. Patrick had trouble sleeping so he was taking downers as well. It was a dangerous combination and Aaron was afraid it was getting the better of his normally affable buddy.

Three more weeks and it will all be over, Aaron thought. Then, the band would sign a deal, make some magic in the studio and hopefully have as much success on the charts as they were having in the clubs.

The Joint in the Woods was barely half full that night for the show. Woodstock was close enough to Parsippany to draw the club's regular crowd out of town. Three days of peace and love upstate had killed business in the greater metropolitan area for the entire weekend.

In between shows, the band continued to watch the news reports and sulk about missing the concert of the century.

Aaron startled himself by daydreaming about playing in front of half a million people, just like Hendrix was at Woodstock. Could his new band really ever get that big? And if they did, could they handle it? Could he handle it? Aaron lived in constant conflict between his need for anonymity and his need for an audience.

Aaron thought about the Beatles, who had to give up playing live shows. They had paid a huge price for their unprecedented fame and wealth. John Lennon took a lot of criticism for suggesting the Beatles "were bigger than Jesus," but Aaron knew there was a lot of truth in what he said. The Beatles were so popular that their every move was documented, discussed and judged by millions of fans. Privacy was impossible. Their slightest missteps became front-page news.

He wondered if the Beatles longed for the days when they could just plug in and play somewhere without inciting a riot. Dewey called it "paying your dues." To Aaron, the Carnival tour had been welcome therapy. For the first time in three years, he was doing what he loved almost every night, just like the old days.

The only problem was, the bigger the future appeared to be, the better the odds that his past would come back into play. He'd been lucky so far. No one was looking for Aaron Lowe. And everyone seemed to have forgotten Willie Taylor.

The band wheeled south down Interstate 95 for a week of stops in the D.C. area. From there, it was further south to Florida, then back West and a merciful ending to their exhausting debut tour.

The long ride home gave Aaron time to think more about where he was, where he had been and where his future was taking him. A few blurry faces came back into focus. Betty. Bobby. Winnie. Tina. Carlo. Andy Rush. And Patsy. What would Patsy say if he saw his nephew's killer taking a bow on Ed Sullivan? Would his mother recognize him after all these years?

Surely, Bobby would have loved touring the country with this friendly gang, just like they planned for a few fleeting hours before everything went to hell.

One night, as the caravan turned towards home, Aaron finally cried for his brother. Thankfully, Claire didn't ask why. She just held him and stroked his long hair. Aaron closed his eyes and pretended he was in Betty's arms.

CHAPTER 38

Three long months of touring had paid handsome dividends for Carnival. By the time they got back to San Francisco, no less than six major recording labels were competing to sign them.

Lenny Hayes and Golden Gate won the sweepstakes. The group still had scars from the Victorian Manner fiasco, but Lenny had never lied to them, a rarity in the record business. He was a good egg and his contacts had jump-started their successful launch.

Gerald asked his older brother, a San Francisco lawyer and anti-war activist, to review the contract. By industry standards, it was fair and generous. There was a nice guaranteed advance and a back door for both parties if things didn't work out. Golden Gate would absorb the recording costs and underwrite the next tour.

A press release dated October 1, 1969, announced the band had signed to Golden Gate and would begin recording its first album later that month. Fans could expect the album in the stores in time for Christmas.

This time, things went smoothly in the studio. Aaron and Patrick had a long talk about responsibility and Patrick showed up every day, sober and ready to rock.

Garrett Townsend happily accepted an invitation to rejoin the band. Aaron and Gerald both felt that Garrett's contribution would be the final piece of the Carnival puzzle. Gerald had been listening to the Band and loved how Garth Hudson's trippy Lowrey organ took the edge off what was otherwise a blue-collar bar band. Garrett's Hammond B-3 could have the same effect on Carnival.

No one blamed Garrett for being loyal to Eric and Helena. The Victorian Manner had been their band. Garrett had been hired by Lenny with their blessing. It was his first big break and he felt he owed them something.

No attempt had been made to contact Dolores Herrera. She had always been more interested in doing her own thing than submitting herself to the dynamics of a group effort. Claire found out Dolores had moved to New York to develop her career as a performance artist. Word was she was living in Greenwich Village.

"There's a good fit," Gerald said when he heard the news. "Maybe she can join the Velvet Underground."

Carnival's first album, "Step Right Up," was released in mid-December and enjoyed slow but steady sales. The first side offered four of Aaron's songs, plus a rolling uptempo arrangement of Chuck Berry's "Promised Land" that showcased the band's tight four-part harmonies.

The band stretched out on the second side, which featured one of Gerald's long instrumentals, one of Patrick's humorous folktunes and a marathon cover of John Lee Hooker's "Boom Boom."

"The Dead Don't Have to Worry" was released as a single and got some play on Top Forty AM stations across the country. Carnival got more exposure on the FM side of the dial when free-format DJs started spinning the longer tracks on Side Two.

Critics praised the record as a strong first effort. Aaron enjoyed reading the reviews, which compared Carnival to the Band, the Dead, the Allman Brothers, Steve Miller and even Led Zeppelin. From his own perspective, Carnival sounded like Carnival. He took the comparisons as a compliment, but was determined to make the Carnival sound so unique that in the future, new bands would be compared to them.

Armed with a louder sound system and a brighter light show, Carnival returned to the road for a tour that would last at least six months. This time, most of the gigs were in larger theaters and college halls that could hold three thousand or more. They gave the fans their money's worth, playing at least three hours on most occasions.

The band's growing reputation for putting on a great live show helped to sustain strong record sales throughout the year. "Step Right Up" never cracked the Top Ten, but by the end of the tour, which dragged on until late October, the record was certified Gold for selling half a million copies.

Back in San Francisco, the exhausted ensemble rested on its laurels for the rest of the year. Most of the band members took advantage of their fledgling celebrity status. They accepted VIP treatment at clubs and sometimes got to jam with other bands onstage. Patrick and Dewey, the most outgoing members of the band, took the lead in putting a public face on Carnival. They made on-air visits to the most popular FM stations on the West Coast and worked as guest artists on recordings by some of the biggest bands in the Bay area.

Large sums of money were finally flowing in and the members of Carnival had a good time spending it. Gerald bought the one thing he had always wanted: a Steinway grand piano. Patrick bought a small house in Santa Cruz and took up surfing. Dewey also bought a house in Santa Cruz but held on to the warehouse, which he hoped to one day transform into a nightclub. Sean David took off to Hawaii to vacation and maybe buy some land. His mother was from the islands and he spent part of his childhood there.

Garrett dropped thousands of dollars on new equipment, including a state-of-the-art Mini Moog synthesizer, and began to explore the new frontier of electronic music.

Fans and music journalists, though, wanted to know more about the enigmatic singer, songwriter and guitar wizard Aaron Lowe. By all accounts, he was the band's leader. He wrote and sang most of the band's original songs and was clearly the band's leader on stage. His guitar solos were becoming the stuff of legend. He got credits on the album for playing half a dozen different instruments. Yet he never gave interviews and was rarely seen at public events other than his own gigs.

Aaron's refusal to court the spotlight drove Claire up the wall. She wanted people to know he was responsible for the band's success. She wanted to dress up, hold his arm and be seen rubbing shoulders with the A-list.

"I have everything I want and more," he told her. "I'm earning a living doing what I love to do. I control my own fate. I have my freedom. I have plenty of money. And I want to hang onto my privacy, too. Is that so hard to understand?"

Partly to pacify Claire, he did allow himself one indulgence, a bright red 1970 Chevy Corvette convertible. It broke his heart to trade in the Mustang, but the old girl was looking her age. There was never enough time to properly care for his prized Pony, which he originally bought to piss off his mother. He had no garage so he was forced to park it on the street, where it was dinged and dented on a regular basis.

The Mustang also was, with the exception of his treasured Les Paul, the last physical remnant of his life in Las Vegas. His memories of Las Vegas rarely induced sentiment, but giving up the Mustang stirred a lot of emotions that he had long since suppressed.

The powerful, elegant 'Vette, though, was an effective cure for the blues. Aaron loved to cruise the Pacific Coast Highway. He'd pop the top and drive for hours, listening to the radio and dreaming up lyrics for new songs.

Sometimes, Claire would go with him, but he usually preferred to take his drives alone. Truth was, he often took a drive just to get away from her. He had thought more than once about breaking up with Claire. She was intelligent, fiercely loyal to him and dedicated to the band. She had proven to be a fantastic manager and had played a large role in their success.

Still, Claire was moody, manipulative and terribly needy. She wanted things he didn't. She wanted him to be something he wasn't. She was so obsessed with making Aaron a star that she never took satisfaction in her own accomplishments.

Guilt prevented Aaron from breaking up with Claire. He thought he owed her for getting him to this comfortable point in life. Besides, if they broke up, it might throw the entire Carnival operation into turmoil. The band had pledged to stick together and for Aaron, that meant sticking with Claire, too.

He recalled how some of his past career decisions had affected other people. His brother was dead and his mother had lost both her sons. Betty had been left alone to care for a sickly mother.

He was determined to make any personal sacrifice necessary to ensure that his new friends, these good people who depended on him for so much, would not suffer for his greed. So Aaron returned Claire's loyalty and kept writing songs. A second album was recorded, then a third. Each sold respectable numbers, but Carnival's growing fame was largely fostered on the concert stage. They were drawing bigger and bigger crowds, filling arenas in a few big cities and headlining large outdoor festivals in the summer.

By the end of 1972, Carnival had sold more than two million records and had performed for nearly as many people. The band had made half a dozen television appearances and had appeared on the cover of Rolling Stone and Creem magazines. They had crossed the Atlantic and made their debuts in Europe and Great Britain.

Life was good. *Almost too good*, was the feeling that nagged Aaron night and day. Whether it was a premonition, or merely experience, he knew what he knew and always tried to be prepared for life around the corner.

Chapter 39

When gossips are short on facts, they fill in the blanks with fiction. Aaron's reputation as a mystery man fueled the frenzy for information about him. People didn't know the truth so they made things up.

Tired of the rumors, lies and speculation, some of which were wilder than his reality, Aaron was forced to pour a little water on the fire. He strategically granted a few interviews and became an expert at deflecting the more probing questions about his personal life.

"Well, I've really led a dull life, to tell you the truth." That was one of his favorite lines. "I was just a regular kid leading an uneventful life. Moved around some. Small towns, only a few neighbors. Probably wouldn't even remember me."

Then he would change the subject to music and insist he was one among many who made Carnival so successful.

It seemed to work. He wasn't quite as mysterious any more. *He was boring.* The rumors about Aaron Lowe began to fade. None of the reporters had dug deep enough to unveil any inconsistencies in his story.

At least not yet.

Aaron sometimes wondered about the real Aaron Lowe. Was he ever a real person? The guy who sold him his fake papers back in 1966 said he stole names from infant obituaries published in newspapers all across the country. The documents were forged, not stolen. All Aaron knew for sure was that his new identity had never been questioned.

At least not yet.

Carnival continued to record and tour regularly for the

next three years. Record sales continued to take a back seat to ticket sales. The band could book multiple shows in some big cities and still not satisfy the demand.

Lenny suggested that some shorter, simpler songs might make better singles and increase their airplay on pop music stations. He also suggested that the fans wanted fewer covers and more original songs.

This incensed Gerald, who said the band wouldn't compromise its purpose just to sell a few more records. Aaron agreed. Carnival was popular enough for his needs. They had plenty of money and fame. The last thing Aaron wanted was to be the Beatles and become so popular that their concerts were drowned out by screaming fans.

It was Patrick who came up with the suggestion that led to Carnival's best-selling record.

"If they don't like what we do in the studio, then let's record what we do onstage," he said.

"*Why didn't I think of that?*" everyone else said.

"Carnival Live in '75" was released in early 1976 and went on to sell nearly four million copies in North America alone. It was a double album containing more than eighty minutes of classic Carnival in its prime.

"A *value-priced* double album," Patrick always liked to emphasize.

DJs around the country were more than happy to play live tracks from one of the world's most accomplished live bands. Carnival's fan base seemed to triple overnight. Worldwide sales of the record topped six million.

Riding the wave of unprecedented popularity, the band toured nonstop for the next eighteen months. Carnival was on top of the world. Three sold-out nights at Madison Square Garden. Two more at the Spectrum in Philadelphia. Two-nighters in Chicago, Detroit, Dallas, Atlanta, Miami and Memphis. Ten dates in Canada.

The highlight of the tour was a festival on Cape Cod that drew 150,000 fans. Carnival headlined the all-day event, which was filmed for a documentary feature.

Then the band went back to Europe for a dozen shows, followed by twelve more in Japan and the Far East.

Completing their circle of the globe, Carnival returned to California for three shows at the Los Angeles Forum, followed by stops in San Diego, Portland and Seattle. Finally, they made a triumphant return to San Francisco, where they made their debut at the Cow Palace. Over the next two weeks, they performed ten sold-out concerts to more than 100,000 of their friends and neighbors at the legendary arena.

The tour ended just in time. While the hometown fans celebrated everything that was Carnival, the band members were at each other's throats. Old friends Dewey Davis and Sean David argued constantly. Gerald Abernathy and Garrett Townsend accused one another of screwing up the arrangements.

Claire was a constant annoyance and Aaron was tired of the other guys yelling at him to "handle her." He tried to avoid the whole scene by finding places to hide in every city. It got to the point that no one ever saw him except for the sound check and the show.

Worst of all, Patrick had reverted to his old habits. He had also picked up a new one: cocaine. He'd snort a few lines before a show, play brilliantly, then swallow quaaludes when he couldn't get to sleep. When he couldn't get his hands on drugs, he drank Vodka straight out of the bottle.

By the time they got back to San Francisco, his playing had started to slip. He even collapsed one night after the set and couldn't play the encore. Everyone agreed that Patrick had finally crossed the line and it was time to let him know.

Aaron and Gerald were still trying to drum up the courage to confront Patrick when the tour finally came to a merciful end. Patrick just needed to rest. So did they all.

The band had spent eight years scaling the summit of stardom. They had worked hard. They had stuck together. They had achieved wealth and fame together. They had gotten a little older together.

Now, they agreed that the best way to stick together was to spend a little time apart. Claire reluctantly issued a press release informing the public that Carnival would not record or tour for at least a year.

Chapter 40

As Carnival sat out the rest of 1977 and all of 1978, the music industry experienced monumental changes. "Classic" rock 'n' roll bands already were on the ropes in the fight against disco. Donna Summer, the Bee Gees and Chic were keeping dance music on the top of the charts. Even the Stones were dabbling in disco and Rod Stewart was strutting around like a dancehall queen, asking "Do You Think I'm Sexy?"

Now, a flood of punk and new wave bands were coming up fast from behind with an admirably minimalist approach to making records. And the kids were eating it up.

The generation of bands from the '60s and '70s that indulged in marathon jams, endless solos and other forms of excess were being dismissed as dinosaurs. Dazzling the fans with musical virtuosity didn't work anymore. The hottest new music was coming from bands like the Ramones, who only seemed to know three chords, and the B-52s, whose lead guitarist played with four strings.

The loyal Carnival lovers didn't give in to fashion and patiently waited out their favorite band's hiatus. The most faithful fans began to call themselves "Carnies." Some of the Carnies had seen a hundred or more Carnival concerts, following the band from town to town and even country to country. They pitched tents together as close to the concert as they could and the encampments often looked like actual Carnivals.

The Carnies kept in touch with each other by holding conventions and publishing newsletters dedicated to all things Carnival. They sold and swapped bootleg tapes of concerts through a special page of classified ads. They shared reams of rumors that the band was about to reunite. Sometimes, hundreds of fans would show up at some club because they heard the band was going to do a surprise set.

Claire subscribed to many of the newsletters to keep her finger on the pulse of Carnival's constituency. The band's temporary retirement had her bouncing off the walls. She was scared to death that the fans would lose interest if the band remained in neutral much longer. The newsletters indicated otherwise. Still, she knew how fickle the public could be. Sooner or later, people would forget about Carnival and they would have to start from scratch.

Current events played a feature role in bringing the band back together. A nuclear accident at Three-Mile Island in Pennsylvania had ignited a firestorm of protest across the country in early 1979. Claire had been burning nervous energy by getting involved with many political causes, especially the environment and the no-nukes movement. Most of her anti-nuclear efforts had been focused on protesting the proliferation of nuclear missiles during the Cold War.

The accident at Three-Mile Island, which occurred as "The China Syndrome" was dramatizing a nuclear-meltdown scenario in movie theaters from coast to coast, brought the anti-nuclear movement into the heartland. Even some of the more conservative Americans, who had been reluctant to protest against the government, were willing to protest a private industry spewing toxic waste into their backyards.

The movement gained more momentum when famous musicians, actors and other celebrities attached themselves to the cause. Benefit concerts were being planned in many large cities around the country. Claire was asked to organize one in San Francisco.

Naturally, she thought this would be a great excuse to bring Carnival back together. Aaron agreed the timing was perfect and the cause was worthy. He helped Claire plead her case to the rest of the band.

Patrick had a new girlfriend, Sheila, who was helping him to manage his bad habits. Aaron had stuck up for Patrick when some of the band members wanted him fired. Now that he was back on his feet, he was fiercely loyal to Aaron and would deny him nothing.

Dewey agreed to do the benefit and nothing more. "We'll see about the rest," he said. Sean followed Dewey's lead as he always did, even when they were pissed at each other.

Gerald and Garrett were still feuding. Gerald finally committed to the benefit, so Garrett decided to sit it out.

That left Aaron to double on the organ, which added to his lore as Carnival made its triumphant return at the Cow Palace. The band quickly shook off the rust and fell into the old groove. They played for three hours and took four encores. The Carnies were in ecstasy.

The explosive performance convinced the skeptics in and out of the band that Carnival still had the goods. One reviewer said it was like they had never left.

The only obvious change seemed to be the absence of Dewey's trademark afro. He'd been thinning up top for years and finally gave in to heredity. He showed up for the first rehearsal with a smooth, shaved skull.

"You know, you ain't so big and bad without the 'fro, bro," Patrick teased. "I don't know why I let you intimidate me all those years."

"I still got two feet to kick your ass with," Dewey said.

"I don't know, you're looking a little chunky, too. You can't kick an ass you can't catch," Patrick said.

"I'll just wait till you get drunk and trip over your own ego," Dewey said. "Then your boney white ass is mine."

Gerald had lost a lot of his hair as well. He didn't bother covering it up. With his receding hairline and wire-rim glasses, he looked more like an accountant than a rock star. Sean David covered *his* bald spot with a fashionable French beret.

Aaron remained trim and fit. His long, wiry blonde hair

was still as thick as his dark red beard. The wrinkles around his eyes, in contrast, gave away his well-over-thirty status. He always looked like he just spent a month in the hot desert sun. Worry lines, Claire called them.

Claire never stopped looking great. She made it her business to be beautiful. She could pass for ten years younger and scowled at people who asked her age.

They were all over thirty and facing fierce competition from regiments of hungry young bands who were warned not to trust their elders. The benefit concert had put them back on the map, but was there enough interest out there to sustain a full-fledged comeback?

The Carnie cult guaranteed that the band would sell a lot of tickets. Plans were under way for a big tour that would begin at the Cow Palace on New Year's Eve. Carnival would then load the trucks and launch a nationwide tour that would last at least six months.

Garrett finally caved in and agreed to re-enlist. Aaron convinced Gerald to be a team player and extend an olive branch to his keyboard rival.

"Remember what you said," Aaron told him. "We can only make it if we stick together."

Aaron had accumulated enough songs during the layoff to fill half a dozen new albums. The best of the bunch would be among the first new original Carnival songs to be recorded in more than five years. The new Carnival album, "Answering the Call," was released in November of 1979.

Critics offered faint praise for the record, noting some "interesting new songs from Aaron Lowe" while they huffed again how the band sounded exactly the same as it had 10 years ago. Overall, "It's another example of why Carnival was always known better for its live shows."

Oddly enough, the album did produce the band's first top-40 single. Aaron wrote "Hiding From the Sun" to explain why they took such a long break.

Spend your day in darkness
Waiting for the night
Spend the night inside a room
With blinding colored light
Try to sleep but something tries
To keep you from your dream
Try to feel but nothing's real
It all gets so obscene

Every day it's getting harder
Just to get it done
Tough to see the light when you are
Hiding from the Sun

Take a long vacation
Find a private sandy shore
Try to find a reason
Not to do it anymore
Maybe you can find a way
To make it on your own
Take a chance to learn just what
It means to be alone

Every day it's getting harder
Just to get it done
Tough to see the light when you are
Hiding from the Sun

The haunting ballad hit broke into the Top Twenty just before Christmas. Unfortunately, album sales lagged behind the single. Once again, Carnival would have to make its biggest impact from the concert stage.

"Think it's too soon to do another live album?" Patrick wise-cracked.

Claire countered the new record's commercial failure with some savvy management. She forged an informal alliance between the band's management and the Carnies. The name, address and phone number of the official Carnie Club was printed in the liner notes of the new album and she donated band merchandise to the organization for giveaway promotions.

It was good business and gave rise to the most loyal assembly of fans any band could hope for. Newspapers, magazines and TV news reporters began to document and analyze the unique relationship between Carnival and its Carnies. This meant more free publicity for the tour. Demand for tickets became so high that some of the promoters were talking about moving the shows into stadiums instead of arenas.

This development troubled Aaron, who had never been comfortable with the move up to arenas. He had grown up playing in a lounge with his audience close enough to touch. The sound was terrible in most arenas and the crowd was as distant as a rumor. For these and other reasons, he referred to the arenas as "the pits." Now, he was balking at the prospect of jumping from "the pits" to "the canyons."

"We all agreed that playing the smaller places was a lot more fun," he argued. "We all hate playing shows where the first row was thirty feet from the stage and the last row was on the other side of town. We hate the acoustics in the pits. It's only going to be worse in stadiums."

Aaron, though, was the only one left who valued music more than money. The rest of Carnival could not resist the temptation to make the move up to stadiums. It made no sense to play three arena shows in a town that could offer you the same fee for one stadium show. Even Claire broke ranks with Aaron and agreed that playing stadiums was the logical move.

Aaron reluctantly went along with the majority. Carnival's 1980 World Tour began in March at The Los Angeles Forum. The tour continued to play the pits until June, when the warmer weather allowed for stadium shows and even larger outdoor field festivals.

The biggest concert of the tour was a Labor Day Jam at massive JFK Stadium in Philadelphia. Ninety thousand fans packed the retired football stadium for a final celebration of summer.

It was everything Aaron hated about trying to make meaningful music in these mammoth, acoustically challenged temples. The remnants of a nor'easter were still whipping the Delaware Valley. Temperatures were in the fifties until midday, when a bright sun came out and glared into the eyes of the opening bands. Two hours later, a dangerous thunderstorm came from the west and blacked out the sky. Lightning broke through the sudden darkness and the show had to be stopped for more than an hour.

No matter what the weather was doing, the sound kept bouncing around the stadium and the multiple echoes completely wrecked the mix. The weather, the delays and the annoying acoustics were talking a toll on the crowd as well. It had been a long day for them. Traffic to the stadium was terrible. Anyone who wasn't parked by 10 a.m. probably missed the first hour of the concert, which presented four other bands before Carnival took the stage at 8 p.m.

Standing for hours in the rain and wind, many of the fans passed the time with too many drugs and too much alcohol. The medical tent was filled with casualties of both by mid-afternoon and medics were unable to cope with the overflow.

Carnival did its best to comfort the fans. The set was determined by the results of a postcard poll that let Carnies vote for their favorite songs. They played on a massive stage colored brightly with a space-age light show. Special FAA permits had to be obtained for the red and green laser beams they fired high into the night sky.

Aaron loathed every minute of it. The comfort of the band and its audience had been ignored in the pursuit of spectacle and economic efficiency.

"This is a good way to make a quick buck," Aaron said.

"But people aren't going to go home and tell other people what a good time they had. They'll just bitch and moan about the lousy weather, the lousy sound and how long it took to get home. This is all about the here and now. The next time, the fans may think twice about coming back. And I swear to God, next time Carnival plays a canyon, I won't be there, either."

Claire tried to pacify Aaron by adding a few smaller shows to the end of the tour. The finale would be two shows at the Cow Palace, which Aaron always enjoyed because he could sleep in his own bed after the show.

The rest of the band responded as well. Carnival played its very best at each Cow Palace show. They dumped the lasers, the custom, experimental "Tryptophonic" sound system that didn't work and just rocked the joint with a stack of Marshall column speakers.

After the final concert, the band lounged in the dressing room, celebrating the end of a long hard journey. Even Aaron was in a festive mood. He shared a bottle of champagne with Patrick without giving his friend the usual lecture about old habits.

He had sunk deep into the corner of a soft old couch when he saw one of the roadies pushing toward him through the party. It was Jerry, the "weightlifter guy," who could lift the Marshalls all by himself.

"Aaron, you taking visitors?" he said.

"That depends on the visitor," Aaron said. "Is he friend or foe? What does he offer for an audience with the Carnival King?"

Everyone laughed, not at the joke but rather the idea of Aaron actually making a joke. He'd been a pill ever since the tour began.

"I don't know, never seen him before," Jerry said. "Says to tell you Mr. Rush is here to see him."

CHAPTER 41

"*Mr. Rush!*" Patrick said. "Far out. Is he related to *Dr. Feelgood?*"

Then he looked at Aaron, who had gone pale and quiet.

"Dude, are you OK? This guy from the I.R.S. or something?"

"I'm cool," Aaron said as he sat up and looked toward the door. "Old friend."

He turned to Claire, who was watching him closely.

"Jerry, where is he? Is he here?"

"He's outside by the stage. Want me to bring him in?"

"No … I'll come out."

Jerry led his boss out of the dressing room and down the hallway leading to the stage. Claire jumped up and followed them. "An old friend?" she said, looking curious beyond words. "Can I tag along?"

Aaron wanted to meet his former mentor by himself, but his mind was too cluttered to think of an excuse to get rid of her. He took Claire's hand and followed Jerry. When they entered the rotunda, he saw Andy's remarkably familiar face standing patiently among a crowd of fans hoping to get backstage.

The crowd began to scream and surge when they recognized their favorite guitar payer. Aaron stopped short, then motioned for Jerry to bring the man back to him.

When Aaron and Andy Rush came face to face, both of them forgot how to speak. Claire cheerfully broke the silence and offered her hand. "Hi, I'm Claire Hall. We'll all be old before Aaron introduces us."

The man extended his hand to Claire, then to Aaron. "Hi,

I'm Andy Rush," he said. Then he turned back to Aaron, smiled and shook his head. "Hey there, little Mozart. You remember your old teacher?"

Aaron kept gripping Andy's hand and inspected him for signs of the years past. Bald on top, Andy had a ponytail in back, liberally streaked with gray, but the face was unmistakable.

"I'm just a little shocked, you know?" Aaron said. "It's been a long time."

"Ah, so you do remember," Andy said. "You keeping up with your old lessons? I guess you must be. I hear you make a pretty good living doing this."

Claire held tightly onto Aaron's arm and studied both men.

"You were Aaron's music teacher? Really?" she asked.

"Well, I was the teacher, but he probably taught me more than I taught him. He was a natural if there ever was one."

"This is truly amazing," Aaron said. "Did you see the show?"

"I've seen a lot of your shows," Andy said. "Tonight was one of the best. You guys have something special. You should be really proud."

They had to shout to be heard above the noisy crowd.

"We should get out of here," Aaron said. "Go someplace where we can talk. Do you have a couple of … weeks?"

Andy laughed. "It's already past my bedtime, but it's not a school night. What did you have in mind?"

"Why don't we just go home?" Claire said. "It's a beautiful night. We can order some pizza, drink some wine and hang out on the balcony."

Aaron was thinking more about a cafe or some other quiet place where he and Andy could talk alone, but it was clear that Claire wasn't going to miss this for the world. Home was as good a place as any.

Back at the apartment, they skipped the pizza and opened a bottle of red wine. Andy and Aaron spoke in circles on the balcony as Claire sat quietly in the corner. Andy caught on that Claire didn't know anything about Willie Taylor, Weekend Willie or Las Vegas. He framed his questions by asking what Aaron had done since he graduated from high school.

After about an hour, Claire stood up and said her good-nights. "I can tell you guys want to talk alone."

She kissed Aaron and turned to go inside. "You boys stay up as late as you want. I'm exhausted. Andy, it was nice to meet you. You can sleep here tonight if you like. Aaron, there's fresh pillows and blankets in the front closet. You can make a bed for him on the couch."

Aaron and Andy smoked cigarettes and drank some more wine as they heard Claire prepare for bed. When the lights in the bedroom dimmed, Aaron got up and moved closer to his old friend. They spoke in hushed tones.

"I gather she doesn't know?" Andy said.

"Nobody knows," Aaron said. "I'm not sure I believe any of it happened. It's like a book that I read about somebody else's life. Some kind of tragedy. Very disturbing while you're reading it, then you reach the end and look for another story to read."

"And no one ever found you? No one ever found out?"

"Amazing, huh? It took a couple of years before I could sleep through the night. I kept waiting for that knock on the door. Or that guy who comes up on you from behind. That's why I hate crowds. So many people out there. Who is the one? Who might recognize me? Who's going to follow me into the alley?"

"Aaron ... do I call you Aaron?"

"Absolutely. Willie Taylor died a long time ago ... so did his brother."

Aaron thought of his brother and started to choke up.

"I'm sorry, Aaron. I didn't mean to open old wounds."

"No ... no, I'm the one who's sorry. I'm really glad to see you. You just kind of took me by surprise. I'm really, truly glad to see you."

Aaron went back inside and opened another bottle of wine. A wave of questions filled his head.

"How did you find me, anyway?" he asked.

"*Ha*! You kids always think you can fool the teacher," Andy said. "The first time I heard one of your records, I said, Hey, that's Willie Taylor!"

Andy smiled and filled his glass. "No, not really. To tell you the truth, I never heard a Carnival record until that live one you put out. Wasn't really my kind of music. I still go for jazz, you know?

"But that live album, that was something else. A lot of my friends were playing it. 'Listen to these guys,' they told me. 'Listen to the improvisation. These guys can really play. Especially the lead guitar player.'

"So I finally got into it and started to look at the photos on the cover. And this guitar player looks kind of familiar. And the more I listened, the more it's driving me crazy. Why does this sound so familiar? Then I'm reading the liner notes and I see that this guy Aaron Lowe plays every instrument in the band at one time or another. I couldn't help but wonder, but I didn't think much more about it until I see this other photo of you playing. Close up. And I know it's you."

Aaron's eyes asked. "What exactly was it that gave me away?"

"The guitar, man. The Les Paul. I know my guitars. You did an amazing job hiding yourself, Willie. I'm sorry, I mean Aaron. You don't look anything like you used to. But the guitar hasn't aged a day. You took really good care of it. I could have picked it out of a Gibson warehouse.

"Damn, I've had that thing almost twenty years. It's like a part of me."

Andy gave him a serious look. "So is Willie Taylor."

Aaron hunched his shoulders and looked out towards the bay. "I know. It's just hard to think about. I *had* to turn my back on all of that. All of you. I didn't want to, you know. I was going to leave town anyway, but I never thought I wouldn't be able to go back ... like, ever."

"I understand ... Aaron," Andy said, pausing before emphasizing his student's new name. "You don't have to justify what you did."

"Did Betty understand?"

Andy shifted in his seat. Time to get comfortable. They were wading deep into the unhappy past.

"It was hard for her, but she understood. Eventually."

"Did you guys talk much? Did you stay friends?"

"Yes we did, for a long time. She did have a hard time of it, Aaron. She felt guilty about breaking up with you. She wondered if things would have been different if she hadn't thrown you out. She said she didn't do enough."

"I cheated on her. She had every right to dump me."

"Having the right to dump you didn't make it any easier for her. What you did didn't make her love you any less. She loved you something awful, and she never wanted anything more than to be with you. She just thought you needed to figure that out on your own. She prayed you would. And that you would come back. When you didn't, and she never even heard from you, she feared the worst. That maybe Carlo's boys caught up with you. I worried about that a few times myself."

Aaron tried to pace on the tiny balcony but there wasn't enough room. He felt like he was trapped in a cage.

"I guess you guys must have talked a lot. I'm glad that you had each other. I didn't have *anyone* to confide in."

"You know, Aaron, if you don't want to talk about this, I'll understand," Andy said, his voice suddenly stern. "But if all I'm doing is making you feel sorry for yourself, then maybe it's time for me to go. From where I'm standing, things worked out for you pretty well. Some people weren't as lucky as you."

"I'm sorry. That's not what I mean. I want to know."

Andy stood up and stretched his legs. "I'm sorry, too. I'm

not here to lecture you. I'm glad you're living a good life. I'm proud of what you have accomplished as a musician. But you have to understand. Betty and I kind of fell in together and formed a little support group. She needed a lot of help after you left, and I was the only one left that she could trust. I leaned on her some as well. We were very close. She means a lot to me."

Slightly surprised and very curious, Aaron studied Andy's face as he spoke so warmly about his first love, perhaps the only true love Aaron would ever know.

"Did you guys ever think about, you know, *getting together*?" Aaron asked.

Andy laughed. "No, Aaron, we never became romantic. That wasn't possible."

"Why not?"

"Aaron, I'm gay. I thought you would have figured that out a long time ago."

Aaron felt like an idiot. He was always too self-absorbed to notice the feelings of other people. Even his closest friends.

"So you see, it was hard for me, too. I loved you too, Aaron. I was always conflicted because I was your teacher. And you and Betty seemed so happy, at least until things got out of hand. I knew we would never be together, but I loved you just the same. I still do."

Aaron lit a cigarette and took a deep drag. "I had no idea. You were my best friend."

"Relax. That was always enough for me. Friends was fine. Besides, back then I was never very comfortable with my sexuality. I thought I was some sort of deviant. Got to the point where I avoided intimate relationships, period. The last thing I wanted was to bring you over to my side of the fence. You and Betty were so happy, and I was genuinely happy for both of you. Anyone could see you two belonged together."

Aaron began to choke up again. How could he have left such beautiful people behind without so much as a phone call?

"And look how it all turned out. God, you must think I'm horrible. Here I am, big fucking rock star, traveling the world, and I do nothing for the people who made it possible. You guys were there when I needed you. You saved my life.

"You have to understand, Andy. I was scared, man. My brother was dead and a bunch of fucking maniacs were after me. I was wanted for murder. I didn't know what to do. I was afraid that if I even sent a postcard, they would find me.

"For a long time, I told myself that getting in touch with you guys would put you in danger. After a while, though, I realized I just felt too guilty. I had made such a mess of things. Betty, you, you'd both be better off without me. I didn't deserve you. If I came back, all I would do is screw your life up more than I had already.

"You know, from time to time, I would think, 'maybe now.' But as time went by, I came to believe that Willie Taylor was dead. And what good would it do to have him come back to life?

"I'm sorry, I'm so sorry for all of it."

"Willie, you made your share of mistakes, but no more than most of us. You weren't responsible for your brother's death. You didn't deserve to have your life ripped away from you like that. You had the right to at least try and work things out with Betty.

"You did what you had to do to survive. You made a new life for yourself. That's more than a lot of us could have done in your situation. You're entitled to enjoy your success."

Aaron was exhausted, but there was so much more that he needed to know.

"So, did Betty make a new life for herself?"

Andy winced as though the question were a punch.

"She's quite a woman, your Betty," he said. "But it's never been easy for her. She took such good care of her mother for years. Amanda finally died about five years ago, and Betty went a little crazy. Having someone to take care of kept her focused. After Amanda was gone, she went right out and looked for someone else. She ended up with this really shitty guy, Mitch. Some kind of Teamster. He would get drunk, beat her up and then beg for forgiveness. She got a night job as a blackjack dealer just so she wouldn't be around when he came home.

"Then, about two years ago, she had a baby, a boy. Had to give up her job. She was really depressed. Mitch didn't like her talking to me, either. He came home one night when I was over and he thought we were having an affair. She told him I was gay and that made things worse. He threatened to kick my faggot ass if he ever saw me with her again.

"Anyway, I was ready to get out of Vegas myself. Have you been back at all? It's so much bigger, so much more crowded. Gaming Control chased all the mobsters out of town. That opened the door for the banks and big corporations. And Howard Hughes. All that money in the middle of the fucking desert."

"So you moved?"

"Yeah, I moved to San Francisco about a year ago." Andy laughed. "I got a job teaching music theory at San Francisco State. I'm a professor now. Much better situation all around. Should have done it years ago."

"That's great! So you've been in town for a year?"

"Yeah, I live in the Mission."

"And it took you this long to look me up?"

"Well, I had some relocation issues of my own, Willie. *Aaron*. Sorry, that's going to take some getting used to. And besides, you spend a lot of time on the road. You're a hard man to pin down."

"Have you talked to Betty since you moved? How's she doing now?"

"I've only talked to her a couple of times in the last year. She said everything is fine, but I doubt it."

"She had a baby, huh? *Wow*."

"Yeah, Travis. A real cute kid, just like his mother."

"Have you told her anything about me?"

"No. I thought about it, though. I didn't know if it would make things better or worse. For either of you. You both have your own lives, and your own relationships. That's one of the reasons I wanted to talk to you. Now you know everything and I'm off the hook. You can decide for yourself whether or not to contact her."

"Do you think I should?"

"Whoa, man, I have no idea. It's a unique situation. And it's been a long time. I don't like keeping things from her, but like I said, we don't talk all that much anymore. I'll say this much, though. She probably could use a friend."

"I don't know if she would really think of me as a friend."

"I guess you may be right about that. I'm not sure Claire would appreciate it, either."

Claire! Aaron hoped that she was sleeping soundly. She would have enough questions for him in the morning. He would need some time to decide how much to tell her.

"Tell me about her," Andy said. "She's the manager, right? She's a big part of your operation?"

"Yeah, she's done a really good job," Aaron said. "She's great with the details. She knows a lot of people and she can always get them to go along with whatever she wants."

"Does that include you?"

Aaron didn't answer.

"I'm sorry," Andy said. "That's none of my business. I just picked up a vibe from you guys that seemed a little off. You've been together how long?"

"Almost twelve years."

"And yet you never told her about your past? I'm sorry. Again, none of my business."

"No, you're right. It is a little strange. She's a good person, she's just ... I'm just ... I don't know. We're more like partners. We're used to each other. We take care of each other."

"I'll bet if I asked her the same question, I'd get a totally different answer. She's crazy about you. I can tell. She'd do anything for you."

"And I would do anything for her."

"Except be honest with her."

"Yeah, except that. What am I supposed to do, tell her I've been a fugitive all these years? I'm trying not to screw up her life like I did with Betty, OK?"

Andy shook his head and looked out over the bay.

"You got a great view here. All I can see from my place is more houses that look just like mine. And it's probably time I got back there. Let you get some sleep. You look tired."

Aaron had to agree. "Look, can we pick this up tomorrow? There's so much more I want to ask you."

They slipped off the patio, then tiptoed quietly through the bedroom, being careful not to wake Claire. At the front door, Aaron remembered another subject that couldn't wait.

"Andy, one more thing," Aaron said. "My mother ..."

Andy shook his head. "I don't really know. I would see her here and there, but we never even waved hello. After the big boys who ran the Full House left town, I never saw her again. I assume she went back to Chicago with Patsy. I'm sorry. I wish I could tell you more."

Aaron shook Andy's hand, then hugged him like a long-lost relative. "Don't be sorry, man. I appreciate everything you've done for me. I really needed ... *something*. A friend. An old friend. Man, when was the last time I could refer to anyone as an old friend?"

"Well, Aaron, any friend of Willie Taylor's is a friend of mine." Andy wrote down his phone number on a slip of paper and Aaron did the same for him. "Any time you want to talk. Or anything else. Just give me a call. Hey, maybe we can get together some time and make some music. You could teach me how to play some of those big hits of yours."

Late the next morning, Aaron and Claire quietly sipped their coffee at the Gold Mine Café. Neither one bothered to look at the menu. Finally, after the waitress came around for refills, Claire cautiously broke the silence.

"You must be really tired," she said, stroking the back of his hand with her fingers. "How late did you guys stay up?"

"I don't know," Aaron said. "I could see the sun was coming up."

"You must have had a lot to talk about. How long has it been since you talked to him?"

"Not since I moved here. A long, long time."

"Did you guys have some sort of falling out?"

"Not really. Claire, it's kind of complicated. There's a lot about me that you don't know."

"I'm quite aware of that, Aaron. I always thought that was the way you wanted it. I figured you would tell me in your own time. I just didn't figure it would take you this long."

"Yeah, well, I'm sorry about that." Maybe it was time to get it off his chest. Andy had made a good point. If he cared for her enough to spend twelve years together, she deserved to know everything.

Aaron and Claire finished their coffee and headed for the park. They walked for hours as Aaron filled Claire in on the life and times of Willie Taylor Jr., from the Kiddie Cowboy to Weekend Willie, the one-hit wonder and crown prince of the Regal Lounge.

"And these criminals, they're still after you?" she asked quietly, trying desperately to look calm.

"I don't know, really," he said. "Andy said they got kicked out of Vegas. I don't know if they are looking for me, but I'll bet they haven't forgotten what happened. I wouldn't want them to find me, that's for sure."

"And the police?"

"Same thing, I imagine. It's been so long, Claire. I don't know what to make of all this."

"Why do you think he's reaching out to you after all this time? What does he want?"

"I don't think he *wants* anything. He's a very close friend, Claire. He's done so much for me. He's the one who gave me the Les Paul. Hell, I owe him my life."

"And now, maybe he wants you to do something for him?"

"Claire, why do you have to be so suspicious of everyone? He's my friend. Is that so hard to believe? If he wanted something, *anything*, I'd gladly give it to him. I hope he does. He's earned it a thousand times over."

"I just worry about some guy who comes out of nowhere, who knows you're rich and famous, and he knows all this stuff about you. Stuff that could get you in big trouble. Stuff that could get you thrown in jail, or even killed."

"He's not just some guy, and he's not going to blackmail me, Claire! Jesus! It blows my mind that you would even think of such a thing!"

Claire sat on a bench and began to sob.

"I'm sorry, I don't mean to be like this," she said. "This is just a lot to take in all at once. And the first thing I thought of is how he could hurt you. I'm afraid, Aaron. Everything you've worked for. He could ruin everything."

"Claire, that's not going to happen. I promise you. But you have to understand, no one else can know about this. You have to promise me you won't say anything to anyone."

Claire pushed him away with both hands. Her fear had turned to anger.

"You have all this trust in him, and you're worried about me giving up your precious little secrets. How am I supposed to feel about *that*?"

It never ceased to amaze Aaron how annoying Claire could be, especially when she was right. He put his arms around her and held tight until the tension drained from her body.

"I'm sorry, Claire," he said. "That's not what I meant at all. Believe me, I understand how hard it is to hear all of this. I lived through it. And it's been a lifetime since I could bear to think about it. I still don't want to think about some of it. Hell, I almost forgot to ask him about my mother."

"I thought your parents were dead."

"Yeah, well, it's going to take a long time to tell you everything. I left my mother behind in Vegas. I never knew my father. Try to understand. I never meant to deceive you. It was the only way I could deal with the past and make a new life. The life we have together."

"I just don't want to lose you, Aaron. Can you understand that?"

"Nothing bad is going to happen, Claire. To me, or to you, or to us. I promise. OK?"

Claire curled up in his embrace and held on for dear life.

"I won't let anything happen to us," she said. "*I won't.*"

CHAPTER 42

Over the next few weeks, Aaron and Andy spent a lot of time catching up, hashing out the old days as they forged a brand-new friendship.

They talked a lot about music. Fourteen years of bands and trends had come and gone since they had last swapped records. They both worshipped Jimi Hendrix. Had he lived, Andy was certain Hendrix would have been playing jazz fusion today.

Andy hated most of the California bands. What could Aaron say about that? He was in charge of one.

Andy was prejudiced in favor of the modern bands that embraced the limitless possibilities of jazz. Weather Report, Chick Corea's Return to Forever. Any band that Miles Davis put together. Even Frank Zappa. Most of it left Aaron bored.

They agreed that punk and new wave were fads, and that real music lovers would come back to the bands with real musicians. There were some exceptions, though. English groups like Rockpile and Graham Parker and the Rumour were throwbacks to the raucous rock-and-roll, rhythm-and-blues spirit of the fifties and sixties. And that guy from Dire Straits could really play the guitar.

They both appreciated how George Thorogood and the Destroyers were turning a new generation on to the blues. Andy told Aaron about Triple Threat, a band he'd seen in Austin that featured an incredible young blues guitar player named Stevie Ray Vaughan.

"Better watch out for this kid, little Mozart," Andy told Aaron. "You ain't the teenage prodigy you used to be."

Andy's teasing touched a nerve. Aaron had been holding

his breath since he left Las Vegas. Now that Andy had brought him up to date, Aaron felt the last fourteen years go whizzing by like a summer squall. In just a few weeks, he went from a young man who was robbed of his childhood to a middle-aged music fossil who couldn't remember when he became an adult.

"You're not quite middle-aged," Andy said. "Take a look at me. This is middle age."

Aaron had promised Claire that nothing bad would happen. Still, things had changed. Aaron was a different person. He was finally confidant that no one was looking for him, at least not very hard. He was more outgoing. He'd spend the morning and afternoon talking to Andy about his future plans, then come home and talk to Claire about the old days.

Of course, Claire could only talk to Aaron about these confidential matters. When friends asked her what had gotten into Aaron, she had to lie. Sometimes she told them he was wiring up on cocaine.

Aaron hoped Claire would appreciate being in on his most intimate secrets. That he trusted her enough to open all his baggage right in front of her.

Instead, she became more tense and angry than ever. She hated being the third wheel as he frolicked with the "Ghost of Christmas Past," which was what she called Andy. She hated having to keep Aaron's secrets from everybody else.

"I feel like fucking Lois Lane," she said. "Only I'm in love with your secret identity."

Aaron didn't dare point out the inaccuracy of the Lois Lane allusion. He could tell Claire was having a hard time. She avoided Andy like he was a disease and sulked when Aaron left to spend time with him.

"Can't you find him a boyfriend or something?" she would ask. "It shouldn't be that hard in this town."

Could it be that Claire was jealous of Andy? Or was she jealous of a past that she had played no part in? Aaron remembered his bad trip at Big Sur years ago. Did she remember the names he had probably shouted out that night?

Aaron held back the more intimate details about Betty and Tina. Betty was just some girl he had already broken up with. Tina was only discussed in the context of the trouble she caused.

He was sure Claire would eventually press him for details about the women in his past, but for now, her mind was already on overload. That was his fault and he realized that he was taking his present lover for granted. He was so preoccupied of late with his past that he was ignoring his present.

The weather was turning as cold as Claire, so Aaron suggested they should spend some time in a warm place. They accepted a longstanding open invitation to visit Sean David in Hawaii. Sean had bought an entire pineapple plantation in Oahu, complete with a colonial estate and a cozy carriage house where visitors could enjoy some privacy.

Claire was ecstatic. They so rarely traveled when the band was not touring. She loved the idea of having Aaron all to herself. Ironically, Sean was in San Francisco, so they got to stay in the luxurious main house.

The two-week vacation stretched into a month. Claire didn't even bother wearing bathing suits on the private beach. She laughed when Aaron didn't follow suit. He feared sunburn in sensitive places.

They swam, explored the beach and took naps together in a huge hammock on the shady back porch, which stretched from one end of the house to the other. They smoked some powerful "Maui Waui" and drank rum with fresh pineapple juice while watching the sun rise over the Pacific.

They made love on the beach, but they couldn't find a comfortable position in the hammock. Fortunately, the guestroom had a king-size waterbed and an even better view of the ocean. Once they got the hang of the waterbed, they would retire right after dinner and spend the rest of the night building up an appetite for breakfast.

"Can we buy our own place here, Aaron?" Claire asked. "Do we have that much money?"

"I don't know about a place like this," he said. "Sean has every dime invested in this operation. But I'm sure we could afford something nice."

"Now I understand why Sean spends as much time here as he can. It's like a fantasy."

"And the pineapple farm makes a nice profit. No doubt, he's got the life down here," Aaron agreed. "But you know, it's time we got back to work. We were supposed to start recording last week."

"I know, I know, but it's not like the rest of the guys are in any hurry," Claire said. "They haven't served us with a subpoena or anything, have they?"

"No, but I'm getting a little itchy. Andy and I had been working on some new songs and ... " Aaron tried and failed to stop himself mid-sentence. He looked at Claire. She was already up and packing.

"Fine, we can leave tonight and be home by morning," she said. *Oh, shit*, Aaron thought.

"Claire, please don't be like that. You know I want to be with you. Haven't we had a wonderful time down here?"

"Yes, but you're an important man and important people are waiting for you to come and do important things with them. And I have to take care of all the little business details so you can go do your important work."

"Let's just spend a few more days here. Then we'll go back. Wouldn't you like to stay a few more days?"

"Whatever, Aaron. Whatever you want."

"This trip was never about what I want. I thought *we* wanted to get away."

"Well, we did get away. And now it's time to go back. Let's just go, Aaron. I understand, There's not enough to do down here to keep you busy. You need to work. You need to make music."

Aaron knew he wasn't going to dig his way out of this one, so he started packing his own things.

"Tell you what. We'll get the new album done and then come back for a few weeks before the next tour. I promise. Maybe we can talk to someone about real estate."

"Fine, Aaron. I'm fine. Do you want to call the airline or shall I?"

The sessions for the new Carnival album began two weeks late. The plan was to record some new songs Aaron had co-written with Andy. Aaron wanted his old teacher in the studio to help fine-tune the arrangements and hoped he would sit in on some of the sessions.

Some of the others joined Claire in concern about this new stranger who seemed to have so much influence on their leader. Andy co-wrote most of the music, so the songs had a jazz flavor that strayed far from the band's signature sound.

Gerald pressed Claire for details. She snapped back and told him to ask Aaron for himself.

He didn't have to. On the first day of the sessions, Aaron introduced Andy to the group and explained that they had indeed written some songs that would hopefully stretch the band in new directions.

"We're not changing our sound," he said. "We're just expanding a little. Everybody says our records don't sell because we always sound the same. We should at least get some credit for trying something new."

The band felt better once they got a chance to work with Andy for a few days. The professor knew his stuff. He tried hard not to disrupt the band's routine in the studio. For the most part, he played the role of volunteer jazz coach, helping out only when someone asked. He did write some jazzy horn charts for a couple of songs and played along with the five-piece horn section.

Aaron was thrilled to give his mentor the first recording credit of his career. Claire simmered as Andy easily blended with the Carnival clan. There was even some talk that he would lead a horn section to complement the new songs on the next tour.

Claire's worst fears began to materialize after the new album, "Blue Notes," was released in the spring of 1981. Positive reviews did nothing to encourage sales. The record barely cracked the Top 40. Eight weeks after its debut, it had fallen out of the Top 100.

One review typified the critical analysis by the music press:

> "No one ever questioned the fact that Carnival could play blues-based rock with the best of them. 'Blue Notes' proves they can play jazz, blues or anything else they put their minds to. The horns expand their impact as an ensemble, and the pristine recording should get someone a Grammy."

Carnival's new sound attracted some new fans, but the Carnies didn't know what to make of it. Word of mouth suggested that you might want to skip this one and save your money for concert tickets.

Patrick summed up the group's reaction in typically blunt fashion. "What the fuck? Are we doomed to play the same old songs, the same old way, for the rest of our lives?"

"Depends on how many records you want to sell," said Aaron, who liked the record and didn't care how many people bought it. He was proud of what the band, and Andy, had accomplished together. He was ready to hit the road, see how the songs sounded live and then move on to the next project.

Others were more concerned that the new sound was grinding the gears in the Carnival machine.

"Again, it depends on how many tickets you want to sell," Aaron countered. "Patrick, we're only doomed to one style if we want to fill the canyons with those whacked-out Carnies who insist the '70s never ended. Somebody needs to tell them that the war is over and Nixon resigned.

"What's wrong with playing clubs and colleges? Let's just go out there and have some fun. Dewey, I promise you'll make enough to cover child support."

Dewey thumped his bass drum like he was playing a funeral march.

"Child support, *shit*. My oldest is starting college in the fall. Columbia. Ivy League. Can you believe that shit? Gonna cost me a fortune."

Once again, Aaron found himself in the minority. Even Sean David, who rarely voiced opinions on band matters, spoke up.

"Aaron, I never understand why you always want to scale everything down. We've played more than a thousand gigs. How much more do you expect us to grow? We've got a good thing here. Three or four months on tour every year. Two more months in the studio. The rest of the time, we can do what we want because we got rich playing these huge gigs that you hate so much. Are they really so bad that you can't suck it up forty or fifty nights a year?

"No one questions you're the leader of the band. You always get to call the shots in the studio. But you're always the first one to say that no one person in the band is more important than another. That we have to stick together. Don't make us feel guilty because we want to play bigger shows and make more money. We all do this for a living. Why should we feel guilty about doing well?"

"Because we're wasting the chance to challenge ourselves, to improve and to make better music," Aaron said. "I know that might sound pretentious, but that's what makes me want to be a musician. The chance to explore, to study new ideas, add them to your own and, every once in a while, you might achieve something great."

"Been there, done that, bro," Dewey said. "Ivy league. Gonna cost me a fortune."

"Music isn't everything," Sean argued. I've got other

things to do. And I've got a payroll to meet back at the farm. Every damn week."

"Come on, Lowe-man, just relax and go with the flow," Patrick said. "It'll be fun. I promise. Then you and Claire can go back and pick pineapples with Sean."

Claire bit her lip as the rest of the band lobbied Aaron. She already knew the new album and the new sound were scaring off concert promoters. Most of them were suggesting that the band should think smaller and play the summer festival circuit. Stadium shows were a huge investment risk for promoters and falling out of favor in general. They were a headache to produce and few, if any, turned much of a profit for the organizers. Arena shows carried a similar risk. The summer "sheds" and outdoor festivals didn't pay quite as much, but they did offer a decent guarantee.

This time, Aaron will get his way, Claire thought. Carnival would *have to* play in front of some smaller crowds this summer, and share the bill at bigger shows, because Andy's influence was dragging the band to the bottom of the Billboard charts like a lead tuba. If he was allowed to continue, it wouldn't be long before the band was back slumming in the clubs, playing for beers and a piece of the door.

Chapter 43

Carnival spent several weeks that spring rehearsing the new songs and getting used to the new horn section, led by Andy Rush, the band's new unofficial member. Relieved of the pressure to fill up stadiums, as Claire predicted, the band felt free to do as it pleased.

Aaron was right about one thing. It was fun to evolve. Gerald began to embrace the complexity of jazz and spent long nights listening to classic jazz records for inspiration.

"I can't believe it took me this long to discover Thelonious Monk," he told Andy one night. "Beethoven and Mozart were amateurs."

Two weeks before the tour was scheduled to begin, Aaron left rehearsals early with a terrible headache. He went home, took two aspirin and a long shower, then drew down the shades to block the bright midday sun.

He woke up several hours later when he heard Claire come in through the front door. From the dark bedroom, he could hear her pacing around the apartment. He got up when he thought he heard her crying.

When he reached the kitchen, he was shocked to see Claire hovering over the sink, frantically trying to wash some blood off her new white silk blouse. Her face was red and her hair was a mess. She *was* crying.

"Honey, what happened? Are you OK?"

Claire was so surprised to see Aaron that she spun around, knocking a wine glass and bottle to the floor. Aaron worked his bare feet around the broken glass to get closer to Claire.

"I ... I, what are you doing home at this hour?" she

stammered. "What time is it?"

Claire didn't wait for an answer. She ran by him into the bathroom and tried to put her hair and face back together.

"Claire, what happened?"

Claire closed the bathroom door and shouted, "Baby, I'm OK, just give me a minute."

Five minutes later she came out and gave Aaron a hug. She smiled, but Aaron could feel her whole body shaking.

"I'm OK, baby. I just had a little scare. There was an accident over on Market Street. A hit-and-run. A pickup truck hit someone ... a kid, a little Chinese girl. She ... she was right next to me on the corner ... and this truck cuts right into us. I got out of the way, but he knocked the girl into the middle of the street. I tried to help her until the ambulance arrived. I tried to help, I did, but I couldn't. She ... she just kept bleeding, and it wouldn't stop."

She spoke slower as she finished the story, then she sat down and took a deep breath.

"That's why I'm such a mess," she said almost apologetically.

Aaron sat down and drew her into his arms. "But you're OK?" She nodded yes. "Thank God, right?"

Aaron led Claire to the couch and went to find some shoes so he could sweep up the broken glass. Then he opened a new bottle of wine and poured some for Claire.

"What about the little girl?" Aaron asked.

Claire gave him a funny look. "Who?"

Aaron worried she might still be in shock.

"The Chinese girl. Did she die?"

"Yes. *No.* I don't know. They took her away."

"Did you have to give the police a statement?"

"*Oh yes*, they had me there forever. I was an eyewitness. He almost hit *me*, Aaron."

Aaron turned on the TV and tuned into the news. There was no mention of a hit-and-run in the Mission or anywhere else.

Claire lit a joint. *Fine*, he thought. That will help her relax and get some sleep.

An hour later, Claire was dozing on the couch when the phone rang. Aaron answered. A police detective asked for him.

"I think you want my girlfriend, Claire Hall," he said.

"Sir, are you Aaron Lowe?" the voice asked.

"Yes. It was my girlfriend Claire who witnessed the accident. She's sleeping now. Can you call back in the morning?"

"Mr. Lowe, there seems to be some kind of misunderstanding. I don't know about your girlfriend or her accident. I'm looking for you. Do you know an Andy Rush?"

Aaron was having trouble following the detective. The headache was still pounding his skull.

"Yes, what about him?"

"You're a friend of his?"

"Yeah, yes, what's going on?"

"Well, I'm sorry to have to tell you this. Mr. Rush was murdered in his apartment. Your phone number was on a piece of paper taped to his refrigerator."

Aaron's head felt like it was in a vice. The detective's voice seemed to trail off. *What did he say about Andy?*

"Mr. Lowe, are you still there?"

"Yes, yes. Did you say Andy is *dead*?"

"I'm sorry, yes. When was the last time you saw him?"

"Just a few hours ago. We were rehearsing. I went home early. What happened?"

"Rehearsing? With your band? Carnival, right?"

"Yes. We were rehearsing. Andy's an old friend of mine. He's working with the band now."

"You work together?"

"Yes. With the band. Oh, Jesus!"

"Mr. Lowe, we were hoping you could come down to the station and help us out with a few things."

"What kind of things?"

"Help with our investigation."

It was beginning to sink in. *Oh, man, this is for real.*

"Look, my girlfriend witnessed a terrible accident today, a traffic accident, and she's really shaken up. I need to take care of her. And I, um, I guess I'm going to have to make some calls. For Andy. Can it wait until morning?"

"Mr. Lowe, we're conducting a murder investigation here. Every second matters. We really need to talk to you. We could send a car if you like."

Grief and indecision were churning his stomach. Could Andy really be dead? Maybe it was a mistake. He needed to make some calls. And how could he wake Claire, drop another bomb on her and then take off to meet with the police?

"Look, give me an hour," he said. "I'll come over after I get someone to look after my girlfriend."

Aaron called Patrick and Sheila to come and stay with Claire. When they arrived, he told Patrick to call the rest of the band and let them know about Andy.

When he got to the police station, he was met at the front desk by Detective Warnock, a large man with large biceps that strained the short sleeves of his white dress shirt. He was about forty-five, with a craggy face that matched his coarse, salt-and-pepper crew cut.

"Thanks for coming down, Mr. Lowe," he said. "I'm the one who spoke with you on the phone."

He led Aaron down a hall into an isolated interview room. It was hot and stuffy inside. Aaron was about to ask them to open a window when he saw the steel grates that made the windows inaccessible.

"What can I do to help?" Aaron asked. "Do you know what happened?"

Detective Warnock sat down, took a pen out of his chest pocket and began to write on a notepad.

"We were hoping you could help us with that. OK, just for the record, please state your name and address."

The request made Aaron a little nervous. Aaron habitually rationed out personal information with meticulous care.

"Aaron Lowe, 2102 Jefferson Street, Apartment 2."

"You're Aaron Lowe of the rock-and-roll band Carnival?"

"Yes."

"And you knew the deceased from the band? He was a member?"

"Yes, well, no. I've known him for a long time. He used to be my teacher. He moved to San Francisco last year and looked me up. We've been working together ever since. He's not an official member of the band, but he's working with us at the moment."

The deceased. Oh, God, Andy. Aaron fought the shock and choked back the tears. Detective Warnock scribbled on his notepad.

"When was the last time you saw him?" the detective asked.

"This morning, late morning, at rehearsal," Aaron. "I told you that on the phone."

"Are you sure that's the last time you saw him?"

"That's the last time I saw anyone! I had a headache. I went right home and took a nap."

"So you were home around four in the afternoon?"

"Yes, I was sleeping."

"Were you home alone, or was there someone there with you?"

"You mean like a witness? What's the difference?"

"Please just answer the question."

"No. I was alone until Claire, my girlfriend, Claire, came home."

"What time was that?"

"I don't know. Maybe five or six. About two hours before you called. What time was that?"

Detective Warnock's questions seemed pointless. Then he began to understand.

"Am I some kind of suspect?" he asked.

Detective Warnock stood up and grabbed a plastic bag off the top of a file cabinet. He turned around and dropped it on the table.

"Can you tell me what this is?" the detective asked.

Aaron opened the bag and pulled out three sheets of white paper, stapled and folded. It was a copy of the schedule for Carnival's upcoming summer tour. Aaron's name was handwritten, in ink, in the upper right corner of the first page.

It was Claire's handwriting.

"It looks like our tour schedule. Where did you get it?"

"It was in Mr. Rush's apartment on the kitchen floor. We asked around. They were distributed to your band at your rehearsal today."

"Who told you that?"

"One of the studio employees, not that it matters. How do you suppose it got to his apartment?"

Aaron had no answer. "I don't know. Maybe he was given my copy by mistake. I have no idea."

"Well, there was another copy there with his name on it. Are you sure you weren't there this afternoon, Mr. Lowe?"

"*No!* Look, I don't mean to be rude, but I'm not sure I can help you with this."

"We appreciate any help you can give us. Tell me, you and Mr. Rush. You were friends, you say?"

"Yes. Very good friends."

"And that's all?"

"What do you mean, *that's all*?"

"Well, it's come to our attention that the deceased was, well, homosexual."

I can't believe this, Aaron thought.

"And you think we were lovers or something? Look, you guys are so far off the mark. I'm not gay and Andy wasn't my lover. I don't know if he even had a lover. And I don't know what his being gay has to do with any of this."

"Well, my experience is that these things happen sometimes with homosexuals. Statistics show a high level of violence in those, ah, relationships. So we have to ask."

"You guys are really something. You realize you're in San Francisco, right? This isn't Nazi Germany."

Aaron got up to leave, but Detective Warnock grabbed him by the collar and slammed him back down in the chair.

"Let me tell you something, you smart-assed rock star piece of shit! This is my case, and I don't like it when people are murdered, even little faggots like your buddy there. And right now, you're my only suspect. So keep your mouth shut and answer the questions. Otherwise I'm gonna search you, and I guarantee I'll find something that I can throw your ass in jail for."

"*Fascist*! I came in here on my own. Because you said you needed help. Now I'm leaving. If you have any more questions, you can call my lawyer!"

Aaron got up again. This time, he wasn't stopped. He dashed out of the room and out of the building. He didn't stop until he turned the corner. There, away from prying eyes, he leaned against a wall and tried to catch his breath.

So much had happened in a few hours that Aaron really hadn't had time to think. First reality: His dear friend and mentor was dead. Second reality: He was a suspect in Andy's murder. Why?

Third reality: The evidence being thrown in his face had come from Claire. Why would she give his copy of the tour schedule to Andy?

Aaron began to shiver. Even his bones felt cold.

Where was that accident Claire told him about?

He hailed a cab and took it to the offices of the San Francisco Chronicle. He asked for Dennis Worthy, a reporter who covered the music beat in his spare time and had written many stories about Carnival. Dennis came down to reception and rushed him through the busy newsroom to a private conference room.

Dennis had heard about Andy Rush and assumed that's what Aaron was there to talk about. Instead, Aaron asked him to check on reports of a hit-and-run accident in the Mission District.

It took Dennis a few anxious minutes to report back.

"I checked the police blotter, man," he said. "There's no news of anything like what you described, anywhere in the city."

Aaron's bones felt colder. His mouth was as dry as cotton.

"What's this all about, Aaron?" Dennis asked. "What about Andy Rush? Do you know what happened?"

"Dennis, I appreciate your help," Aaron said. "Tell you what. When we get a chance to figure all this out, I'll give you an exclusive on the whole thing, OK?"

"Sure, bro, sure," the happy reporter said. "You won't forget?"

"Promise. Thanks." With that, Aaron was out the door again for another round of hyperventilating on the sidewalk.

Aaron tried to convince himself he was wrong as he walked all the way home. He *had* to be wrong. Things like this couldn't happen twice in one lifetime.

When he got back home, Patrick and Sheila were in the kitchen.

"Claire woke up and was kind of disoriented," Sheila said. "She was all upset that you weren't here. I gave her a Valium so she could sleep. I hope that's alright."

"She's sleeping now?" Aaron asked.

"Like a baby, man," Patrick said. "What happened to her?"

"She said she was almost hit by a truck, and that some little girl was hit right in front of her. I don't know, I checked, and ..." Aaron cut himself off right there. He needed to work this out with Claire first.

"And what about you, are you OK? What did the cops want?" Patrick asked.

"Andy was murdered right in his apartment. I'm a suspect!" Aaron said.

"Son of a bitch! What's wrong with them?"

"I don't know. They found my tour schedule there. Tell me something, did you guys get the schedule today at rehearsal?"

"Yeah, Claire came by and handed them out. Why?"

Aaron stuck his head in the bedroom to make sure Claire was asleep.

"Did she ask why I wasn't there?"

"I don't remember, man. She was kind of distracted and a little hyper. You know how she is sometimes. Strange, though, she left with Andy. They were all chatty-friendly and stuff, which was kind of weird."

Aaron opened a beer. He hoped it might wash away the bitter taste in his mouth. He used to think that was the taste of adrenaline, but had learned it was merely a reaction to anxiety.

"Look, thanks a lot for coming over," he said. "I can take it from here."

"You sure you're OK, Lowe-man?" Patrick asked. "You don't look so hot."

"Why don't I come by in the morning and check on Claire?" Sheila asked. "Maybe I can run some errands for her or something."

Aaron gave Sheila a kiss on the forehead. "No, thanks, we'll be OK. You take care of that man of yours."

Aaron finished his beer, opened another and spent the rest of the night on the balcony strumming a guitar. He played some of the songs Andy and he had written together. When he screwed up the bridge chords, he expected to hear Andy let him know about it. He teared up when the silence went unbroken.

Every once in a while, he'd get up and check on Claire. She was still as a painting, sleeping like her world was in order.

When the sun came up, Aaron set the coffee to brew and

went to take a shower. When he returned, Claire was in the living room, on the sofa, wrapped in a blanket and sipping from a steaming cup. She was watching the morning news on television.

"Hi, baby," she said. "I was just checking to see if they had the accident on the news."

Aaron sat in an easy chair, as far from her as he could get without leaving the room.

"How do you feel?"

"Much better, thank you. Sheila gave me a Valium and *poof!* Knocked me right out. I should do that more often."

Aaron looked at the TV. "So, anything on the news?"

"No, can you imagine, an awful thing like that?"

"It's not in the papers, either."

Claire looked at Aaron. He looked tired.

"How is that possible? I guess a hit-and-run isn't big news these days. There's so much crime and violence."

Aaron almost laughed. "There sure is. You can never be too careful in this town."

Claire moved to the other end of the sofa so she could reach his hand. "Baby, you look like you had a long night. Did you stay up all night watching out for me?"

"Yeah, something like that," he said as he pulled back his hand from hers.

Claire sat up. "Baby, what's the matter? Is there something wrong?"

Aaron stared right at her. "Andy. He was murdered yesterday. Stabbed in the back in his apartment. The police called right after you fell asleep last night."

Claire began to breathe harder and reached out once more for Aaron's hand. He kept it beyond her reach. "Oh, no! Oh, Aaron! How could this happen?"

"Like you said, Claire, San Francisco's going to hell. So much crime and violence."

Claire averted his stare. She used the coffee cup to warm her hands.

"Did you say the police called you? Why would they do that?"

"Because they think I killed him."

Claire dropped the hot coffee in her lap and jumped up. "Shit! Shit!"

She scurried to the closet and grabbed a towel to soak up the mess. Aaron was motionless, watching her every move.

"Aaron, are they out of their minds? How could they think that?"

"Cause I went home early. Cause I don't have an alibi. Cause they found my copy of the tour schedule on his kitchen floor."

Claire's eyes darted across the room to her leather work bag, which was lying on the floor near the front door.

"Lose something?" Aaron asked.

"No. I just wanted to make sure I still had my bag. I don't remember much from last night."

"Well, you seem to remember the accident well enough."

"How could I forget? Oh, Aaron, I'm so sorry. I've been so worried about the little girl that I don't even know, and your friend is dead."

"He was your friend, too," Aaron snapped. "He was everybody's friend. He never hurt anybody."

"Of course not, Aaron," Claire said. "Please don't be short with me. I'm just as upset as you are."

"Yeah, but not about Andy."

"What's that supposed to mean? How could you say such a thing? I admit I had my doubts about Andy, but I never would have wished him any harm!"

"No Claire, you never settle for wishes. You want something to happen, you just take charge and make it happen."

"Aaron, I don't understand what you're talking about. Look, I know you're upset, but everything's going to be OK. We won't miss one horn."

No wonder he felt so cold. Claire was a Popsicle. No

regret. No remorse. Andy was just one lousy horn. Plenty more where he came from.

Aaron jumped from his seat and stared down at her.

"One horn! My best friend is dead and the cops think I killed him! Claire, how could you do this?"

"How could I … do what?"

Aaron screamed so loud that Claire coiled in her seat. *"Stop it! Stop it!* Stop treating me like I'm some sort of an idiot!" He grabbed her by the arm and pulled her to her feet. Now, they were eye to eye. "Don't lie to me! Tell me what happened with you and Andy!"

Claire became hysterical. Her eyes were wild with fear. "Aaron, don't … don't look at me like that!"

"Tell me what happened! Tell me what you did!"

Claire broke from Aaron's grasp and sat back down on the sofa. She hugged a pillow in her lap and stared at the floor. She started to talk, then fell silent again. She reached for a cigarette, lit it and took a long drag.

"Aaron, please, you have to believe me. I never meant for this to happen. I … I was at the rehearsal to hand out the tour schedules. The rehearsal was just breaking up and Andy and I just started talking. We had never really talked, me and him, without you around. We got started on you and Las Vegas. I wanted to hear some of the stories for myself. He invited me to his place for a cup of tea and some more talk."

Claire put out her half-smoked cigarette and unconsciously lit another.

"We were having a nice chat. Everything was fine. But then we ended up arguing … about the band. I finally told him he was messing with your head, and he was messing up the band. That he didn't understand you. That he didn't understand the situation. How important the band is to you. How many people depend on you. It wasn't some sandbox for you guys to play in. All that jazz. That's not what people want from Carnival. Everything was all screwed up, and it was his fault.

"*Somebody* had to tell him, Aaron. *Somebody* had to do something about him. He was going to ruin *everything!*"

Aaron cut her off sharply. "That's not your decision, Claire. You had no right."

Claire laughed and her eyes widened. "That's what he said. He said he wasn't going to argue with me about it. That he would take it up with you. Well, he had fucked everything else up. Now he was going to come between you and me. How could I let him do that? What right did he have to do that?"

"Claire, we could have worked it out," Aaron said, shaking his head. "He didn't want to break us up. He would have quit the band before doing anything like that."

"That's the problem, Aaron, you're so naïve," she said. "You were his ticket into the band. He was going to be a big, famous musician, just like you. You think he would have given all that up so easily? He would have done anything, said anything, to keep what you gave him!

"He told me to leave and turned his back on me. *Turned his back on me!* I tried to stop him and he pushed me away. We were in the kitchen and these knives were right there on the counter. I was just defending myself!"

"Defending yourself?" Aaron said. "Against someone trying to push you away? Claire, what have you done? What have you done to all of us?"

Aaron walked out to the balcony. Claire followed closely behind. She reached out to touch him, but he turned away.

"Claire, what are we going to do?"

She came to him again and put her arms around him. He was too exhausted to push her away. Instead, he just stood there, arms limp at his side.

"Aaron, please try to understand," she said. "Please don't hate me. I never meant to hurt him. I was just so angry. I was afraid he was going to ruin your career. I didn't mean to hurt him."

"My career? Do you think I care about my career? Claire,

I'm a musician. That's all I am. Luckier than most. If I never worked another day, we still have enough money to live on for the rest of our lives. If and when Carnival goes bust, I'm still a musician. That's all I ever was. Andy was my friend. My teacher. My savior. Getting to play music with him, having him join the band, I've never been happier.

"And now, he's gone. My girlfriend killed him, and the cops want to blame me. Claire, what are we gonna do?"

"Baby, I swear, everything will be OK," Claire said. She was still holding him tightly, as though he would float off the balcony if she let go. "I'm sure the police will clear you. You'll see. This will all go away. I'll confess if I have to."

Aaron broke her hug pushed her away. "Claire, don't you get it? This will never be OK! I'm not worried about the cops. What about Andy? And what about you? What am I going to do about you?"

"What do you mean, Aaron? Please don't hate me. I'm sorry! I'm sorry! I did a terrible thing. I know that. But it was an accident. I love you so much, baby. Please don't give up on me! We can get through this!"

Aaron remembered when Betty said those same words to him. *Please don't give up on me.* He gave up on Betty twice without even realizing it. Once, when he cheated on her with Tina. Again, when he never sent for her after leaving Las Vegas.

This time, he knew what he had to do, and he would do it with his eyes wide open.

"Claire, I can't even look at you without getting sick. I have to get out of here. I have to figure a few things out. The only thing I know for sure is that we can never make this right."

"Aaron, please, don't!" Claire cried. "I did it for you! Don't leave me!"

Aaron grabbed an overnight bag and threw some clothes inside. He packed some notebooks, then he packed the Les Paul in its case.

"You did this for yourself, Claire," he said. "If you knew me at all, if you really loved me, you would understand. But you don't. And you never will."

"Aaron, I'll *die* if you leave me. I swear to God, I'll kill myself!"

"Right now, I really don't care," Aaron said. "I'm going. I've got to go bury my friend."

CHAPTER 44

By the time Andy Rush was put to rest, the police had removed Aaron from their list of subjects. They had interviewed nearly everyone associated with the band and were satisfied that Aaron wasn't the type to commit violence, especially on his oldest and closest friend. There was no motive and the evidence was more coincidental than circumstantial.

Detective Warnock was inclined to believe that Andy Rush was the victim of a homosexual lover. "You pick up some degenerate in a bar. What do you expect?"

Claire was never considered as a suspect. The police made a few more token inquiries and put the case on the back burner.

Aaron briefly considered outing Detective Warnock and his astonishing ignorance to Dennis Worthy at the Chronicle, but was too scared to stir the pot. The last thing he needed was for the San Francisco Police Department to start digging into his past. He also was afraid that a proper investigation of Andy's murder could and should lead to Claire. Maybe he was rationalizing for his own benefit, but he did not see how getting her busted would help anyone.

Aaron took care of the funeral arrangements. Andy's only family was an estranged sister and she could not be located. Andy said he hadn't left a lot of close friends behind in Las Vegas, so Aaron did not feel obliged to make any inquiries.

He felt an urge to contact Betty, but how could he? *Hi Betty, long time, how you been? By the way, my girlfriend just murdered Andy Rush and got away with it. Want to come to the funeral?*

Andy's body was cremated and the band joined Aaron in a ceremony to cast the ashes into the Pacific. Afterwards, Dewey opened the warehouse for a small party. The band climbed on the old stage and played some slow blues. Gerald played a sad Thelonious Monk piano piece he had been practicing. Dewey's sister cooked for everyone. Patrick predictably drank too much whiskey and told stupid Irish jokes.

Claire did not attend any of the memorial events. Aaron was staying with Dewey in Santa Cruz. He told everyone that Claire and he should have split long ago and his friend's death had inspired him to make some changes in his life.

Sheila told Aaron she had called Claire, who said she was leaving town to visit her family. No one else brought it up. All they wanted to know was whether Aaron was up to playing or if he wanted to postpone the tour. It was up to him. Aaron said that getting out of town for a while was probably the best thing they could do right now.

Carnival tried to rock away its troubles on the road. The first few gigs were nothing short of spectacular. The band was playing with a passionate sense of urgency. The "Blue Note" songs, like most of Carnival's music, sounded better in a live setting. The fans actually loved the jazzy new songs and the bold, brassy horn section.

Aaron tried to administer some self-therapy by writing more new songs. He matched a set of lyrics to one of Andy's unused melodies and the result was "A Single Reason Why." The band knew it was important for Aaron to get some of these feelings out, so they quickly learned the song and put it into the set.

Aaron tearfully introduced the song to a faithful gathering of Carnies in Austin. A few details of the Andy Rush incident had been published in the Carnie Club newsletter, so the fans had been expecting something like this.

"I had the privilege over the last few months to work with my old teacher, Andy Rush," he said before 10,000 silent fans.

"He was a like a brother to me. A father, a mentor. If it wasn't for him, I probably would not be with you here today."

A swell of polite applause rose from the amphitheater. Aaron bowed his head and waited for quiet.

"When we finally had the opportunity to work together, I realized how much he still had to offer. There was so much more that he could teach me. And he was happy to give, to give to all of us up here. I know some people aren't crazy about the new record, that it didn't sound like Carnival. But he taught us how to try something new, and I think we did a pretty good job."

Aaron paused again as the crowd applauded once more.

"We're going to play some of those songs tonight, with the new horn section that he put together for us. Unfortunately, Andy can't be here. We lost him a few weeks ago. So on this tour, we play with heavy hearts. We miss him terribly, but we'll remember him well tonight. I hope you'll join us.

"This is a new one, just for him."

I don't know which way to go
I don't know which way to turn
When all that you knew before is gone
Time to find some new things to learn

Study hard and try to understand
How it all got so far out of hand
Try to count the stars up in the sky
Try to find a single reason why

I can't find my way again
I can't find my only friend
Adding up what has been lost
Hard to justify the cost

Pray for guidance but it doesn't come
Wonder when you'll see the rising sun
Try to catch the eagle when she flies
Try to find a single reason why

I can't help but stand in wonder
When the lightning follows thunder ...

Aaron's biggest problem at the moment was getting sleep. Sheila copped him some Valium, which helped a little. Trouble was, when he did sleep, the dreams did more damage than the insomnia. He kept seeing Claire and Betty fighting with Andy. Then they fought with each other.

When Aaron was awake, he fought to keep his mind from reliving the nightmares. Sometimes, he wrestled with guilt about Claire. If only he could have been more sensitive to her needs. If only he could have seen what she was capable of. All the signs had been there.

Then again, he had never met a more needy and demanding person than Claire Hall. She always believed she knew what he wanted, or needed, better than he did himself. She refused to accept his priority of music over recognition. She measured her success through his, and she measured success by record sales and concert grosses. She literally made a career of it.

Aaron tried so many times to explain to her that material success didn't matter. It wasn't his fault that the lesson never took. And her ambition was no excuse for murder.

His guilt was no match for his anger. Aaron thought again about turning Claire into the police. Andy deserved some justice and his prized student was in a position to deliver. Still, the scandal would affect so many people. Carnival might not ever recover from such a bloody black cloud. And the media would be all over the story. Aaron still had to worry about other scars from his past that might be exposed by the investigative undertow.

Once again, he was trapped. Only this time, it was Claire who would have to live with the fear of discovery. Aaron's own experience told him that this familiar purgatory would be punishment enough. Her emotional prison would deliver some small measure of the justice owed to Andy.

And Claire would do her time alone. Aaron could never reconcile with her. He wondered if he ever really did love her. At the moment, he could not be sure. Loyalty might have kept him by her side, but not under these unimaginable circumstances. No, there would be no reconciliation. When the tour was over, Aaron would meet with her and give her any property or money she wanted. Then they would go their separate ways.

Two weeks into the tour, the Valium was kicking in as Aaron showered in his room at the St. Louis Hilton. It was well past midnight. The show that night had gone well. He was hoping for a long, quiet rest when the phone rang.

"Hi, baby. Are you alone?" It was Claire. Her voice was faint and sweet.

"Hi, Claire," was all he could think to say.

"How was the show tonight, baby? Everything go OK?"

"Sure. It was fine."

"Is the hotel OK? I made all the arrangements, you know."

The Valium was doing its job, so Aaron had trouble keeping his focus. This was the first time they had spoken since he walked out. He wondered why she was making small talk about hotel accommodations.

"Everything here is fine, Claire. How about you?"

Claire laughed. It was more of a giggle, really. "Well, I'm glad you're comfortable. You need your rest."

"To tell you the truth, Claire, I'm not getting a lot of rest these days."

"You having nightmares, baby? Something keeping you up at night?"

God, she was *taunting* him.

"Something, or someone, maybe? Are you alone?" she asked again.

"Come on, Claire. Don't be like that. What do you really want?"

"I'm all alone here, baby. All warm and comfy. Nice bottle of wine. I feel so sleepy, you know? I wish you were here with me."

Aaron could tell she was wasted. Probably on her second bottle of wine.

"Claire, why don't you sleep it off? We should both get some sleep. If you really want to talk, you can call me in the morning."

"Oh, I don't think I can do that. I'll probably be, um, *indisposed* by then. Places to go, you know? That sort of thing."

Her words were beginning to slur. Aaron began to worry. Normally, when Claire drank too much, she went right to sleep. "Where are you going, Claire? Where are you going tomorrow?"

"No tomorrow, baby, just tonight. I'm going to my final reward. Or my final punishment. *Whatever*. They'll sort it out when I get there. I don't really care anymore."

Oh, shit. Oh, shit. What had she done now?

"Claire, did you take something?"

"Baby, I took a life. *You know*. The teacher. Your precious teacher. I stabbed him in the back. Sooner or later, I stab everybody in the back. *You know*. Psycho bitch would probably kill for her boyfriend. As a matter of fact, she did."

The Valium in his blood couldn't stop the growing panic. "Claire, I'm going to call someone, OK? I'm gonna have someone come over and help you. You need some help."

"*Psycho bitch!* That's what everybody thinks, right? Always butting in where I don't belong. Those fucking friends of yours. They have no idea. They'd be playing high school sock hops if it wasn't for me."

"Nobody's angry with you, Claire." Aaron tried to keep a

calm voice. "They don't know what happened. I haven't said a word. And they know how much you did for them. For the band."

"But what about you, Aaron? I don't give a shit what they think about me. What about you?"

"Claire, we can talk about all this when you feel better. I'm gonna call someone." He wished someone would come by his room. He didn't want to hang up on her. He needed someone else to call an ambulance.

"I would do anything for you, Aaron. I would do anything for *us*. I killed for you! Do you understand? Both times, I did it for you!"

Both times? What did that mean?

"What do you mean by that, Claire? What do you mean, both times?"

She giggled again. "*Eric*, silly. Eric and Helena. You think they drove off that cliff all by themselves? You see, Aaron? You're not the only one who can keep a secret."

Aaron fought to remember the circumstance of the accident that killed the leaders of the Victorian Manner. *Oh, no. It couldn't be.*

"Claire, you need to be careful what you say. You don't want any more trouble."

"Spiked their coffee thermos. There was enough LSD to trip out a whole Carnie convention." She laughed loud and long. "Must have been some wild ride. I envy them, really. At least they died together."

"Claire, don't talk about dying. Don't talk about any of this. You don't need this kind of trouble."

"Ooh, is it trouble you're worried about? Don't worry, baby, I won't say anything about your Weekend Willie thing. I won't narc you out. I wouldn't do anything to hurt you, baby. You know that."

"Claire, I'm talking about *you*. I don't want you to get into trouble. It doesn't have to be that way. I'm gonna call someone."

Her voice was fading. "I don't know, Aaron. I think it's time to go. Don't worry, baby. All your secrets are safe with me."

Aaron could hear the phone drop to the floor. "Claire! Claire!"

Aaron hung up and quickly rang the front desk to contact the San Francisco Police. Then he called Patrick and Sheila down the hall. They rushed over and the three of them anxiously waited for the phone to ring.

An hour later, the police called and said Aaron's apartment was empty. Claire was nowhere to be found.

The police called again the next afternoon. They told Aaron that Claire's mother had called from San Diego. She was desperately trying to reach him.

She told him that Claire had overdosed on a handful of powerful Tuinal tablets at her mother's home. She was dead when they found her the next morning in her old bedroom.

Carnival hastily cancelled a week of concerts and returned home, as a group, to San Francisco. From there, they flew to San Diego on a private charter plane arranged by Lenny Hayes.

Claire's family was handling the funeral arrangements. The band got an icy reception from the Halls. Aaron had only met Claire's family once, more than ten years ago. Claire used to battle constantly with her mother on the phone. After a while, she finally stopped calling.

Mrs. Hall cursed Aaron for dumping Claire and firing her as manager of the band. He tried to tell her that Claire left on her own. That he would have done something if he thought she was suicidal.

That wasn't entirely the truth. The truth was even worse. The truth was more than Mrs. Hall could take. Aaron knew that better than anybody, so he wasn't about to add to her troubles. She needed to believe that Aaron was the villain, so he let her.

Claire's family visited Aaron's sins upon the entire

Carnival delegation. The Halls and the band parted ways at the church. Patrick and Dewey stuck to Aaron like bodyguards during the long trip home. They swatted the gnats from the press who were swarming at the airports to catch Aaron in a state of public grief.

Aaron was spent from the ordeal. He felt like someone had tipped his life over and everything that mattered came spilling out. From his current perspective, Bobby had just died. Now he had lost Andy and Claire in the blink of an eye.

His past and his present had been wiped out. How could he even hope for a peaceful future? Sooner or later, everything he touched became tainted by tragedy. The future was nothing more than another disaster waiting to happen. He thought about going somewhere far away, before someone else's life was darkened by his shadow.

Chapter 45

Claire was right about one thing. Her precision skills as a manager played a crucial role in Carnival's success. Without her around to handle the business end of things, the band's operation began to unravel.

Lenny assigned one of his most trusted young assistants, Marty Sherman, to take Claire's place. Marty was immediately overwhelmed by the immense scope of managing Carnival's massive enterprise. More than thirty people made their living from the band, including roadies, sound technicians, lighting designers and, of course, musicians. Claire had even set up a health plan for everyone on the payroll.

Business was already falling off following the commercial failure of "Blue Notes." And the band, reeling from the combination punch of losing Andy and Claire, had lost much of its enthusiasm for touring. In the end, Marty had little choice but to cancel the remainder of Carnival's 1981 tour.

When Marty tried to put together a set of live dates for the summer of 1982, he was unable to scare up much interest from the concert promoters who were normally eager to bring in Carnival. Marty was told that the band didn't have the following it once had. They should think about doing small theaters, maybe even find a bigger band to open for.

Aaron was in no hurry to get back onstage. The idea of being a warm-up act wasn't going to help change his mind.

Following the aborted tour, Aaron didn't pick up a guitar for three months. Instead, he passed the days by getting wasted with Patrick. He was more inexperienced than most of his peers as a stoner, so he sought guidance from his old friend and new drinking buddy. They sat around his old apartment for days at a time, drinking vodka and beer, smoking bongs of pot and hash and gulping down the occasional downer.

Aaron didn't share Patrick's taste for cocaine. He didn't like the effects. He had enough trouble sleeping as it was. Sheila was a weekend heroin user and helped Aaron with his first fix. He liked the high, but couldn't handle the needle. It also made him sick to his stomach, so he stuck with the smoke and alcohol.

When the pity party had gone on too long, Dewey stepped in and read them all the riot act. He was especially angry with Aaron for helping Patrick hop off the wagon.

"Damn, bro, you don't need to be giving him excuses to get high," Dewey said to Aaron. "He worships you. He follows your lead. You tell him it's cool to get high, that's all he need to hear. And we both know he can't handle it. From the looks of it, bro, you can't handle it, either."

Aaron got the message. If he didn't care about himself, he needed to care about Patrick. He didn't want another notch in his bad-luck belt.

The best way to break the pattern with Patrick was to put some distance between them. Once the spring thaw kicked in, Aaron traded in his old Corvette for a newer model and began to drive the highways of America. He traveled alone for weeks, down the West Coast into Mexico and across the American Southwest. Just for the hell of it, he followed Route 66 from end to end. Then he headed south to New Orleans and followed the fabled "Blues Highway" 61 back north, through the fabled crossroads of Clarksdale in Mississippi and onto Memphis. While he was there, he visited Elvis Presley's estate, Graceland, which had just been opened to the public.

He took the tour with a group of strangers who dutifully waited on a line for hours to get inside. A few people recognized him and he politely accommodated their request for autographs. The second question always was, "Did you ever meet Elvis?"

No, he had never met Elvis, although both musicians shared a history of conquering Las Vegas. But he had an idea how hard life must have been for the King. He imagined Graceland as an empty fortress, with Elvis wandering the halls after his wife and child moved out. How lonely it must have been for him there. How terrible that the place where he died so horribly had been turned into some sort of theme park.

The sadness swelled inside him as cheerful young guides ushered his group from one room to the next. By the time they got to the Jungle Room, he couldn't take it anymore and broke away from the tour. On the way back, he drove by the tiny Memphis storefront of the shuttered Sun Studios, where Elvis and so many of his music heroes had cut their first records. Aaron thought it must have been a much happier place to be than Graceland was. It was a narrow, cramped little building bursting with music. To Aaron, it looked like heaven. *That's the place for me*, he thought.

The visit to Memphis seemed to release Aaron from a few of his demons. Perhaps it was the inspirational vision of Sun Studios. Perhaps it was the realization that Aaron had not quite sunk to the lows that Elvis did before he finally succumbed to the anguish.

No matter how bad things get in the future, I don't think they'll ever be able to charge admission to my apartment, he thought. The very idea let him laugh for the first time in months. Maybe it was time to give the future a try.

The next morning, he turned west and headed for home. He really wanted to play some music. When he got back to San Francisco, he summoned the band members and tried to bring everyone together. It took a couple of days to assemble the troops. On a warm day in late June, Dewey opened the warehouse and called his sister in to cook for the gang. For the first few sessions, Carnival avoided playing most of their own songs. It was more fun to warm up with Chuck Berry and Willie Dixon.

For two long days, they played whatever felt good. Patrick taught Aaron some of the old jug band songs he used to play with the Moonshiners. Garrett showed off his new synthesizers and programmed some new wave beats for the band to jam with. Dewey passed around samples of his newest vice, Cuban cigars. Dewey's sister cooked up tall pots of spicy jambalaya, large skillets of cornbread and bottomless bowls of salad. Sean had crates of fresh pineapple delivered from his farm and the gang devoured it until everyone was sticky.

Playing music, any music, helped Aaron to feel alive again. After a few days, he was ripping hot solos like nothing had happened. The band fell in right behind him.

Still, he shuddered when the others talked about another tour. Going back to the old routine would be hard. The old routine had always included Claire.

"Come on, Lowe-man, what else are we gonna do?" Patrick said. "Go back to your place and get wasted? Let's play some music, man. That's what we do. We suck at everything else. Who cares if we have to play smaller gigs? Hell, at this point, I don't care if we open for Air Supply at the Oshkosh Legion Hall. Let's just go do our thing."

Aaron had to laugh. After years of preaching against playing bigger shows, here was Patrick begging him to accept a scaled-down tour.

In a way, he was still numb, and maybe that was for the best. Experience was helping him to detach from the reality of recent events. Andy was dead and there was nothing he could do about it. Claire had paid the price for her sins. The scale was as balanced as it was going to get.

"Well, I don't know about Air Supply, but I'm up for it if you are," Aaron said. "Dewey, how about Neil Diamond? You still got his number?"

Carnival never seriously considered offering its services as an opening band. They were used to playing three hours or more. Knocking out forty-five minute sets in front of some other band's fans was no way to get back in the game.

Better to headline their own shows. They could still make good money filling three- or four-thousand seaters. They could still be the masters of their own destiny.

The band returned to the road in the fall of 1982. Now that Carnival had abandoned the pits and canyons, Aaron found it easier to connect with the fans in the more intimate venues. Watching the faces of people absorb his music was the best drug he had ever known. With the front row arm's-length from the stage, he even recognized some of the older Carnies and could see they were digging the environment as well.

He also knew the Carnies knew about Claire and Andy. He was comfortable sharing his pain with them. He cried to them through his music and they cried back by clapping, cheering and lighting matches before the encore.

Speaking directly about the tragedies was more difficult. He avoided any direct reference to Andy or Claire when addressing the audience. He rarely spoke about them to anyone, even the boys in the band. All his anger, guilt and grief was packed away after every show along with the rest of the equipment. The next night, he would make his way to the stage, strap on the Les Paul and play his guts out all over again.

But the casual fans who weren't interested in band gossip didn't understand what was going on. For all they knew, it was the band's natural evolution that made them sound better than ever. Those fans didn't really care. They just knew they wanted more.

Word of mouth continued to spread during the tour. Carnival was back and in peak form. Demand for tickets began to grow. The last half of the four-month comeback tour was completely sold out. Extra shows were added in cities when the schedule allowed.

The final shows back in San Francisco were filmed for the band's first video release. After the tour ended, the full-length concert video sold well enough that a separate video of the band performing "A Single Reason Why" was issued as the band's first video single.

At the same time, the media latched on to the story about Aaron writing the song as a tribute to a lost companion. Given that Claire's death had followed so closely to Andy's, and had received far more press coverage, the world simply assumed the song was for her as well.

The misguided sentiment was more than America could resist. "A Single Reason Why" was quickly rereleased as a 45 and the hot new music-video cable TV station, YFM, was playing the video night and day. On Valentine's Day, 1983, it became Carnival's first Number One record.

The band's profile skyrocketed on the coattails of their big hit. Major television networks were begging to book the band on their late-night talk and variety shows. Promoters who had given the band a cold shoulder the last time around were calling to mend fences and get Carnival, and the Carnies, back inside their rotundas.

The single produced yet another dividend when "A Single Reason Why" received three Grammy nominations, for "Best Record," "Best Song" and "Best Performance by a Group or Duo."

Aaron had rubber-stamped the video and single releases. He never anticipated the reaction they would receive. Now, he was mortified that the entire nation was following his story. Suddenly, even people who had never heard of the band knew who Aaron Lowe was. He couldn't walk down a street without people rushing him for autographs and telling him how sorry they were about his girlfriend.

God, if they only knew the truth, Aaron thought. About the song. About Claire and Andy.

About him.

He grew nauseous at the prospect of having to accept a Grammy and make a speech with millions of people watching his every move on TV. He reluctantly agreed to attend the ceremony, if only because his absence would have created yet another sensational story.

Fortunately for Aaron, Michael Jackson and the Police bogarted the Grammies that year. It was the year of "Thriller" and "Synchronicity." Carnival and its grateful leader left the ceremony empty-handed.

The media frenzy for Carnival eventually burnt to embers and gave Aaron a chance to catch his breath. But the damage, as he saw it, was already done. The band already had upscaled its tour plans once again and booked a long arena tour that would start in the summer and carry over well into 1985, if not longer.

There was nothing Aaron could do about it. Video hits, Grammy nominations and chart-topping records had attracted an army of managers, publicists and executives who weren't going to let Carnival Incorporated rest on its laurels. It was time to cash in.

Aaron could have torpedoed the whole thing just by telling the truth. In the end, he couldn't bring himself to wreck it for everyone else just for a little peace of mind. What good would that do? Either way, he was lost. He'd carry the burden like a good bluesman and let the others reap their hard-earned rewards.

CHAPTER 46

Swimming in a river of fame and sympathy, Aaron went with the current and tried to keep his head above water.

Carnival stayed on the road for most of the next two years, performing concerts in twenty countries on five continents. While the rest of the band reveled in the spotlight, Aaron punched the clock. He reliably showed up and did his job every night, then went back to his room, wherever that was. The highway motor inn rooms were now downtown suites, so he enjoyed more creature comfort than he was used to. But the loneliness was a cancer. He had withdrawn from everyone, even Patrick.

Aaron's friends gave him his space. After all, he was staying sharp, showing up for every gig and hitting all the right notes. If he wanted to talk, if he asked for help, they would be there for him. If all he wanted to do was sulk about being a huge rock star, they would gladly let him be. The Carnival soap opera had gone on too long for all of them. Each member coped in his own way.

Meanwhile, some of the tour managers were worried about security, logistics and other practical concerns. Promoters were getting flak from local government officials about the Carnies who invaded their cities like a wave of refugees whenever Carnival came to town. Their passionate disciples were camping out in public parks, crashing ticket lines and scalping tickets back to locals to cover their expenses.

The Carnies, though, were guaranteed revenue, so everyone looked the other way and hoped for the best. Marty went one step further and embraced Claire's philosophy of catering to the Carnie Club, whose latest suggestion was to remove the seating from the arena floors. The Carnies wanted to be on their feet, free to roam, dance and move with the music. There were plenty of reserved seats in the mezzanine for those who wanted to sit.

It was a good idea on paper that didn't work in practice. Hard-core Carnies were lining up outside the arena the night before the concert in hopes of being able to grab the best spots on the floor. With nothing to do but sit and wait, a lot of the kids were drinking heavily and gobbling drugs like popcorn.

When the doors to the show were opened, thousands of wasted fans made a mad dash to the front of the stage, then aggressively defended their positions against insurgents.

The band was never around to see these conflicts but could not miss the bad vibes in some arenas when they arrived to play. Scattered fights would break out on the floor. Security responded with increasingly physical tactics. They busted heads and hauled the offenders to jail. Carnie casualties filled the emergency rooms of nearby hospitals, usually with no insurance coverage.

Some towns were threatening the band with lawsuits for failing to control their concerts. Other municipal councils discussed blocking the band from playing within their borders.

Marty, who now commanded a full staff of tour management, told the band not to worry. "It's only rock and roll," he said. "Kids will be kids. There's always going to be some problems when you bring this many people together. I can handle it. Let me handle it."

The conflicts escalated one fateful night at Joe Louis Arena in Detroit in the summer of 1986. The problems began the night before, when the Carnies invaded several of the downtown Motor City parks. A few of Detroit's street gangs had gone into the scalping business and were charging top-dollar for tickets, which caused a few angry confrontations. Out of their element and out of their league, several Carnies took vicious beatings when they stood up to the local hoodlums. Hundreds of the visitors had to flee when the gang-bangers decided to forcibly evict them from their temporary shanty town.

The tension carried over the next night to the arena. Rival gangs were mixing it up as they competed for good spots to scalp tickets. Carnies, stung by the violent reception they had received in Detroit, were mixing it up with local fans who showed up late and tried to cut the line.

Extra security was brought in and clashed with everyone outside as the fans impatiently waited for the doors to open. Every skirmish kept the doors closed a little longer. Normally, the doors opened an hour before showtime. This night, the crowd was kept outside until five minutes before the concert was scheduled to start.

Things were so bad outside that officials thought seriously about cancelling the show. Eventually, it was decided a cancellation would guarantee a riot, so the best thing to do would be to let the kids in and get what they came for.

Opening the doors failed to end the conflicts. They merely relocated to the rotunda. Fighting broke out in at least half a dozen different spots on the floor. One fight escalated into an all-out rumble between the Carnies and a large group of locals that included some of the gang members.

Suddenly, screams could be heard throughout the arena. One of the Carnies had been stabbed and his friends had cornered the gang member who wielded the knife. When the assailant's gang brothers came to rescue him, one of them pulled a gun and fired directly into the advancing crowd.

All hell broke loose. Everyone on the floor frantically surged towards the exit, which was blocked by hundreds of people still trying to get in. The fans in the lower-tier seats watched in horror as the people on the floor trampled each other. Some of them tried to lift people over the wall to safety. For most, there was no escape. Security guards, pinned on either side of the melee, could do little to break the logjam.

It took nearly three hours to disperse the worst riot Detroit had seen since the 1960s. TV news crews descended on the scene and recorded the carnage for the whole world to see. Three people were dead, including an unarmed security guard who got caught in the middle of the scrum. At least thirty people had been hurt, including two teenagers who were in critical condition. More than fifty more were arrested. Two more people were injured in a brawl at the jail.

Aaron and the rest of the band were blissfully unaware of the calamity until they heard the screams and then the shots. They tried to take the stage to plead for calm but were held back by security. Long before the riot had ended, Carnival was ushered out the back and whisked away in limousines.

Back at the hotel, they watched the news in horror along with the rest of America. The next day, the morning talk shows continued their reports, along with background stories on Carnival and similar incidents that were occurring more frequently at concerts and festivals around the country.

The members of Carnival had all experienced their share of turmoil, but the riots in Detroit were beyond comprehension. Even if they weren't the cause for the mayhem, they were wading neck-deep in the middle of a national tragedy.

Carnival became the poster band for everything that was wrong with modern youth, modern music and the decay of society in general. They didn't have to cancel the rest of the tour. It was cancelled for them, one show after the other.

Their suddenly open schedule gave them time to field the harvest of lawsuits that followed. Concert promoters and the City of Detroit lined up to aim the blame at Carnival, while lawyers representing the dead and injured fans were suing the band, the city and the promoters.

For Aaron, it was the final straw. He had always argued against the big shows for his own selfish reasons. It never occurred to him that such deadly aggression could occur at a concert.

Playing music had always been his refuge. When nothing else was going right, there was always a stage where he could play his guitar and make everyone feel better. Now, he couldn't even do that without people getting hurt.

Over the next year, the band and its management settled dozens of lawsuits resulting from the riot in Detroit. Insurance covered some of the damages. More money was drained from the band in the form of legal expenses and lost revenue. By the time everything was sorted out, each member of Carnival had lost millions.

Aaron volunteered even more of his fortune to start up a fund to aid the victims. All of the band members followed suit. The gesture left them bent, but not broke, opening the door for critics to say "It was the *least* they could do." The public criticism added to the backlash against the band and its dysfunctional extended family of Carnies.

Still, the musicians were the only ones who had coughed up so much as a dime of their own money to try and set things right. The whole affair embittered the group. All they did was play music people loved and now they were being treated like terrorists.

The victim's fund turned out to be the band's final collaboration. The other members hoped that with time, Carnival would be able to pick up where it left off. Their leader didn't see the point.

"I think we've done all that we can do together," he told them. "I love you all, but I think the foundation of Carnival has been corrupted. All I ever wanted to do was make a living playing music. What we do isn't music anymore. Everything we do gets blown so far out of proportion that the music slips through the cracks. It's lost all its meaning.

"And now, we're always going to be connected to this horrible, horrible tragedy. People may forgive, but they won't forget. I just can't live that way."

Late in 1986, Aaron left his only living friends behind. The parting was amicable. Most of the guys knew he was right.

The wheels had fallen off the Carnival wagon. It was time to try something else. They could still walk away as friends. They could all still walk away with enough money to live comfortably for the rest of their lives. That was more than most of their peers could say.

"Maybe there will be another time for us," Aaron said hopefully as he shared hugs with his band of brothers.

A few weeks later, the remaining members of Carnival announced they were disbanding. By then, Aaron was already preparing to leave his home of the last 20 years.

He didn't know where he wanted to go, just as he knew he wasn't coming back. So he traded in his Corvette for a roomy Jeep Cherokee. He packed whatever possessions he could in the Jeep and gave everything else away, just as Winnie had done when she moved her family to Las Vegas.

There wasn't very far to go west, so he headed east on Interstate 80, which could take him all the way to New York.

His first stop was across the Nevada border, just outside of Reno. As he continued his journey the next morning, he saw a road sign for Route 95 South and Las Vegas.

It occurred to him that in all his travels with Carnival, he had never been back to Vegas since he left the city as a young man in 1966. For a few minutes, he lingered with thoughts of going home. Then he remembered the trip with Betty to Oceanside, where the Kiddie Cowboy was quickly forgotten. There was no home for him there anymore. There was no home for him anymore in San Francisco. If he wanted to go home now, he would have to find it first.

He stuck to Route 80. Maybe he could find a new life somewhere along the way that would replace the two lives he had already lived and lost.

Third time's a charm, he told himself. *That's what they say.*

PART THREE

CHAPTER 47

From California to New York City, down the East Coast and back up again, Aaron patiently searched for a place where he could disappear.

Not as he had vanished after leaving Las Vegas two decades ago. He no longer felt the frantic need to hide.

He wanted to *settle*. Just be a regular person living a regular life. He didn't want to be the Kiddie Cowboy, Weekend Willie or Aaron Lowe.

He wanted to be "That guy Aaron, you know, the one who lives over there. We met him at that thing."

Even with the lawsuits and memorial fund contributions, Aaron was still financially independent. His accountant put his net worth at nearly two million dollars. And his residuals and royalties would probably provide a steady income for many years to come.

It was enough that he could live just about anywhere he wanted and do just about anything he wanted to do. All he had to do now was figure out the where and the what.

He spent a few months in Manhattan and experienced the warm-blooded pulse of the city that never sleeps. After a while, though, he began to see New York as a poor substitute for San Francisco, louder and not nearly as pretty.

No, he needed more of a change. He had lived in cities since he was a kid. He wanted a different experience.

Aaron always loved living near the ocean, yet he rarely had the time to hit the beach and feel the water between his toes. Now he had more time than ever, and the hot weather made the city unbearable, so he did what everyone else there did and went to the shore.

Aaron accepted an offer from one of Lenny's friends to use his beach house in Point Pleasant, one of the more popular destinations on the busy New Jersey shoreline. The beach house turned out to be a cramped condominium, but it had all the creature comforts he needed. It was situated right across the street from the quiet southern end of the Boardwalk. Since the condo was located on the third floor, he could see and hear the ocean from the bedroom and balcony, just as he could from his apartment in San Francisco, only much closer.

There was one important difference to living there as opposed to living in San Francisco. No one recognized him in Point Pleasant, especially with his shaggy long hair cut short and his beard trimmed neat and tight. What's more, he got the feeling that if they did know who he was, they wouldn't care. New Jersey residents seemed to get more worked up about traffic and taxes than they did about celebrities.

Once Aaron got used to the unique New Jersey tradition of paying for admission to the beach, he spent nearly every day there. Being a West Coaster, he enjoyed the novelty of watching the sun *rise* over the ocean. He started out taking long morning walks up and down the shoreline. Later, he began to jog the same course. He also gave up smoking. Physically, he could never remember feeling better.

Later in the day, Aaron liked to swim out as far as the lifeguards would let him, then turn around, tread water and look to the shore. On a warm weekend afternoon, he could see a tide of humanity cresting against the shoreline. It stretched in each direction as far as he could see. Sometimes, he estimated that hundreds of thousands of people were within his sightline.

And no one except the lifeguards paid him any mind.

This was the anonymity he was looking for. *This could work*, he thought. Here, he was just another grain of sand.

He stayed in the condo after Labor Day weekend marked the official end of summer. Within a few weeks, Point Pleasant was like a ghost town. He could walk the Boardwalk for hours on a cool, cloudy day and only see a few people.

From one extreme to another, Aaron thought. *Either way, it works for me.*

The real estate agents he met with suggested he check out some of the quieter residential towns farther south and along Barnegat Bay. They didn't understand that he was used to noise and people. All he needed was a place where he wouldn't be bothered.

He finally found the perfect home, a three-bedroom contemporary ranch right on a stretch of private beach just south of Point Pleasant in Bay Head. He could have his privacy, yet he was only a mile from the familiar Point Pleasant Boardwalk. He was even closer to Bay Head's quieter, noncommercial boardwalk that Aaron grew to love for its relative tranquility year-round.

God, he loved boardwalks. For walkers, it was a level, soft, forgiving footpath. And in Point Pleasant, Seaside and other tourist destinations, each side of the Boardwalk presented a completely different environment. Look one way and the ocean breeze greeted your face. When the mood struck, you could veer off to the shoreline and let the waves massage your tired feet. Or you could sit on a bench and read while the sun warmed your body.

Look the other way and a Great Wall of earthly pleasures blocked your view of the workaday world. Good food, bad food. Clams and custard. Pizza and taffy. Gift shops full of cheap T-shirts and flying toys being demonstrated by noisy barkers. Midways and arcades where you could play bizarre games of chance for even stranger prizes. Amusement parks with Ferris wheels to take you a hundred feet above the fray.

As long as Aaron avoided the psychics and palm readers who could tell him his past and his present, he was always happy to be on the Boardwalk.

He learned that boardwalks were conceived in Atlantic City back in 1870 to solve a simple problem: how to prevent people from tracking beach sand into the luxury oceanfront hotels. By the turn of the century, the Boardwalk — and the commercial establishments built along its route — became a vacation destination on its own.

With due respect to Thomas Edison, Aaron thought boardwalks to be greater than anything ever invented in New Jersey.

His new home was rather ugly, just a long, wide shoebox with a small wood deck attached to the backside facing the ocean. The bedrooms, bathroom and the laundry room were all off to the front side. The rest of the house was one large, loft-like space with a countertop island to separate the kitchen from the living room.

It was simple. It was perfect for a man craving the simple life. Here, he could *settle*.

He took pictures of the view from his deck and sent them to his friends back in San Francisco, along with a note containing his address and phone number.

"This is what I am now," the note said. "This is where I am if you want to visit."

Having successfully traded coasts, Aaron eased comfortably into his new life. He put a lot of thought and effort into keeping busy. His long walks on the Boardwalk and jogs on the beach evolved into a new obsession with fitness. He bought an expensive exercise machine and incorporated a rigorous weight workout to his routine. As soon as the water warmed up enough in late spring, he added a long daily swim to his regimen.

With some help from contractors, Aaron also threw himself into home improvement. He hired carpenters and cabinetmakers to help him remodel the kitchen. He thought he might like to learn how to cook and wanted to be surrounded with all the modern conveniences. He shadowed the electrician as the man upgraded the house's wiring and installed track lighting throughout the kitchen and living room.

Aaron learned quickly and built a brand-new terraced

deck all by himself. The upper level was wider, with steps down to a beach-level platform complete with a foot shower. Aaron christened it as his own tiny boardwalk.

Over the winter, Aaron purchased his first computer, an Apple Macintosh. He installed a word processing program to start a journal, which he faithfully wrote in every day.

Aaron was acquiring new habits to replace the ones he left behind. The Les Paul and the rest of his guitars rested in their cases, stored in the third bedroom that he had not yet furnished. He sometimes hesitated as he walked by the closed door, then quickly found something else to do. The very idea of making music was still distasteful to him. He rarely even listened to music. Instead, he watched television. For the first time in his life, he followed sports. He grew to love football. At first, he rooted for Joe Montana and the Forty-Niners, the NFL front-runners from his beloved San Francisco. Then he remembered he was living in Giant country, so he switched his allegiance to LT and Phil Simms.

Aaron found it easy to stay busy, which helped him pass the sleepless nights. Insomnia was the one old habit he couldn't seem to shake. Sometimes, the soothing rhythm of the waves would lull him under, but that left him vulnerable to the nightmares. *You can change everything except the past,* he thought. And the past was always waiting there for him when he slept.

Sometimes when he couldn't sleep and ran out of things to do, he would take a drive to Atlantic City. He wasn't much of a gambler, but the casinos were open all night and he enjoyed playing cards. The band used to kill many an hour in the tour bus by playing small-stakes poker. Dewey often claimed that he could live off the money he took from his Carnival brothers playing seven-card stud.

One warm and restless night, Aaron was scouting the blackjack tables at the Showboat, Atlantic City's newest casino hotel, when he heard a laugh that sounded very familiar. It belonged to a woman, a smooth, melodic warble that trailed off with a sweet, lazy sigh.

The seats at the tables around him were full, with crowds of people standing behind the players. Aaron had to look from several angles to see all the faces.

None of the ladies looked familiar. Then he took a closer look at one of the dealers. She was a petite, attractive blond, about his age. She seemed to know many of the players at the table and they seemed to know her. There was more laughter, then he heard her speak.

Her seductive Georgia drawl dripped honey all over the table and the men sitting in front of her were lapping up every drop.

Aaron moved closer to the game and read the signs. A black sign on the table listed a one-hundred-dollar minimum bet. These boys were playing for some real money.

A rectangular plastic tag pinned to the dealer's colorful vest told everyone her name.

Betty.

CHAPTER 48

Aaron felt a bit woozy, so he moved away from the tables and found a seat in the slot parlor. After a few minutes, he went back for another look. No, he wasn't hallucinating, it *was* Betty Tilden, dealing blackjack like a seasoned veteran while she tactfully deflected the advances from her little class of high-rollers.

"Mr. White, you're making me blush," she said to one of the men. "You know we're not allowed to fraternize with the guests. Now, you boys want to play cards or not?"

Aaron cautiously inched closer the table, trying to blend with a dozen other spectators. It was the hottest action in the room. The men were wagering stacks of black hundred-dollar chips on every hand and doubling down when the odds were in their favor. The rabble booed when Betty burned the table by drawing to twenty-one and hooted with delight when she went bust.

After an hour or so, the bettors slowed down and the crowd began to disperse. Aaron left to use the bathroom and consider his next move. He went to the sink and let the water flow until it was ice cold, then threw some on his face. It wasn't working. He had been up for two nights. That's why he was here in the first place.

Aaron desperately needed to rest and think, so he booked a room. Upstairs, he took a long shower, then laid down. At first, thinking about Betty stirred up old demons, but after a while, the prospect of seeing her again warmed the cool, stiff sheets under him. Finally, the fatigue of nearly forty-two hours awake dragged him into a deep sleep.

The next morning, Aaron woke with the sun and headed

straight for the Boardwalk. He walked briskly from one end of Casino Row to the other, hoping the exercise would clear his mind. Gulls swarmed about, picking at the garbage from the night before that was still waiting to be swept up. The gulls made such a racket that at times, you couldn't hear the music blaring from speakers outside of every casino. Between the casinos, where the speakers weren't so loud, it was easy to hear the waves crashing on the shore.

Sometimes, the Boardwalk in Atlantic City reminded him of his early days in the Haight, with so many sounds competing for his attention as he walked to nowhere in particular.

A thousand questions followed him along the slanted wooden thoroughfare. What would he say to her? What *could* he say to her? Would she even recognize him? She hadn't the night before. They never even made eye contact.

Aaron thought about the forces of circumstance that led to this incredible coincidence. He had moved to New Jersey to start a new life. Was she here for the same reason? And he could not forget that their history was part of the past he had left behind. Could they possibly fit into each other's future?

Aaron wondered if Betty ever thought about him anymore. If there was some small part of her waiting for him to return. Maybe she would be better off if he left her alone. He remembered when he was passing through Reno and saw the road signs pointing to Las Vegas. He had the choice to drive south and answer the questions he was asking now. He chose not to. *Why*? And why should he change his mind now, just because the mountain had come to Mohammed, or at least had met him halfway?

He tried to reclaim some balance in his routine. He took a swim in the ocean, then went to the hotel spa for a hard, sweaty workout. The questions wouldn't go away. They needed to be answered. Fate had not gone to all this trouble only to be denied.

That night, Aaron went back to the Showboat and looked

for Betty. He found her at the same table. Some of the high rollers from the night before were back as well.

He kept his distance, still unsure of his next move. When the action at the table attracted another big crowd, he allowed himself to slide a little closer. From his new vantage point, he could examine Betty without attracting attention to himself. He studied her features, her movements, her voice. He had forgotten how much he loved the sound of her voice. Somehow she had hung onto that sensual Southern cadence she inherited mainly from her Nana. It was like music to him.

Her dealer's uniform, which fit the casino's theme of a Mississippi River boat, wasn't very flattering. Still, he could tell that time had been kind to her. Betty still had the same lean-but-round build. Last night, she had let her shoulder-length hair fall freely. Tonight, it was tied back in a ponytail, which flattered her high, round cheeks. She was an unfamiliar shade of blonde, more honey-gold than the natural platinum he remembered. With the exception of a few thin wrinkles around her eyes, her skin was smooth and flawless. And she still had that cute upper lip, curled up like Cupid's bow.

Standing there in the wings, Aaron found himself falling in love all over again. The men at the table were equally smitten. They didn't seem to mind that they were taking a beating. Betty and the house were having a good night.

"Don't blame me," she said diplomatically. "I make better tips when you guys win."

The crowd gradually dwindled when the men began to ration their bets. When Betty began a shuffle break, the last of the high rollers left, leaving just one player on the far corner. She was a thin, wrinkled old woman with badly dyed blonde hair and a cigarette held between two shaky, boney yellow fingertips. Aaron saw Betty wince from the smoke.

"Honey, can you call me a waitress?" the woman asked. "I could kill for a seven and seven. The drink, honey, not the cards."

Betty passed the request to a pit boss, then resumed her

elaborate shuffling routine. As she mixed the decks, she startled Aaron by speaking to him.

"So, why don't you join us ladies?" She finally looked up, smiled, then winked at the old lady.

"Huh? You mean me?" Aaron fumbled for words, just as he did when he first met her.

"Well, you've been standing there for the last two nights, so I thought you might like to try your luck."

Damn. He was busted.

"I don't know," he said. "A hundred dollars is a lot to bet on one hand. I've just been enjoying the action."

"You like the action, do you?"

It occurred to Aaron that he would have to either play or leave, so he took a seat. "OK, let's play some cards," he said.

Betty finished shuffling, let the old lady cut the shoe, and stood back. Aaron sat there politely, waiting for her to deal. *Why was she looking at him like that?*

"Place your bets," she gently instructed.

Oh, yeah. "I need some chips," he said, digging into his pockets for some cash. He came up with two hundred and thirty dollars and offered it to Betty. She gave him a funny look, handed him back thirty dollars and folded the rest into a slot. *"Changing two hundred,"* she called out. A pit boss came by, curious about a new player asking for only two chips at a hundred-dollar table.

He won the first hand, then lost three straight, leaving him with thirty dollars and a red face. "That was quick," he said, smiling.

"It sure was," she said, laughing. "Maybe you should try the slots."

"I'll be back," Aaron said as he left the table and headed for the lobby. He found an ATM machine, punched in the maximum — eight hundred dollars — then returned to the table.

Betty was gone. He noticed a new shift of dealers had come in to take over. Then he spotted her walking out the

Boardwalk exit with another female dealer.

Aaron followed and found them leaning against a Boardwalk railway, chatting as the other woman lit a cigarette. He tossed caution to the wind and walked straight up to them.

"Break time, eh?" he said, smiling.

Both women look startled. "Um, do we have a problem here?" the other woman said in a thick New Jersey accent.

Betty touched the other woman's arm and said, "It's all right, Annie." She looked straight up at Aaron. "He's OK. He just doesn't know that you're not supposed to be following the dealers around on their breaks."

She kept staring at him, hoping he would get the message.

"Security keeps a close eye on us, you know, even out here."

Oh, shit, Aaron thought. *They think I'm some kind of pervert stalker.*

"So why don't you just go back inside and let us take our break, OK?" Annie said sternly. "Or do I have to call them over?"

Betty continued to stare at Aaron. "Now, don't be rude, Annie. Look at him. He won't do anything ungentlemanly, will you, Mr. ..."

"Lowe ... Aaron."

Suddenly, Annie became terribly excited. "Oh my God, oh my God, oh my God! Betty, do you know who this is?" She turned towards Aaron. "Oh my God! You're Aaron Lowe!"

Betty cocked her head, looked at her friend, then looked back at Aaron.

"Aaron Lowe?" she asked.

"You know, the guy from the Carnival!" Annie exclaimed. "The band. *You know*, 'A Single Reason Why.' Oh my God!"

Aaron stood there with a sheepish grin on his face. At least she wasn't going to sic security on him.

"What are you doing here? Are you doing a concert here?" Annie said as sweetly as her nail-and-hammer voice would allow.

"I'm just, well, I live in Jersey now," he said. "I come down here sometimes. I love the Boardwalk."

"Isn't it wonderful?" Betty said. "I could stay out here for hours. Too bad we only have five more minutes."

"I'm embarrassed to ask, but could you possibly give me an autograph?" Annie asked. "I'm a really big fan of yours. My ex-husband has all your albums. We saw you guys in Philadelphia once. JFK Stadium. What a show!"

"Yeah, I remember that one," he said, laughing to himself as he recalled that horrible, squall-scarred gig in Philly's historic canyon. "That was quite a night."

She pulled a small notepad from her bag and opened it to the back page. "Make it out to Ann, please. Oh my God, this is unbelievable!"

Aaron signed as instructed, returned the notepad and smiled.

"I mean it, I'm a really big Carnival fan," Annie said. "When are you guys going to get back together?"

Aaron had to force a smile this time. "I don't know. Someday, maybe. It's kinda complicated."

A light went on in Annie's brain. "Oh yeah. That thing in Detroit. I saw it on the news. It must have been terrible."

Thankfully, Betty changed the subject. "Annie, we gotta go."

"Oh my God!" Annie squealed, then ran back into the Showboat. Betty waited a moment, turned back to Aaron, smiled and held out her hand. "It was nice to meet you, Mr. Lowe."

Aaron took her hand and held it softly for a moment. "Call me Aaron. It was nice to meet you, too, … "

"Betty," she said. "Just like it says on the name tag."

"*Betty*," he said.

Aaron thought better about following Betty back inside. That *would* be stalking, he reasoned. Instead, he took a seat on a nearby bench. About an hour later, Betty came back out.

When she saw him there, she came over and joined him on the bench, leaving a respectable distance between them.

"Mr. Lowe. Still breathing the salt air, I see. Don't you want to go back inside and lose some more money?"

Aaron couldn't help beaming at the very sight of her. "I'm … not much of a gambler, really. I just come down here sometimes when I can't sleep."

"Well, I'm not sure how much sense that makes. You sleep better down here?"

Aaron laughed. "I always loved your sense of humor."

Betty turned her head like a confused puppy. "Excuse me?"

He hadn't meant to say that out loud. He was having trouble keeping it all inside.

"I … I just feel like I know you."

Now she was looking shy and confused at the same time. "Mr. Lowe … Aaron, don't make too much of this, but you seem familiar to me in some way, too. I don't know why. Is it possible that we have met before?"

How about that? Aaron thought. Maybe this would be easier than he thought.

"Do I look familiar?" he asked.

She studied him intensely for a while. "Something about the eyes."

She broke off her stare and laughed at herself. "I don't know. And I don't have my glasses, either. I probably saw you on television or something. Carnival, right? That's what Annie said. I'm sorry, I don't really follow the new bands all that closely. I just listen to what's on the radio. But I think I know that song Annie mentioned — what was it, 'A Reason Why?' That sounds very familiar."

"Actually, Carnival isn't all that new. We split up almost two years ago. We're old, old news."

Aaron looked out at the ocean and cleared his throat. He could see the waves emerging out of the darkness, then crashing on the shore.

"Look, I don't know if this is the time or place, but … " he stopped himself mid-sentence. *This is going to be hard*, he thought.

"Betty, maybe you don't remember me, but I could never forget you. You're from Las Vegas, right?"

He had startled her already. "How did you … you know me from Las Vegas?"

"From a long time ago."

A few silent seconds passed. Then her eyes popped with recognition. She turned pale, then jumped back in her seat. Her mouth opened wide, as though she was about to scream, but her voice came out as a breathy whisper.

"Willie?"

He didn't say anything. His eyes told her she was right.

"Willie?" she asked again.

Again, Aaron said nothing. Betty reached out to him, then pulled back. She spun off the bench and backed up a step.

"I don't believe it. This cannot possibly be happening."

"Betty, I know. I don't believe it myself. I came down here and there you were. I had no idea …"

Betty kept backing up until she bumped into a couple strolling on the Boardwalk. She stared at them, apologized, then stared back at Willie. She looked horrified.

"This is … *I can't handle this*," she said. She looked at her watch. "I've got to go. I've got to go. I'm … "

She turned away and hurried back into the Showboat.

Aaron didn't follow her. He understood exactly how she felt. He could use a few minutes alone, too. He took off his shoes and walked slowly across the sand to the shoreline, until the foamy seawater seeped between his toes. It was unusually warm. Funny how it always felt warmer at night.

After a few minutes, he returned to the bench and waited, hoping Betty would return as well. A few more moments passed before he saw her come back out of the Showboat, carrying a small gym bag. She looked around, saw him and took a slow, unsteady path across the Boardwalk in his direction. Aaron stood up but was afraid to say anything for fear of scaring her away again.

She looked him over from head to foot, then leaned on the Boardwalk railing. "I kinda freaked out in there," she said, looking somewhat embarrassed. "They told me to take the rest of the night off."

"I'm sorry, Betty," Aaron said. He wanted to hold her so bad that it ached. "I didn't mean to upset you."

"Huh?" she said in an excited voice.

"I hope I didn't get you in trouble."

"No, no, it's alright, I'm just ... oh, God, Willie, is it really you? Where in heaven ... *where have you been?*"

Tears welled in her eyes until a few trickled slowly down her rosy cheeks. She smiled weakly and tried to hold it together. "Oh, well, dumb question, I guess. You're some kind of big rock star. Everyone seems to know who you are except *me*. Annie's in there showing off the autograph you gave her.

"Oh, Willie, what are you doing here?"

"I guess it must be fate, Betty. I live up the Shore by Point Pleasant. I had no idea you were here. I know it's crazy, but here we are."

"Here we are, here we are," she said faintly, almost as if she were singing a lullaby. "And what are we supposed to do now?"

Aaron gently took her hand. "Why don't we just get some coffee?"

Betty chose to have an iced tea instead. "I'm quite sufficiently wired at the moment, thank you," she said. They got their drinks to go and walked from one end of the Boardwalk to the other, talking slowly through the past 22 years. Aaron gave her the outline of his adult life. Hiding out from the cops and the mob in San Francisco. Assuming a new identity. His eventful career as a musician. A longtime, frequently rocky relationship that ended badly, followed by Claire's suicide. The awful business in Detroit, his retirement and his new beachfront hideaway.

Betty told him about the long, hard years of caring for her mother. A bad marriage to the wrong man. Having a child. Travis was ten years old now and her pride and joy. She endured the humiliation of a husband who cheated on her often and beat her even more. But when he started beating Travis, she had him arrested, filed for divorce and escaped to Atlantic City. The Showboat was only too happy to hire an experienced Las Vegas blackjack dealer just before its grand opening last year.

They did the math and realized both of them had relocated to New Jersey within months of each other. What were the odds of that?

"It was a bit of a shock coming out here," she said. "I had lived in Las Vegas for my entire life, almost, anyway. New Jersey is so different. So much faster. Everyone is always so busy. But the ocean. Don't you just love it? It's so much more alive than the desert. Look at the moon. It controls the tides, you know. How is that possible? It really makes you wonder."

She took off her shoes and left them on the edge of the Boardwalk. She motioned for Aaron to follow. They walked across the beach, all the way to the shoreline, then headed south. The surf foamed above their ankles and dampened the cuffs of their pants.

The noise of the waves muted Betty's rising voice.

"Willie, it took me a long time to get over you," she said. "What are you doing here? And why now?"

"Betty, I told you, this just happened. I don't know why either of us is here."

"But it did happen. You're here. I'm here. Where do we go from here?"

"Where do you want to go?"

"I don't know. I don't know if I want to go back *there*, you know? We've been talking and talking about what happened since you left Las Vegas. But we haven't talked about what happened *before* you left. Or why you never came back."

Aaron instinctively reached for a cigarette, then

remembered he had given them up. She was asking some difficult questions.

"Betty, I've been asking myself the same thing for more than twenty years. I don't really have an answer. I messed things up so badly. I guess I thought you were better off without me."

"Well, I wish you had let me make that decision for myself."

"And what would you have decided back then? I was in big trouble. I had to get out of town. I had to leave everything I knew behind. My brother was dead, and I couldn't even contact my mother for fear of being found out. What would you have decided to do? If I asked you to come with me — your unfaithful, no-good fugitive ex-boyfriend — would you have done it?"

Betty turned her back to Aaron, hoping he wouldn't see the tears were flowing again.

"To tell you the truth, I don't know. I loved you so much, and I wanted to be with you so badly. But I was scared, too. You were mixed up in something that I didn't understand, and it frightened me. I don't know what I would have done, Willie, but you never gave me the option, so what's the difference?"

"I'm sorry, Betty. I'm so sorry for everything. We were both so young, and life was so damn complicated back then. How did everything get so complicated?"

Betty let Aaron put his arms around her, then he felt her collapse into his embrace. "Oh Willie, I waited so long for you to come back, but it seems like a lifetime since I gave up hoping. Is this a dream, or is it really you?"

It felt as if she would drop to the ground if he let her go. Not that he was about to. He wanted to hold on to her forever.

"I don't really know who I am, Betty, but I feel a lot better here with you."

CHAPTER 49

The summer of 1988 was a long time in coming for Aaron and Betty. He had no qualms about following the path fate had laid out for him. She was a little more cautious.

"I've got my boy to think about," she told him early in their new courtship.

So they took it slowly at first, as though a chaperone was watching and waiting for them to make a false move. Betty accepted "dates" from Aaron and would meet with him a few hours before or after her shift at the Showboat.

They never went anywhere. They just walked the Boardwalk — a comfortable and effective neutral ground — trading stories and generally getting to know each other as adults.

It took a while, but Aaron told her *everything*. That was how it was when they were first together, he thought. And ever since they split up, there had never been anyone else he could tell *everything* to. Certainly not Claire. His life with Claire was a symphony of secrets.

It was more than his desire to respect Betty with total honesty. It was his desperate need to *unload*. And she was so easy to talk to. She already knew his oldest secrets. He knew he could trust her with the rest.

Betty admitted she often had to fight depression and, for a little while after her mother died, she danced with her demons.

"I was getting wasted and picking up guys like some kind of nympho whore," she said. "That was around the time I met Mitch. He was a Teamster. He drank too much, but so did I. He made decent money and he didn't gamble, which put him a notch above most of the men I met. So when I got pregnant, we figured we might as well get married.

"Mitch was the type of husband who never let his wife get in the way of a good time. I stopped drinking and smoking for the baby and once Travis came along, I had to stay home. He didn't see it that way. When I caught him cheating on me, he started smacking me around like it was my fault.

"I'm not proud of any of it, but I did get Travis out of the deal. God, I just love him so much, and I love being a momma."

"I'd love to meet him," Aaron kept saying.

"I'm not quite ready for that yet," she kept replying. "I'm still not sure what to make of all this."

After about a month of "dates," Betty finally agreed to bring the men in her life together. On her day off, she brought Travis to her usual meeting spot with Aaron on the Boardwalk by Convention Hall.

Aaron noticed Travis was big for his age. He was a husky five feet tall, wearing shorts, a Showboat T-shirt and a Philadelphia Phillies cap. He reminded Aaron of his big brother at that age.

The boy shyly clung to his mother's side as she made the introductions. She smiled as she watched both of them fumble for words.

Betty had packed a picnic lunch and a blanket for the beach. The adults sat back and relaxed when Travis left them to ride the waves on his boogie board.

"He seems like a great kid," Aaron said. "I guess his father must have been a big guy."

"A big jerk is what he was," she said. "At least Travis didn't get his daddy's disposition. He's as sweet as my Nana's peach cobbler."

She opened the cooler and pulled out some sandwiches. "Ham and Swiss, mayo, no mustard, right?"

"How could you remember that?" Aaron was astounded. He despised mustard. God, what a woman.

"You know, I've never introduced Travis to any of my gentlemen friends before," she said. "He still thinks it was his fault that his daddy was the way he was."

Aaron smiled. "Is that what I am?"

"What?"

"Your gentleman friend?"

Betty smiled, then opened a jar of pickles. "Well, you *used* to be."

"Seriously, what did you tell him about me?"

"Well, I told him that I knew you way back when and that we had bumped into each other here. I told him it was fun for grownups to catch up on old times. He's a kid. He doesn't really get how we could spend so much time catching up. I told him that he'll understand when he's old enough to have stuff to catch up on."

Aaron looked down to the water's edge. Travis was safe and far from earshot.

"What if you told him I love his mother like I've never loved anyone else, and I want her back in my life? Would he understand that?"

"Oh, Willie … "

"You know, maybe it's time you started calling me Aaron."

She forced back a tear, then laughed. "I'll call you what I please, Mr. Willie Taylor."

"Well, you did introduce me to Travis as Mr. Lowe."

"Did I? Oh, this is all so complex. I don't want my life to be so complex."

"Neither do I. I spent so many years letting other people complicate my life. But when I'm with you, it all feels so simple, so natural. Like this is the way it's supposed to be. And you know what? For the first time since I can remember, I can sleep like a normal person. Nightmares are gone, too."

"Willie, there's a part of me that wants to believe this could work. But there's also a part of me that's scared to death. And I'm still worried about what Travis will make of all this. You've got to understand, none of this is easy for me. You may be sleeping like a big old baby, but I haven't had a decent night's sleep since you showed up."

A scream from the shore shattered their conversation. They turned and saw Travis tumbling head over heels into the surf. Aaron jumped up and sprinted to the shoreline to grab the boy out of the vicious undertow.

Betty got there a second later. "Travis! Are you OK? Is he OK? Oh, *baby!*"

Travis coughed hard to clear his throat, then shook his head like a wet dog.

"*Wow*, that was *intense!*" he said, grinning widely. "Where's my boogie board?"

Aaron laughed, then put an arm around Betty. "I don't know much about kids, but I think he's OK."

"I'm OK," Travis said. "I'm *fine!*"

Betty was laughing and crying at the same time. "Oh God, Travis, you scared the life out of me! Oh, my! You need to be more careful."

"I will, mom," Travis said before running off to retrieve his board.

She looked up at Aaron, then leaned against him. "Well, aren't you our handsome knight in shining armor?" She kissed him gently on the lips. It was their first kiss in more than two decades. "I think I need to sit down. I do believe I'm getting a case of the vapors."

Betty leaned on Aaron as they walked back to the blanket. He helped her sit down, then sat beside her. She was quiet for a few moments, then leaned forward and kissed him again, longer, but just as gently as before. They stared at each other, sharing a warm glow that both remembered well.

"Do you think you could do me one more favor, Willie?"

"Anything," he said eagerly.

"Get rid of the beard."

CHAPTER 50

Travis was too old to be grounded. Otherwise, the mess he made in the laundry room would have wrecked his weekend plans.

Betty sighed and reluctantly gathered his greasy coveralls into a basket. "I'm not going to wash them, you know!" she shouted down the hall, hoping to wake her son before noon.

It was a typical summer Saturday on the Jersey Shore. The weekend crowd had jammed every road and taken every parking spot in town, legal or otherwise. Clumps of beachgoers were parading by private homes like refugees, lugging beach chairs and umbrellas and pulling coolers on squeaky wheels.

Travis was fast asleep. His band, Riptide, had played until two in the morning at a Jersey Shore nightclub. Betty couldn't remember which one, but it was always a late night when the band played on weekends. The poor kid was up at dawn the day before and put in ten hours at the Chopper Shop before coming home, grabbing a bite and heading right back out for the gig.

His mother admired how hard he worked. She just didn't like it when he dumped a week's worth of filthy work uniforms on the laundry room floor, as if he expected them to be magically cleaned by Sunday night.

Of course, they always were. By the time he woke up, he would have just enough time for a quick swim, some dinner and then it was off to the Saturday night gig. If Betty didn't wash them, they wouldn't get washed.

"Hello! Mrs. Lowe?" Good, Betty thought. Roxy was here. She could help with her boyfriend's laundry.

"In the laundry room, Rox," Betty called out. "Wake up Big Boy, will you please?"

Betty went back to the kitchen and put on a fresh pot of coffee. A few minutes later, Roxy and a bleary-eyed Travis joined her. "Coffee," Travis mumbled. He tugged his T-shirt down over his ample belly, pulled up his sweat pants and flopped into a kitchen chair that creaked in protest of bearing his two-hundred-and-fifty-pound girth.

"How was the gig, baby?" his mother asked.

"Rockin' as usual," he said, rubbing his eyes. "Breakfast, please. With meat."

"I made some hash from the leftover ham," Betty said. "How about that and some eggs?"

"I love you," he said. "Roxy, watch what she does. Watch and learn."

"*You* watch and learn, young man," Betty said. "The way you eat, you need to learn how to feed yourself."

"When is dad coming home?" he asked.

"He said he would try to be home by two," Betty said. "But only if he can get someone to stay and close."

"Why doesn't he just close on the weekends in the summer? He hardly does any business."

"Because he's got some good customers who can only get there on the weekend. It's good for business."

"So what? We're not gonna starve if the business goes bad."

"He enjoys working at the Exchange. He wants to hand it over to you someday."

"Well, I'm happy at the Chopper Shop and they pay better than he does. Anyway, I need him to bring home a few parts. The pickup on my Stratocaster is messed up. I need him to fix it before tonight."

"Why don't you just go down there?"

"Because I'm tired and I can't deal with the traffic."

Betty served both kids a big helping of hash and scrambled eggs, then made herself a cup of tea. She watched with wonder as her son cleaned his plate in less than two minutes flat. God, but the boy could eat.

And so the pattern that began right after her son's high school graduation continued at the Lowe residence. Betty found it to be a happy rut. Maybe it was time for Travis to move out and maybe get a place with Roxy. They were very much in love and very well-suited for each other. Roxy was no raving beauty, but she was a sweet, resourceful girl who worked two jobs and helped her single mother care for two younger brothers.

Travis wasn't exactly a matinee idol, either. He could easily be mistaken for a stereotypical biker or metalhead and, in truth, he was a little of each. Betty could have killed him when he tattooed a big Riptide logo on his arm.

He also was a gifted motorcycle mechanic who put in at least fifty hours a week at the Chopper Shop. On the weekends, he strapped on his guitar and played with Riptide, which was considered to be one of the best unsigned bands on the Jersey Shore music scene.

He didn't drink or do drugs, he stayed out of trouble and he was saving money for the future. He might not ever cure cancer, but he was a well-adjusted and responsible young man, his laundry deficiencies notwithstanding. Travis still was Betty's pride and joy, although his stepfather also had a lot to do with how well he turned out.

Travis had called Aaron "Dad" ever since his mother reunited with her old boyfriend. A few months after meeting Aaron on the Boardwalk, Betty and Travis moved to Bay Head. In the spring of 1989, nearly twenty-eight years after their first date, Aaron and Betty finally got married. It was a small wedding, at least when measured by attendance, but the reception was a loud and lively affair. All the former members of Carnival flew in for the occasion. The happy reunion lasted until dawn as the party moved from the catering hall — ironically named the Victorian Manor — back to the beach house.

They avoided playing music or any talk of reforming the band and stuck to swapping stories of their adventures since breaking up three years earlier. Patrick had recorded two solo albums and was earning a respectable reputation as a singer-songwriter. Gerald was writing music for the movies. Garrett had moved to the other side of the glass and was now a successful record producer. He often worked with Dewey, who still was one of the busiest session drummers in the business. And the nightclub Dewey opened in his old warehouse was one of the hottest spots in San Francisco.

Other than Sean David, who was now a full-time pineapple farmer in Hawaii, Aaron was the only alumnus of Carnival who wasn't making music professionally. He had found something better to do. He was going to be a husband and father. He was going to put their needs above his.

"As a musician, I achieved and exceeded every goal and ambition I ever had," he told his friends. "But as a person, I was a complete failure. I still love music, but now's my chance to make a real difference in people's lives. People that matter to me a great deal."

He also took the opportunity to tell his trusted bandmates about his former life as Willie Taylor. He needed them to know about his history with Betty so they could understand how much she meant to him. Just how important it was to give her, and Travis, a better lot in life.

His confessions stopped short of the sordid details surrounding the deaths of Andy Rush and Claire Hall. Some secrets were better left buried deep in the ground. Betty flipped out when she heard about that episode and it took her weeks to recover.

Of course, he swore his friends to secrecy about the rest of it. There was no statute of limitations on murder and Aaron didn't want to take any chances.

About a year after the wedding, Aaron had fixed everything around the house that needed fixing, so he searched for a new diversion. He found it when he saw a "For

Sale" sign in the window of a music shop in downtown Point Pleasant Borough. He bought it in a quick cash deal and renamed it Lowe's Music and Instrument Exchange. While the shop did a small amount of retail business, Aaron's passion was to buy old guitars, fix them up and sell them cheap to struggling musicians who couldn't afford to buy new.

At first, Travis would spend hours at the shop helping his stepfather. They adored each other so much that Betty would sometimes weep with joy when she watched them work and play together.

Aaron also spent long hours teaching Travis how to play the guitar and the boy was a quick learner. He formed Riptide when he was only sixteen. He still didn't have a driver's license, so Aaron had to drive him to the gigs. As long as he was there, Aaron made himself useful by running the band's mix board.

Having a famous rock musician as a father and roadie helped Riptide get through a few doors other bands could not. By the time Travis graduated high school, his band had enough experience and contacts to consider going full-time.

The other members were willing, but Travis said no.

Aaron wondered why and offered to make some calls on the band's behalf.

"I still have some influence, you know," he told Travis. "I could probably get you guys a recording deal. You're good enough to have a real shot in the business. Why not give it a try while you're still young? You may never get another chance like this. It could be a great experience for you."

By then, Travis had fallen in love with Roxanne and motorcycles. He had a good job at the Chopper Shop. He was having fun playing weekend gigs at the Shore.

"Why would I trade all of that to be some kind of international rock star?" he said. "How'd that work out for you, Dad? How did that work out for Mom? I'm happy with my life. Why would I want to give it all up and do what you did?"

Out of the mouth of babes, Aaron thought. Even a babe who was known to his friends as Big Boy.

A few years later, Travis was inhaling his second plate of hash when he stopped to answer the phone. "International House of Pancakes. Big Boy speaking, how can I help you?" he asked.

He listened for a moment, said, "Uh, he's not here right now," then listened a little longer.

"Is this some kind of joke? Ian, is that you?"

Travis started waving madly to his mother. "Paper and pencil! Quick!"

He wrote down some names and numbers. "Yeah, I'm his stepson. I have a band, too … Yeah, he's great. So are you guys. My dad took me to see you at Giants Stadium. Yeah, sure! I'm sure it'll be fine … I'll make sure he gets the message … Yeah, he'll be home tonight. Yeah, thanks!"

Betty stood Behind Travis with hands on her hips. "What in heaven was that all about?"

"Um, what are we having for dinner Tuesday night?"

"What? How do I know? Why?"

Travis started a grin that slowly made its way from one ear to the other.

"Because Rollo and Rex from 2Night are coming to dinner."

CHAPTER 51

2Night was probably the most famous and most influential band in the free world. Fifteen years ago as a brash group of teenagers from Glasgow, they put Scotland on the rock 'n' roll map with their raw-but-passionate sound. As the years went by, their music became more sophisticated and popular, but it never lost its edge. When they paid musical tribute to classic bands from the sixties and seventies, newer bands tried to copy them, creating a line of rock lineage that was linked through four decades.

The charismatic lead singer and songwriter, Roland MacPherson, aka Rollo, became the grand sage of the international music scene, producing records for bands all around the world, organizing benefit concerts and speaking out on behalf of many human-rights organizations.

Rex Harrington, the band's lead guitarist, kept a slightly lower profile and was known as the brains behind the group. He was the one who took Rollo's ideas and turned them into records that the critics gushed over and the public bought by the millions.

2Night's live show was legendary, filling the stage with massive video screens, theatrical sets and a supporting cast that sometimes numbered in the hundreds. Aaron and Travis saw their show at Giants Stadium two years earlier, and Travis remembered Aaron saying, "Compared to these guys, Pink Floyd's show is a few firecrackers in the back yard."

As usual, Betty couldn't place the band. She knew Carnival, Riptide and Bruce Springsteen, and not much else.

"Mom, believe me, this is like Jesus going to Egypt," said Travis, who never went to Sunday School. "This is totally over-the-top."

He quickly called his stepfather at the shop, but Aaron was already on his way home. He arrived a few minutes later and got a full report.

"Did they say what they wanted?" he asked suspiciously.

"Dad, they want to meet you. Rollo said they were big fans of yours."

"Well, that's very flattering, but they wouldn't come all this way just to fall at my feet. Believe me, Travis, my music never had that kind of effect on people."

That night, a 2Night staff assistant called on Rollo's behalf to schedule a visit. Rollo and Rex wanted to come by and pay their respects on Tuesday night. He asked Aaron not to make a fuss. They just wanted to meet with him and discuss a business proposition.

The assistant did not say what kind of business, leaving Aaron a little apprehensive about the meeting. This wasn't the first time he had been contacted by producers and other musicians. There had been plenty of offers to come out of retirement and get back into the business. Aaron turned all of them down without a second thought. Like his stepson, he was happy and wasn't about to mess up a good thing.

Still, he liked 2Night's music and respected Rollo and Rex as dedicated musicians. He remembered reading a magazine article about them when they first came out. Rex was quoted as saying Aaron Lowe and Carnival were among his most significant musical influences.

"There was a band that always got a raw deal because their records weren't as good as their live shows. But the night I saw them play was the night I decided I wanted to be a musician. I wanted to *be* Aaron Lowe."

So Aaron put his misgivings aside and agreed to accept their visit. Betty spent the afternoon cooking up a southern feast of pan-fried chicken, homemade potato salad and lots of fresh Jersey corn on the cob.

Travis made sure to come home from work on time and

even took a shower before dinner. Rex and Rollo finally arrived half an hour late in a black custom Range Rover. It was driven by a large man in a dark suit who looked as though he doubled as a bodyguard. The man stayed outside and in the vehicle.

"Damn, Dad, you're a rock star, you oughta get one of those, too," said Travis as he went to answer the door.

"The ride or the goon?" Aaron asked with a wink.

Rollo and Rex were polite, affable guests who fell victim to Betty's cooking.

"It's a good thing my girlfriend isn't here to see me eating this," Rollo said in his thick Scottish brogue while wiping chicken grease off his fingers with a paper napkin. "She's a hard-core vegan."

After dinner, the party moved outside to the patio and the guests explained the reason for their visit.

"I know you don't care for the spotlight and I respect that," Rollo said. "But I think it's important that people know about what you accomplished as a musician. We feel like we owe you a huge debt, and would like to repay that debt. We're in a position to do anything we want. Record anything we want. We want to put together an album of songs with some of the musicians who have influenced us. Steve Miller said he would do it. So did Van Morrison and Robbie Robertson. We'd like to bring you in as well.

"It wouldn't take a lot of your time, maybe a week or two in New York City. We would be working with each of the guests separately, so for that time, it would just be you and us. First-class studio, first-class accommodations. And, at the risk of insulting you, we would pay you handsomely for the privilege."

Betty and Travis sat anxiously as Aaron considered the incredible opportunity in front of him. At first, he said that he wouldn't feel right about reviving old Carnival songs without bringing the entire band in. They argued that he had written, arranged and sung the songs they wanted to do and, logistically, it would be difficult to work all six Carnival members into the project. They wanted him, and only him, to come in and duet with Rollo on "The Dead Don't Have to Worry." Then, he could play on a few other more obscure Carnival classics. Maybe add a few fresh guitar solos. Two or three of the tracks would then be chosen for the CD.

"What the hell, Dad?" Travis said. "What are you thinking about? Just do it!"

Aaron looked at Travis. The kid was about to bust wide open.

"Tell you what, if I can bring my boy along, you've got yourself a guitar player. Two, actually."

"Smashing! Absolutely smashing!" Rex said. "You can bring anyone you like. Maybe you can get Betty here to send some of that chicken with you."

Aaron christened the occasion by pulling his old Les Paul out of the attic. His favorite guitar, which had been with him for thirty-seven years, had rested quietly in its case for the last dozen. In the meantime, Aaron's guitar playing had been limited to lessons with Travis and some noodling to test guitars at the shop.

It all came back to him quickly, even though age had allowed some arthritis to stiffen his fingers. The Les Paul wasn't quite as lucky. It had been ravaged by time. The strings, of course, were shot. And the salty sea air had corroded the pickups. They would have to be replaced. Fortunately, no one was better at reconditioning Les Pauls than Aaron Lowe. All the technical skills he had learned since his days of hanging with Flash at KVLY had been finely honed over the past decade at the Exchange.

The sessions with 2Night were beyond anything Aaron could have imagined. For one thing, he had not been inside a recording studio for more than a decade. He was amazed that the industry-standard reel-to-reel master tape machines had been replaced by computers and digital recording devices. He was like a kid in a candy store as Rex showed off his custom guitar synthesizers, which could make his six strings sound like anything from a pipe organ to a jackhammer.

Aaron was at first alarmed by the number of people there. There was an army of producers, engineers, technicians and assistants. A separate room had been set up for the media covering the sessions as a major event. Another room was reserved for interviews. Still another was set up as a dining room with a gourmet buffet.

A film crew was on hand to record the entire event for a documentary.

"Don't worry, mate, they all work for us," Rollo told him. "Any time you want them out of your hair, just yell. Or throw a chair at them. And don't forget, you're just a small part of this, as are we. We've got six other guest artists coming in over the next three months. This won't turn into some cheesy A&E Biography of Aaron Bloody Lowe."

Eventually, they got around to playing some music and Aaron could feel warm blood flowing into veins he had long forgotten. 2Night had rehearsed nearly a dozen Carnival songs and could play them to perfection. Of course, they tweaked a few of the arrangements to update them for modern tastes and for 2Night's signature sound, which were more or less the same thing.

Rex and Aaron traded lead vocals on "The Dead Don't Have to Worry," and Aaron plugged his Les Paul into Rex's guitar synthesizer and played the kind of complex, melodic solo he was famous for. The new hardware gave his guitar an eerie echo, but there was no mistaking that Aaron Lowe was pulling the strings.

They spent the next two weeks laying down tracks for four songs, then spent their final week together playing around with the mix. In between sessions, the band coaxed old war stories out of Aaron. They were so nice to him, and to Travis, that Aaron almost volunteered a few episodes that could have gotten him in a lot of trouble. It was Travis who pinched him back to reality when he started to blab about seeing the Rat Pack perform in Vegas back in the early 1960s.

Aaron was genuinely sorry when the sessions came to an end.

"I've really got to thank you guys," he said to Rollo and Rex. "You talked me into doing something I never would have done otherwise, and it turned out to be one of the most enjoyable experiences of my career. It's nice to know I still have a few licks in me."

"You know, Aaron, there's a lot of people out there that would love to hear you and Carnival play again," Rollo said. "We could help you set it all up. We've got a whole production company. We'd be happy to have you open some of our U.S. shows next summer. You know what would really be outrageous? We're supposed to headline Woodstock '99 next summer. Maybe we could put both bands together and jam all night. Complete the circle and all that."

Aaron was tempted until Rollo mentioned Woodstock. He imagined hundreds of thousands of people tramping through the mud, screaming for Carnival to get off the stage and make way for 2Night.

"Rollo, like I said, this was a lot more fun than I expected," Aaron replied. "But playing rock star is something I left behind a long time ago."

"You don't have to be a rock star, Aaron," Rollo argued. "You just have to be a musician. And I know you well enough by now that you can't help but be a musician."

Aaron smiled. "Rollo, I learned the hard way that you can't be a proper musician *and* a star. Musicians are like vampires. Too much limelight and they burn to ashes."

Rollo looked a little miffed. "Well, we seem to do bloody well enough."

Aaron tried to explain himself a little better.

"That's different, you're different," he said. "I don't mean to imply you guys aren't serious musicians. You guys are great. I could learn a lot from you. But you're *more* than musicians. You're entertainers. You have a sense of how to put all the elements of the performing arts together. You have vision. You have an agenda.

"I'm just a guy who can play some. I don't know about the rest of it. All I know is music. And when it all got so big that the music barely mattered, well … take my word for it. What is it that Neil Young sang? That it's better to burn out than to rust? I think it's the other way around. Just call me Rusty."

Rollo laughed and offered his hand one more time.

"Well, as long as you're happy," he said. "But the offer stands, my word to God. Just call me if you change your mind."

Chapter 52

For someone who had spent most of his life in the entertainment industry, Aaron was incredibly clueless about how it worked. His mother handled his early career. When he became Aaron Lowe, Claire took care of the business side of Carnival.

So once again, left to his own devices, Aaron found himself neck-deep in the muck.

2Night released their long-awaited tribute album, "Legacies," just in time for the Christmas season of 1998. Just like their last three CDs, it debuted on the charts at Number One and stayed there through the holidays.

Aaron only appeared on three tracks, but it was enough to introduce him, and some of Carnival's greatest hits, to a whole new generation of fans. Golden Gate Records, now a subsidiary of Global America, Inc., quickly capitalized by releasing a CD of Carnival's greatest hits. If that wasn't enough, you could upgrade to the four-CD box set of Carnival classics, B-sides and unreleased live recordings. Both were very popular with the kids who followed the new wave of "jam" bands.

Back home, Aaron nervously tried to resume his business as usual. It was no use. The media spread news of the band like wildfire. Fans began to crowd the Exchange, making it impossible to conduct regular business. Someone published the Lowe's home address on the Internet and it became common to have strangers knocking on their front door at strange hours.

Aaron was furious, more so because it was his own fault. How could he not see this coming?

Patrick, Gerald and Dewey called to congratulate Aaron and gauge his interest in a reunion tour. For years, he had been the only holdout. He was eternally grateful that they understood his reasons for wanting to stay home. Things were different now. Carnival was in demand. Aaron was playing Carnival songs with other people and had earned a pretty penny doing so.

"Lowe-man, if you can play with them, why can't you play with us?" Patrick said. "And right now, we're bigger than the Backstreet Boys. If not now, when? We ain't getting any younger."

Patrick presented a good argument. Aaron never imagined how big his thing with 2Night would be. If he had, he never would have done it. But the damage had been done, his old band mates were feeling slighted and his precious privacy was shot to hell.

To make matters worse, Rollo told him that Carrie Mann called to request an interview for a segment of "The Phoenix Café" devoted to Carnival. She told him some of the Carnival alumni had already agreed to appear.

"You can't blame them," Betty told her husband. "They're proud of Carnival. They don't have your reasons for ducking the spotlight."

"Sounds like you think I should go along with it," Aaron observed with surprise.

"Well, I don't know about that. I've seen that show a few times and it's horrible. That Carrie Mann is such a bitch. She dredges up the worst gossip and throws it in people's faces. And they sit there, crying about how they screwed up, and endure the torture because YFM can make them famous again.

"Putting the band back together might not be such a bad idea. You're not the person you used to be, Aaron. It might not be so bad. You might even enjoy yourself. And it would mean so much to your friends."

"You may be right. It was great to play again, even in the studio, and now that I'm warmed up, I might as well follow up with Carnival. I guess maybe I owe it to them. But what about us? And Travis? What about our life?"

"Well, Aaron, things are already topsy-turvy around here. Maybe if you give the people what they want, they'll leave you alone."

"That's not my experience, sweetheart. That's not the way it works."

"Maybe not. I wasn't around for all those years when you were a big whatever. But I know you. The music matters so much to you. And if you don't do this, you'll always wonder '*what if?*'

"Look, don't worry about Travis and me. We can take care of things here. Do what your heart tells you. We'll be here when you get home."

Later that afternoon, as expected, Aaron got a call from Carrie Mann. She told him that everyone else in the band had agreed to appear on "The Phoenix Café" but it wouldn't work if he didn't join them.

Smart girl, Aaron thought. She must have done her homework. She knew he would be the toughest nut to crack, so she got the rest of the band in her corner first.

Aaron agreed to her terms, as long as the compensation included the custom "Phoenix Café" tour package. He called Rollo back and gave him the all-clear to participate as well. As for the offer to open for 2Night, Aaron gratefully declined. "I'm going to leave the stadiums to you guys. I'm just not comfortable with the big crowds. YFM is going to book us into some real nice clubs and concert halls. That's where we belong."

Aaron did accept one other offer from Rollo. "You're going to need a manager, mate. Someone who will protect your interest through the process. I've got a guy on staff who can help you. His name is Eli Kinder. I'll have him give you a call."

YFM scheduled the taping for early May in New York City. The idea was to interview the band as a group, and then

Carrie Mann would sit down and talk to each member separately.

Aaron was looking forward to seeing his old friends and excited about making music with them for the first time in several years. He would endure the interviews. Betty said he was a different person. She was right. And this different person could handle the media circus.

The group interview was hilarious. Everyone laughed about old times, receding hairlines and expanding waistlines.

"By the end of the tour, they'll be wheeling us out there," Patrick said. "Don't forget to have plenty of oxygen there for Dewey."

"And young women," Dewey said. "I seem to remember beautiful, eager young women."

Three days later, Aaron came back for his one-on-one with Carrie Mann. He was the last interview. By the time he got there, the rest of the group had left town. They would reconvene next month in San Francisco to rehearse for the tour.

Carrie greeted him warmly and escorted him to the set. She was taller than she looked on television. "Can I get you anything? Coffee, tea, some mineral water?"

"Water's good," he said as he settled in the tall chair opposite hers. He mentioned that it wasn't very comfortable and was told it prevented people from slouching, which looked bad on television.

As the taping began, Carrie loosened up with a few softballs about the Summer of Love and the Victorian Manner. Aaron knew the tougher questions were coming and he wasn't disappointed. She asked about the pain of losing his best friend and his longtime girlfriend in the space of a few short weeks. She grilled him about Detroit, asking how it felt to be at the epicenter of such a violent episode and if he felt responsible in any way.

Aaron felt he was doing a pretty good job of saying the right things. He peeked at his watch. They had been at it for forty-five minutes. Carrie promised to keep the interview to an hour.

I'm home-free, he thought happily.

Then, Carrie pulled the pin and dropped the grenade in his lap.

"Aaron, there's only one more thing I'd like to know," she said. "Does the name *Weekend Willie* mean anything to you?"

The room suddenly began to spin. Aaron could see lips moving, but could hear no sound. A loud ringing in his ears shattered the silence. It was a rapid, off-key ring, like the unforgiving clamor of an old wind-up alarm clock.

What did she say? The ringing was so loud that he could barely hear his own thoughts.

"Did you hear the question?"

Of course he heard the question. It was still ringing in his head like a damn church bell.

Aaron tried to regroup as the room spun faster and the bell rang louder.

"I'm sorry, who?"

"*Weekend Willie.* Does that name mean anything to you?"

"Uh, no. I mean, not really. Should it?"

"And ... *go to commercial!*" he heard someone shout. The segment was being taped, but was being staged as though it was live. The timed breaks helped to preserve continuity when it was all edited together.

The break gave Aaron a chance to catch his breath. Two minutes later, he was right back on the hot seat. Back on the set, Aaron could see Eli still arguing with the show's producer in a distant corner of the studio.

"*And we're on in five, four three, two, one ...* " and the red light on the camera went back on.

Carrie smiled at the camera. "We're talking to Aaron Lowe, leader of the classic rock band, Carnival. Aaron, I've been doing some digging and I've made an odd connection. Some of our audience may remember the name Weekend Willie, one of the more infamous one-hit wonders in rock and roll history. His real name was Willie Taylor Jr., a child musical prodigy who started out singing on the radio in California back in the 1950s. By the time he was fourteen, he had started a tremendously popular lounge act with his brother, Bobby, in Las Vegas at the Full House Hotel and Casino. In 1966, he released his first record, "Betty Are You Ready?" which became a Number One hit.

"What a lot of people don't know is that a few months later, before he got a chance to make another record, Willie Taylor disappeared from sight after he was implicated in a shooting that left two people dead. One of those people was Carlo Bucco, a young man reportedly tied to organized crime. The other was Willie's brother, Bobby, who also died of a gunshot wound.

"Weekend Willie was never seen or heard from again, and a mysterious legend was born. No one ever knew what happened to him. Was he involved in the shootings? Did the mob hunt him down? Or was he able to put the slip on them, and the police, and find a way to hide his true identity?

"Aaron, does any of this sound familiar to you?"

Aaron simply relaxed. He knew he was beaten.

"It's a fascinating story, Carrie," he said dryly. "Why don't you tell us how it comes out?"

Carrie licked her lips and went in for the kill.

"Well, a few weeks ago, I followed up a rumor that made its way to my desk. You've always been a man of mystery. You've always been tight-lipped about your past. But I dug up some interviews that you gave many years ago. In those interviews, you said that you grew up in Southern California. San Clemente, I think you said it was? Well, there's no record of an Aaron Lowe attending school in San Clemente. In fact, there's no record of an Aaron Lowe living anywhere in California until 1966, about a month after Willie Taylor disappeared.

"Oceanside," Aaron said with a matter-of-fact tone. "Get your facts straight. I lived in Oceanside."

"Well, in that interview, you said San Clemente. A little deception, a little misdirection on your part, perhaps?" she smirked. "Bottom line, Aaron, is that your history begins where Willie Taylor's ends. Now, I've got some photos here of Willie Taylor, or Weekend Willie, back in Las Vegas. Can we put that up on the monitor? Boy, does he look familiar."

Carrie stopped talking to observe Aaron's reaction. He just sat there, motionless, with the blank expression of a poker champion. Inside, he was busted, boned and filleted.

Carrie broke off the stare fight and filled the dead air. "OK, I've got some more evidence linking you and ..."

Aaron calmly interrupted her.

"Carrie, look, if you were me back then, well, anyone would have done the same thing. I didn't do anything wrong. I didn't commit any crime. I didn't shoot anyone, even in self-defense. My life was in danger, so I left town and found a place to hide. I changed my name so they couldn't find me. I got on with my life. I never denied being Willie Taylor. No one ever asked me. I didn't think anyone really knew or cared about Weekend Willie."

"Well, the Las Vegas Police wanted you for questioning."

"I didn't kill anybody. I didn't hurt anybody and I wasn't involved in committing any sort of crime. I assume that the police figured that out for themselves. Why do you even bring it up, Carrie? Are there any warrants out for me, or for Willie Taylor? I'll bet if there was, you would be waving it in front of the camera right now."

Carrie smiled and returned the volley.

"As a matter of fact, I spoke to a detective in Las Vegas, who said that the case file indicated you were cleared as a suspect. But you were wanted for questioning as a likely witness. After all, the shootings took place in your hotel room! Anyway, you may be relieved to hear that the case file left the Las Vegas Police very little to follow up on, so they have no plans to reopen the case."

"That's great, Carrie. Best news I heard all day. Anything

else you want to talk about?"

News of Carrie Mann's salacious scoop leaked to the press before the show aired a week after the taping.

Patrick called to apologize. The old Moonshiner was pretty sure that he was Carrie Mann's secret source.

"I *might* have let something slip about Weekend Willie. I'm so sorry," he said. "To tell you the truth, I was a little wasted when she called to get some background. She got me going on about how wild things were back then, and I guess I tried to impress her with some wild stories. Have to admit, she was smokin' hot, am I right? Anyway, that whole Weekend Willie thing was the wildest story of them all, and it just kind of slipped out. I'm so sorry, Lowe-man."

Naturally, the interview sparked a firestorm across the nation. Sensational journalism didn't get much more sensational than this. Carrie Mann had solved a thirty-three-year-old cold case and revealed to America that one famous celebrity was actually *two*.

Overnight, Aaron became the poster boy for the phrase "truth is stranger than fiction." Network morning shows attacked the story from every angle. One of them dug up Sammy Llanes and Jimmy Rose from the old Taylor Brothers band. In a live interview, both of them claimed Aaron, or at least Willie Taylor, owed them back pay and thirty-three years' worth of interest.

Another reporter scooped the competition by digging up records that Winnie had Willie declared dead in 1974. She was living in Chicago at the time as Mrs. Pasquale Bucco. Andy's suspicions about his mother's whereabouts had been accurate.

As Willie's only surviving relative, Winnie sued Harrison Records to collect the royalties on "Betty Are You Ready?" and a followup single that never charted. Aaron never knew about them and was surprised to learn those 45s had become popular collector's items at vinyl record shows.

"Good for Winnie," Aaron told Betty. "She always knew

how to play all the angles."

Otherwise, the furor drove Aaron into the kind of deep depression that he hadn't experienced since the Carnival days. This time, though, Betty was there to bring him out of it.

"You know what's pretty cool?" she told him. "I've heard 'Betty Are You Ready?' on the radio four times in the last week. I always loved that song."

Aaron's scowl told her that he didn't share her amusement.

"Come on, Aaron, that secret's been eating at you since you were nineteen years old. Isn't it about time you let it go? Nobody except you cares about what happened back then. You don't have to hide anymore. And after a little while, everyone will forget about Weekend Willie, and you can go back to being Aaron Lowe, less a little emotional baggage. You'll see. Madonna will put out another sex book, or some rappers will shoot at each other, and everyone will forget about your moldy old story.

"Either way, I promise that you won't get away from me this time. I'm going to get you one of those ankle bracelets so I can track you with the GPS on my Acura."

Aaron wasn't as sure that this would blow over so quickly. Still, Betty was doing a good job cheering him up.

"Well, I guess if you can handle it, I can handle it," he said, smiling weakly.

Betty put her arms around him and held on until he relaxed. "It's time you realized, Mr. Willie Taylor. You're not alone anymore. You were alone for so long, but you're never going to be alone, ever again. We'll handle it together."

CHAPTER 53

Betty was right as usual. A few tumultuous weeks after the Aaron Lowe segment of "The Phoenix Café" aired, the world forgot about his twisted tale and went back to obsessing over the fast-approaching new millennium and potential Y2K computer meltdowns.

With his latest fifteen minutes of fame behind him, Aaron could focus on rehearsals for the upcoming Carnival reunion. The "Phoenix" producers lived up to their end of the bargain. A five-week, 20-date tour had been organized to the most precise detail. The band would start off by playing half a dozen dates on the West Coast and would end just before Christmas with a weekend engagement at the Taj Mahal in Atlantic City. The final stop fit perfectly into the manufactured storyline of Aaron beginning and ending his career in a casino.

"I guess they forgot about the Kiddie Cowboy," Aaron said during rehearsals.

"Kiddie Cowboy was never wanted for capping a wiseguy, Homes," Dewey said. "Ain't no headlines there."

With a documentary crew following their every step, Carnival basked in glory as they blazed a triumphant trail across America. Betty and Travis joined Aaron for the big finale in Atlantic City and Aaron coaxed Travis up on stage for the encore. Rollo and Rex showed up as well and gave the crowd the thrill of a lifetime when they jammed with Carnival and a nervous-but-ecstatic Travis on a medley of Chuck Berry rockers.

Betty and Travis headed home right after the final concert. Travis had to rehearse with Riptide for a big New Year's Eve gig. The band had the midnight slot in an all-night marathon of local bands at Birch Hill, one of the biggest clubs on the Jersey Shore circuit.

Aaron stayed overnight for one final party before everyone went back to their own lives. As the celebration petered out, Rollo cornered Aaron and his bandmates with a tempting proposition.

"Guys, I told Aaron a few months ago that I wanted Carnival to open for us on our summer stadium tour," he said. "I understood his reasons then and I understand them now. Those big shows aren't always a lot of fun, especially for the musicians. But I still want to play with you guys, and give our fans a chance to see who made us love rock and roll in the first place. And I think I have the perfect compromise.

"You may know we're playing Madison Square Garden on New Year's Eve. Big millennium bash and all that. It's gonna be a huge thing. We already got half a million people signed up for pay-per-view. This is a chance for all the people who couldn't get tickets to your Phoenix tour to see you play live one more time. And maybe a few of those wankers, the ones who only know you as '*that band with the Weekend Willie mystery guy,*' will get to see that Carnival's music is a lot more interesting than the stuff they read about you on the gossip pages."

"Whoa, count me out," Aaron protested. "I told you guys, this is it for me, and I mean it."

"What summer tour?" Dewey said. "I didn't hear about no summer tour."

"Dewey, never mind, because it's not gonna happen," Aaron said.

"Like I said, Aaron, I understand," Rollo continued. "But the Garden is a whole different thing. This is going to be history. You guys are all warmed up. No tour meetings, no rehearsal. One-and-done. Just come to the Garden, play an hour and maybe come out and jam with us at midnight."

Aaron was floored by Rollo's offer. Here was the leader of

the biggest band in the world and he was willing to shake up the program at his big millennium gig, just for one more chance to jam with Carnival.

"Lowe-man, I know how you feel," Patrick said. "And I know that right now, I'm the last one who should be asking you for favors. But *shit*, Lowe-man, think about it. We can go out in a blaze of glory. People will be watching this on video a thousand years from now. Swear to God, man, if you do this, I'll never ask you for anything ever again."

The others made similar petitions and promises. Aaron's resistance was dissolving once again. *Just one more.* Then he remembered his promise to mix the sound for Riptide that same night at Birch Hill.

Just like old times, he thought. *I have to decide if the music is more important than everything else in my life.*

"Let me think about it for a few days, OK?" he said. "I need to talk to my family."

The next morning, the band exchanged a last round of laughs and hugs before going their separate ways. Aaron promised to get back to them soon about the Garden.

On his way to the parking deck, Aaron's mind wandered as he reviewed his choices. *Just one more*, he thought. He remembered what Rollo said. *"This is going to be history."*

His mind was too occupied to notice two tall, well-dressed men coming up behind him as he approached the parking deck elevator. They caught up with him as the elevator doors were closing and jumped inside at the last minute.

"Mr. Lowe?" one of them asked.

They didn't look like fans. They looked more like businessmen. Or cops. Whatever they were, they were bigger than he was.

"*Yeah*," he said cautiously. "Do I know you guys?"

"Mr. Lowe, we work for someone you used to know. Patsy Bucco. If you've got the time, he'd like a word with you."

The elevator shuddered to a stop and opened to Aaron's

floor on the deck. He took a closer look at the men, then looked around for possible escape routes. There were no witnesses to discourage them from doing anything bold. Their granite expressions never wavered. His face flushed and his mouth filled with a sharp, bitter taste.

He remembered what Betty had said when his past was outed on national television. *"Nobody except you cares about what happened back then."*

Nobody except Patsy Bucco. If ever there was a man who should not be underestimated, it was Patsy. Aaron had to admire his stepfather's persistence. It took more than 30 years for Aaron to let his guard down, but Patsy was a patient man. Apparently, he had a long memory as well. Obviously, he still had a long reach.

Aaron studied the two men closely. They weren't going to go away empty-handed. "What if I said no?" Aaron asked.

"Would you deny your stepfather this small favor?" one of them said.

"What if I said no?" Aaron asked again.

"Then we'll let you be on your way," the man said. "But let me ask you something. Man to man. You wonder what he wants with you, but you're afraid to find out. Am I right?"

"OK," Aaron said. "What's your point?"

"The point is, if you go home now, you'll still be wondering what he wants with you," the man said. "And you'll still be afraid."

Aaron thought he heard a double meaning in the man's argument. He had a good point. Aaron would always wonder what Patsy wanted. But was the man suggesting that if Aaron didn't volunteer to see Patsy, then Patsy might take more direct action to initiate their reunion?

"Where is he? Where does he want to meet?"

The man smiled. "That's the beauty of it. He's right here in A.C. He lives maybe half a mile from here. A few blocks down the Boardwalk. He's hoping you'll have lunch with him."

Aaron resigned to the inevitable. *Amazing*, he thought. Patsy Bucco, living right here in Atlantic City. Go figure.

"Funny thing about this town," Aaron told the man. "Fate seems to find me here. OK. Let's go see Patsy."

Patsy lived in the top-floor penthouse of a high-rise Boardwalk condominium just south of Casino Row. It took less than a minute for the men to take Aaron by limousine from one parking deck to the other. Inside the building, the man used a key card to access a private elevator.

When they arrived, the condo appeared uninhabited. The place reminded Aaron of a typical luxury hotel suite, only much larger. There were marble columns everywhere, and marble walls and floors that amplified every step they took. On one side of the open space, there was a large wet bar and a wide door opening to a spacious kitchen. On the other side, a hallway decorated with paintings and floor sculptures angled away from the main room. In the middle, there was sofa-and-easy-chair seating for at least a dozen people. Each seat had a panoramic postcard view of the ocean and Boardwalk.

"I'll let Patsy know you're here," said the man who did all the talking.

Aaron noticed there was a balcony beyond the glass wall of windows. *Long way down*, Aaron thought. He tugged on the handle of the sliding glass door in the middle. It was stuck.

"Watch yourself there, Willie, you open that door and the wind will knock you right on your *coolie*. Lousy bit of engineering, if you ask me."

Aaron turned around and saw a small, slight old man shuffling slowly into the living room. *Patsy*?

"Well, well, well, ain't you a sight for sore eyes," the man said. This time, while the voice was weak, Aaron placed it for certain. It *was* Patsy. Half of him, anyway. Aaron remembered Patsy never acted like a tough, but he sure looked like one. He used to be as thick and hard as a turnpike toll booth. The old man in front of him now barely came up to his shoulders and couldn't weigh much more than one hundred pounds. His skin was dark and a little yellow, and his sunken cheeks were almost black. His thick, gray hair was neatly trimmed and matted firmly to his skull. Or was he wearing a hairpiece? His eyes were cloudy but still gave away obvious signs of physical pain.

"Patsy. It's really you," Aaron said.

"What's left of me, kid," Patsy said. "Damn cancer got me. The doctors say they can fix it, but the cure is worse than the disease."

He came right up to Aaron and put on a large, thick pair of glasses so he could inspect him more closely. Finally, he took off the glasses, took a step back, and offered his hand.

"Aaron Lowe, is it?" Patsy said. "*Hmmm.* That's a pretty good disguise, but I coulda picked you out of a crowd in the dark. Those eyes. You got them from your mother."

Winnie. Jesus! Aaron had completely forgotten.

"Patsy, what about her?" Aaron asked. "What about my mother? Is she here?"

"She's here, Willie," Patsy said. "She's not well, but she's still here. She's just up from a nap, and the nurse is in there taking care of her. She'll be ready in a few minutes. All in good time, son. For now, let's you and I talk for a while."

Patsy slowly headed for the living room and settled into the corner of a sofa. Aaron followed him and sat on the edge of the chair nearest to his stepfather. He was still anxious. What was Patsy going to do with him? And now, *my God*, he was going to see Winnie. That alone was enough to distract him from his darkest fears.

"I understand you did pretty well for yourself since leaving Las Vegas," Patsy said. "A big star, a respected musician. Tell me something, was it worth it?"

"Worth what, Patsy?" Aaron said. "I don't understand."

"Was it worth all the sacrifice? Was it worth putting your career ahead of everything else in your life? Was it worth leaving so much behind?"

"Patsy, I didn't have much choice. I never looked for

trouble. All I ever wanted was to play my music ... Patsy, I'm sorry for what happened. I'm sorry about Carlo, about Tina, about leaving the way I did. But I never asked for any of it. And I didn't know what else to do."

Patsy grimaced and his body tightened in pain. Aaron wasn't sure if it was the disease or the conversation that was causing his distress. Either way, he felt for the old guy. Patsy had always been good to him.

"Patsy, can I get you something?" he said.

Patsy raised a hand and waved him off. "I'll be alright in a minute. I'm actually used to this."

As if on cue, a servant in a white coat came in the room carrying an old-fashioned pitcher of iced tea and two tall glasses on a tray. He placed it on the table between Aaron and Patsy and poured the glasses full.

"Thank you, Miguel," Patsy said. Miguel smiled and left. "How about some lunch? I said I wanted to have lunch with you, but right now, I just can't eat. How about you? Anything you want."

"No, no thanks, I'm good," Willie said. "I'm sorry you feel so bad."

"Good kid, that Miguel," Patsy said. "His mother has been cooking for us for years. He helps out here in the summer. Goes to Penn. Gonna be an engineer. We're helping out with the tuition. Makes his mother so proud."

Aaron couldn't miss the parallel. "I guess it must have been hard on Winnie, losing me and Bobby like that," he said. "I'm sorry for that, too."

"Son, I need to stop you right there." Patsy's voice had suddenly regained its old verve, so much that it startled his houseguest. *Here it comes*, Aaron thought.

"All this feeling sorry! All this regret you've been carrying around for thirty years! That's not what I brought you here for. I'm not asking for any apologies."

Aaron wasn't following him, but he was getting the sense that Patsy wasn't out for revenge.

"Patsy, what do you want me to say?"

Patsy glared at him, then settled back in his seat.

"I want you to be happy to see me, son," he said. "I want you to be happy for the chance to see your mother. I want you to be relieved that all your secrets are out, and you can live the rest of your life in peace."

Aaron was dumbfounded. This was quite a moment, one he would most certainly never forget. So long in coming. And it was just beginning.

"Patsy, it is good to see you," Aaron said. "And it is a relief to know that I can live the rest of my life with your blessing."

"And your mother?" Patsy asked.

"I'm still trying to process that one," Aaron said. "I've been a different person for a long time. It's hard to relate to Willie Taylor. Or his mother. They had an unusual relationship. It wasn't a typical mother-and-child dynamic. I was her meal ticket. She manipulated me to achieve her own goals."

"That's rather harsh, don't you think? She was your mother. She looked out for you. She was proud of you."

"And what about Bobby? He wasn't a prodigy. He couldn't fill a room. And because of that, she treated him like yesterday's newspaper. Yeah, she treated me like a little prince. But I always wondered, if I didn't make all that money, would she have bothered? Or would I have been in the outhouse with my brother?"

Patsy sighed. "I guess you have a point there. Just the same, she did love you very much, Willie. And it broke her heart to lose you."

"And what about Bobby?"

"She loved him, too. It was a terrible thing, what happened to your brother. It was hard on all of us. You're right, Willie. Your mother could be a very selfish woman. Very self-centered. But you weren't there to see how hard it was to lose her sons. It changed her, profoundly."

"I'm sorry, Patsy. It must have been hard for you, too. To lose Carlo, I mean."

"Carlo? Yes, I suppose it was. It was harder to know that his sister was involved. Tina never really recovered from that, you know. She fell into the drinking, and the drugs, and that whole Studio 54 scene. Went from one man to the next. Finally got the HIV and died a terrible death. Must be ten years now, maybe more. I try not to think about it.

"But they made their own choices, she and her brother, and they had to accept the consequences, just like everybody else."

Patsy read the surprise and sadness on Aaron's face.

"Yes, I know that Tina shot her brother. We knew exactly what happened. We worked closely with the cops back then. We investigated the shooting together. We also know what Carlo did to you, and that he and Bobby shot each other. We knew everything. You were never in any danger of being arrested."

Aaron felt foolish and relieved at the same time. It was a strange sensation. He looked at his iced tea. "You have anything stronger than this around here?"

Patsy laughed. "Sure, kid. Help yourself to the bar. I could use a drink myself. Those goddamn doctors. Can't even have a glass of wine at dinner."

Aaron found some chilled beer in the refrigerator behind the bar. The cold, bubbly brew soothed his throat.

"So I guess I never had to leave town, change my name and do everything I did for the last thirty-three years," Aaron said. The noose had been removed from his neck, but the irony still covered him like a shroud.

"Well, I wouldn't go quite that far," Patsy said. "Carlo had a lot of friends and some of them would have loved nothing better than to get their hands on you. They might have even defied me. Who knows? Carlo, may he rest in peace, was a punk, and he surrounded himself with punks. Those boys had no sense of honor. They didn't have any sense at all. And they all got what they deserved, sooner or later. Just like Carlo did, if you get my drift. So you don't have to worry about them, either.

"Anyways, if you had come to me back then, I would have sent you out of town myself. I might have even sent you to that guy in Los Angeles with the fake ID's."

Patsy had startled Aaron once again.

"You knew about that?" Aaron said.

"Sure I did," Patsy said. "Kid, back in the day, when the cops really wanted to find someone, they came to us."

"So you knew all along ..."

"Who you were? Where you were? What you were doing? I knew everything. I always had an eye on you. I even know that girlfriend of yours killed your friend, the music teacher."

Aaron took a long sip of his beer. Patsy was really something else.

"And you never said a word?"

"I never told anyone. Not even your mother because she never could keep her mouth shut. All I told her was that I got you out of the country and she would have to accept that you could not come back.

"It was true enough. You were in a bad situation. You paid a price far greater than any of your mistakes should have cost. But you found a way through the darkness and made a new life for yourself. You earned your freedom. You were entitled to make your own decisions.

"Which gets me back to my first question. Was what you gave up worth what you gained? That's the measure of a man's life. What did he learn, what did he gain, and what was the price? That's the thing that interests me.

"Let me tell you something, son. We all make decisions, and we all regret some of them. God knows I came to regret some of the things I've done, and I may burn in Hell for a lot of them. I don't know, son. It was a different time. I can't justify the things I did back in the day, but I feel I've done some good."

"I got out of the business a long time ago, Willie. Took a little nest egg with me, invested it in the bull market and made a goddamn fortune. Gave away most of it, but there was plenty left over for me and your mother. We moved here about 15 years ago. Back to the place where I first saw her. God, she was a beauty.

"By the way, sorry about those guys and all the cloak-and-dagger getting you here. I still try to keep a low profile myself. Still very careful even what I say on the phone. Old habits and all that."

Aaron wondered where Winnie was. "You said she had a nurse? What's wrong with her?"

Patsy shook his head. "She's got the Alzheimer's, Willie. On a good day, she knows who I am, at least in the morning before she gets tired. She doesn't remember much else. She knows the ocean is right out there, but she doesn't know where she is. She's been like this for a couple of years. She needs round-the-clock care now. Thank God I can provide it for her. Those nursing homes are, well, they might as well just dig the hole, if you ask me. At least here, she's home. She's got the best of care. And she's got me."

Patsy winced, then took a sip of tea. "For the time-being."

As if on cue, a nurse appeared from the hallway with Winnie, who was confined to a wheelchair. Aaron was shocked to see his mother in such a weak and helpless state. He remembered how the room would shake when she made her entrance. If you lost her in a crowd, all you had to do was spot the commotion and you would find her right in the middle.

This time, there was no fanfare as she was wheeled quietly into the room. Dressed in a thick sweater and covered with a blanket, Aaron couldn't even make out the outline of her once-proud body. A scarf covered her gray hair. All he could see of her was a thin, wrinkled neck and a blank expression.

"There's my girl!" Patsy said as he struggled to stand up.

He excused the nurse, gave Winnie a kiss on the cheek, and wheeled her closer to Aaron.

"Winnie, you have a visitor," Patsy said sweetly. "It's your son, Willie."

Winnie looked at Patsy, then at Aaron.

"*Patsy?*" she said weakly.

"That's right, sweetheart. I'm your Patsy. And this is your son, Willie."

Aaron got up, kneeled in front of her and took her hand.

"Mom, it's me, *Willie,*" he said. She stared right past him, smiling slightly. She didn't recognize him. She didn't even seem to know he was there.

"It's … it's good to see you, Mom." Aaron could feel the tears welling in his eyes.

"*Patsy?*" Winnie said. "Patsy, what time is it? Is it time yet?"

"It's lunchtime, sweetheart, and your son has come to visit you," Patsy said. "Isn't that wonderful?"

"Are we going out tonight?" she asked.

Patsy sighed and stroked her head. "I was hoping she would recognize you. I hoped having you here might snap her out of it some. But I'm not surprised. The doctors, they counsel you. Don't get your hopes up too much."

Both men now had tears in their eyes. "But how can you not hope?" Patsy said. "How can you just give up?"

Patsy turned away from Aaron to wipe his eyes and blow his nose.

"Your mother and I, we were lucky to find each other. Boy, we sure had some times. She could be a real piece of work. But she was so full of life. Completely fearless in her own way. That's what I loved about her. I don't know what my life would have been like without her. I'd probably be in a ditch somewhere by now. Or in a prison cell. She gave me a reason to put all that crap behind me. Now, that's one decision I'll never regret."

Patsy turned around and looked down at Aaron, still

kneeling at his mother's side.

"The way I see it, you start your life out as an empty vessel. And in the end, we're measured by what we fill the vessel with. Sometimes we stumble and the vessel tips over. We lose some of ourselves. But if we have enough strength and character, and we remember to learn from our mistakes, we can get back on our feet. Continue the journey. And keep filling the vessel.

"So, Willie, what's in your vessel? Are you satisfied with your life? Or is your vessel full of regret? Do you miss what you left behind? Was it all worth it? These are the things that matter. These are the things that interest me."

Aaron thought about what Patsy was asking. If you asked him ten years ago, his answer would be quite different. Up to that point, his vessel had been filled many times with accomplishment, but something always tipped it over, leaving him empty of everything except regret.

Now, he was content. His career had completed a full circle and his life was full of love. And now, thanks to Patsy, he could finally put his oldest fears to rest.

"Patsy, there will always be some regret," he said. "Right now, I regret that I can't tell Winnie that I'm alright. That Betty and I found each other again. Of course, I guess you knew that, too.

"I don't know, Patsy. I've lived with regret my entire life. Somewhere along the way, I learned how to put it aside and keep going. I learned to do more than live with my mistakes. I learned *from* them. Eventually, all that experience must have paid off. Betty did the rest. Betty and my stepson, Travis. You should see him, Patsy. Big lump of a kid, happy as a clam, fixing motorcycles and playing his guitar. He's got a nice girlfriend, too. They're very happy together.

"I offered to set his band up, use my contacts to get them a record deal. Give him a shot at the big-time. He didn't want any part of it. It wasn't that he was too proud to let me help him. It wasn't that he wanted to make it on his own. He thinks he's already made it. And you know what? He's right. He's found some things that he is good at, and he likes doing them, so that's what he does. That's all he wants and all he needs. It's not an extraordinary life. But he makes his contribution, you know? He doesn't need anything else. He doesn't need to be a star. He's happy. We could all learn a thing or two from him about ambition."

"Yes, yes, ambition!" Patsy said. "Did you ever read Shakespeare? 'Richard the Third?' Ambition isn't much different than revenge. It can consume you. And it will often bring you to a bad end."

"Well, I don't know much about Shakespeare," Aaron said. "But my ambition, and giving in to the ambition of others, has consumed me many times. It's brought me to bad ends more often than I'd like to admit. When Betty came back into my life, right here in this town, it was like a miracle. I was finally able to break the pattern. And I've been happy ever since."

"I'm very happy for you, Willie. All of you," Patsy said. "You've learned your lessons very well. You hang on to that woman. You know what makes you happy? Making her happy. And making you happy is what does it for her. That's what love is all about. You can't fill the vessel by yourself."

Aaron smiled at the old man. Another regret suddenly popped into his head. If only he had stayed in touch with Patsy. If only he could have benefited from his counsel for all those years. Maybe there would have been less regret to learn from.

"You're a very wise man, Patsy," Aaron said. "I wish I had given you more of a chance to be my stepfather."

Patsy raised his eyebrows. "Well, maybe we still have a little time for that. There's one more thing I need to tell you, son. As I said, I'm a wealthy man and, as it turns out, I have no heirs. No blood heirs, anyway. And I have to face the possibility that your mother may very well outlive me. So I must ask for your help.

"I'm going to have the lawyers change my will and leave everything to you and your family. All I ask is that when I'm gone, you'll see to your mother's care. That, and maybe you'll bring that family of yours here for a visit. I want to meet that boy of yours. And it would be wonderful to see Betty again."

Aaron was humbled by Patsy's gesture. "Patsy, I don't need the money, but I'll be proud to be your heir. And I'll be just as proud to take care of mom, if and when that time comes. We'll take care of you, too. We'll be there for you every step of the way."

Patsy struggled to stand up, so Aaron rose and held out his hand to help him. Once both men were on their feet, they stood there for a while with their hands gripped tight. "Life is full of surprises, isn't it?" Patsy said.

"You never know what's around the corner," Aaron said, smiling. "You just never know."

CHAPTER 54

Aaron's conversation with Patsy had cleared the bases. His past was past. His vessel was upright. His future was a blank page. He could control his own destiny.

Patsy's advice also made easy work of his next hard decision.

"2Night doesn't need me to help them christen the new millennium," he told everyone who needed to know. "They can do that all by themselves. My kid needs someone to mix the sound at *his* millennium gig. I'll be a lot more useful there."

Aaron and his family spent Christmas Eve with Patsy and Winnie. Patsy sent them home with a trunkload of presents, including an old framed poster from the Full House advertising "The Taylor Brothers, appearing nightly at the Regal Lounge."

At home on Christmas morning, the Lowe family exchanged presents and then prepared for the big evening feast. Betty had invited all the boys from Riptide, and their girlfriends, over for dinner.

Aaron waited until everyone was there to bring out one last present for Travis. He did a lousy wrapping job, so the surprise only lasted as long as it took him to haul it out of the closet.

"Honestly, Aaron, I would have wrapped it for you," Betty said.

"I wanted it to be a surprise for you, too," he replied.

Travis was too excited to say anything. He knew what was inside the large, wrinkly package.

"Your Les Paul," Travis said in a low voice. "You sure about this?"

"More sure than I've ever been about anything," Aaron said. "You just take good care of her. She's seen a lot in her life. Been a lot of places. Played a lot of songs. You listen to her. She can teach you a lot about life."

"Yes sir, I will," Travis said, shaking his head in disbelief.

"Did you ever hear him so quiet?" Betty whispered to Aaron as Travis showed off his new guitar to the band. "You really got him with that one."

"It's nice to have someone to give it to," Aaron said as he pulled Betty under the mistletoe and gave her a soft kiss.

"I love you, Mr. Willie Taylor," she said.

"I love *you*, Mrs. Lowe," he replied.

Six days later, Aaron and Betty headed up the shore to Old Bridge about ten in the evening. They got to Birch Hill just before eleven.

"Where have you guys been?" Travis said anxiously as he let them in the side door. "We're going on in fifteen minutes, for Chrissakes!"

"Relax, boy. The less time I work, the less you'll have to pay me," Aaron said.

Travis relaxed a bit and smiled. "You know the deal, Dad," he said. "We can't pay you cash, but you can help yourself to beer and groupies."

"Travis!" his mother said. "Don't give him any ideas. Besides, he has to drive home. But you can get your mother a Bud Light."

An hour later, Travis, playing his stepfather's old Les Paul, and Riptide were rocking the crowd with a few Pearl Jam covers. As the final seconds ticked down to midnight, and the year 2000, the band switched gears and went into a loud, grunged-up arrangement of "Auld Lang Syne." When the song was over, Travis shaded his eyes from the spotlight so he could see Aaron and Betty. Once he made sure they were there together, he stepped to the microphone. There was a little feedback, so Aaron twirled a knob on the board to clear it up.

"All right! Right now we're going to do a special song for a special couple. Some of you may know that my dad, Aaron Lowe, used to have his own band. And now, he's our only roadie. He's right there, working the board for us. Dad, stand up and take a bow. *Aaron Lowe,* everybody!"

Aaron rose halfway out of his seat and accepted a polite ovation.

Travis continued, "Are there any Carnival fans out there?"

It wasn't a Carnival kind of crowd, but there were enough cheers that Aaron wasn't completely humiliated.

"Any Weekend Willie fans out there?" This time, the cheer was a little louder.

Aaron gave Travis a dirty look, then turned to Betty. "I thought you said people would forget about that?"

"Patience, sugar," she said. "You'll be a has-been before you know it."

Travis laughed at the crowd's reaction, then continued his speech.

"Well, actually, he's my stepfather, but he's the only dad I've ever known. And at the risk of ruining my rep, I've got something to say. Dad, I love you. And it's because of you that I'm up here tonight."

Travis was in his glory and playing to the crowd like Mick Jagger. *"And I love being up here!"* he bellowed.

"My dad is the best guitar player I ever heard and he taught me everything I know. He was a great songwriter, too, and once upon a time, he wrote a song for my mother. She's here tonight as well, right next to my dad. How about some love for *Betty Lowe!*"

Travis waited once more for the applause to die down.

"Anyway, right now we're going to play that song for you. Dad, I hope you don't mind, we kicked it up a little."

Travis shot off a quick, loud guitar riff.

"Dad, are you ready?"

Aaron raised one arm in the air, then put the other around Betty.

"Betty, are you ready?"

Betty kissed Aaron, then waved both of her arms in the air.

Travis waved back, turned to his band and counted off.

"One – two – three – four!"

AUTHOR'S NOTE

Fine, I'll admit it. I'm a frustrated musician.

Since I was old enough to walk, nothing has moved my soul more than music. As a young lad, I loved to stay up late watching scary movies and creature features, tapping my toes like a Motown backup singer to the rhythm of things that go bump in the night. But let me listen to "Teen Angel" or "Leader of the Pack," which set superficial tragedy and death to music, and the nightmares would rip at my slumber like a chainsaw.

A deficiency of hand-eye coordination and the inability to focus on one task for more than 15 minutes at a time conspired against my becoming the next Eric Clapton (or Mickey Mantle, which would have been my second choice). I eventually found my calling as a journalist known for his ability to handle a wide range of topics. But the arts and entertainment beat, particularly the performing arts, was my passion.

As the years passed, I became better known for my expertise in theater rather than music, but music was still my master. So when it came time to focus my attention on a novel, music was the natural target.

My expansive tastes might be too much for some of my friends (my typical segues from John Lee Hooker to Roxy Music, P-Funk, Alison Krauss and King Sunny Ade drive them nuts), but my passion for so many styles, and the instinctive need to research each one, has imprinted my brain with a vast storehouse of music history, with the lines between the artists clearly drawn.

Want to know the six degrees of separation between Led Zeppelin and Loudon Wainwright III? Hell, I can do it in three.

"One-Hit Willie" is an attempt to put some of those links to good use. While my characters frequently intersect with actual milestones in music history, many of their fictional backstories and adventures also are based in part on the lives and experiences of the artists who inspired their creation. The fun in reading their story, I hope, is piecing it all together like a puzzle.

I also tapped into my decades of research, along with my hundreds of interviews with these fabulous artists over the years, to illustrate a valuable lesson I learned along the way: Talent, fame and wealth alone will not make you happy. Without some balance, the vessel that is your life will always tip to one side, and will never stay full.

It still frustrates me that I cannot make music, but writing this novel has helped to remind me that I was lucky enough to find my true calling and, with the support of the friends and family who give me balance, there's a happy song in my heart.

Made in the USA
Lexington, KY
22 January 2013